DOCTOR SLEEP

'A magnificent sequel to one of the finest horror yarns written . . . Brilliant' – *Daily Express*

'This is the master on top form, drawing his readers in with his amazing storytelling power – first with the tension, then with the richness and details of the scene-setting and characterisation' – *Daily Mail*

'Both an excellent sequel to *The Shining* and a strong novel in its own right, this is one of King's best books in the last decade' – *SciFi Bulletin*

'A superbly well-engineered ride, full of satisfying twists and switch-backs [while] the novel's deepest shiverings depend on no made-up devils' – *Guardian*

PRAISE FOR DOCTOR SLEEP

'King is a very remarkable and singular writer. He can catch dialogue, throw away an observation or mint a simile, sometimes, brilliantly . . . Storytelling is everything – and by golly does he know how to carry the reader' – *Observer*

'*Doctor Sleep* is a warm, entertaining novel by a man who is no longer the prisoner of his demons, but knows where to find them when he needs to call on them' – *Daily Telegraph*

'*Doctor Sleep* is King expertly returning to the milieu of his most beloved novels, combining not just elements from the original *The Shining* but themes and imagery familiar from King's books, including *Carrie, Salem's Lot, Firestarter* and *It*. It also has a structure King has often utilised before, with a group of essentially good people having to band against a gang of baddies but within this structure King works masterful variations, showing just with a brilliant storyteller he is' – *Sunday Express*

PRAISE FOR DOCTOR SLEEP

'King has written a sequel, the tale of what happened to little Danny when he grew up. Need one say more? It cannot fail . . . the best thing to emerge from King's glittering, warped imagination is of mundane, small-town America corrupted by hidden forces . . . you cannot but respect his ruthless expertise as a storyteller . . . even those of us who would never freely pick up a Stephen King must genuflect to a master' – *The Times*

'A thrilling ride of page-turning suspense' – *Sunday Express*

'Wild ectoplasmic partly decayed vampire horses would not tear from me the story of what happens next, but let me assure you King is a pro: by the end of this book your fingers will be mere stubs of their former selves, and you will be looking askance at the people in the supermarket line, because if they turn around they might have metallic eyes. King's inventiveness and skill show no signs of slacking: *Doctor Sleep* has all the virtues of his best work' – Margaret Atwood, *New York Times*

PRAISE FOR DOCTOR SLEEP

'[A] brilliant sequel . . . King [is] a genius at transforming the ordinary into the utterly horrific . . .' – *Evening Standard*

'A gripping, powerful novel, all the more so for being patently heartfelt' – *Financial Times*

'For the truth is, there are few writers who have such a way with character (and that character delivered through authorial peeks into thought and feeling, is so important in his books . . .) Once his stories get their hooks into you, they're impossible to put down' – *SFX*

ABOUT THE AUTHOR

There is a reason why Stephen King is one of the bestselling writers in the world, *ever*. Described by Frances Fyfield in the *Daily Express* as 'one of those natural storytellers' and by the *Daily Telegraph* as 'genuinely masterful', Stephen King writes stories that draw you in and are *impossible to put down*.

King is the author of more than sixty books, all of them worldwide bestsellers including the popular classics *Carrie*, *Misery* and *The Shining*, to which *Doctor Sleep* is the sequel.

Many of his books and novellas have been turned into celebrated films, television series and streamed events, including *Doctor Sleep*, *Gerald's Game*, *IT* and *The Shining*.

King was the recipient of the 2003 National Book Foundation Medal for Distinguished Contribution to American Letters, in 2007 he won the Grand Master Award from the Mystery Writers of America and in 2015 received America's National Medal of Arts. He lives with his wife, Tabitha King, in Maine.

By Stephen King and published by
Hodder & Stoughton

NOVELS:

Carrie
'Salem's Lot
The Shining
The Stand
The Dead Zone
Firestarter
Cujo
Cycle of the Werewolf
Christine
Pet Sematary
IT
The Eyes of the Dragon
Misery
The Tommyknockers
The Dark Half
Needful Things
Gerald's Game
Dolores Claiborne
Insomnia
Rose Madder
Desperation
Bag of Bones
The Girl Who Loved Tom Gordon
Dreamcatcher
From a Buick 8
Cell
Lisey's Story
Duma Key
Under the Dome
11.22.63
Doctor Sleep
Mr Mercedes
Revival
Finders Keepers
End of Watch
Sleeping Beauties (with Owen King)
The Outsider
Elevation
The Insitute

The Dark Tower I: The Gunslinger
The Dark Tower II:
The Drawing of the Three
The Dark Tower III: The Waste Lands
The Dark Tower IV: Wizard and Glass
The Dark Tower V: Wolves of the Calla
The Dark Tower VI: Song of Susannah
The Dark Tower VII: The Dark Tower
The Wind through the Keyhole:
A Dark Tower Novel

As Richard Bachman

Thinner
The Running Man
The Bachman Books
The Regulators
Blaze

STORY COLLECTIONS:

Night Shift
Different Seasons
Skeleton Crew
Four Past Midnight
Nightmares and Dreamscapes
Hearts in Atlantis
Everything's Eventual
Just after Sunset
Stephen King Goes to the Movies
Full Dark, No Stars
The Bazaar of Bad Dreams

NON-FICTION:

Danse Macabre
On Writing (A Memoir of the Craft)

STEPHEN KING

DOCTOR SLEEP

HODDER

Grateful acknowledgement is made for permission to print excerpts from the following copyrighted material:

The Big Book of Alcoholics Anonymous © 1939, 1955, 1976, 2001 by
Alcoholics Anonymous World Services, Inc. All rights reserved.

"Y.M.C.A" written by Henri Belolo, Jacques Morali & Victor Willis © Can't Stop Music/Scorpio Music, S.A.

'A Game of Chess' from *The Waste Land* by T.S. Eliot © The Estate of T.S. Eliot. Reprinted by permission
of Faber & Faber Ltd. Publishing Company. *Collected Poems 1909–1962* by T.S. Eliot. Copyright © 1936 by
Houghton Mifflin Harcourt Publishing Company. Copyright © renewed 1964 by Thomas Stearns Eliot.
Reprinted by permission of Houghton Mifflin Harcourt Publishing Company. All rights reserved.

Keeley, Edmund: *George Sefaris*. © 1967 Princeton University Press, 1995 renewed PUP/revised edition.
Reprinted by permission of Princeton University Press.

"Shorts" © 1940 by W.H. Auden, renewed © 1974 by The Estate of W.H. Auden, from
COLLECTED POEMS OF W.H. AUDEN by W.H. Auden. Used by permission of Random House, Inc.
and Curtis Brown, Ltd. Any third party use of this material, outside of this publication, is prohibited.
Interested parties must apply directly to Random House, Inc. for permission.

THE WRECK OF THE EDMUND FITZGERALD Words and Music by
GORDON LIGHTFOOT © 1976 (Renewed) MOOSE MUSIC LTD. Used by
Permission of ALFRED MUSIC PUBLISHING CO., INC. All Rights Reserved.

"Ancient Music" by Ezra Pound, from PERSONAE, copyright © 1926 by Ezra Pound.
Reprinted by permission of New Directions Publishing Corp. and Faber & Faber Ltd.

Copyright © 2013 by Stephen King

First published in Great Britain in 2013 by Hodder & Stoughton
An Hachette UK company

This paperback edition published in 2019

The right of Stephen King to be identified as the Author of the Work
has been asserted by him in accordance with the Copyright,
Designs and Patents Act 1988.

A Hodder Paperback

8

A CIP catalogue record for this title is available from the British Library

A Format ISBN 978 1 529 37506 0
B Format ISBN 978 1 529 37507 7
epub ISBN 978 1 444 76119 1

Typeset in Bembo by Palimpsest Book Production Ltd, Falkirk, Stirlingshire

Printed and bound in Great Britain by Clays Ltd, Elcograf S.p.A.

Hodder & Stoughton policy is to use papers that are natural,
renewable and recyclable products and made from wood grown in
sustainable forests. The logging and manufacturing processes are expected
to conform to the environmental regulations of the country of origin.

Hodder & Stoughton
Carmelite House
50 Victoria Embankment
London EC4Y 0DZ

www.hodder.co.uk

When I was playing my primitive brand of rhythm guitar with a group called the Rock Bottom Remainders, Warren Zevon used to gig with us. Warren loved gray t-shirts and movies like *Kingdom of the Spiders*. He insisted I sing lead on his signature tune, 'Were-wolves of London', during the encore portion of our shows. I said I was not worthy. He insisted that I was. 'Key of G', Warren told me, 'and howl like you mean it. Most important of all, *play like Keith*.'

I'll never be able to play like Keith Richards, but I always did my best, and with Warren beside me, matching me note for note and laughing his fool head off, I always had a blast.

Warren, this howl is for you, wherever you are. I miss you, buddy.

We stood at the turning point. Half-measures availed us nothing.

                          – The Big Book of Alcoholics Anonymous

If we were to live, we had to be free of anger. [It is] the dubious luxury of normal men and women.

                          – The Big Book of Alcoholics Anonymous

PREFATORY MATTERS

FEAR stands for fuck everything and run.

– Old AA saying

LOCKBOX

1

On the second day of December in a year when a Georgia peanut farmer was doing business in the White House, one of Colorado's great resort hotels burned to the ground. The Overlook was declared a total loss. After an investigation, the fire marshal of Jicarilla County ruled the cause had been a defective boiler. The hotel was closed for the winter when the accident occurred, and only four people were present. Three survived. The hotel's off-season caretaker, John Torrance, was killed during an unsuccessful (and heroic) effort to dump the boiler's steam pressure, which had mounted to disastrously high levels due to an inoperative relief valve.

Two of the survivors were the caretaker's wife and young son. The third was the Overlook's chef, Richard Hallorann, who had left his seasonal job in Florida and come to check on the Torrances because of what he called 'a powerful hunch' that the family was in trouble. Both surviving adults were quite badly injured in the explosion. Only the child was unhurt.

Physically, at least.

2

Wendy Torrance and her son received a settlement from the corporation that owned the Overlook. It wasn't huge, but enough to get them by for the three years she was unable to work because of back injuries. A lawyer she consulted told her that if she were willing to hold out and play tough, she might get a great deal more, because the corporation was anxious to avoid a court case. But she, like the corporation, wanted only to put that disastrous winter in Colorado behind her. She would convalesce, she said, and she did, although back injuries plagued her until the end of her life. Shattered vertebrae and broken ribs heal, but they never cease crying out.

Winifred and Daniel Torrance lived in the mid-South for a while, then drifted down to Tampa. Sometimes Dick Hallorann (he of the powerful hunches) came up from Key West to visit with them. To visit with young Danny especially. They shared a bond.

One early morning in March of 1981, Wendy called Dick and asked if he could come. Danny, she said, had awakened her in the night and told her not to go in the bathroom.

After that, he refused to talk at all.

3

He woke up needing to pee. Outside, a strong wind was blowing. It was warm – in Florida it almost always was – but he did not like that sound, and supposed he never would. It reminded him of the Overlook, where the defective boiler had been the very least of the dangers.

He and his mother lived in a cramped second-floor tenement apartment. Danny left the little room next to his mother's and crossed the hall. The wind gusted and a dying palm tree beside the building clattered its leaves. The sound was skeletal. They always left the bathroom door open when no one was using the shower or the toilet, because the lock was broken. Tonight the door was closed. Not because his mother was in there, however. Thanks to facial injuries she'd suffered at the Overlook, she now snored – a soft *queep-queep* sound – and he could hear it coming from her bedroom.

Well, she closed it by accident, that's all.

He knew better, even then (he was possessed of powerful hunches and intuitions himself), but sometimes you had to know. Sometimes you had to *see*. This was something he had found out at the Overlook, in a room on the second floor.

Reaching with an arm that seemed too long, too stretchy, too *boneless*, he turned the knob and opened the door.

The woman from Room 217 was there, as he had known she would be. She was sitting naked on the toilet with her legs spread and her pallid thighs bulging. Her greenish breasts hung down like deflated balloons. The patch of hair below her stomach was gray.

Her eyes were also gray, like steel mirrors. She saw him, and her lips stretched back in a grin.

Close your eyes, Dick Halloran had told him once upon a time. *If you see something bad, close your eyes and tell yourself it's not there and when you open them again, it will be gone.*

But it hadn't worked in Room 217 when he was five, and it wouldn't work now. He knew it. He could *smell* her. She was decaying.

The woman – he knew her name, it was Mrs Massey – lumbered to her purple feet, holding out her hands to him. The flesh on her arms hung down, almost dripping. She was smiling the way you do when you see an old friend. Or, perhaps, something good to eat.

With an expression that could have been mistaken for calmness, Danny closed the door softly and stepped back. He watched as the knob turned right . . . left . . . right again . . . then stilled.

He was eight now, and capable of at least some rational thought even in his horror. Partly because, in a deep part of his mind, he had been expecting this. Although he had always thought it would be Horace Derwent who would eventually show up. Or perhaps the bartender, the one his father had called Lloyd. He supposed he should have known it would be Mrs Massey, though, even before it finally happened. Because of all the undead things in the Overlook, she had been the worst.

The rational part of his mind told him she was just a fragment of unremembered bad dream that had followed him out of sleep and across the hall to the bathroom. That part insisted that if he opened the door again, there would be nothing there. Surely there wouldn't be, now that he was awake. But another part of him, a part that *shone*, knew better. The Overlook wasn't done with him. At least one of its vengeful spirits had followed him all the way to Florida. Once he had come upon that woman sprawled in a bathtub. She had gotten out and tried to choke him with her fishy (but terribly strong) fingers. If he opened the bathroom door now, she would finish the job.

He compromised by putting his ear against the door. At first there was nothing. Then he heard a faint sound.

Dead fingernails scratching on wood.

Danny walked into the kitchen on not-there legs, stood on a chair, and peed into the sink. Then he woke his mother and told her not to go into the bathroom because there was a bad thing there. Once that was done, he went back to bed and sank deep beneath the covers. He wanted to stay there forever, only getting up to pee in the sink. Now that he had warned his mother, he had no interest in talking to her.

His mother knew about the no-talking thing. It had happened after Danny had ventured into Room 217 at the Overlook.

'Will you talk to Dick?'

Lying in his bed, looking up at her, he nodded. His mother called, even though it was four in the morning.

Late the next day, Dick came. He brought something with him. A present.

4

After Wendy called Dick – she made sure Danny heard her doing it – Danny went back to sleep. Although he was now eight and in the third grade, he was sucking his thumb. It hurt her to see him do that. She went to the bathroom door and stood looking at it. She was afraid – Danny had made her afraid – but she had to go, and she had no intention of using the sink as he had. The image of how she would look, teetering on the edge of the counter with her butt hanging over the porcelain (even if there was no one there to see), made her wrinkle her nose.

In one hand she had the hammer from her little box of widow's tools. As she turned the knob and pushed the bathroom door open, she raised it. The bathroom was empty, of course, but the ring of the toilet seat was down. She never left it that way before going to bed, because she knew if Danny wandered in, only ten percent awake, he was apt to forget to put it up and piss all over it. Also, there was a smell. A bad one. As if a rat had died in the walls.

She took a step in, then two. She saw movement and whirled, hammer upraised, to hit whoever

(*whatever*)

was hiding behind the door. But it was only her shadow. Scared of her own shadow, people sometimes sneered, but who had a better right than Wendy Torrance? After the things she had seen and been through, she knew that shadows could be dangerous. They could have teeth.

No one was in the bathroom, but there was a discolored smear on the toilet seat and another on the shower curtain. Excrement was her first thought, but shit wasn't yellowish-purple. She looked more closely and saw bits of flesh and decayed skin. There was more on the bathmat, in the shape of footprints. She thought them too small – too *dainty* – to be a man's.

'Oh God,' she whispered.

She ended up using the sink after all.

5

Wendy nagged her son out of bed at noon. She managed to get a little soup and half a peanut butter sandwich into him, but then he went back to bed. He still wouldn't speak. Hallorann arrived shortly after five in the afternoon, behind the wheel of his now ancient (but perfectly maintained and blindingly polished) red Cadillac. Wendy had been standing at the window, waiting and watching as she had once waited and watched for her husband, hoping Jack would come home in a good mood. And sober.

She rushed down the stairs and opened the door just as Dick was about to ring the bell marked TORRANCE 2A. He held out his arms and she rushed into them at once, wishing she could be enfolded there for at least an hour. Maybe two.

He let go and held her at arm's length by her shoulders. 'You're lookin fine, Wendy. How's the little man? He talkin again?'

'No, but he'll talk to you. Even if he won't do it out loud to start with, you can—' Instead of finishing, she made a finger-gun and pointed it at his forehead.

'Not necessarily,' Dick said. His smile revealed a bright new pair of false teeth. The Overlook had taken most of the last set on the night the boiler blew. Jack Torrance swung the mallet that took Dick's dentures and Wendy's ability to walk without a hitch in her stride, but they both understood it had really been the Overlook.

'He's very powerful, Wendy. If he wants to block me out, he will. I know from my own experience. Besides, it'd be better if we talk with our mouths. Better for him. Now tell me everything that happened.'

After she did that, Wendy took him into the bathroom. She had left the stains for him to see, like a beat cop preserving the scene of a crime for the forensic team. And there *had* been a crime. One against her boy.

Dick looked for a long time, not touching, then nodded. 'Let's see if Danny's up and in the doins.'

He wasn't, but Wendy's heart was lightened by the look of gladness that came into her son's face when he saw who was sitting beside him on the bed and shaking his shoulder.

(*hey Danny I brought you a present*)

(*it's not my birthday*)

Wendy watched them, knowing they were speaking but not knowing what it was about.

Dick said, 'Get on up, honey. We're gonna take a walk on the beach.'

(*Dick she came back Mrs Massey from Room 217 came back*)

Dick gave his shoulder another shake. 'Talk out loud, Dan. You're scarin your ma.'

Danny said, 'What's my present?'

Dick smiled. 'That's better. I like to hear you, and Wendy does, too.'

'Yes.' It was all she dared say. Otherwise they'd hear the tremble in her voice and be concerned. She didn't want that.

'While we're gone, you might want to give the bathroom a cleaning,' Dick said to her. 'Have you got kitchen gloves?'

She nodded.

'Good. Wear them.'

6

The beach was two miles away. The parking lot was surrounded by tawdry beachfront attractions – funnel cake concessions, hotdog stands, souvenir shops – but this was the tag end of the season, and none were doing much business. They had the beach itself almost entirely to themselves. On the ride from the apartment, Danny had held his present – an oblong package, quite heavy, wrapped in silver paper – on his lap.

'You can open it after we talk a bit,' Dick said.

They walked just above the waves, where the sand was hard and gleaming. Danny walked slowly, because Dick was pretty old. Someday he'd die. Maybe even soon.

'I'm good to go another few years,' Dick said. 'Don't you worry about that. Now tell me about last night. Don't leave anything out.'

It didn't take long. The hard part would have been finding words to explain the terror he now felt, and how it was mingled with a suffocating sense of certainty: now that she'd found him, she'd never leave. But because it was Dick, he didn't need words, although he found some.

'She'll come back. I know she will. She'll come back and come back until she gets me.'

'Do you remember when we met?'

Although surprised at the change of direction, Danny nodded. It had been Hallorann who gave him and his parents the guided tour on their first day at the Overlook. Very long ago, that seemed.

'And do you remember the first time I spoke up inside your head?'

'I sure do.'

'What did I say?'

'You asked me if I wanted to go to Florida with you.'

'That's right. And how did it make you feel, to know you wasn't alone anymore? That you wasn't the only one?'

'It was great,' Danny said. 'It was so great.'

'Yeah,' Hallorann said. 'Yeah, course it was.'

They walked in silence for a bit. Little birds – peeps, Danny's mother called them – ran in and out of the waves.

'Did it ever strike you funny, how I showed up when you needed me?' He looked down at Danny and smiled. 'No. It didn't. Why would it? You was just a child, but you're a little older now. A *lot* older in some ways. Listen to me, Danny. The world has a way of keeping things in balance. I believe that. There's a saying: When the pupil is ready, the teacher will appear. I was your teacher.'

'You were a lot more than that,' Danny said. He took Dick's hand. 'You were my friend. You saved us.'

Dick ignored this . . . or seemed to. 'My gramma also had the shining – do you remember me telling you that?'

'Yeah. You said you and her could have long conversations without even opening your mouths.'

'That's right. She taught me. And it was her *great*-gramma that taught her, way back in the slave days. Someday, Danny, it will be your turn to be the teacher. The pupil will come.'

'If Mrs Massey doesn't get me first,' Danny said morosely.

They came to a bench. Dick sat down. 'I don't dare go any further; I might not make it back. Sit beside me. I want to tell you a story.'

'I don't want stories,' Danny said. 'She'll come back, don't you get it? She'll come *back* and come *back* and come *back*.'

'Shut your mouth and open your ears. Take some instruction.' Then Dick grinned, displaying his gleaming new dentures. 'I think you'll get the point. You're far from stupid, honey.'

7

Dick's mother's mother – the one with the shining – lived in Clearwater. She was the White Gramma. Not because she was Caucasian, of course, but because she was *good*. His father's father lived in Dunbrie, Mississippi, a rural community not far from Oxford. His wife had died long before Dick was born. For a man of color in that place and time, he was wealthy. He owned a funeral parlor. Dick and his parents visited four times a year, and young Dick Hallorann hated those visits. He was terrified of Andy Hallorann, and called him – only in his own mind, to speak it aloud would have earned him a smack across the chops – the Black Grampa.

'You know about kiddie-fiddlers?' Dick asked Danny. 'Guys who want children for sex?'

'Sort of,' Danny said cautiously. Certainly he knew not to talk to strangers, and never to get into a car with one. Because they might do stuff to you.

'Well, old Andy was more than a kiddie-fiddler. He was a damn sadist, as well.'

'What's that?'

'Someone who enjoys giving pain.'

Danny nodded in immediate understanding. 'Like Frankie Listrone at school. He gives kids Indian burns and Dutch rubs. If he can't make you cry, he stops. If he can, he *never* stops.'

'That's bad, but this was worse.'

Dick lapsed into what would have looked like silence to a passerby, but the story went forward in a series of pictures and connecting phrases. Danny saw the Black Grampa, a tall man in a suit as black as he was, who wore a special kind of

(*fedora*)

hat on his head. He saw how there were always little buds of spittle at the corners of his mouth, and how his eyes were red-rimmed, like he was tired or had just gotten over crying. He saw how he would take Dick – younger than Danny was now, probably the same age he'd been that winter at the Overlook – on his lap. If they weren't alone, he might only tickle. If they were, he'd put his hand between Dick's legs and squeeze his balls until Dick thought he'd faint with the pain.

'Do you like that?' Grampa Andy would pant in his ear. He smelled of cigarettes and White Horse scotch. 'Coss you do, every boy likes that. But even if you don't, you dassn't tell. If you do, I'll hurt you. I'll burn you.'

'Holy shit,' Danny said. 'That's gross.'

'There were other things, too,' Dick said, 'but I'll just tell you one. Grampy hired a woman to help out around the house after his wife died. She cleaned and cooked. At dinnertime, she'd slat out everything on the table at once, from salad to dessert, because that's the way ole Black Grampa liked it. Dessert was always cake or puddin. It was put down on a little plate or in a little dish next to your dinnerplate so you could look at it and want it while you plowed through the other muck. Grampa's hard and fast rule was you could *look* at dessert but you couldn't *eat* dessert unless you finished every bite of fried meat and boiled greens and mashed potatoes. You even had to clean up the gravy, which was lumpy and didn't have much taste. If it wasn't all gone, Black Grampa'd hand me a hunk of bread and say "Sop er up with that, Dickie-Bird,

make that plate shine like the dog licked it." That's what he called
me, Dickie-Bird.

'Sometimes I couldn't finish no matter what, and then I didn't
get the cake or the puddin. He'd take it and eat it himself. And
sometimes when I *could* finish all my dinner, I'd find he'd smashed
a cigarette butt into my piece of cake or my vanilla puddin. He
could do that because he always sat next to me. He'd make like it
was a big joke. "Whoops, missed the ashtray," he'd say. My ma and
pa never put a stop to it, although they must have known that even
if it was a joke, it wasn't a fair one to play on a child. They just
made out like it was a joke, too.'

'That's really bad,' Danny said. 'Your folks should have stood up
for you. My mom does. My daddy would, too.'

'They were scairt of him. And they were right to be scairt. Andy
Hallorann was a bad, bad motorcycle. He'd say, "Go on, Dickie, eat
around it, that won't poison ya." If I took a bite, he'd have Nonnie
– that was his housekeeper's name – bring me a fresh dessert. If I
wouldn't, it just sat there. It got so I could never finish my meal,
because my stomach would get all upset.'

'You should have moved your cake or puddin to the other side
of your plate,' Danny said.

'I tried that, sure, I wasn't born foolish. He'd just move it back,
saying dessert went on the right.' Dick paused, looking out at the
water, where a long white boat was trundling slowly across the
dividing line between the sky and the Gulf of Mexico. 'Sometimes
when he got me alone he bit me. And once, when I said I'd tell
my pa if he didn't leave me alone, he put a cigarette out on my
bare foot. He said, "Tell him that, too, and see what good it does
you. Your daddy knows my ways already and he'll never say a word,
because he yella and because he wants the money I got in the bank
when I die, which I ain't fixing to do soon."'

Danny listened in wide-eyed fascination. He had always thought
the story of Bluebeard was the scariest of all time, the scariest there
ever could be, but this one was worse. Because it was true.

'Sometimes he said that he knew a bad man named Charlie Manx,
and if I didn't do what he wanted, he'd call Charlie Manx on the
long-distance and he'd come in his fancy car and take me away to

a place for bad children. Then Grampa would put his hand between my legs and commence squeezing. "So you ain't gonna say a thing, Dickie-Bird. If you do, ole Charlie will come and keep you with the other children he done stole until you die. And when you do, you'll go to hell and your body will burn forever. Because you peached. It don't matter if anybody believes you or not, peaching is peaching."

'For a long time I believed the old bastard. I didn't even tell my White Gramma, the one with the shining, because I was afraid she'd think it was my fault. If I'd been older I would've known better, but I was just a kid.' He paused. 'There was something else, too. Do you know what it was, Danny?'

Danny looked into Dick's face for a long time, probing the thoughts and images behind his forehead. At last he said, 'You wanted your father to get the money. But he never did.'

'No. Black Grampa left it all to a home for Negro orphans in Alabama, and I bet I know why, too. But that's neither here nor there.'

'And your good gramma never knew? She never guessed?'

'She knew there was *something*, but I kep it blocked away, and she left me alone about it. Just told me that when I was ready to talk, she was ready to listen. Danny, when Andy Hallorann died – it was a stroke – I was the happiest boy on earth. My ma said I didn't have to go to the funeral, that I could stay with Gramma Rose – my White Gramma – if I wanted to, but I wanted to go. You bet I did. I wanted to make sure old Black Grampa was really dead.

'It rained that day. Everybody stood around the grave under black umbrellas. I watched his coffin – the biggest and best one in his shop, I have no doubt – go into the ground, and I thought about all the times he'd twisted my balls and all the cigarette butts in my cake and the one he put out on my foot and how he ruled the dinner table like the crazy old king in that Shakespeare play. But most of all I thought about Charlie Manx – who Grampa had no doubt made up out of whole cloth – and how Black Grampa could never call Charlie Manx on the long-distance to come in the night and take me away in his fancy car to live with the other stolen boys and girls.

'I peeped over the edge of the grave – "Let the boy see," my pa said when my ma tried to pull me back – and I scoped the coffin down in that wet hole and I thought, "Down there you're six feet closer to hell, Black Grampa, and pretty soon you'll be all the way, and I hope the devil gives you a thousand with a hand that's on fire."'

Dick reached into his pants pocket and brought out a pack of Marlboros with a book of matches tucked under the cellophane. He put a cigarette in his mouth and then had to chase it with the match because his hand was trembling and his lips were trembling, too. Danny was astounded to see tears standing in Dick's eyes.

Now knowing where this story was headed, Danny asked: 'When did he come back?'

Dick dragged deep on his cigarette and exhaled smoke through a smile. 'You didn't need to peek inside my head to get that, did you?'

'Nope.'

'Six months later. I came home from school one day and he was laying naked on my bed with his half-rotted prick all rared up. He said, "You come on and sit on this, Dickie-Bird. You give me a thousand and I'll give you *two* thousand." I screamed but there was no one there to hear it. My ma and pa, they was both working, my ma in a restaurant and my dad at a printing press. I ran out and slammed the door. And I heard Black Grampa get up . . . *thump* . . . and cross the room . . . *thump-thump-thump* . . . and what I heard next . . .'

'Fingernails,' Danny said in a voice that was hardly there. 'Scratching on the door.'

'That's right. I didn't go in again until that night, when my ma and pa were both home. He was gone, but there were . . . leavings.'

'Sure. Like in our bathroom. Because he was going bad.'

'That's right. I changed the bed myself, which I could do because my ma showed me how two years before. She said I was too old to need a housekeeper anymore, that housekeepers were for little white boys and girls like the ones she took care of before she got her hostessing job at Berkin's Steak House. About a week later, I see ole Black Grampa in the park, a-settin in a swing. He had his suit on, but it was all covered with gray stuff – the mold that was growing on it down in his coffin, I think.'

'Yeah,' Danny said. He spoke it in a glassy whisper. It was all he could manage.

'His fly was open, though, with his works stickin out. I'm sorry to tell you all this, Danny, you're too young to hear about such things, but you need to know.'

'Did you go to the White Gramma then?'

'Had to. Because I knew what you know: he'd just keep comin back. Not like . . . Danny, have you ever seen dead people? *Regular* dead people, I mean.' He laughed because that sounded funny. It did to Danny, too. 'Ghosts.'

'A few times. Once there were three of them standing around a railroad crossing. Two boys and a girl. Teenagers. I think . . . maybe they got killed there.'

Dick nodded. 'Mostly they stick close to where they crossed over until they finally get used to bein dead and move on. Some of the folks you saw in the Overlook were like that.'

'I know.' The relief in being able to talk about these things – to someone who *knew* – was indescribable. 'And this one time there was a woman at a restaurant. The kind, you know, where they have tables outside?'

Dick nodded again.

'I couldn't see through that one, but no one else saw her, and when a waitress pushed in the chair she was sitting in, the ghost lady disappeared. Do you see them sometimes?'

'Not for years, but you're stronger in the shining than I was. It goes back some as you get older—'

'Good,' Danny said fervently.

'—but you'll have plenty left even when you're grown up, I think, because you started with so much. Regular ghosts aren't like the woman you saw in Room 217 and again in your bathroom. That's right, isn't it?'

'Yes,' Danny said. 'Mrs Massey's *real*. She leaves pieces of herself. You saw them. So did Mom . . . and she doesn't shine.'

'Let's walk back,' Dick said. 'It's time you saw what I brought you.'

8

The return to the parking lot was even slower, because Dick was winded. 'Cigarettes,' he said. 'Don't ever start, Danny.'

'Mom smokes. She doesn't think I know, but I do. Dick, what did your White Gramma do? She must have done something, because your Black Grampa never got you.'

'She gave me a present, same like I'm gonna give you. That's what a teacher does when the pupil is ready. Learning itself is a present, you know. The best one anybody can give or get.

'She wouldn't call Grampa Andy by his name, she just called him' – Dick grinned – 'the *preevert*. I said what you said, that he wasn't a ghost, he was real. And she said yes, that was true, because I was *making* him real. With the shining. She said that some spirits – angry spirits, mostly – won't go on from this world, because they know what's waiting for them is even worse. Most eventually starve away to nothing, but some of them find food. "That's what the shining is to them, Dick," she told me. "Food. You're feeding that preevert. You don't mean to, but you are. He's like a mosquito who'll keep circling and then landing for more blood. Can't do nothing about that. What you *can* do is turn what he came for against him."'

They were back at the Cadillac. Dick unlocked the doors, then slid behind the steering wheel with a sigh of relief. 'Once upon a time I could've walked ten miles and run another five. Nowadays, a little walk down the beach and my back feels like a hoss kicked it. Go on, Danny. Open your present.'

Danny stripped off the silver paper and discovered a box made of green-painted metal. On the front, below the latch, was a little keypad.

'Hey, neat!'

'Yeah? You like it? Good. I got it at the Western Auto. Pure American steel. The one White Gramma Rose gave me had a padlock, with a little key I wore around my neck, but that was long ago. This is the nineteen eighties, the modern age. See the number pad? What you do is put in five numbers you're sure you won't forget, then push the little button that says SET. Then, anytime you want to open the box, you punch your code.'

Danny was delighted. 'Thanks, Dick! I'll keep my special things in it!' These would include his best baseball cards, his Cub Scouts Compass Badge, his lucky green rock, and a picture of him and his father, taken on the front lawn of the apartment building where they'd lived in Boulder, before the Overlook. Before things turned bad.

'That's fine, Danny, I want you to do that, but I want you to do something else.'

'What?'

'I want you to know this box, inside and out. Don't just look at it; touch it. Feel it all over. Then stick your nose inside and see if there's a smell. It needs to be your closest friend, at least for a while.'

'Why?'

'Because you're going to put another one just like it in your mind. One that's even more special. And the next time that Massey bitch comes around, you'll be ready for her. I'll tell you how, just like ole White Gramma told me.'

Danny didn't talk much on the ride back to the apartment. He had a lot to think about. He held his present – a lockbox made of strong metal – on his lap.

9

Mrs Massey returned a week later. She was in the bathroom again, this time in the tub. Danny wasn't surprised. A tub was where she had died, after all. This time he didn't run. This time he went inside and closed the door. She beckoned him forward, smiling. Danny came, also smiling. In the other room, he could hear the television. His mother was watching *Three's Company*.

'Hello, Mrs Massey,' Danny said. 'I brought you something.'

At the last moment she understood and began to scream.

10

Moments later, his mom was knocking at the bathroom door. 'Danny? Are you all right?'

'Fine, Mom.' The tub was empty. There was some goo in it, but Danny thought he could clean that up. A little water would send it right down the drain. 'Do you have to go? I'll be out pretty soon.'

'No. I just . . . I thought I heard you call.'

Danny grabbed his toothbrush and opened the door. 'I'm a hundred percent cool. See?' He gave her a big smile. It wasn't hard, now that Mrs Massey was gone.

The troubled look left her face. 'Good. Make sure you brush the back ones. That's where the food goes to hide.'

'I will, Mom.'

From inside his head, far inside, where the twin of his special lockbox was stored on a special shelf, Danny could hear muffled screaming. He didn't mind. He thought it would stop soon enough, and he was right.

11

Two years later, on the day before the Thanksgiving break, halfway up a deserted stairwell in Alafia Elementary, Horace Derwent appeared to Danny Torrance. There was confetti on the shoulders of his suit. A little black mask hung from one decaying hand. He reeked of the grave. 'Great party, isn't it?' he asked.

Danny turned and walked away, very quickly.

When school was over, he called Dick long-distance at the restaurant where Dick worked in Key West. 'Another one of the Overlook People found me. How many boxes can I have, Dick? In my head, I mean.'

Dick chuckled. 'As many as you need, honey. That's the beauty of the shining. You think my Black Grampa's the only one *I* ever had to lock away?'

'Do they die in there?'

This time there was no chuckle. This time there was a coldness in Dick's voice the boy had never heard before. 'Do you care?'

Danny didn't.

When the onetime owner of the Overlook showed up again shortly after New Year's – this time in Danny's bedroom closet – Danny was ready. He went into the closet and closed the door. Shortly afterward, a second mental lockbox went up on the high mental shelf beside the one that held Mrs Massey. There was more pounding, and some inventive cursing that Danny saved for his own later use. Pretty soon it stopped. There was silence from the Derwent lockbox as well as the Massey lockbox. Whether or not they were alive (in their undead fashion) no longer mattered.

What mattered was they were never getting out. He was safe.

That was what he thought then. Of course, he also thought he would never take a drink, not after seeing what it had done to his father.

Sometimes we just get it wrong.

RATTLESNAKE

1

Her name was Andrea Steiner, and she liked movies but she didn't like men. This wasn't surprising, since her father had raped her for the first time when she was eight. He had gone on raping her for that same number of years. Then she had put a stop to it, first popping his balls, one after the other, with one of her mother's knitting needles, and then putting that same needle, red and dripping, in her rapist-sire's left eyesocket. The balls had been easy, because he was sleeping, but the pain had been enough to wake him in spite of her special talent. She was a big girl, though, and he was drunk. She had been able to hold him down with her body just long enough to administer the coup de grâce.

Now she had years eight times four, she was a wanderer on the face of America, and an ex-actor had replaced the peanut farmer in the White House. The new fellow had an actor's unlikely black hair and an actor's charming, untrustworthy smile. Andi had seen one of his movies on TV. In it, the man who would be president played a guy who lost his legs when a train ran over them. She liked the idea of a man without legs; a man without legs couldn't chase you down and rape you.

Movies, they were the thing. Movies took you away. You could count on popcorn and happy endings. You got a man to go with you, that way it was a date and he paid. This movie was a good one, with fighting and kissing and loud music. It was called *Raiders of the Lost Ark*. Her current date had his hand under her skirt, high up on her bare thigh, but that was all right; a hand wasn't a prick. She had met him in a bar. She met most of the men she went on dates with in bars. He bought her a drink, but a free drink wasn't a date; it was just a pickup.

What's this about? he'd asked her, running the tip of his finger over her upper left arm. She was wearing a sleeveless blouse, so the tattoo showed. She liked the tattoo to show when she was out looking for a date. She wanted men to see it. They thought it was kinky. She had gotten it in San Diego the year after she killed her father.

It's a snake, she said. *A rattler. Don't you see the fangs?*

Of course he did. They were *big* fangs, out of all proportion to the head. A drop of poison hung from one.

He was a businessman type in an expensive suit, with lots of combed-back presidential hair and the afternoon off from whatever paper-pushing crap he did for work. His hair was mostly white instead of black and he looked about sixty. Close to twice her age. But that didn't matter to men. He wouldn't have cared if she was sixteen instead of thirty-two. Or eight. She remembered something her father had said once: *If they're old enough to pee, they're old enough for me.*

Of course I see them, the man who was now sitting beside her had said, *but what does it mean?*

Maybe you'll find out, Andi replied. She touched her upper lip with her tongue. *I have another tattoo. Somewhere else.*

Can I see it?

Maybe. Do you like movies?

He had frowned. *What do you mean?*

You want to date me, don't you?

He knew what that meant − or what it was supposed to mean. There were other girls in this place, and when they spoke of dates, they meant one thing. But it was not what Andi meant.

Sure. You're cute.

Then take me on a date. A real *date. Raiders of the Lost Ark is playing at the Rialto.*

I was thinking more of that little hotel two blocks down, darlin. A room with a wetbar and a balcony, how does that sound?

She had put her lips close to his ear and let her breasts press against his arm. *Maybe later. Take me to the movies first. Pay my way and buy me popcorn. The dark makes me amorous.*

And here they were, with Harrison Ford on the screen, big as a skyscraper and snapping a bullwhip in the desert dust. The old guy with the presidential hair had his hand under her skirt but she had a tub of popcorn placed firmly on her lap, making sure he could get most of the way down the third base line but not quite to home plate. He was trying to go higher, which was annoying because she wanted to see the end of the movie and find out what was in the Lost Ark. So . . .

2

At 2 p.m. on a weekday, the movie theater was almost deserted, but three people sat two rows back from Andi Steiner and her date. Two men, one quite old and one appearing on the edge of middle age (but appearances could be deceiving), flanked a woman of startling beauty. Her cheekbones were high, her eyes were gray, her complexion creamy. Her masses of black hair were tied back with a broad velvet ribbon. Usually she wore a hat – an old and battered tophat – but she had left it in her motorhome this day. You didn't wear a tall topper in a movie theater. Her name was Rose O'Hara, but the nomadic family she traveled with called her Rose the Hat.

The man edging into middle age was Barry Smith. Although one hundred percent Caucasian, he was known in this same family as Barry the Chink, because of his slightly upturned eyes.

'Now watch this,' he said. 'It's interesting.'

'The *movie's* interesting,' the old man – Grampa Flick – grunted. But that was just his usual contrariness. He was also watching the couple two rows down.

'It better be interesting,' Rose said, 'because the woman's not all that steamy. A little, but—'

'There she goes, there she goes,' Barry said as Andi leaned over and put her lips to her date's ear. Barry was grinning, the box of gummy bears in his hand forgotten. 'I've watched her do it three times and I still get a kick out of it.'

3

Mr Businessman's ear was filled with a thatch of wiry white hairs and clotted with wax the color of shit, but Andi didn't let that stop her; she wanted to blow this town and her finances were at a dangerously low ebb. 'Aren't you tired?' she whispered in the disgusting ear. 'Don't you want to go to sleep?'

The man's head immediately dropped onto his chest and he began to snore. Andi reached under her skirt, plucked up the relaxing hand, and placed it on the armrest. Then she reached into Mr Businessman's expensive-looking suitcoat and began to rummage. His wallet was in the inside left pocket. That was good. She wouldn't have to make him get up off his fat ass. Once they were asleep, moving them could be tricky.

She opened the wallet, tossed the credit cards on the floor, and looked for a few moments at the pictures – Mr Businessman with a bunch of other overweight Mr Businessmen on the golf course; Mr Businessman with his wife; a much younger Mr Businessman standing in front of a Christmas tree with his son and two daughters. The daughters were wearing Santa hats and matching dresses. He probably hadn't been raping them, but it was not out of the question. Men would rape when they could get away with it, this she had learned. At her father's knee, so to speak.

There was over two hundred dollars in the bill compartment. She had been hoping for even more – the bar where she had met him catered to a better class of whore than those out by the airport – but it wasn't bad for a Thursday matinee, and there were always men who wanted to take a good-looking girl to the movies, where a little heavy petting would only be the appetizer. Or so they hoped.

4

'Okay,' Rose murmured, and started to get up. 'I'm convinced. Let's give it a shot.'

But Barry put a hand on her arm, restraining her. 'No, wait. Watch. This is the best part.'

5

Andi leaned close to the disgusting ear again and whispered, 'Sleep deeper. As deep as you can. The pain you feel will only be a dream.'

She opened her purse and took out a pearl-handled knife. It was small, but the blade was razor-sharp. 'What will the pain be?'

'Only a dream,' Mr Businessman muttered into the knot of his tie.

'That's right, sweetie.' She put an arm around him and quickly slashed double Vs into his right cheek – a cheek so fat it would soon be a jowl. She took a moment to admire her work in the chancy light of the projector's colored dream-beam. Then the blood sheeted down. He would wake up with his face on fire, the right arm of his expensive suitcoat drenched, and in need of an emergency room.

And how will you explain it to your wife? You'll think of something, I'm sure. But unless you have plastic surgery, you'll see my marks every time you look in the mirror. And every time you go looking for a little strange in one of the bars, you'll remember how you got bitten by a rattlesnake. One in a blue skirt and a white sleeveless blouse.

She tucked the two fifties and five twenties into her purse, clicked it shut, and was about to get up when a hand fell on her shoulder and a woman murmured in her ear. 'Hello, dear. You can see the rest of the movie another time. Right now you're coming with us.'

Andi tried to turn, but hands seized her head. The terrible thing about them was that they were *inside*.

After that – until she found herself in Rose's EarthCruiser in a going-to-seed campground on the outskirts of this Midwestern city – all was darkness.

6

When she woke up, Rose gave her a cup of tea and talked to her for a long time. Andi heard everything, but most of her attention was taken up by the woman who had abducted her. She was a presence, and that was putting it mildly. Rose the Hat was six feet tall, with long legs in tapered white slacks and high breasts inside a t-shirt branded with the UNICEF logo and motto: *Whatever It Takes To Save a Child*. Her face was that of a calm queen, serene and untroubled. Her hair, now unbound, tumbled halfway down her back. The scuffed tophat cocked on her head was jarring, but otherwise she was the most beautiful woman Andi Steiner had ever seen.

'Do you understand what I've been telling you? I'm giving you an opportunity here, Andi, and you should not take it lightly. It's been twenty years or more since we've offered anyone what I'm offering you.'

'And if I say no? What then? Do you kill me? And take this . . .' What had she called it? 'This steam?'

Rose smiled. Her lips were rich and coral pink. Andi, who considered herself asexual, nonetheless wondered what that lipstick would taste like.

'You don't have enough steam to bother with, dear, and what you *do* have would be far from yummy. It would taste the way the meat from a tough old cow tastes to a rube.'

'To a what?'

'Never mind, just listen. We won't kill you. What we'll do if you say no is to wipe out all memory of this little conversation. You will find yourself on the side of the road outside some nothing town – Topeka, maybe, or Fargo – with no money, no identification, and no memory of how you got there. The last thing you'll remember is going into that movie theater with the man you robbed and mutilated.'

'He deserved to be mutilated!' Andi spat out.

Rose stood on her tiptoes and stretched, her fingers touching the roof of the RV. 'That's your business, honeydoll, I'm not your psychiatrist.' She wasn't wearing a bra; Andi could see the shifting punctuation marks of her nipples against her shirt. 'But here's something to consider: we'll take your talent as well as your money and your no doubt bogus indentification. The next time you suggest that a man go to sleep in a darkened movie theater, he'll turn to you and ask what the fuck you're talking about.'

Andi felt a cold trickle of fear. 'You can't do that.' But she remembered the terribly strong hands that had reached inside her brain and felt quite sure this woman could. She might need a little help from her friends, the ones in the RVs and motor homes gathered around this one like piglets at a sow's teats, but oh yes – she could.

Rose ignored this. 'How old are you, dear?'

'Twenty-eight.' She had been shading her age since hitting the big three-oh.

Rose looked at her, smiling, saying nothing. Andi met those

beautiful gray eyes for five seconds, then had to drop her gaze. But what her eyes fell upon when she did were those smooth breasts, unharnessed but with no sign of a sag. And when she looked up again, her eyes only got as far as the woman's lips. Those coral-pink lips.

'You're thirty-two,' Rose said. 'Oh, it only shows a little – because you've led a hard life. A life on the run. But you're still pretty. Stay with us, live with us, and ten years from now you really will be twenty-eight.'

'That's impossible.'

Rose smiled. 'A hundred years from now, you'll look and feel thirty-five. Until you take steam, that is. Then you'll be twenty-eight again, only you'll feel ten years younger. And you'll take steam often. Live long, stay young, and eat well: those are the things I'm offering. How do they sound?'

'Too good to be true,' Andi said. 'Like those ads about how you can get life insurance for ten dollars.'

She wasn't entirely wrong. Rose hadn't told any lies (at least not yet), but there were things she wasn't saying. Like how steam was sometimes in short supply. Like how not everyone lived through the Turning. Rose judged this one might, and Walnut, the True's jackleg doctor, had cautiously concurred, but nothing was sure.

'And you and your friends call yourself—?'

'They're not my friends, they're my family. We're the True Knot.' Rose laced her fingers together and held them in front of Andi's face. 'And what's tied can never be untied. You need to understand that.'

Andi, who already knew that a girl who has been raped can never be unraped, understood perfectly.

'Do I really have any other choice?'

Rose shrugged. 'Only bad ones, dear. But it's better if you want it. It will make the Turning easier.'

'Does it hurt? This Turning?'

Rose smiled and told the first outright lie. 'Not at all.'

7

A summer night on the outskirts of a Midwestern city.

Somewhere people were watching Harrison Ford snap his bullwhip;

somewhere the Actor President was no doubt smiling his untrustworthy smile; here, in this campground, Andi Steiner was lying on a discount-store lawn recliner, bathed in the headlights of Rose's EarthCruiser and someone else's Winnebago. Rose had explained to her that, while the True Knot owned several campgrounds, this wasn't one of them. But their advance man was able to four-wall places like this, businesses tottering on the edge of insolvency. America was suffering a recession, but for the True, money was not a problem.

'Who is this advance man?' Andi had asked.

'Oh, he's a very winning fellow,' Rose had said, smiling. 'Able to charm the birdies down from the trees. You'll meet him soon.'

'Is he your special guy?'

Rose had laughed at that and caressed Andi's cheek. The touch of her fingers caused a hot little worm of excitement in Andi's stomach. Crazy, but there it was. 'You've got a twinkle, don't you? I think you'll be fine.'

Maybe, but as she lay here, Andi was no longer excited, only scared. News stories slipped through her mind, ones about bodies found in ditches, bodies found in wooded clearings, bodies found at the bottom of dry wells. Women and girls. Almost always women and girls. It wasn't Rose who scared her – not exactly – and there were other women here, but there were also men.

Rose knelt beside her. The glare of the headlights should have turned her face into a harsh and ugly landscape of blacks and whites, but the opposite was true: it only made her more beautiful. Once again she caressed Andi's cheek. 'No fear,' she said. 'No fear.'

She turned to one of the other women, a pallidly pretty creature Rose called Silent Sarey, and nodded. Sarey nodded back and went into Rose's monster RV. The others, meanwhile, began to form a circle around the lawn recliner. Andi didn't like that. There was something *sacrificial* about it.

'No fear. Soon you'll be one of us, Andi. One *with* us.'

Unless, Rose thought, *you cycle out. In which case, we'll just burn your clothes in the incinerator behind the comfort stations and move on tomorrow. Nothing ventured, nothing gained.*

But she hoped that wouldn't happen. She liked this one, and a sleeper talent would come in handy.

Sarey returned with a steel canister that looked like a thermos bottle. She handed it to Rose, who removed the red cap. Beneath was a nozzle and a valve. To Andi the canister looked like an unlabeled can of bug spray. She thought about bolting up from the recliner and running for it, then remembered the movie theater. The hands that had reached inside her head, holding her in place.

'Grampa Flick?' Rose asked. 'Will you lead us?'

'Happy to.' It was the old man from the theater. Tonight he was wearing baggy pink Bermuda shorts, white socks that climbed all the way up his scrawny shins to his knees, and Jesus sandals. To Andi he looked like Grandpa Walton after two years in a concentration camp. He raised his hands, and the rest raised theirs with him. Linked that way and silhouetted in the crisscrossing headlight beams, they looked like a chain of weird paperdolls.

'We are the True Knot,' he said. The voice coming from that sunken chest no longer trembled; it was the deep and resonant voice of a much younger and stronger man.

'*We are the True Knot*,' they responded. '*What is tied may never be untied*.'

'Here is a woman,' Grampa Flick said. 'Would she join us? Would she tie her life to our life and be one with us?'

'Say yes,' Rose said.

'Y-Yes,' Andi managed. Her heart was no longer beating; it was thrumming like a wire.

Rose turned the valve on her canister. There was a small, rueful sigh, and a puff of silver mist escaped. Instead of dissipating on the light evening breeze, it hung just above the canister until Rose leaned forward, pursed those fascinating coral lips, and blew gently. The puff of mist – looking a bit like a comic-strip dialogue balloon without any words in it – drifted until it hovered above Andi's upturned face and wide eyes.

'We are the True Knot, and we endure,' Grampa Flick proclaimed.

'*Sabbatha hanti*,' the others responded.

The mist began to descend, very slowly.

'We are the chosen ones.'

'*Lodsam hanti*,' they responded.

'Breathe deep,' Rose said, and kissed Andi softly on the cheek. 'I'll see you on the other side.'

Maybe.

'We are the fortunate ones.'

'*Cahanna risone hanti.*'

Then, all together: 'We are the True Knot, and we . . .'

But Andi lost track of it there. The silvery stuff settled over her face and it was cold, cold. When she inhaled, it came to some sort of tenebrous life and began screaming inside her. A child made of mist – whether boy or girl she didn't know – was struggling to get away but someone was cutting. *Rose* was cutting, while the others stood close around her (in a knot), shining down a dozen flashlights, illuminating a slow-motion murder.

Andi tried to bolt up from the recliner, but she had no body to bolt with. Her body was gone. Where it had been was only pain in the shape of a human being. The pain of the child's dying, and of her own.

Embrace it. The thought was like a cool cloth pressed on the burning wound that was her body. *That's the only way through.*

I can't, I've been running from this pain my whole life.

Perhaps so, but you're all out of running room. Embrace it. Swallow it. Take steam or die.

8

The True stood with hands upraised, chanting the old words: *sabbatha hanti, lodsam hanti, cahanna risone hanti.* They watched as Andi Steiner's blouse flattened where her breasts had been, as her skirt puffed shut like a closing mouth. They watched as her face turned to milk-glass. Her eyes remained, though, floating like tiny balloons on gauzy strings of nerve.

But they're going to go, too, Walnut thought. *She's not strong enough. I thought maybe she was, but I was wrong. She may come back a time or two, but then she'll cycle out. Nothing left but her clothes.* He tried to recall his own Turning, and could only remember that the moon had been full and there had been a bonfire instead of headlights. A bonfire, the whicker of horses . . . and the pain. Could you actually remember pain? He didn't think so. You knew there was such a thing, and that you had suffered it, but that wasn't the same.

Andi's face swam back into existence like the face of a ghost above a medium's table. The front of her blouse plumped up in curves; her skirt swelled as her hips and thighs returned to the world. She shrieked in agony.

'*We are the True Knot and we endure,*' they chanted in the criss-crossing beams of the RVs. '*Sabbatha hanti. We are the chosen ones,* lodsam hanti. *We are the fortunate ones,* cahanna risone hanti.' They would go on until it was over. One way or the other, it wouldn't take long.

Andi began to disappear again. Her flesh became cloudy glass through which the True could see her skeleton and the bone grin of her skull. A few silver fillings gleamed in that grin. Her disembodied eyes rolled wildly in sockets that were no longer there. She was still screaming, but now the sound was thin and echoing, as if it came from far down a distant hall.

9

Rose thought she'd give up, that was what they did when the pain became too much, but this was one tough babe. She came swirling back into existence, screaming all the way. Her newly arrived hands seized Rose's with mad strength and bore down. Rose leaned forward, hardly noticing the pain.

'I know what you want, honeydoll. Come back and you can have it.' She lowered her mouth to Andi's, caressing Andi's upper lip with her tongue until the lip turned to mist. But the eyes stayed, fixed on Rose's.

'*Sabbatha hanti,*' they chanted. '*Lodsam hanti. Cahanna risone hanti.*'

Andi came back, growing a face around her staring, pain-filled eyes. Her body followed. For a moment Rose could see the bones of her arms, the bones in the fingers clutching hers, then they were once more dressed in flesh.

Rose kissed her again. Even in her pain Andi responded, and Rose breathed her own essence down the younger woman's throat.

I want this one. And what I want, I get.

Andi began to fade again, but Rose could feel her fighting it. Getting on top of it. Feeding herself with the screaming life-force she had breathed down her throat and into her lungs instead of trying to push it away.

Taking steam for the first time.

10

The newest member of the True Knot spent that night in Rose O'Hara's bed, and for the first time in her life found something in sex besides horror and pain. Her throat was raw from the screaming she'd done on the lawn recliner, but she screamed again as this new sensation – pleasure to match the pain of her Turning – took her body and once more seemed to render it transparent.

'Scream all you want,' Rose said, looking up from between her thighs. 'They've heard plenty of them. The good as well as the bad.'

'Is sex like this for everybody?' If so, what she had missed! What her bastard father had stolen from her! And people thought *she* was a thief?

'It's like this for us, when we've taken steam,' Rose said. 'That's all you need to know.'

She lowered her head and it began again.

11

Not long before midnight, Token Charlie and Baba the Russian were sitting on the lower step of Token Charlie's Bounder, sharing a joint and looking up at the moon. From Rose's EarthCruiser came more screams.

Charlie and Baba turned to each other and grinned.

'Someone is likin it,' Baba remarked.

'What's not to like?' Charlie said.

12

Andi woke in the day's first early light with her head pillowed on Rose's breasts. She felt entirely different; she felt no different at all.

She lifted her head and saw Rose looking at her with those remarkable gray eyes.

'You saved me,' Andi said. 'You brought me back.'

'I couldn't have done it alone. You wanted to come.' *In more ways than one, honeydoll.*

'What we did after . . . we can't do it again, can we?'

Rose shook her head, smiling. 'No. And that's okay. Some experiences absolutely cannot be topped. Besides, my man will be back today.'

'What's his name?'

'He answers to Henry Rothman, but that's just for the rubes. His True name is Crow Daddy.'

'Do you love him? You do, don't you?'

Rose smiled, drew Andi closer, kissed her. But she did not answer.

'Rose?'

'Yes?'

'Am I . . . am I still human?'

To this Rose gave the same answer Dick Hallorann had once given young Danny Torrance, and in the same cold tone of voice: 'Do you care?'

Andi decided she didn't. She decided she was home.

MAMA

1

There was a muddle of bad dreams – someone swinging a hammer and chasing him down endless halls, an elevator that ran by itself, hedges in the shapes of animals that came to life and closed in on him – and finally one clear thought: *I wish I were dead.*

Dan Torrance opened his eyes. Sunlight shot through them and into his aching head, threatening to set his brains on fire. The hangover to end all hangovers. His face was throbbing. His nostrils were clogged shut except for a tiny pinhole in the left one that allowed in a thread of air. Left one? No, it was the right. He could breathe through his mouth, but it was foul with the taste of whiskey and cigarettes. His stomach was a ball of lead, full of all the wrong things. *Morning-after junkbelly*, some old drinking buddy or other had called that woeful sensation.

Loud snoring from beside him. Dan turned his head that way, although his neck screamed in protest and another bolt of agony shot him through the temple. He opened his eyes again, but just a little; no more of that blazing sun, please. Not yet. He was lying on a bare mattress on a bare floor. A bare woman lay sprawled on her back beside him. Dan looked down and saw that he was also alfresco.

Her name is . . . Dolores? No. Debbie? That's closer, but not quite—

Deenie. Her name was Deenie. He had met her in a bar called the Milky Way, and it had all been quite hilarious until . . .

He couldn't remember, and one look at his hands – both swollen, the knuckles of the right scuffed and scabbed – made him decide he didn't want to remember. And what did it matter? The basic scenario never changed. He got drunk, someone said the wrong thing, chaos and bar-carnage followed. There was a dangerous dog inside his head. Sober, he could keep it on a leash. When he drank, the leash disappeared. *Sooner or later I'll kill someone.* For all he knew, he had last night.

Hey Deenie, squeeze my weenie.

Had he actually said that? He was terribly afraid he had. Some of it was coming back to him now, and even some was too much. Playing eightball. Trying to put a little extra spin on the cue and scratching it right off the table, the little chalk-smudged sonofabitch bouncing and rolling all the way to the jukebox that was playing – what else? – country music. He seemed to remember Joe Diffie. Why had he scratched so outrageously? Because he was drunk, and because Deenie was standing behind him. Deenie had been squeezing his weenie just below the line of the table and he was showing off for her. All in good fun. But then the guy in the Case cap and the fancy silk cowboy shirt had laughed, and that was his mistake.

Chaos and bar-carnage.

Dan touched his mouth and felt plump sausages where normal lips had been when he left that check-cashing joint yesterday afternoon with a little over five hundred bucks in his front pants pocket.

At least all my teeth seem to be—

His stomach gave a liquid lurch. He burped up a mouthful of sour gunk that tasted of whiskey and swallowed it back. It burned going down. He rolled off the mattress onto his knees, staggered to his feet, then swayed as the room began to do a gentle tango. He was hungover, his head was bursting, his gut was filled with whatever cheap food he'd put in it last night to tamp down the booze . . . but he was also still drunk.

He hooked his underpants off the floor and left the bedroom with them clutched in his hand, not quite limping but definitely favoring his left leg. He had a vague memory – one he hoped would never sharpen – of the Case cowboy throwing a chair. That was when he and Deenie-squeeze-my-weenie had left, not quite running but laughing like loons.

Another lurch from his unhappy gut. This time it was accompanied by a clench that felt like a hand in a slick rubber glove. That released all the puke triggers: the vinegar smell of hardcooked eggs in a big glass jar, the taste of barbecue-flavored pork rinds, the sight of french fries drowning in a ketchup nosebleed. All the crap he'd crammed into his mouth last night between shots. He was going to spew, but the images just kept on coming, revolving on some nightmare gameshow prize wheel.

What have we got for our next contestant, Johnny? Well, Bob, it's a great big platter of GREASY SARDINES!

The bathroom was directly across a short stub of hall. The door was open, the toilet seat up. Dan lunged, fell on his knees, and spewed a great flood of brownish-yellow stuff on top of a floating turd. He looked away, groped for the flush, found it, pushed it. Water cascaded, but there was no accompanying sound of draining water. He looked back and saw something alarming: the turd, probably his own, rising toward the pee-splashed rim of the toilet bowl on a sea of half-digested bar-snacks. Just before the toilet could overspill, making this morning's banal horrors complete, something cleared its throat in the pipe and the whole mess flushed away. Dan threw up again, then sat on his heels with his back against the bathroom wall and his throbbing head lowered, waiting for the tank to refill so he could flush a second time.

No more. I swear it. No more booze, no more bars, no more fights. Promising himself this for the hundredth time. Or the thousandth.

One thing was certain: he had to get out of this town or he might be in trouble. *Serious* trouble was not out of the question.

Johnny, what have we got for today's grand prize winner? Bob, it's TWO YEARS IN STATE FOR ASSAULT AND BATTERY!

And . . . the studio audience goes wild.

The toilet tank had quieted its noisy refill. He reached for the handle to flush away The Morning After, Part Two, then paused, regarding the black hole of his short-term memory. Did he know his name? Yes! Daniel Anthony Torrance. Did he know the name of the chick snoring on the mattress in the other room? Yes! Deenie. He didn't recall her last name, but it was likely she had never told him. Did he know the current president's name?

To Dan's horror, he didn't, not at first. The guy had a funky Elvis haircut and played the sax – quite badly. But the name . . . ?

Do you even know where you are?

Cleveland? Charleston? It was one or the other.

As he flushed the toilet, the president's name arrived in his head with splendid clarity. And Dan wasn't in either Cleveland *or*

Charleston. He was in Wilmington, North Carolina. He worked as an orderly at Grace of Mary Hospital. Or had. It was time to move on. If he got to some other place, some *good* place, he might be able to quit the drinking and start over.

He got up and looked in the mirror. The damage wasn't as bad as he'd feared. Nose swelled but not actually broken – at least he didn't think so. Crusts of dried blood above his puffy upper lip. There was a bruise on his right cheekbone (the Case cowboy must have been a lefty) with the bloody imprint of a ring sitting in the middle of it. Another bruise, a big one, was spreading in the cup of his left shoulder. That, he seemed to remember, had been from a pool cue.

He looked in the medicine cabinet. Amid tubes of makeup and cluttered bottles of over-the-counter medicine, he found three prescription bottles. The first was Diflucan, commonly prescribed for yeast infections. It made him glad he was circumcised. The second was Darvon Comp 65. He opened it, saw half a dozen capsules, and put three in his pocket for later reference. The last scrip was for Fioricet, and the bottle – thankfully – was almost full. He swallowed three with cold water. Bending over the basin made his headache worse than ever, but he thought he would soon get relief. Fioricet, intended for migraine and tension headaches, was a guaranteed hangover killer. Well . . . almost guaranteed.

He started to close the cabinet, then took another look. He moved some of the crap around. No birth control ring. Maybe it was in her purse. He hoped so, because he hadn't been carrying a rubber. If he'd fucked her – and although he couldn't remember for sure, he probably had – he'd ridden in bareback.

He put on his underwear and shuffled back to the bedroom, standing in the doorway for a moment and looking at the woman who had brought him home last night. Arms and legs splayed, everything showing. Last night she had looked like the goddess of the Western world in her thigh-high leather skirt and cork sandals, her cropped top and hoop earrings. This morning he saw the sagging white dough of a growing boozegut, and the second chin starting to appear under the first.

He saw something worse: she wasn't a woman, after all. Probably not jailbait (please God not jailbait), but surely no more than twenty and maybe still in her late teens. On one wall, chillingly childish, was a poster of KISS with Gene Simmons spewing fire. On another was a cute kitten with startled eyes, dangling from a tree branch. HANG IN THERE, BABY, this poster advised.

He needed to get out of here.

Their clothes were tangled together at the foot of the mattress. He separated his t-shirt from her panties, yanked it over his head, then stepped into his jeans. He froze with the zipper halfway up, realizing that his left front pocket was much flatter than it had been when he left the check-cashing joint the previous afternoon.

No. It can't be.

His head, which had begun to feel the teeniest bit better, started to throb again as his heartbeat picked up speed, and when he shoved his hand into the pocket, it brought up nothing but a ten-dollar bill and two toothpicks, one of which poked under his index finger-nail and into the sensitive meat beneath. He hardly noticed.

We didn't drink up five hundred dollars. No way we did. We'd be dead if we drank up that much.

His wallet was still at home in his hip pocket. He pulled it out, hoping against hope, but no joy. He must have transferred the ten he usually kept there to his front pocket at some point. The front pocket made it tougher for barroom dips, which now seemed like quite the joke.

He looked at the snoring, splayed girl-woman on the mattress and started for her, meaning to shake her awake and ask her what she'd done with his fucking money. *Choke* her awake, if that was what it took. But if she'd stolen from him, why had she brought him home? And hadn't there been something else? Some other adventure after they left the Milky Way? Now that his head was clearing, he had a memory — hazy, but probably valid — of them taking a cab to the train station.

I know a guy who hangs out there, honey.

Had she really said that, or was it only his imagination?

She said it, all right. I'm in Wilmington, Bill Clinton's the president, and we went to the train station. Where there was indeed a guy. The kind who likes to do his deals in the men's room, especially when the customer has a slightly rearranged face. When he asked who teed off on me, I told him—

'I told him he should mind his beeswax,' Dan muttered.

When the two of them went in, Dan had been meaning to buy a gram to keep his date happy, no more than that, and only if it wasn't half Manitol. Coke might be Deenie's thing but it wasn't his. Rich man's Anacin, he'd heard it called, and he was far from rich. But then someone had come out of one of the stalls. A business type with a briefcase banging his knee. And when Mr Businessman went to wash his hands at one of the basins, Dan had seen flies crawling all over his face.

Deathflies. Mr Businessman was a dead man walking and didn't know it.

So instead of going small, he was pretty sure he'd gone big. Maybe he'd changed his mind at the last moment, though. It was possible; he could remember so little.

I remember the flies, though.

Yes. He remembered those. Booze tamped down the shining, knocked it unconscious, but he wasn't sure the flies were even a part of the shining. They came when they would, drunk or sober.

He thought again: *I need to get out of here.*

He thought again: *I wish I were dead.*

2

Deenie made a soft snorting sound and turned away from the merciless morning light. Except for the mattress on the floor, the room was devoid of furniture; there wasn't even a thrift-shop bureau. The closet stood open, and Dan could see the majority of Deenie's meager wardrobe heaped in two plastic laundry baskets. The few items on hangers looked like barhopping clothes. He could see a red t-shirt with SEXY GIRL printed in spangles on the front, and a denim skirt with a fashionably frayed hem. There were two pairs of sneakers, two pairs of flats, and one pair of strappy high-heel fuck-me shoes. No cork sandals, though. No sign of his own beat-up Reeboks, for that matter.

Dan couldn't remember them kicking off their shoes when they came in, but if they had, they'd be in the living room, which he *could* remember – vaguely. Her purse might be there, too. He might have given her whatever remained of his cash for safekeeping. It was unlikely but not impossible.

He walked his throbbing head down the short hall to what he assumed was the apartment's only other room. On the far side was a kitchenette, the amenities consisting of a hotplate and a bar refrigerator tucked under the counter. In the living area was a sofa hemorrhaging stuffing and propped up at one end with a couple of bricks. It faced a big TV with a crack running down the middle of the glass. The crack had been mended with a strip of packing tape that now dangled by one corner. A couple of flies were stuck to the tape, one still struggling feebly. Dan eyed it with morbid fascination, reflecting (not for the first time) that the hungover eye had a weird ability to find the ugliest things in any given landscape.

There was a coffee table in front of the sofa. On it was an ashtray filled with butts, a baggie filled with white powder, and a *People* magazine with more blow scattered across it. Beside it, completing the picture, was a dollar bill, still partly rolled up. He didn't know how much they had snorted, but judging by how much still remained, he could kiss his five hundred dollars goodbye.

Fuck. I don't even like coke. And how did I snort it, anyway? I can hardly breathe.

He hadn't. *She* had snorted it. He had rubbed it on his gums. It was all starting to come back to him. He would have preferred it stay away, but too late.

The deathflies in the restroom, crawling in and out of Mr Businessman's mouth and over the wet surfaces of his eyes. Mr Dealerman asking what Dan was looking at. Dan telling him it was nothing, it didn't matter, let's see what you've got. It turned out Mr Dealerman had plenty. They usually did. Next came the ride back to her place in another taxi, Deenie already snorting from the back of her hand, too greedy — or too needy — to wait. The two of them trying to sing 'Mr Roboto.'

He spied her sandals and his Reeboks right inside the door, and here were more golden memories. She hadn't kicked the sandals off, only dropped them from her feet, because by then he'd had his hands planted firmly on her ass and she had her legs wrapped around his waist. Her neck smelled of perfume, her breath of barbecue-flavored pork rinds. They had been gobbling them by the handful before moving on to the pool table.

Dan put on his sneakers, then walked across to the kitchenette, thinking there might be instant coffee in the single cupboard. He didn't find coffee, but he did see her purse, lying on the floor. He thought he could remember her tossing it at the sofa and laughing when it missed. Half the crap had spilled out, including a red imitation leather wallet. He scooped everything back inside and took it over to the kitchenette. Although he knew damned well that his money was now living in the pocket of Mr Dealerman's designer jeans, part of him insisted that there must be *some* left, if only because he needed some to be left. Ten dollars was enough for three drinks or two six-packs, but it was going to take more than that today.

He fished out her wallet and opened it. There were some pictures – a couple of Deenie with some guy who looked too much like her not to be a relative, a couple of Deenie holding a baby, one of Deenie in a prom dress next to a bucktoothed kid in a gruesome blue tux. The bill compartment was bulging. This gave him hope until he pulled it open and saw a swatch of food stamps. There was also some currency: two twenties and three tens.

That's my money. What's left of it, anyway.

He knew better. He never would have given some shitfaced pickup his week's pay for safekeeping. It was hers.

Yes, but hadn't the coke been her idea? Wasn't she the reason he was broke as well as hungover this morning?

No. You're hungover because you're a drunk. You're broke because you saw the deathflies.

It might be true, but if she hadn't insisted they go to the train station and score, he never would have *seen* the deathflies.

She might need that seventy bucks for groceries.

Right. A jar of peanut butter and a jar of strawberry jam. Also a loaf of bread to spread it on. She had food stamps for the rest.

Or rent. She might need it for that.

If she needed rent money, she could peddle the TV. Maybe her dealer would take it, crack and all. Seventy dollars wouldn't go very far on a month's rent, anyway, he reasoned, even for a dump like this one.

That's not yours, doc. It was his mother's voice, the last one he needed to hear when he was savagely hungover and in desperate need of a drink.

'Fuck you, Ma.' His voice was low but sincere. He took the money, stuffed it in his pocket, put the billfold back in the purse, and turned around.

A kid was standing there.

He looked about eighteen months old. He was wearing an Atlanta Braves t-shirt. It came down to his knees, but the diaper underneath showed anyway, because it was loaded and hanging just above his ankles. Dan's heart took an enormous leap in his chest and his head gave a sudden terrific whammo, as if Thor had swung his hammer in there. For a moment he was absolutely sure he was going to stroke out, have a heart attack, or both.

Then he drew in a deep breath and exhaled. 'Where did *you* come from, little hero?'

'Mama,' the kid said.

Which in a way made perfect sense – Dan, too, had come from his mama – but it didn't help. A terrible deduction was trying to form itself in his thumping head, but he didn't want anything to do with it.

He saw you take the money.

Maybe so, but that wasn't the deduction. If the kid saw him take it, so what? He wasn't even two. Kids that young accepted everything adults did. If he saw his mama walking on the ceiling with fire shooting from her fingertips, he'd accept that.

'What's your name, hero?' His voice was throbbing in time with his heart, which still hadn't settled down.

'Mama.'

Really? The other kids are gonna have fun with that when you get to high school.

'Did you come from next door? Or down the hall?'

Please say yes. Because here's the deduction: if this kid is Deenie's, then she went out barhopping and left him locked in this shitty apartment. Alone.

'Mama!'

Then the kid spied the coke on the coffee table and trotted toward it with the sodden crotch of his diaper swinging.

'Canny!'

'No, that's not candy,' Dan said, although of course it was: nose candy.

Paying no attention, the kid reached for the white powder with one hand. As he did, Dan saw bruises on his upper arm. The kind left by a squeezing hand.

He grabbed the kid around the waist and between the legs. As he swung him up and away from the table (the sodden diaper squeezing pee through his fingers to patter on the floor), Dan's head filled with an image that was brief but excruciatingly clear: the Deenie look-alike in the wallet photo, picking the kid up and shaking him. Leaving the marks of his fingers.

(*Hey Tommy what part of* get the fuck out *don't you understand?*)

(*Randy don't he's just a baby*)

Then it was gone. But that second voice, weak and remonstrating, had been Deenie's, and he understood that Randy was her older brother. It made sense. Not every abuser was the boyfriend. Sometimes it was the brother. Sometimes the uncle. Sometimes

(*come out you worthless pup come out and take your medicine*) it was even dear old Dad.

He carried the baby – Tommy, his name was Tommy – into the bedroom. The kid saw his mother and immediately began wriggling. 'Mama! Mama! *Ma*ma!'

When Dan set him down, Tommy trotted to the mattress and crawled up beside her. Although sleeping, Deenie put her arm around him and hugged him to her. The Braves shirt pulled up, and Dan saw more bruises on the kid's legs.

The brother's name is Randy. I could find him.

This thought was as cold and clear as lake ice in January. If he handled the picture from the wallet and concentrated, ignoring the pounding of his head, he probably *could* find the big brother. He had done such things before.

I could leave a few bruises of my own. Tell him the next time I'll kill him.

Only there wasn't going to be a next time. Wilmington was done. He was never going to see Deenie or this desperate little apartment again. He was never going to think of last night or this morning again.

This time it was Dick Halloran's voice. *No, honey. Maybe you can put the things from the Overlook away in lockboxes, but not memories. Never those. They're the real ghosts.*

He stood in the doorway, looking at Deenie and her bruised boy. The kid had gone back to sleep, and in the morning sun, the two of them looked almost angelic.

She's no angel. Maybe she didn't leave the bruises, but she went out partying and left him alone. If you hadn't been there when he woke up and walked into the living room . . .

Canny, the kid had said, reaching for the blow. Not good. Something needed to be done.

Maybe, but not by me. I'd look good showing up at DHS to complain about child neglect with this face, wouldn't I? Reeking of booze and puke. Just an upstanding citizen doing his civic duty.

You can put her money back, Wendy said. *You can do that much.*

He almost did. Really. He took it out of his pocket and had it right there in his hand. He even strolled it over to her purse, and the walk must have done him good, because he had an idea.

Take the coke, if you've got to take something. You can sell what's left for a hundred bucks. Maybe even two hundred, if it hasn't been stomped on too much.

Only, if his potential buyer turned out to be a narc — it would be just his luck — he'd wind up in jail. Where he might also find himself nailed for whatever stupid shit had gone down in the Milky Way. The cash was way safer. Seventy bucks in all.

I'll split it, he decided. *Forty for her and thirty for me.*

Only, thirty wouldn't do him much good. And there were the food stamps — a wad big enough to choke a horse. She could feed the kid with those.

He picked up the coke and the dusty *People* magazine and put them on the kitchenette counter, safely out of the kid's reach. There was a scrubbie in the sink, and he used it on the coffee table, cleaning up the leftover shake. Telling himself that if she came stumbling out while he was doing it, he would give her back her goddam money. Telling himself that if she went on snoozing, she deserved whatever she got.

Deenie didn't come out. She went on snoozing.

Dan finished cleaning up, tossed the scrubbie back in the sink, and thought briefly about leaving a note. But what would it say? *Take better care of your kid, and by the way, I took your cash?*

Okay, no note.

He left with the money in his left front pocket, being careful not to slam the door on his way out. He told himself he was being considerate.

3

Around noon – his hangover headache a thing of the past thanks to Deenie's Fioricet and a Darvon chaser – he approached an establishment called Golden's Discount Liquors & Import Beers. This was in the old part of town, where the establishments were brick, the sidewalks were largely empty, and the pawnshops (each displaying an admirable selection of straight razors) were many. His intention was to buy a very large bottle of very cheap whiskey, but what he saw out front changed his mind. It was a shopping cart loaded with a bum's crazy assortment of possessions. The bum in question was inside, haranguing the clerk. There was a blanket, rolled up and tied with twine, on top of the cart. Dan could see a couple of stains, but on the whole it didn't look bad. He took it and walked briskly away with it under his arm. After stealing seventy dollars from a single mother with a substance abuse problem, taking a bum's magic carpet seemed like small shit indeed. Which might have been why he felt smaller than ever.

I am the Incredible Shrinking Man, he thought, hurrying around the corner with his new prize. *Steal a few more things and I will vanish entirely from sight.*

He was listening for the outraged caws of the bum – the crazier they were, the louder they cawed – but there was nothing. One more corner and he could congratulate himself on a clean getaway.

Dan turned it.

4

That evening found him sitting at the mouth of a large stormdrain on the slope beneath the Cape Fear Memorial Bridge. He had a room, but there was the small matter of stacked-up back rent, which he had absolutely promised to pay as of 5 p.m. yesterday. Nor was that all. If he returned to his room, he might be invited to visit a certain fortresslike municipal building on Bess Street, to answer questions about a certain bar altercation. On the whole, it seemed safer to stay away.

There was a downtown shelter called Hope House (which the winos of course called Hopeless House), but Dan had no intention of going there. You could sleep free, but if you had a bottle they'd take it away. Wilmington was full of by-the-night flops and cheap motels where nobody gave a shit what you drank, snorted, or injected, but why would you waste good drinking money on a bed and a roof when the weather was warm and dry? He could worry about beds and roofs when he headed north. Not to mention getting his few possessions out of the room on Burney Street without his landlady's notice.

The moon was rising over the river. The blanket was spread out behind him. Soon he would lie down on it, pull it around him in a cocoon, and sleep. He was just high enough to be happy. The takeoff and the climb-out had been rough, but now all that low-altitude turbulence was behind him. He supposed he wasn't leading what straight America would call an exemplary life, but for the time being, all was fine. He had a bottle of Old Sun (purchased at a liquor store a prudent distance from Golden's Discount) and half a hero sandwich for breakfast tomorrow. The future was cloudy, but tonight the moon was bright. All was as it should be.

(*Canny*)

Suddenly the kid was with him. Tommy. Right here with him. Reaching for the blow. Bruises on his arm. Blue eyes.

(*Canny*)

He saw this with an excruciating clarity that had nothing to do with the shining. And more. Deenie lying on her back, snoring. The red imitation leather wallet. The wad of food stamps with US DEPARTMENT OF AGRICULTURE printed on them. The money. The seventy dollars. Which he had taken.

Think about the moon. Think about how serene it looks rising over the water.

For a while he did, but then he saw Deenie on her back, the red imitation leather wallet, the wad of food stamps, the pitiful crumple of cash (much of it now gone). Most clearly of all he saw the kid reaching for the blow with a hand that looked like a starfish. Blue eyes. Bruised arm.

Canny, he said.

Mama, he said.

Dan had learned the trick of measuring out his drinks; that way the booze lasted longer, the high was mellower, and the next day's headache lighter and more manageable. Sometimes, though, the measuring thing went wrong. Shit happened. Like at the Milky Way. That had been more or less an accident, but tonight, finishing the bottle in four long swallows, was on purpose. Your mind was a blackboard. Booze was the eraser.

He lay down and pulled the stolen blanket around him. He waited for unconsciousness, and it came, but Tommy came first. Atlanta Braves shirt. Sagging diaper. Blue eyes, bruised arm, starfish hand.

Canny. Mama.

I will never speak of this, he told himself. *Not to anyone.*

As the moon rose over Wilmington, North Carolina, Dan Torrance lapsed into unconsciousness. There were dreams of the Overlook, but he would not remember them upon waking. What he remembered upon waking were the blue eyes, the bruised arm, the reaching hand.

He managed to get his possessions and went north, first to upstate New York, then to Massachusetts. Two years passed. Sometimes he helped people, mostly old people. He had a way of doing that. On too many drunk nights, the kid would be the last thing he thought of and the first thing that came to mind on the hungover mornings-after. It was the kid he always thought of when he told himself he was going to quit the drinking. Maybe next week; next month for sure. The kid. The eyes. The arm. The reaching starfish hand.

Canny.

Mama.

PART ONE
ABRA

CHAPTER ONE
WELCOME TO TEENYTOWN

1

After Wilmington, the daily drinking stopped.

He'd go a week, sometimes two, without anything stronger than diet soda. He'd wake up without a hangover, which was good. He'd wake up thirsty and miserable – *wanting* – which wasn't. Then there would come a night. Or a weekend. Sometimes it was a Budweiser ad on TV that set him off – fresh-faced young people with nary a beergut among them, having cold ones after a vigorous volleyball game. Sometimes it was seeing a couple of nice-looking women having after-work drinks outside some pleasant little café, the kind of place with a French name and lots of hanging plants. The drinks were almost always the kind that came with little umbrellas. Sometimes it was a song on the radio. Once it was Styx, singing 'Mr Roboto.' When he was dry, he was completely dry. When he drank, he got drunk. If he woke up next to a woman, he thought of Deenie and the kid in the Braves t-shirt. He thought of the seventy dollars. He even thought of the stolen blanket, which he had left in the stormdrain. Maybe it was still there. If so, it would be moldy now.

Sometimes he got drunk and missed work. They'd keep him on for a while – he was good at what he did – but then would come a day. When it did, he would say thank you very much and board a bus. Wilmington became Albany and Albany became Utica. Utica became New Paltz. New Paltz gave way to Sturbridge, where he got drunk at an outdoor folk concert and woke up the next day in jail with a broken wrist. Next up was Weston, after that came a nursing home on Martha's Vineyard, and boy, *that* gig didn't last long. On his third day the head nurse smelled booze on his breath and it was seeya, wouldn't want to beya. Once he crossed the path of the True Knot without realizing it. Not in the top part of his mind, anyway, although lower down – in the part that *shone* – there was something. A smell, fading and unpleasant, like the smell of burned rubber on a stretch of turnpike where there has been a bad accident not long before.

From Martha's Vineyard he took MassLines to Newburyport. There he found work in a don't-give-much-of-a-shit veterans' home, the kind of place where old soldiers were sometimes left in wheelchairs outside empty consulting rooms until their peebags overflowed onto the floor. A lousy place for patients, a better one for frequent fuckups like himself, although Dan and a few others did as well by the old soldiers as they could. He even helped a couple get over when their time came. That job lasted awhile, long enough for the Saxophone President to turn the White House keys over to the Cowboy President.

Dan had a few wet nights in Newburyport, but always with the next day off, so it was okay. After one of these mini-sprees, he woke up thinking *at least I left the food stamps*. That brought on the old psychotic gameshow duo.

Sorry, Deenie, you lose, but nobody leaves empty-handed. What have we got for her, Johnny?

Well, Bob, Deenie didn't win any money, but she's leaving with our new home game, several grams of cocaine, and a great big wad of FOOD STAMPS!

What Dan got was a whole month without booze. He did it, he guessed, as a weird kind of penance. It occurred to him more than once that if he'd had Deenie's address, he would have sent her that crappy seventy bucks long ago. He would have sent her twice that much if it could have ended the memories of the kid in the Braves t-shirt and the reaching starfish hand. But he didn't have the address, so he stayed sober instead. Scourging himself with whips. *Dry* ones.

Then one night he passed a drinking establishment called the Fisherman's Rest and through the window spied a good-looking blonde sitting alone at the bar. She was wearing a tartan skirt that ended at mid-thigh and she looked lonely and he went in and it turned out she was newly divorced and wow, that was a shame, maybe she'd like some company, and three days later he woke up with that same old black hole in his memory. He went to the

veterans' center where he had been mopping floors and changing
lightbulbs, hoping for a break, but no dice. Don't-give-much-of-a-
shit wasn't quite the same as don't-give-*any*-shit; close but no cigar.
Leaving with the few items that had been in his locker, he recalled
an old Bobcat Goldthwait line: 'My job was still there, but somebody
else was doing it.' So he boarded another bus, this one headed for
New Hampshire, and before he got on, he bought a glass container
of intoxicating liquid.

He sat all the way in back in the Drunk Seat, the one by the
toilet. Experience had taught him that if you intended to spend a
bus trip getting smashed, that was the seat to take. He reached into
the brown paper sack, loosened the cap on the glass container of
intoxicating liquid, and smelled the brown smell. That smell could
talk, although it only had one thing to say: *Hello, old friend.*

He thought *Canny.*

He thought *Mama.*

He thought of Tommy going to school by now. Always assuming
good old Uncle Randy hadn't killed him.

He thought, *The only one who can put on the brakes is you.*

This thought had come to him many times before, but now it
was followed by a new one. *You don't have to live this way if you
don't want to. You can, of course . . . but you don't have to.*

That voice was so strange, so unlike any of his usual mental dialogues,
that he thought at first he must be picking it up from someone else
– he could do that, but he rarely got uninvited transmissions anymore.
He had learned to shut them off. Nevertheless he looked up the aisle,
almost positive he would see someone looking back at him. No one
was. Everyone was sleeping, talking with their seatmates, or staring
out at the gray New England day.

You don't have to live this way if you don't want to.

If only that were true. Nevertheless, he tightened the cap on the
bottle and put it on the seat beside him. Twice he picked it up. The
first time he put it down. The second time he reached into the bag
and unscrewed the cap again, but as he did, the bus pulled into the
New Hampshire welcome area just across the state line. Dan filed
into the Burger King with the rest of the passengers, pausing only
long enough to toss the paper bag into one of the trash containers.

Stenciled on the side of the tall green can were the words IF YOU NO LONGER NEED IT, LEAVE IT HERE.

Wouldn't that be nice, Dan thought, hearing the clink as it landed. *Oh God, wouldn't that be nice.*

2

An hour and a half later, the bus passed a sign reading WELCOME TO FRAZIER, WHERE THERE'S A REASON FOR EVERY SEASON! And, below that, HOME OF TEENYTOWN!

The bus stopped at the Frazier Community Center to take on passengers, and from the empty seat next to Dan, where the bottle had rested for the first part of the trip, Tony spoke up. Here was a voice Dan recognized, although Tony hadn't spoken so clearly in years.

(this is the place)

As good as any, Dan thought.

He grabbed his duffel from the overhead rack and got off. He stood on the sidewalk and watched the bus pull away. To the west, the White Mountains sawed at the horizon. In all his wanderings he had avoided mountains, especially the jagged monsters that broke the country in two. Now he thought, *I've come back to the high country after all. I guess I always knew I would.* But these mountains were gentler than the ones that still sometimes haunted his dreams, and he thought he could live with them, at least for a little while. If he could stop thinking about the kid in the Braves t-shirt, that is. If he could stop using the booze. There came a time when you realized that moving on was pointless. That you took yourself with you wherever you went.

A snow flurry, fine as wedding lace, danced across the air. He could see that the shops lining the wide main street catered mostly to the skiers who'd come in December and the summer people who'd come in June. There would probably be leaf-peepers in September and October, too, but this was what passed for spring in northern New England, an edgy eight weeks chrome-plated with cold and damp. Frazier apparently hadn't figured out a reason for this season yet, because the main drag – Cranmore Avenue – was all but deserted.

Dan slung the duffel over his shoulder and strolled slowly north. He stopped outside a wrought-iron fence to look at a rambling Victorian home flanked on both sides by newer brick buildings. These were connected to the Victorian by covered walkways. There was a turret at the top of the mansion on the left side, but none on the right, giving the place a queerly unbalanced look that Dan sort of liked. It was as if the big old girl were saying *Yeah, part of me fell off. What the fuck. Someday it'll happen to you.* He started to smile. Then the smile died.

Tony was in the window of the turret room, looking down at him. He saw Dan looking up and waved. The same solemn wave Dan remembered from his childhood, when Tony had come often. Dan closed his eyes, then opened them. Tony was gone. Had never been there in the first place, how could he have been? The window was boarded up.

The sign on the lawn, gold letters on a green background the same shade as the house itself, read HELEN RIVINGTON HOUSE.

They have a cat in there, he thought. *A gray cat named Audrey.*

This turned out to be partly right and partly wrong. There *was* a cat, and it was gray, but it was a neutered tom and its name wasn't Audrey.

Dan looked at the sign for a long time – long enough for the clouds to part and send down a biblical beam – and then he walked on. Although the sun was now bright enough to twinkle the chrome of the few slant-parked cars in front of Olympia Sports and the Fresh Day Spa, the snow still swirled, making Dan think of something his mother had said during similar spring weather, long ago, when they had lived in Vermont: *The devil's beating his wife.*

3

A block or two up from the hospice, Dan stopped again. Across the street from the town municipal building was the Frazier town common. There was an acre or two of lawn, just beginning to show green, a bandstand, a softball field, a paved basketball half-court, picnic tables, even a putting green. All very nice, but what interested him was a sign reading

VISIT TEENYTOWN
FRAZIER'S 'SMALL WONDER'
AND RIDE THE TEENYTOWN RAILWAY!

It didn't take a genius to see that Teenytown was a teeny replica of Cranmore Avenue. There was the Methodist church he had passed, its steeple rising all of seven feet into the air; there was the Music Box Theater; Spondulicks Ice Cream; Mountain Books; Shirts & Stuff; the Frazier Gallery, Fine Prints Our Specialty. There was also a perfect waist-high miniature of the single-turreted Helen Rivington House, although the two flanking brick buildings had been omitted. Perhaps, Dan thought, because they were butt-ugly, especially compared to the centerpiece.

Beyond Teenytown was a miniature train with TEENYTOWN RAILWAY painted on passenger cars that were surely too small to hold anyone larger than toddler size. Smoke was puffing from the stack of a bright red locomotive about the size of a Honda Gold Wing motorcycle. He could hear the rumble of a diesel engine. Printed on the side of the loco, in old-fashioned gold flake letters, was THE HELEN RIVINGTON. Town patroness, Dan supposed. Somewhere in Frazier there was probably a street named after her, too.

He stood where he was for a bit, although the sun had gone back in and the day had grown cold enough for him to see his breath. As a kid he'd always wanted an electric train set and had never had one. Yonder in Teenytown was a jumbo version kids of all ages could love.

He shifted his duffel bag to his other shoulder and crossed the street. Hearing Tony again – and seeing him – was unsettling, but right now he was glad he'd stopped here. Maybe this really was the place he'd been looking for, the one where he'd finally find a way to right his dangerously tipped life.

You take yourself with you, wherever you go.

He pushed the thought into a mental closet. It was a thing he was good at. There was all sorts of stuff in that closet.

4

A cowling surrounded the locomotive on both sides, but he spied a footstool standing beneath one low eave of the Teenytown Station, carried it over, and stood on it. The driver's cockpit contained two sheepskin-covered bucket seats. It looked to Dan as if they had been scavenged from an old Detroit muscle car. The cockpit and controls also looked like modified Detroit stock, with the exception of an old-fashioned Z-shaped shifter jutting up from the floor. There was no shift pattern; the original knob had been replaced with a grinning skull wearing a bandanna faded from red to pallid pink by years of gripping hands. The top half of the steering wheel had been cut off, so that what remained looked like the steering yoke of a light plane. Painted in black on the dashboard, fading but legible, was TOP SPEED 40 DO NOT EXCEED.

'Like it?' The voice came from directly behind him.

Dan wheeled around, almost falling off the stool. A big weathered hand gripped his forearm, steadying him. It was a guy who looked to be in his late fifties or early sixties, wearing a padded denim jacket and a red-checked hunting cap with the earflaps down. In his free hand was a toolkit with PROPERTY OF FRAZIER MUNICIPAL DEPT Dymo-taped across the top.

'Hey, sorry,' Dan said, stepping off the stool. 'I didn't mean to—'

'S'all right. People stop to look all the time. Usually model-train buffs. It's like a dream come true for em. We keep em away in the summer when the place is jumpin and the *Riv* runs every hour or so, but this time of year there's no we, just me. And I don't mind.' He stuck out his hand. 'Billy Freeman. Town maintenance crew. The *Riv*'s my baby.'

Dan took the offered hand. 'Dan Torrance.'

Billy Freeman eyed the duffel. 'Just got off the bus, I 'magine. Or are you ridin your thumb?'

'Bus,' Dan said. 'What does this thing have for an engine?'

'Well now, that's interesting. Probably never heard of the Chervrolet Veraneio, didja?'

He hadn't, but knew anyway. Because *Freeman* knew. Dan didn't think he'd had such a clear shine in years. It brought a ghost of delight that went back to earliest childhood, before he had discovered how dangerous the shining could be.

'Brazilian Suburban, wasn't it? Turbodiesel.'

Freeman's bushy eyebrows shot up and he grinned. 'Goddam right! Casey Kingsley, he's the boss, bought it at an auction last year. It's a corker. Pulls like a sonofabitch. The instrument panel's from a Suburban, too. The seats I put in myself.'

The shine was fading now, but Dan got one last thing. 'From a GTO Judge.'

Freeman beamed. 'That's right. Found em in a junkyard over Sunapee way. The shifter's a high-hat from a 1961 Mack. Nine-speed. Nice, huh? You lookin for work or just lookin?'

Dan blinked at the sudden change of direction. *Was* he looking for work? He supposed he was. The hospice he'd passed on his amble up Cranmore Avenue would be the logical place to start, and he had an idea – didn't know if it was the shining or just ordinary intuition – that they'd be hiring, but he wasn't sure he wanted to go there just yet. Seeing Tony in the turret window had been unsettling.

Also, Danny, you want to be a little bit farther down the road from your last drink before you show up there askin for a job application form. Even if the only thing they got is runnin a buffer on the night shift.

Dick Halloran's voice. Christ. Dan hadn't thought of Dick in a long time. Maybe not since Wilmington.

With summer coming – a season for which Frazier most definitely had a reason – people would be hiring for all sorts of things. But if he had to choose between a Chili's at the local mall and Teenytown, he definitely chose Teenytown. He opened his mouth to answer Freeman's question, but Halloran spoke up again before he could.

You're closing in on the big three-oh, honey. You could be runnin out of chances.

Meanwhile, Billy Freeman was looking at him with open and artless curiosity.

'Yes,' he said. 'I'm looking for work.'

'Workin in Teenytown, wouldn't last long, y'know. Once summer comes and the schools let out, Mr Kingsley hires local. Eighteen to twenty-two, mostly. The selectmen expect it. Also, kids work cheap.' He grinned, exposing holes where a couple of teeth had once resided.

'Still, there are worse places to make a buck. Outdoor work don't look so good today, but it won't be cold like this much longer.'

No, it wouldn't be. There were tarps over a lot of stuff on the common, but they'd be coming off soon, exposing the superstructure of small-town resort summer: hotdog stands, ice cream booths, a circular something that looked to Dan like a merry-go-round. And there was the train, of course, the one with the teeny passenger cars and the big turbodiesel engine. If he could stay off the sauce and prove trustworthy, Freeman or the boss – Kingsley – might let him drive it a time or two. He'd like that. Farther down the line, when the municipal department hired the just-out-of-school local kids, there was always the hospice.

If he decided to stay, that was.

You better stay somewhere, Hallomann said – this was Dan's day for hearing voices and seeing visions, it seemed. *You better stay somewhere soon, or you won't be able to stay anywhere.*

He surprised himself by laughing. 'It sounds good to me, Mr Freeman. It sounds really good.'

5

'Done any grounds maintenance?' Billy Freeman asked. They were walking slowly along the flank of the train. The tops of the cars only came up to Dan's chest, making him feel like a giant.

'I can weed, plant, and paint. I know how to run a leaf blower and a chainsaw. I can fix small engines if the problem isn't too complicated. And I can manage a riding mower without running over any little kids. The train, now . . . that I don't know about.'

'You'd need to get cleared by Kingsley for that. Insurance and shit. Listen, have you got references? Mr Kingsley won't hire without em.'

'A few. Mostly janitorial and hospital orderly stuff. Mr Freeman—'

'Just Billy'll do.'

'Your train doesn't look like it could carry passengers, Billy. Where would they sit?'

Billy grinned. 'Wait here. See if you think this is as funny as I do. I never get tired of it.'

Freeman went back to the locomotive and leaned in. The engine, which had been idling lazily, began to rev and send up rhythmic jets of dark smoke. There was a hydraulic whine along the whole length of *The Helen Rivington*. Suddenly the roofs of the passenger wagons and the yellow caboose – nine cars in all – began to rise. To Dan it looked like the tops of nine identical convertibles all going up at the same time. He bent down to look in the windows and saw hard plastic seats running down the center of each car. Six in the passenger wagons and two in the caboose. Fifty in all.

When Billy came back, Dan was grinning. 'Your train must look very weird when it's full of passengers.'

'Oh yeah. People laugh their asses off and burn yea film, takin pitchers. Watch this.'

There was a steel-plated step at the end of each passenger car. Billy used one, walked down the aisle, and sat. A peculiar optical illusion took hold, making him look larger than life. He waved grandly to Dan, who could imagine fifty Brobdingnagians, dwarfing the train upon which they rode, pulling grandly out of Teenytown Station.

As Billy Freeman rose and stepped back down, Dan applauded. 'I'll bet you sell about a billion postcards between Memorial Day and Labor Day.'

'Bet your ass.' Billy rummaged in his coat pocket, brought out a battered pack of Duke cigarettes – a cut-rate brand Dan knew well, sold in bus stations and convenience stores all over America – and held it out. Dan took one. Billy lit them up.

'I better enjoy it while I can,' Billy said, looking at his cigarette. 'Smoking'll be banned here before too many more years. Frazier Women's Club's already talkin about it. Bunch of old biddies if you ask me, but you know what they say – the hand that rocks the fuckin cradle rules the fuckin world.' He jetted smoke from his nostrils. 'Not that most of *them* have rocked a cradle since Nixon was president. Or needed a Tampax, for that matter.'

'Might not be the worst thing,' Dan said. 'Kids copy what they see in their elders.' He thought of his father. The only thing Jack Torrance had liked better than a drink, his mother had once said, not long before she died, was a dozen drinks. Of course what Wendy had liked was her cigarettes, and they had killed her. Once upon a time Dan had promised himself he'd never get going with that habit, either. He had come to believe that life was a series of ironic ambushes.

Billy Freeman looked at him, one eye squinted mostly shut. 'I get feelins about people sometimes, and I got one about you.' He pronounced *got* as *gut*, in the New England fashion. 'Had it even before you turned around and I saw your face. I think you might be the right guy for the spring cleanin I'm lookin at between now and the end of May. That's how it feels to me, and I trust my feelins. Prob'ly crazy.'

Dan didn't think it was crazy at all, and now he understood why he had heard Billy Freeman's thoughts so clearly, and without even trying. He remembered something Dick Hallorann had told him once – Dick, who had been his first adult friend. *Lots of people have got a little of what I call the shining, but mostly it's just a twinkle – the kind of thing that lets em know what the DJ's going to play next on the radio or that the phone's gonna ring pretty soon.*

Billy Freeman had that little twinkle. That gleam.

'I guess this Cary Kingsley would be the one to talk to, huh?'

'Casey, not Cary. But yeah, he's the man. He's run municipal services in this town for twenty-five years.'

'When would be a good time?'

'Right about now, I sh'd think.' Billy pointed. 'Yonder pile of bricks across the street's the Frazier Municipal Building and town offices. Mr Kingsley's in the basement, end of the hall. You'll know you're there when you hear disco music comin down through the ceiling. There's a ladies' aerobics class in the gym every Tuesday and Thursday.'

'All right,' Dan said, 'that's just what I'm going to do.'

'Got your references?'

'Yes.' Dan patted the duffel, which he had leaned against Teenytown Station.

'And you didn't write them yourself, nor nothin?'

Danny smiled. 'No, they're straight goods.'

'Then go get im, tiger.'

'Okay.'

'One other thing,' Billy said as Dan started away. 'He's death on drinkin. If you're a drinkin man and he asts you, my advice is . . . lie.'

Dan nodded and raised his hand to show he understood. That was a lie he had told before.

6

Judging by his vein-congested nose, Casey Kingsley had not always been death on drinkin. He was a big man who didn't so much inhabit his small, cluttered office as wear it. Right now he was rocked back in the chair behind his desk, going through Dan's references, which were neatly kept in a blue folder. The back of Kingsley's head almost touched the downstroke of a plain wooden cross hanging on the wall beside a framed photo of his family. In the picture, a younger, slimmer Kingsley posed with his wife and three bathing-suited kiddos on a beach somewhere. Through the ceiling, only slightly muted, came the sound of the Village People singing 'YMCA', accompanied by the enthusiastic stomp of many feet. Dan imagined a gigantic centipede. One that had recently been to the local hairdresser and was wearing a bright red leotard about nine yards long.

'Uh-huh,' Kingsley said. 'Uh-huh . . . yeah . . . right, right, right . . .'

There was a glass jar filled with hard candies on the corner of his desk. Without looking up from Dan's thin sheaf of references, he took off the top, fished one out, and popped it into his mouth. 'Help yourself,' he said.

'No, thank you,' Dan said.

A queer thought came to him. Once upon a time, his father had probably sat in a room like this, being interviewed for the position of caretaker at the Overlook Hotel. What had he been thinking? That he really needed a job? That it was his last chance? Maybe. Probably. But of course, Jack Torrance had had hostages to fortune. Dan did not. He could drift on for a while if this didn't work out. Or try his luck at the hospice. But . . . he liked the town common. He liked the train, which made adults of ordinary size look like Goliaths. He liked Teenytown, which was absurd and cheerful and somehow brave in its self-important small-town-America way. And he liked Billy Freeman, who had a pinch of the shining and probably didn't even know it.

Above them, 'YMCA' was replaced by 'I Will Survive'. As if he had just been waiting for a new tune, Kingsley slipped Dan's references back into the folder's pocket and passed them across the desk.

He's going to turn me down.

But after a day of accurate intuitions, this one was off the mark. 'These look fine, but it strikes me that you'd be a lot more comfortable working at Central New Hampshire Hospital or the hospice here in town. You might even qualify for Home Helpers – I see you've got a few medical and first aid qualifications. Know your way around a defibrillator, according to these. Heard of Home Helpers?'

'Yes. And I thought about the hospice. Then I saw the town common, and Teenytown, and the train.'

Kingsley grunted. 'Probably wouldn't mind taking a turn at the controls, would you?'

Dan lied without hesitation. 'No, sir, I don't think I'd care for that.' To admit he'd like to sit in the scavenged GTO driver's seat and lay his hands on that cut-down steering wheel would almost certainly lead to a discussion of his driver's license, then to a further discussion of how he'd lost it, and then to an invitation to leave Mr Casey Kingsley's office forthwith. 'I'm more of a rake-and-lawnmower guy.'

'More of a short-term employment guy, too, from the looks of this paperwork.'

'I'll settle someplace soon. I've worked most of the wanderlust out of my system, I think.' He wondered if that sounded as bullshitty to Kingsley as it did to him.

'Short term's about all I can offer you,' Kingsley said. 'Once the schools are out for the summer—'

'Billy told me. If I decide to stay once summer comes, I'll try the hospice. In fact, I might put in an early application, unless you'd rather I don't do that.'

'I don't care either way.' Kingsley looked at him curiously. 'Dying people don't bother you?'

Your mother died there, Danny thought. The shine wasn't gone after all, it seemed; it was hardly even hiding. *You were holding her hand when she passed. Her name was Ellen.*

'No,' he said. Then, with no reason why, he added: 'We're all dying. The world's just a hospice with fresh air.'

'A philosopher, yet. Well, Mr Torrance, I think I'm going to take you on. I trust Billy's judgment – he rarely makes a mistake about people. Just don't show up late, don't show up drunk, and don't show up with red eyes and smelling of weed. If you do any of those things, down the road you'll go, because the Rivington House won't have a thing to do with you – I'll make sure of it. Are we clear on that?'

Dan felt a throb of resentment

(*officious prick*)

but suppressed it. This was Kingsley's playing field and Kingsley's ball. 'Crystal.'

'You can start tomorrow, if that suits. There are plenty of rooming houses in town. I'll make a call or two if you want. Can you stand paying ninety a week until your first paycheck comes in?'

'Yes. Thank you, Mr Kingsley.'

Kingsley waved a hand. 'In the meantime, I'd recommend the Red Roof Inn. My ex-brother-in-law runs it, he'll give you a rate. We good?'

'We are.' It had all happened with remarkable speed, the way the last few pieces drop into a complicated thousand-piece jigsaw puzzle. Dan told himself not to trust the feeling.

Kingsley rose. He was a big man and it was a slow process. Dan also got to his feet, and when Kingsley stuck his ham of a hand over the cluttered desk, Dan shook it. Now from overhead came the sound of KC and the Sunshine Band telling the world that's the way they liked it, oh-ho, uh-huh.

'I hate that boogie-down shit,' Kingsley said.

No, Danny thought. *You don't. It reminds you of your daughter, the one who doesn't come around much anymore. Because she still hasn't forgiven you.*

'You all right?' Kingsley asked. 'You look a little pale.'

'Just tired. It was a long bus ride.'

The shining was back, and strong. The question was, why now?

7

Three days into the job, ones Dan spent painting the bandstand and blowing last fall's dead leaves off the common, Kingsley ambled across Cranmore Avenue and told him he had a room on Eliot Street, if he wanted it. Private bathroom part of the deal, tub and shower. Eighty-five a week. Dan wanted it.

'Go on over on your lunch break,' Kingsley said. 'Ask for Mrs Robertson.' He pointed a finger that was showing the first gnarls of arthritis. 'And don't you fuck up, Sunny Jim, because she's an old pal of mine. Remember that I vouched for you on some pretty thin paper and Billy Freeman's intuition.'

Dan said he wouldn't fuck up, but the extra sincerity he tried to inject into his voice sounded phony to his own ears. He was thinking of his father again, reduced to begging jobs from a wealthy old friend after losing his teaching position in Vermont. It was strange to feel sympathy for a man who had almost killed you, but the sympathy was there. Had people felt it necessary to tell his father not to fuck up? Probably. And Jack Torrance had fucked up anyway. Spectacularly. Five stars. Drinking was undoubtedly a part of it, but when you were down, some guys just seemed to feel an urge to walk up your back and plant a foot on your neck instead of helping you to stand. It was lousy, but so much of human nature was. Of course when you were running with the bottom dogs, what you mostly saw were paws, claws, and assholes.

'And see if Billy can find some boots that'll fit you. He's squirreled away about a dozen pairs in the equipment shed, although the last time I looked, only half of them matched.'

The day was sunny, the air balmy. Dan, who was working in jeans and a Utica Blue Sox t-shirt, looked up at the nearly cloudless sky and then back at Casey Kingsley.

'Yeah, I know how it looks, but this is mountain country, pal. NOAA claims we're going to have a nor' easter, and it'll drop maybe a foot. Won't last long – poor man's fertilizer is what New Hampshire folks call April snow – but there's also gonna be gale-force winds. So they say. I hope you can use a snowblower as well as a leaf blower.' He paused. 'I also hope your back's okay, because you and Billy'll be picking up plenty of dead limbs tomorrow. Might be cutting up some fallen trees, too. You okay with a chainsaw?'

'Yes, sir,' Dan said.

'Good.'

8

Dan and Mrs Robertson came to amicable terms; she even offered him an egg salad sandwich and a cup of coffee in the communal kitchen. He took her up on it, expecting all the usual questions about what had brought him to Frazier and where he had been before. Refreshingly, there were none. Instead she asked him if he had time to help her close the shutters on the downstairs windows in case they really did get what she called 'a cap o' wind'. Dan agreed. There weren't many mottoes he lived by, but one was always get in good with the landlady; you never know when you might have to ask her for a rent extension.

Back on the common, Billy was waiting with a list of chores. The day before, the two of them had taken the tarps off all the kiddie rides. That afternoon they put them back on, and shuttered the various booths and concessions. The day's final job was backing the *Riv* into her shed. Then they sat in folding chairs beside the Teenytown station, smoking.

'Tell you what, Danno,' Billy said, 'I'm one tired hired man.'

'You're not the only one.' But he felt okay, muscles limber and tingling. He'd forgotten how good outdoors work could be when you weren't also working off a hangover.

The sky had scummed over with clouds. Billy looked up at them and sighed. 'I hope to God it don't snow n blow as hard as the radio says, but it probably will. I found you some boots. They don't look like much, but at least they match.'

Dan took the boots with him when he walked across town to his new accommodations. By then the wind was picking up and the day was growing dark. That morning, Frazier had felt on the edge of summer. This evening the air held the face-freezing dampness of coming snow. The side streets were deserted and the houses buttoned up.

Dan turned the corner from Morehead Street onto Eliot and paused. Blowing down the sidewalk, attended by a skeletal scutter of last year's autumn leaves, was a battered tophat, such as a magician might wear. *Or maybe an actor in an old musical comedy*, he thought. Looking at it made him feel cold in his bones, because it wasn't there. Not really.

He closed his eyes, slow-counted to five with the strengthening wind flapping the legs of his jeans around his shins, then opened them again. The leaves were still there, but the tophat was gone. It had just been the shining, producing one of its vivid, unsettling, and usually senseless visions. It was always stronger when he'd been sober for a little while, but never as strong as it had been since coming to Frazier. It was as if the air here were different, somehow. More conducive to those strange transmissions from Planet Elsewhere. Special.

The way the Overlook was special.

'No,' he said. 'No, I don't believe that.'

A few drinks and it all goes away, Danny. Do you believe that?

Unfortunately, he did.

9

Mrs Robertson's was a rambling old Colonial, and Dan's third-floor room had a view of the mountains to the west. That was a panorama he could have done without. His recollections of the Overlook had faded to hazy gray over the years, but as he unpacked his few things, a memory surfaced . . . and it *was* a kind of surfacing, like some nasty organic artifact (the decayed body of a small animal, say) floating to the surface of a deep lake.

It was dusk when the first real snow came. We stood on the porch of that big old empty hotel, my dad in the middle, my mom on one side, me on the other. He had his arms around us. It was okay then. He wasn't drinking then. At first the snow fell in perfectly straight lines, but then the wind picked up and it started to blow sideways, drifting against the sides of the porch and coating those—

He tried to block it off, but it got through.

—those hedge animals. The ones that sometimes moved around when you weren't looking.

He turned away from the window, his arms rashed out in goose-flesh. He'd gotten a sandwich from the Red Apple store and had planned to eat it while he started the John Sandford paperback he'd also picked up at the Red Apple, but after a few bites he rewrapped the sandwich and put it on the windowsill, where it would stay cold. He might eat the rest later, although he didn't think he'd be staying up much past nine tonight; if he got a hundred pages into the book, he'd be doing well.

Outside, the wind continued to rise. Every now and then it gave a bloodcurdling scream around the eaves that made him look up from his book. Around eight thirty, the snow began. It was heavy and wet, quickly coating his window and blocking his view of the mountains. In a way, that was worse. The snow had blocked the windows in the Overlook, too. First just on the first floor . . . then on the second . . . and finally on the third.

Then they had been entombed with the lively dead.

My father thought they'd make him the manager. All he had to do was show his loyalty. By giving them his son.

'His only begotten son,' Dan muttered, then looked around as if someone else had spoken . . . and indeed, he did not feel alone. Not quite alone. The wind shrieked down the side of the building again, and he shuddered.

Not too late to go back down to the Red Apple. Grab a bottle of something. Put all these unpleasant thoughts to bed.

No. He was going to read his book. Lucas Davenport was on the case, and he was going to read his book.

He closed it at quarter past nine and got into another rooming-house bed. *I won't sleep*, he thought. *Not with the wind screaming like that.*

But he did.

10

He was sitting at the mouth of the stormdrain, looking down a scrub-grass slope at the Cape Fear River and the bridge that spanned it. The night was clear and the moon was full. There was no wind, no snow. And the Overlook was gone. Even if it hadn't burned to the ground during the tenure of the Peanut Farmer President, it would have been over a thousand miles from here. So why was he so frightened?

Because he wasn't alone, that was why. There was someone behind him.

'Want some advice, Honeybear?'

The voice was liquid, wavering. Dan felt a chill go rushing down his back. His legs were colder still, prickled out in starpoints of goose-flesh. He could see those white bumps because he was wearing shorts. Of course he was wearing shorts. His brain might be that of a grown man, but it was currently sitting on top of a five-year-old's body.

Honeybear. Who—?

But he knew. He had told Deenie his name, but she didn't use it, just called him Honeybear instead.

You don't remember that, and besides, this is just a dream.

Of course it was. He was in Frazier, New Hampshire, sleeping while a spring snowstorm howled outside Mrs Robertson's rooming house. Still, it seemed wiser not to turn around. And safer – that, too.

'No advice,' he said, looking out at the river and the full moon. 'I've been advised by experts. The bars and barbershops are full of them.'

'Stay away from the woman in the hat, Honeybear.'

What hat? he could have asked, but really, why bother? He knew the hat she was talking about, because he had seen it blowing down the sidewalk. Black as sin on the outside, lined with white silk on the inside.

'She's the Queen Bitch of Castle Hell. If you mess with her, she'll eat you alive.'

He turned his head. He couldn't help it. Deenie was sitting behind him in the stormdrain with the bum's blanket wrapped around her naked shoulders. Her hair was plastered to her cheeks. Her face was bloated and dripping. Her eyes were cloudy. She was dead, probably years in her grave.

You're not real, Dan tried to say, but no words came out. He was five again, Danny was five, the Overlook was ashes and bones, but here was a dead woman, one he had stolen from.

'It's all right,' she said. Bubbling voice coming from a swollen throat. 'I sold the coke. Stepped on it first with a little sugar and got two hundred.' She grinned, and water spilled through her teeth. 'I liked you, Honeybear. That's why I came to warn you. *Stay away from the woman in the hat.*'

'False face,' Dan said . . . but it was Danny's voice, the high, frail, chanting voice of a child. 'False face, not there, not real.'

He closed his eyes as he had often closed them when he had seen terrible things in the Overlook. The woman began to scream, but he wouldn't open his eyes. The screaming went on, rising and falling, and he realized it was the scream of the wind. He wasn't in Colorado and he wasn't in North Carolina. He was in New Hampshire. He'd had a bad dream, but the dream was over.

11

According to his Timex, it was two in the morning. The room was cold, but his arms and chest were slimy with sweat.

Want some advice, Honeybear?

'No,' he said. 'Not from you.'

She's dead.

There was no way he could know that, but he did. Deenie – who had looked like the goddess of the Western world in her thigh-high leather skirt and cork sandals – was dead. He even knew how she had done it. Took pills, pinned up her hair, climbed into a bathtub filled with warm water, went to sleep, slid under, drowned.

The roar of the wind was dreadfully familiar, loaded with hollow threat. Winds blew everywhere, but it only sounded like this in the high country. It was as if some angry god were pounding the world with an air mallet.

I used to call his booze the Bad Stuff, Dan thought. *Only sometimes it's the Good Stuff. When you wake up from a nightmare that you know is at least fifty percent shining, it's the Very Good Stuff.*

One drink would send him back to sleep. Three would guarantee not just sleep but dreamless sleep. Sleep was nature's doctor, and right now Dan Torrance felt sick and in need of strong medicine.

Nothing's open. You lucked out there.

Well. Maybe.

He turned on his side, and something rolled against his back when he did. No, not something. Some*one*. Someone had gotten into bed with him. *Deenie* had gotten into bed with him. Only it felt too small to be Deenie. It felt more like a—

He scrambled out of bed, landed awkwardly on the floor, and looked over his shoulder. It was Deenie's little boy, Tommy. The right side of his skull was caved in. Bone splinters protruded through bloodstained fair hair. Gray scaly muck – brains – was drying on one cheek. He couldn't be alive with such a hellacious wound, but he was. He reached out to Dan with one starfish hand.

'Canny,' he said.

The screaming began again, only this time it wasn't Deenie and it wasn't the wind.

This time it was him.

12

When he woke for the second time – real waking, this time – he wasn't screaming at all, only making a kind of low growling deep in his chest. He sat up, gasping, the bedclothes puddled around his waist. There was no one else in his bed, but the dream hadn't yet dissolved, and looking wasn't enough. He threw back the bedclothes, and that still wasn't enough. He ran his hands down the bottom sheet, feeling for fugitive warmth, or a dent that might have been made by small hips and buttocks. Nothing. Of course not. So then he looked under the bed and saw only his borrowed boots.

The wind was blowing less strongly now. The storm wasn't over, but it was winding down.

He went to the bathroom, then whirled and looked back, as if expecting to surprise someone. There was just the bed, with the covers now lying on the floor at the foot. He turned on the light over the sink, splashed his face with cold water, and sat down on the closed lid of the commode, taking long breaths, one after the other. He thought about getting up and grabbing a cigarette from the pack lying beside his book on the room's one small table, but his legs felt rubbery and he wasn't sure they'd hold him. Not yet, anyway. So he sat. He could see the bed and the bed was empty. The whole room was empty. No problem there.

Only . . . it didn't *feel* empty. Not yet. When it did, he supposed he would go back to bed. But not to sleep. For this night, sleep was done.

13

Seven years before, working as an orderly in a Tulsa hospice, Dan had made friends with an elderly psychiatrist who was suffering from terminal liver cancer. One day, when Emil Kemmer had been reminiscing (not very discreetly) about a few of his more interesting cases, Dan had confessed that ever since childhood, he had suffered from what he called double dreaming. Was Kemmer familiar with the phenomenon? Was there a name for it?

Kemmer had been a large man in his prime – the old black-and-white wedding photo he kept on his bedside table attested to that – but cancer is the ultimate diet program, and on the day of this conversation, his weight had been approximately the same as his age, which was ninety-one. His mind had still been sharp, however, and now, sitting on the closed toilet and listening to the dying storm outside, Dan remembered the old man's sly smile.

'Usually,' he had said in his heavy German accent, 'I am paid for my diagnoses, Daniel.'

Dan had grinned. 'Guess I'm out of luck, then.'

'Perhaps not.' Kemmer studied Dan. His eyes were bright blue. Although he knew it was outrageously unfair, Dan couldn't help imagining those eyes under a Waffen-SS coal-scuttle helmet. 'There's a rumor in this deathhouse that you are a kid with a talent for helping people die. Is this true?'

'Sometimes,' Dan said cautiously. 'Not always.' The truth was *almost* always.

'When the time comes, will you help me?'

'If I can, of course.'

'Good.' Kemmer sat up, a laboriously painful process, but when Dan moved to help, Kemmer had waved him away. 'What you call double dreaming is well known to psychiatrists, and of particular interest to Jungians, who call it *false awakening*. The first dream is usually a lucid dream, meaning the dreamer knows he is dreaming—'

'Yes!' Dan cried. 'But the second one—'

'The dreamer believes he is awake,' Kemmer said. 'Jung made much of this, even ascribing precognitive powers to these dreams . . . but of course we know better, don't we, Dan?'

'Of course,' Dan had agreed.

'The poet Edgar Allan Poe described the false awakening phenomenon long before Carl Jung was born. He wrote, "All that we see or
seem is but a dream within a dream." Have I answered your question?'

'I think so. Thanks.'

'You're welcome. Now I believe I could drink a little juice. Apple,
please.'

14

Precognitive powers . . . but of course we know better.

Even if he hadn't kept the shining almost entirely to himself over
the years, Dan would not have presumed to contradict a dying man
. . . especially one with such coldly inquisitive blue eyes. The truth,
however, was that one or both of his double dreams were often
predictive, usually in ways he only half understood or did not
understand at all. But as he sat on the toilet seat in his underwear,
now shivering (and not just because the room was cold), he understood much more than he wanted to.

Tommy was dead. Murdered by his abusive uncle, most likely.
The mother had committed suicide not long after. As for the rest
of the dream . . . or the phantom hat he'd seen earlier, spinning
down the sidewalk . . .

*Stay away from the woman in the hat. She's the Queen Bitch of Castle
Hell.*

'I don't care,' Dan said.

If you mess with her, she'll eat you alive.

He had no intention of meeting her, let alone messing with her.
As for Deenie, he wasn't responsible for either her short-fused brother
or her child neglect. He didn't even have to carry around the guilt
about her lousy seventy dollars anymore; she had sold the cocaine
– he was sure that part of the dream was absolutely true – and they
were square. More than square, actually.

What he cared about was getting a drink. Getting drunk, not to put
too fine a point on it. Standing-up, falling-down, pissy-assed drunk.
Warm morning sunshine was good, and the pleasant feeling of muscles
that had been worked hard, and waking up in the morning without a

hangover, but the price – all these crazy dreams and visions, not to mention the random thoughts of passing strangers that sometimes found their way past his defenses – was too high.

Too high to bear.

15

He sat in the room's only chair and read his John Sandford novel by the light of the room's only lamp until the two town churches with bells rang in seven o'clock. Then he pulled on his new (new to him, anyway) boots and duffel coat. He headed out into a world that had changed and softened. There wasn't a sharp edge anywhere. The snow was still falling, but gently now.

I should get out of here. Go back to Florida. Fuck New Hampshire, where it probably even snows on the Fourth of July in odd-numbered years.

Halloranns's voice answered him, the tone as kind as he remembered from his childhood, when Dan had been Danny, but there was hard steel underneath. *You better stay somewhere, honey, or you won't be able to stay anywhere.*

'Fuck you, oldtimer,' he muttered.

He went back to the Red Apple because the stores that sold hard liquor wouldn't be open for at least another hour. He walked slowly back and forth between the wine cooler and the beer cooler, debating, and finally decided if he was going to get drunk, he might as well do it as nastily as possible. He grabbed two bottles of Thunderbird (eighteen percent alcohol, a good enough number when whiskey was temporarily out of reach), started up the aisle to the register, then stopped.

Give it one more day. Give yourself one more chance.

He supposed he could do that, but why? So he could wake up in bed with Tommy again? Tommy with half of his skull caved in? Or maybe next time it would be Deenie, who had lain in that tub for two days before the super finally got tired of knocking, used his passkey, and found her. He couldn't know that, if Emil Kemmer had been here he would have agreed most emphatically, but he did. He did know. So why bother?

Maybe this hyperawareness will pass. Maybe it's just a phase, the psychic equivalent of the DTs. Maybe if you just give it a little more time . . .

But time changed. That was something only drunks and junkies understood. When you couldn't sleep, when you were afraid to look around because of what you might see, time elongated and grew sharp teeth.

'Help you?' the clerk asked, and Dan knew

(*fucking shining fucking thing*)

that he was making the clerk nervous. Why not? With his bed head, dark-circled eyes, and jerky, unsure movements, he probably looked like a meth freak who was deciding whether or not to pull out his trusty Saturday night special and ask for everything in the register.

'No,' Dan said. 'I just realized I left my wallet home.'

He put the green bottles back in the cooler. As he closed it, they spoke to him gently, as one friend speaks to another: *See you soon, Danny.*

16

Billy Freeman was waiting for him, bundled up to the eyebrows. He held out an old-fashioned ski hat with ANNISTON CYCLONES embroidered on the front.

'What the hell are the Anniston Cyclones?' Dan asked.

'Anniston's twenty miles north of here. When it comes to football, basketball, and baseball, they're our archrivals. Someone sees that on ya, you'll probably get a snowball upside your head, but it's the only one I've got.'

Dan hauled it on. 'Then go, Cyclones.'

'Right, fuck you and the hoss you rode in on.' Billy looked him over. 'You all right, Danno?'

'Didn't get much sleep last night.'

'I hear that. Damn wind really screamed, didn't it? Sounded like my ex when I suggested a little Monday night lovin might do us good. Ready to go to work?'

'Ready as I'll ever be.'

'Good. Let's dig in. Gonna be a busy day.'

17

It was indeed a busy day, but by noon the sun had come out and the temperature had climbed back into the mid-fifties. Teenytown was filled with the sound of a hundred small waterfalls as the snow melted. Dan's spirits rose with the temperature, and he even caught himself singing ('Young man! I was once in your shoes!') as he followed his snowblower back and forth in the courtyard of the little shopping center adjacent to the common. Overhead, flapping in a mild breeze far removed from the shrieking wind of the night before, was a banner reading HUGE SPRING BARGAINS AT TEENYTOWN PRICES!

There were no visions.

After they clocked out, he took Billy to the Chuck Wagon and ordered them steak dinners. Billy offered to buy the beer. Dan shook his head. 'Staying away from alcohol. Reason being, once I start, it's sometimes hard to stop.'

'You could talk to Kingsley about that,' Billy said. 'He got himself a booze divorce about fifteen years ago. He's all right now, but his daughter still don't talk to him.'

They drank coffee with the meal. A lot of it.

Dan went back to his third-floor Eliot Street lair tired, full of hot food, and glad to be sober. There was no TV in his room, but he had the last part of the Sandford novel, and lost himself in it for a couple of hours. He kept an ear out for the wind, but it did not rise. He had an idea that last night's storm had been winter's final shot. Which was fine with him. He turned in at ten and fell asleep almost immediately. His early morning visit to the Red Apple now seemed hazy, as if he had gone there in a fever delirium and the fever had now passed.

18

He woke in the small hours, not because the wind was blowing but because he had to piss like a racehorse. He got up, shuffled to the bathroom, and turned on the light inside the door.

The tophat was in the tub, and full of blood.

'No,' he said. 'I'm dreaming.'

Maybe double dreaming. Or triple. Quadruple, even. There was something he hadn't told Emil Kemmer: he was afraid that eventually he would get lost in a maze of phantom nightlife and never be able to find his way out again.

All that we see or seem is but a dream within a dream.

Only this was real. So was the hat. No one else would see it, but that changed nothing. The hat was real. It was somewhere in the world. He knew it.

From the corner of his eye, he saw something written on the mirror over the sink. Something written in lipstick.

I must not look at it.

Too late. His head was turning; he could hear the tendons in his neck creaking like old doorhinges. And what did it matter? He knew what it said. Mrs Massey was gone, Horace Derwent was gone, they were securely locked away in the boxes he kept far back in his mind, but the Overlook was still not done with him. Written on the mirror, not in lipstick but in blood, was a single word:

REDRUM

Beneath it, lying in the sink, was a bloodstained Atlanta Braves t-shirt.

It will never stop, Danny thought. *The Overlook burned and the most terrible of its revenants went into the lockboxes, but I can't lock away the shining, because it isn't just inside me, it* is *me. Without booze to at least stun it, these visions will go on until they drive me insane.*

He could see his face in the mirror with **REDRUM** floating in front of it, stamped on his forehead like a brand. This was not a dream. There was a murdered child's shirt in his washbasin and a hatful of blood in his tub. Insanity was coming. He could see its approach in his own bulging eyes.

Then, like a flashlight beam in the dark, Hallorann's voice: *Son, you may see things, but they're like pictures in a book. You weren't helpless in the Overlook when you were a child, and you're not helpless now. Far from it. Close your eyes and when you open them, all this crap will be gone.*

He closed his eyes and waited. He tried to count off the seconds, but only made it to fourteen before the numbers were lost in the roaring confusion of his thoughts. He half expected hands – perhaps those of whoever owned the hat – to close around his neck. But he stood there. There was really nowhere else to go.

Summoning all his courage, Dan opened his eyes. The tub was empty. The washbasin was empty. There was nothing written on the mirror.

But it will be back. Next time maybe it'll be her shoes – those cork sandals. Or I'll see her in the tub. Why not? That's where I saw Mrs Massey, and they died the same way. Except I never stole Mrs Massey's money and ran out on her.

'I gave it a day,' he told the empty room. 'I did that much.'

Yes, and although it had been a busy day, it had also been a good day, he'd be the first to admit it. The *days* weren't the problem. As for the nights . . .

The mind was a blackboard. Booze was the eraser.

19

Dan lay awake until six. Then he dressed and once more made the trek to the Red Apple. This time he did not hesitate, only instead of extracting two bottles of Bird from the cooler, he took three. What was it they used to say? Go big or go home. The clerk bagged the bottles without comment; he was used to early wine purchasers. Dan strolled to the town common, sat on one of the benches in Teenytown, and took one of the bottles out of the bag, looking down at it like Hamlet with Yorick's skull. Through the green glass, what was inside looked like rat poison instead of wine.

'You say that like it's a bad thing,' Dan said, and loosened the cap.

This time it was his mother who spoke up. Wendy Torrance, who had smoked right to the bitter end. Because if suicide was the only option, you could at least choose your weapon.

Is this how it ends, Danny? Is this what it was all for?

He turned the cap widdershins. Then tightened it. Then back the other way. This time he took it off. The smell of the wine was sour, the smell of jukebox music and crappy bars and pointless arguments followed by fistfights in parking lots. In the end, life was as stupid as one of those fights. The world wasn't a hospice with fresh air, the world was the Overlook Hotel, where the party never ended. Where the dead were alive forever. He raised the bottle to his lips.

Is this why we fought so hard to get out of that damned hotel, Danny? Why we fought to make a new life for ourselves? There was no reproach in her voice, only sadness.

Danny tightened the cap again. Then loosened it. Tightened it. Loosened it.

He thought: *If I drink, the Overlook wins. Even though it burned to the ground when the boiler exploded, it wins. If I don't drink, I go crazy.*

He thought: *All that we see or seem is but a dream within a dream.*

He was still tightening the cap and loosening it when Billy Freeman, who had awakened early with the vague, alarmed sense that something was wrong, found him.

'Are you going to drink that, Dan, or just keep jerking it off?'

'Drink it, I guess. I don't know what else to do.'

So Billy told him.

20

Casey Kingsley wasn't entirely surprised to see his new hire sitting outside his office when he arrived at quarter past eight that morning. Nor was he surprised to see the bottle Torrance was holding in his hands, first twisting the cap off, then putting it back on and turning it tight again – he'd had that special look from the start, the thousand-yard Kappy's Discount Liquor Store stare.

Billy Freeman didn't have as much shine as Dan himself, not even close, but a bit more than just a twinkle. On that first day he had called Kingsley from the equipment shed as soon as Dan headed across the street to the Municipal Building. There was a young fella looking for work, Billy said. He wasn't apt to have much in the way of references, but Billy thought he was the right man to help out until Memorial Day. Kingsley, who'd had experiences – good ones – with Billy's intuitions before, had agreed. *I know we've got to have someone*, he said.

Billy's reply had been peculiar, but then *Billy* was peculiar. Once, two years ago, he had called an ambulance five minutes *before* that little kid had fallen off the swings and fractured his skull.

He needs us more than we need him, Billy had said.

And here he was, sitting hunched forward as if he were already riding his next bus or barstool, and Kingsley could smell the wine from twelve yards down the hallway. He had a gourmet's nose for such scents, and could name each one. This was Thunderbird, as in the old saloon rhyme: *What's the word? Thunderbird! . . . What's the price? Fifty twice!* But when the young guy looked up at him, Kingsley saw the eyes were clear of everything but desperation.

'Billy sent me.'

Kingsley said nothing. He could see the kid gathering himself, struggling with it. It was in his eyes; it was in the way his mouth turned down at the corners; mostly it was the way he held the bottle, hating it and loving it and needing it all at the same time.

At last Dan brought out the words he had been running from all his life.

'I need help.'

He swiped an arm across his eyes. As he did, Kingsley bent down and grasped the bottle of wine. The kid held on for a moment . . . then let go.

'You're sick and you're tired,' Kingsley said. 'I can see that much. But are you sick and tired of being sick and tired?'

Dan looked up at him, throat working. He struggled some more, then said, 'You don't know how much.'

'Maybe I do.' Kingsley produced a vast key ring from his vast trousers. He stuck one in the lock of the door with FRAZIER MUNICIPAL SERVICES painted on the frosted glass. 'Come on in. Let's talk about it.'

CHAPTER TWO
BAD NUMBERS

1

The elderly poet with the Italian given name and the absolutely American surname sat with her sleeping great-granddaughter in her lap and watched the video her granddaughter's husband had shot in the delivery room three weeks before. It began with a title card: ABRA ENTERS THE WORLD! The footage was jerky, and David had kept away from anything too clinical (thank God), but Concetta Reynolds saw the sweat-plastered hair on Lucia's brow, heard her cry out '*I am!*' when one of the nurses exhorted her to push, and saw the droplets of blood on the blue drape – not many, just enough to make what Chetta's own grandmother would have called 'a fair show.' But not in English, of course.

The picture jiggled when the baby finally came into view and she felt gooseflesh chase up her back and arms when Lucy screamed, '*She has no face!*'

Sitting beside Lucy now, David chuckled. Because of course Abra *did* have a face, a very sweet one. Chetta looked down at it as if to reassure herself of that. When she looked back up, the new baby was being placed in the new mother's arms. Thirty or forty jerky seconds later, another title-card appeared: HAPPY BIRTHDAY ABRA RAFAELLA STONE!

David pushed STOP on the remote.

'You're one of the very few people who will ever get to see that,' Lucy announced in a firm, take-no-prisoners voice. 'It's embarrassing.'

'It's wonderful,' Dave said. 'And there's one person who gets to see it for sure, and that's Abra herself.' He glanced at his wife, sitting next to him on the couch. 'When she's old enough. And if she wants to, of course.' He patted Lucy's thigh, then grinned at his granny-in-law, a woman for whom he had respect but no great love. 'Until then, it goes in the safe deposit box with the insurance papers, the house papers, and my millions in drug money.'

Concetta smiled to show she got the joke but thinly, to show she didn't find it particularly funny. In her lap, Abra slept and slept. In a way, all babies were born with a caul, she thought, their tiny faces drapes of mystery and possibility. Perhaps it was a thing to write about. Perhaps not.

Concetta had come to America when she was twelve and spoke perfect idiomatic English – not surprising, since she was a graduate of Vassar and professor (now emeritus) of that very subject – but in her head every superstition and old wives' tale still lived. Sometimes they gave orders, and they always spoke Italian when they did. Chetta believed that most people who worked in the arts were high-func-tioning schizophrenics, and she was no different. She knew supersition was shit; she also spat between her fingers if a crow or black cat crossed her path.

For much of her own schizophrenia she had the Sisters of Mercy to thank. They believed in God; they believed in the divinity of Jesus; they believed mirrors were bewitching pools and the child who looked into one too long would grow warts. These were the women who had been the greatest influence on her life between the ages of seven and twelve. They carried rulers in their belts – for hitting, not measuring – and never saw a child's ear they did not desire to twist in passing.

Lucy held out her arms for the baby. Chetta handed her over, not without reluctance. The kid was one sweet bundle.

2

Twenty miles southeast of where Abra slept in Concetta Reynolds's arms, Dan Torrance was attending an AA meeting while some chick droned on about sex with her ex. Casey Kingsley had ordered him to attend ninety meetings in ninety days, and this one, a nooner in the basement of Frazier Methodist Church, was his eighth. He was sitting in the first row, because Casey – known in the halls as Big Casey – had ordered him to do that, too.

'Sick people who want to get well sit in front, Danny. We call the back row at AA meetings the Denial Aisle.'

Casey had given him a little notebook with a photo on the front that showed ocean waves crashing into a rock promontory. Printed above the picture was a motto Dan understood but didn't much care for: NO GREAT THING IS CREATED SUDDENLY.

'You write down every meeting you go to in that book. And anytime I ask to see it, you better be able to haul it out of your back pocket and show me perfect attendance.'

'Don't I even get a sick day?'

Casey laughed. 'You're sick *every* day, my friend – you're a drunk-ass alcoholic. Want to know something my sponsor told me?'

'I think you already did. You can't turn a pickle back into a cucumber, right?'

'Don't be a smartass, just listen.'

Dan sighed. 'Listening.'

'"Get your ass to a meeting," he said. "If your ass falls off, put it in a bag and take it to a meeting."'

'Charming. What if I just forget?'

Casey had shrugged. 'Then you find yourself another sponsor, one who believes in forgetfulness. I don't.'

Dan, who felt like some breakable object that has skittered to the edge of a high shelf but hasn't quite fallen off, didn't want another sponsor or changes of any kind. He felt okay, but tender. Very tender. Almost skinless. The visions that had plagued him following his arrival in Frazier had ceased, and although he often thought of Deenie and her little boy, the thoughts were not as painful. At the end of almost every AA meeting, someone read the Promises. One of these was *We will not regret the past nor wish to shut the door on it.* Dan thought he would *always* regret the past, but he had quit trying to shut the door. Why bother, when it would just come open again? The fucking thing had no latch, let alone a lock.

Now he began to print a single word on the current page of the little book Casey had given him. He made large, careful letters. He had no idea why he was doing it, or what it meant. The word was **ABRA**.

Meanwhile, the speaker reached the end of her qualification and burst into tears, through them declaring that even though her ex was a shit and she loved him still, she was grateful to be straight and sober. Dan applauded along with the rest of the Lunch Bunch, then began to color in the letters with his pen. Fattening them. Making them stand out.

Do I know this name? I think I do.

As the next speaker began and he went to the urn for a fresh cup of coffee, it came to him. Abra was the name of a girl in a John Steinbeck novel. *East of Eden.* He'd read it . . . he couldn't remember where. At some stop along the way. Some somewhere. It didn't matter.

Another thought

(*did you save it*)

rose to the top of his mind like a bubble and popped.

Save what?

Frankie P., the Lunch Bunch oldtimer who was chairing the meeting, asked if someone wanted to do the Chip Club. When no one raised a hand, Frankie pointed. 'How about you, lurking back there by the coffee?'

Feeling self-conscious, Dan walked to the front of the room, hoping he could remember the order of the chips. The first – white for beginners – he had. As he took the battered cookie tin with the chips and medallions scattered inside it, the thought came again.

Did you save it?

3

That was the day the True Knot, which had been wintering at a KOA campground in Arizona, packed up and began meandering back east. They drove along Route 77 toward Show Low in the usual caravan: fourteen campers, some towing cars, some with lawn chairs or bicycles clamped to the backs. There were Southwinds and Winnebagos, Monacos and Bounders. Rose's EarthCruiser – seven hundred thousand dollars' worth of imported rolling steel, the best RV money could buy – led the parade. But slowly, just double-nickeling it.

They were in no hurry. There was plenty of time. The feast was still months away.

4

'Did you save it?' Concetta asked as Lucy opened her blouse and offered Abra the breast. Abby blinked sleepily, rooted a little, then lost interest. *Once your nipples get sore, you won't offer until she asks,* Chetta thought. *And at the top of her lungs.*

'Save what?' David asked.

Lucy knew. 'I passed out right after they put her in my arms. Dave says I almost dropped her. There was no time, Momo.'

'Oh, that goop over her face.' David said it dismissively. 'They stripped it off and threw it away. Damn good thing, if you ask me.' He was smiling, but his eyes challenged her. *You know better than to go on with this,* they said. *You know better, so just drop it.*

She *did* know better . . . and didn't. Had she been this two-minded when she was younger? She couldn't remember, although it seemed she could remember every lecture on the Blessed Mysteries and the everlasting pain of hell administered by the Sisters of Mercy, those banditti in black. The story of the girl who had been struck blind for peeping at her brother while he was naked in the tub and the one about the man who had been struck dead for blaspheming against the pope.

Give them to us when they're young and it doesn't matter how many honors classes they've taught, or how many books of poetry they've written, or even that one of those books won all the big prizes. Give them to us when they're young . . . and they're ours forever.

'You should have saved *il amnio*. It's good luck.'

She spoke directly to her granddaughter, cutting David out entirely. He was a good man, a good husband to her Lucia, but fuck his dismissive tone. And double-fuck his challenging eyes.

'I would have, but I didn't have a chance, Momo. And Dave didn't know.' Buttoning her blouse again.

Chetta leaned forward and touched the fine skin of Abra's cheek with the tip of her finger, old flesh sliding across new. 'Those born with *il amnio* are supposed to have double sight.'

'You don't actually believe that, do you?' David asked. 'A caul is nothing but a scrap of fetal membrane. It . . .'

He was saying more, but Concetta paid no attention. Abra had opened her eyes. In them was a universe of poetry, lines too great to ever be written. Or even remembered.

'Never mind,' Concetta said. She raised the baby and kissed the smooth skull where the fontanelle pulsed, the magic of the mind so close beneath. 'What's done is done.'

5

One night about five months after the not-quite-argument over Abra's caul, Lucy dreamed her daughter was crying – crying as if her heart would break. In this dream, Abby was no longer in the master bedroom of the house on Richland Court but somewhere down a long corridor. Lucy ran in the direction of the weeping. At first there were doors on both sides, then seats. Blue ones with high backs. She was on a plane or maybe an Amtrak train. After running for what seemed like miles, she came to a bathroom door. Her baby was crying behind it. Not a hungry cry, but a frightened cry. Maybe

(*oh God, oh Mary*)

a hurt cry.

Lucy was terribly afraid the door would be locked and she would have to break it down – wasn't that the kind of thing that always happened in bad dreams? – but the knob twisted and she opened it. As she did, a new fear struck her: What if Abra was in the toilet? You read about that happening. Babies in toilets, babies in Dumpsters. What if she were drowning in one of those ugly steel bowls they had on public conveyances, up to her mouth and nose in disinfected blue water?

But Abra lay on the floor. She was naked. Her eyes, swimming with tears, stared at her mother. Written on her chest in what looked like blood was the number 11.

6

David Stone dreamed he was chasing his daughter's cries up an endless escalator that was running – slowly but inexorably – in the wrong direction. Worse, the escalator was in a mall, and the mall was on fire. He should have been choking and out of breath long before he reached the top, but there was no smoke from the fire, only a hell of flames. Nor was there any sound other than Abra's cries, although he saw people burning like kerosene-soaked torches. When he finally made it to the top, he saw Abby lying on the floor like someone's cast-off garbage. Men and women ran all around her, unheeding, and in spite of the flames, no one tried to use the escalator even though it was going down. They simply sprinted aimlessly in all directions, like ants whose hill has been torn open by a farmer's harrow. One woman in stilettos almost stepped on his daughter, a thing that would almost surely have killed her.

Abra was naked. Written on her chest was the number 175.

7

The Stones woke together, both initially convinced that the cries they heard were a remnant of the dreams they had been having. But no, the cries were in the room with them. Abby lay in her crib beneath her Shrek mobile, eyes wide, cheeks red, tiny fists pumping, howling her head off.

A change of diapers did not quiet her, nor did the breast, nor did what felt like miles of laps up and down the hall and at least a thousand verses of 'The Wheels on the Bus'. At last, very frightened now – Abby was her first, and Lucy was at her wits' end – she called Concetta in Boston. Although it was two in the morning, Momo answered on the second ring. She was eighty-five, and her sleep was as thin as her skin. She listened more closely to her wailing great-granddaughter than to Lucy's confused recital of all the ordinary remedies they had tried, then asked the pertinent questions. 'Is she running a fever? Pulling at one of her ears? Jerking her legs like she has to make *merda*?'

'No,' Lucy said, 'none of that. She's a little warm from crying, but I don't think it's a fever. Momo, what should I do?'

Chetta, now sitting at her desk, didn't hesitate. 'Give her another fifteen minutes. If she doesn't quiet and begin feeding, take her to the hospital.'

'What? Brigham and Women's?' Confused and upset, it was all

Lucy could think of. It was where she had given birth. 'That's a hundred and fifty miles!'

'No, no. Bridgton. Across the border in Maine. That's a little closer than CNH.'

'Are you sure?'

'Am I looking at my computer right now?'

Abra did not quiet. The crying was monotonous, maddening, terrifying. When they arrived at Bridgton Hospital, it was quarter of four, and Abra was still at full volume. Rides in the Acura were usually better than a sleeping pill, but not this morning. David thought about brain aneurysms and told himself he was out of his mind. Babies didn't have strokes . . . did they?

'Davey?' Lucy asked in a small voice as they pulled up to the sign reading EMERGENCY DROP-OFF ONLY. 'Babies don't have strokes or heart attacks . . . do they?'

'No, I'm sure they don't.'

But a new idea occurred to him then. Suppose the kiddo had somehow swallowed a safety pin, and it had popped open in her stomach? *That's stupid, we use Huggies, she's never even been near a safety pin.*

Something else, then. A bobby pin from Lucy's hair. An errant tack that had fallen into the crib. Maybe even, God help them, a broken-off piece of plastic from Shrek, Donkey, or Princess Fiona.

'Davey? What are you thinking?'

'Nothing.'

The mobile was fine. He was sure of it.

Almost sure.

Abra continued to scream.

8

David hoped the doc on duty would give his daughter a sedative, but it was against protocol for infants who could not be diagnosed, and Abra Rafaella Stone seemed to have nothing wrong with her. She wasn't running a fever, she wasn't showing a rash, and ultrasound had ruled out pyloric stenosis. An X-ray showed no foreign objects in her throat or stomach, or a bowel obstruction. Basically, she just wouldn't shut up. The Stones were the only patients in the ER at that hour on a Tuesday morning, and each of the three nurses on duty had a try at quieting her. Nothing worked.

'Shouldn't you give her something to eat?' Lucy asked the doctor when he came back to check. The phrase *Ringer's lactate* occurred to her, something she'd heard on one of the doctor shows she'd watched ever since her teenage crush on George Clooney. But for all she knew, Ringer's lactate was foot lotion, or an anticoagulant, or something for stomach ulcers. 'She won't take the breast *or* the bottle.'

'When she gets hungry enough, she'll eat,' the doctor said, but neither Lucy nor David was much comforted. For one thing, the doctor looked younger than they were. For another (this was far worse), he didn't sound completely sure. 'Have you called your pediatrician?' He checked the paperwork. 'Dr Dalton?'

'Left a message with his service,' David said. 'We probably won't hear from him until mid-morning, and by then this will be over.'

One way or the other, he thought, and his mind – made ungovernable by too little sleep and too much anxiety – presented him with a picture as clear as it was horrifying: mourners standing around a small grave. And an even smaller coffin.

9

At seven thirty, Chetta Reynolds blew into the examining room where the Stones and their ceaselessly screaming baby daughter had been stashed. The poet rumored to be on the short list for a Presidential Medal of Freedom was dressed in straight-leg jeans and a BU sweatshirt with a hole in one elbow. The outfit showed just how thin she'd become over the last three or four years. *No cancer, if that's what you're thinking*, she'd say if anyone commented on her runway-model thinness, which she ordinarily disguised with billowing dresses or caftans. *I'm just in training for the final lap around the track.*

Her hair, as a rule braided or put up in complicated swoops arranged to showcase her collection of vintage hair clips, stood out around her head in an unkempt Einstein cloud. She wore no makeup, and even in her distress, Lucy was shocked by how old Concetta looked. Well, of course she was old, eighty-five was *very* old, but until this morning she had looked like a woman in her late sixties at most. 'I would have been here an hour earlier if I'd found someone to come in and take care of Betty.' Betty was her elderly, ailing boxer.

Chetta caught David's reproachful glance.

'Bets is *dying*, David. And based on what you could tell me over the phone, I wasn't all that concerned about Abra.'

'Are you concerned now?' David asked.

Lucy flashed him a warning glance, but Chetta seemed willing to accept the implied rebuke. 'Yes.' She held out her hands. 'Give her to me, Lucy. Let's see if she'll quiet for Momo.'

But Abra would not quiet for Momo, no matter how she was rocked. Nor did a soft and surprisingly tuneful lullabye (for all David knew, it was 'The Wheels on the Bus' in Italian) do the job. They all tried the walking cure again, first squiring her around the small exam room, then down the hall, then back to the exam room. The screaming went on and on. At some point there was a commotion outside – someone with actual visible injuries being wheeled in, David assumed – but those in exam room 4 took little notice.

At five to nine, the exam room door opened and the Stones' pediatrician walked in. Dr John Dalton was a fellow Dan Torrance would have recognized, although not by last name. To Dan he was just Doctor John, who made the coffee at the Thursday night Big Book meeting in North Conway.

'Thank God!' Lucy said, thrusting her howling child into the pediatrician's arms. 'We've been left on our own for *hours*!'

'I was on my way when I got the message.' Dalton hoisted Abra onto his shoulder. 'Rounds here, then over in Castle Rock. You've heard about what's happened, haven't you?'

'Heard what?' David asked. With the door open, he was for the first time consciously aware of a moderate uproar outside. People were talking in loud voices. Some were crying. The nurse who had admitted them walked by, her face red and blotchy, her cheeks wet. She didn't even glance at the screaming infant.

'A passenger jet hit the World Trade Center,' Dalton said. 'And no one thinks it was an accident.'

That was American Airlines Flight 11. United Airlines Flight 175 struck the Trade Center's South Tower seventeen minutes later, at 9:03 a.m. At 9:03, Abra Stone abruptly stopped crying. By 9:04, she was sound asleep.

On their ride back to Anniston, David and Lucy listened to the radio while Abra slept peacefully in her car seat behind them. The news was unbearable, but turning it off was unthinkable . . . at least until a newscaster announced the names of the airlines and the flight numbers of the aircraft: two in New York, one near Washington, one cratered in rural Pennsylvania. Then David finally reached over and silenced the flood of disaster.

'Lucy, I have to tell you something. I dreamed—'

'I know.' She spoke in the flat tone of one who has just suffered a shock. 'So did I.'

By the time they crossed back into New Hampshire, David had begun to believe there might be something to that caul business, after all.

10

In a New Jersey town, on the west bank of the Hudson River, there's a park named for the town's most famous resident. On a clear day, it offers a perfect view of lower Manhattan. The True Knot arrived in Hoboken on September eighth, parking in a private lot which they had four-walled for ten days. Crow Daddy did the deal. Handsome and gregarious, looking about forty, Crow's favorite t-shirt read I'M A PEOPLE PERSON! Not that he ever wore a tee when negotiating for the True Knot; then it was strictly suit and tie. It was what the rubes expected. His straight name was Henry Rothman. He was a Harvard-educated lawyer (class of '38), and he always carried cash. The True had over a billion dollars in various accounts across the world – some in gold, some in diamonds, some in rare books, stamps, and paintings – but never paid by check or credit card. Everyone, even Pea and Pod, who looked like kids, carried a roll of tens and twenties.

As Jimmy Numbers had once said, 'We're a cash-and-carry outfit. We pay cash and the rubes carry us.' Jimmy was the True's accountant.

In his rube days he had once ridden with an outfit that became known (long after their war was over) as Quantrill's Raiders. Back then he had been a wild kid who wore a buffalo coat and carried a Sharps, but in the years since, he had mellowed. These days he had a framed, autographed picture of Ronald Reagan in his RV.

On the morning of September eleventh, the True watched the attacks on the Twin Towers from the parking lot, passing around four pairs of binoculars. They would have had a better view from Sinatra Park, but Rose didn't need to tell them that gathering early might attract suspicion . . . and in the months and years ahead, America was going to be a very suspicious nation: if you see something, say something.

Around ten that morning – when crowds had gathered all along the riverbank and it was safe – they made their way to the park. The Little twins, Pea and Pod, pushed Grampa Flick in his wheelchair. Grampa wore his cap stating I AM A VET. His long, baby-fine white hair floated around the cap's edges like milkweed. There had been a time when he'd told folks he was a veteran of the Spanish-American War. Then it was World War I. Nowadays it was World War II. In another twenty years or so, he expected to switch his story to Vietnam. Verisimilitude had never been a problem; Grampa was a military history buff.

Sinatra Park was jammed. Most folks were silent, but some wept. Apron Annie and Black-Eyed Sue helped in this respect; both were able to cry on demand. The others put on suitable expressions of sorrow, solemnity, and amazement.

Basically, the True Knot fit right in. It was how they rolled.

Spectators came and went, but the True stayed for most of the day, which was cloudless and beautiful (except for the thick billows of dreck rising in Lower Manhattan, that is). They stood at the iron rail, not talking among themselves, just watching. And taking long slow deep breaths, like tourists from the Midwest standing for the first time on Pemaquid Point or Quoddy Head in Maine, breathing deep of the fresh sea air. As a sign of respect, Rose took off her tophat and held it by her side.

At four o'clock they trooped back to their encampment in the parking lot, invigorated. They would return the next day, and the day after that, and the day after that. They would return until the good steam was exhausted, and then they would move on again.

By then, Grampa Flick's white hair would have become iron gray, and he would no longer need the wheelchair.

CHAPTER THREE
SPOONS

1

It was a twenty-mile drive from Frazier to North Conway, but Dan Torrance made it every Thursday night, partly because he could. He was now working at Helen Rivington House, making a decent salary, and he had his driver's license back. The car he'd bought to go with it wasn't much, just a three-year-old Caprice with blackwall tires and an iffy radio, but the engine was good and every time he started it up, he felt like the luckiest man in New Hampshire. He thought if he never had to ride another bus, he could die happy. It was January of 2004. Except for a few random thoughts and images – plus the extra work he sometimes did at the hospice, of course – the shining had been quiet. He would have done that volunteer work in any case, but after his time in AA, he also saw it as making amends, which recovering people considered almost as important as staying away from the first drink. If he could manage to keep the plug in the jug another three months, he would be able to celebrate three years sober.

Driving again figured large in the daily gratitude meditations upon which Casey K. insisted (because, he said – and with all the dour certainty of the Program long-timer – a grateful alcoholic doesn't get drunk), but mostly Dan went on Thursday nights because the Big Book gathering was soothing. Intimate, really. Some of the open discussion meetings in the area were uncomfortably large, but that was never true on Thursday nights in North Conway. There was an old AA saying that went, *If you want to hide something from an alcoholic, stick it in the Big Book*, and attendance at the North Conway Thursday night meeting suggested that there was some truth in it. Even during the weeks between the Fourth of July and Labor Day – the height of the tourist season – it was rare to have more than a dozen people in the Amvets hall when the gavel fell.

As a result, Dan had heard things he suspected would never have been spoken aloud in the meetings that drew fifty or even seventy recovering alkies and druggies. In those, speakers had a tendency to take refuge in the platitudes (of which there were hundreds) and avoid the personal. You'd hear *Serenity pays dividends* and *You can take my inventory if you're willing to make my amends*, but never *I fucked my brother's wife one night when we were both drunk.*

At the Thursday night We Study Sobriety meetings, the little enclave read Bill Wilson's big blue how-to manual from cover to cover, each new meeting picking up where the last meeting had left off. When they got to the end of the book, they went back to 'The Doctor's Statement' and started all over again. Most meetings covered ten pages or so. That took about half an hour. In the remaining half hour, the group was supposed to talk about the material just read. Sometimes they actually did. Quite often, however, the discussion veered off in other directions, like an unruly planchette scurrying around a Ouija board beneath the fingers of neurotic teenagers.

Dan remembered a Thursday night meeting he'd attended when he was about eight months sober. The chapter under discussion, 'To Wives', was full of antique assumptions that almost always provoked a hot response from the younger women in the Program. They wanted to know why, in the sixty-five years or so since the Big Book's original publication, no one had ever added a chapter called 'To Husbands'.

When Gemma T. – a thirtysomething whose only two emotional settings seemed to be Angry and Profoundly Pissed Off – raised her hand on that particular night, Dan had expected a fem-lib tirade. Instead she said, much more quietly than usual, 'I need to share something. I've been holding onto it ever since I was seventeen, and unless I let go, I'll never be able to stay away from coke and wine.'

The group waited.

'I hit a man with my car when I was coming home drunk from a party,' Gemma said. 'This was back in Somerville. I left him lying by the side of the road. I didn't know if he was dead or alive. I still don't. I waited for the cops to come and arrest me, but they never did. I got away with it.'

She had laughed at this the way people do when the joke's an especially good one, then put her head down on the table and burst into sobs so deep that they shook her rail-thin body. It had been Dan's first experience with how terrifying 'honesty in all our affairs' could be when it was actually put into practice. He thought, as he still did every so often, of how he had stripped Deenie's wallet of cash, and how the little boy had reached for the cocaine on the coffee table. He was a little in awe of Gemma, but that much raw honesty wasn't in him. If it came down to a choice between telling that story and taking a drink . . .

I'd take the drink. No question.

2

Tonight the reading was 'Gutter Bravado', one of the stories from the section of the Big Book cheerily titled 'They Lost Nearly All'. The tale followed a pattern with which Dan had become familiar: good family, church on Sundays, first drink, first binge, business success spoiled by booze, escalating lies, first arrest, broken promises to reform, institutionalization, and the final happy ending. All the stories in the Big Book had happy endings. That was part of its charm.

It was a cold night but overwarm inside, and Dan was edging into a doze when Doctor John raised his hand and said, 'I've been lying to my wife about something, and I don't know how to stop.'

That woke Dan up. He liked DJ a lot.

It turned out that John's wife had given him a watch for Christmas, quite an expensive one, and when she had asked him a couple of nights ago why he wasn't wearing it, John said he'd left it at the office.

'Only it's not there. I looked everywhere, and it's just not. I do a lot of hospital rounds, and if I have to change into scrubs, I use one of the lockers in the doctors' lounge. There are combo locks, but I hardly ever use them, because I don't carry much cash and I don't have anything else worth stealing. Except for the watch, I guess. I can't remember taking it off and leaving it in a locker – not at CNH or over in Bridgton – but I think I must have. It's not the expense. It just brings back a lot of the old stuff from the days when

I was drinking myself stupid every night and chipping speed the next morning to get going.'

There were nodding heads at this, followed by similar stories of guilt-driven deceit. No one gave advice; that was called 'crosstalk', and frowned on. They simply told their tales. John listened with his head down and his hands clasped between his knees. After the basket was passed ('We are self-supporting through our own contributions'), he thanked everyone for their input. From the look of him, Dan didn't think said input had helped a whole hell of a lot.

After the Lord's Prayer, Dan put away the leftover cookies and stacked the group's tattered Big Books in the cabinet marked FOR AA USE. A few people were still hanging around the butt-can outside – the so-called meeting after the meeting – but he and John had the kitchen to themselves. Dan hadn't spoken during the discussion; he was too busy having an interior debate with himself.

The shining had been quiet, but that didn't mean it was absent. He knew from his volunteer work that it was actually stronger than it had been since childhood, though now he seemed to have a greater degree of control over it. That made it less frightening and more useful. His co-workers at Rivington House knew he had *something*, but most of them called it empathy and let it go at that. The last thing he wanted, now that his life had begun to settle down, was to get a reputation as some sort of parlor psychic. Best to keep the freaky shit to himself.

Doctor John was a good guy, though. And he was hurting.

DJ placed the coffee urn upside down in the dish drainer, used a length of towel hanging from the stove handle to dry his hands, then turned to Dan, offering a smile that looked as real as the Coffeemate Dan had stored away next to the cookies and the sugar bowl. 'Well, I'm off. See you next week, I guess.'

In the end, the decision made itself; Dan simply could not let the guy go looking like that. He held his arms out. 'Give it up.'

The fabled AA manhug. Dan had seen many but never given a single one. John looked dubious for a moment, then stepped forward. Dan drew him in, thinking *There'll probably be nothing.*

But there was. It came as quickly as it had when, as a child, he had sometimes helped his mother and father find lost things.

'Listen to me, Doc,' he said, letting John go. 'You were worried about the kid with Goocher's.'

John stepped back. 'What are you talking about?'

'I'm not saying it right, I know that. Goocher's? Glutcher's? It's some sort of bone thing.'

John's mouth dropped open. 'Are you talking about Norman Lloyd?'

'You tell me.'

'Normie's got Gaucher's disease. It's a lipid disorder. Hereditary and very rare. Causes an enlarged spleen, neurologic disorders, and usually an early, unpleasant death. Poor kid's basically got a glass skeleton, and he'll probably die before he's ten. But how do you know that? From his parents? The Lloyds live way the hell down in Nashua.'

'You were worried about talking to him – the terminal ones drive you crazy. That's why you stopped in the Tigger bathroom to wash your hands even though your hands didn't need washing. You took off your watch and put it up on the shelf where they keep that dark red disinfectant shit that comes in the plastic squeeze bottles. I don't know the name.'

John D. was staring at him as though he had gone mad.

'Which hospital is this kid in?' Dan asked.

'Elliot. The time-frame's about right, and I did stop in the bath-room near the Pedes nursing station to wash my hands.' He paused, frowning. 'And yeah, I guess there are Milne characters on the walls in that one. But if I'd taken off my watch, I'd remem . . .' He trailed off.

'You *do* remember,' Dan said, and smiled. '*Now* you do. Don't you?'

John said, 'I checked the Elliot lost and found. Bridgton and CNH, too, for that matter. Nothing.'

'Okay, so maybe somebody came along, saw it, and stole it. If so, you're shit out of luck . . . but at least you can tell your wife what happened. And *why* it happened. You were thinking about the kid, *worrying* about the kid, and you forgot to put your watch back on before you left the can. Simple as that. And hey, maybe it's still there. That's a high shelf, and hardly anybody uses what's in those plastic bottles, because there's a soap dispenser right beside the sink.'

'It's Betadine on that shelf,' John said, 'and up high so the kids can't reach it. I never noticed. But . . . Dan, have you ever *been* in Elliot?'

This wasn't a question he wanted to answer. 'Just check the shelf, Doc. Maybe you'll get lucky.'

3

Dan arrived early at the following Thursday's We Study Sobriety meeting. If Doctor John had decided to trash his marriage and possibly his career over a missing seven-hundred-dollar watch (alkies routinely trashed marriages and careers over far less), someone would have to make the coffee. But John was there. So was the watch.

This time it was John who initiated the manhug. An extremely hearty one. Dan almost expected to receive a pair of Gallic kisses on the cheeks before DJ let him go.

'It was right where you said it would be. Ten days, and still there. It's like a miracle.'

'Nah,' Dan said. 'Most people rarely look above their own eyeline. It's a proven fact.'

'How did you *know*?'

Dan shook his head. 'I can't explain it. Sometimes I just do.'

'How can I thank you?'

This was the question Dan had been waiting and hoping for. 'By working the Twelfth Step, dummocks.'

John D. raised his eyebrows.

'Anonymity. In words of one syllable, keep ya fuckin mouth shut.'

Understanding broke on John's face. He grinned. 'I can do that.'

'Good. Now make the coffee. I'll put out the books.'

4

In most New England AA groups, anniversaries are called birthdays and celebrated with a cake and an after-meeting party. Shortly before Dan was due to celebrate his third year of sobriety in this fashion, David Stone and Abra's great-grandmother came to see John Dalton – known in some circles as either Doctor John or DJ – and invite him to another third birthday party. This was the one the Stones were throwing for Abra.

'That's very kind,' John said, 'and I'll be more than happy to drop by if I can. Only why do I feel there's a little more to it?'

'Because there is,' Chetta said. 'And Mr Stubborn here has decided that it's finally time to talk about it.'

'Is there a problem with Abra? If there is, fill me in. Based on her last checkup, she's fine. Fearsomely bright. Social skills terrific. Verbal skills through the roof. Reading, ditto. Last time she was here she read me *Alligators All Around*. Probably rote memory, but still remarkable for a child who's not yet three. Does Lucy know you're here?'

'Lucy and Chetta are the ones who ganged up on me,' David said. 'Lucy's home with Abra, making cupcakes for the party. When I left, the kitchen looked like hell in a high wind.'

'So what are we saying here? That you want me at her party in an observational capacity?'

'That's right,' Concetta said. 'None of us can say for sure that something will happen, but it's more likely to when she's excited, and she's *very* excited about her party. All her little pals from daycare are coming, and there's going to be a fellow who does magic tricks.'

John opened a desk drawer and took out a yellow legal pad. 'What kind of something are you expecting?'

David hesitated. 'That's . . . hard to say.'

Chetta turned to face him. 'Go on, *caro*. Too late to back out now.' Her tone was light, almost gay, but John Dalton thought she looked worried. He thought they both did. 'Begin with the night she started crying and wouldn't stop.'

5

David Stone had been teaching American history and twentieth-century European history to undergraduates for ten years, and knew how to organize a story so the interior logic was hard to miss. He began this one by pointing out that their infant daughter's marathon crying spree had ended almost immediately after the second jetliner had struck the World Trade Center. Then he doubled back to the dreams in which his wife had seen the American Airlines flight number on Abra's chest and he had seen the United Airlines number.

'In Lucy's dream, she found Abra in an airplane bathroom. In mine, I found her in a mall that was on fire. Draw your own conclusions about that part. Or not. To me, those flight numbers seem pretty conclusive. But of what, I don't know.' He laughed without much humor, raised his hands, then dropped them again. 'Maybe I'm afraid to know.'

John Dalton remembered the morning of 9/11 – and Abra's nonstop crying jag – very well. 'Let me get this straight. You believe your daughter – who was then only five months old – had a premonition of those attacks and somehow sent word to you telepathically.'

'Yes,' Chetta said. 'Put very succinctly. Bravo.'

'I know how it sounds,' David said. 'Which is why Lucy and I kept it to ourselves. Except for Chetta, that is. Lucy told her that night. Lucy tells her momo everything.' He sighed. Concetta gave him a cool look.

'You didn't get one of these dreams?' John asked her.

She shook her head. 'I was in Boston. Out of her . . . I don't know . . . transmitting range?'

'It's been almost three years since 9/11,' John said. 'I assume other stuff has happened since then.'

A lot of other stuff had happened, and now that he had managed to speak of the first (and most unbelievable) thing, Dave found himself able to talk about the rest easily enough.

'The piano. That was next. You know Lucy plays?'

John shook his head.

'Well, she does. Since she was in grammar school. She's not great or anything, but she's pretty good. We've got a Vogel that my parents gave her as a wedding present. It's in the living room, which is also where Abra's playpen used to be. Well, one of the presents I gave Lucy for Christmas in 2001 was a book of Beatles tunes arranged for piano. Abra used to lie in her playpen, goofing with her toys and listening. You could tell by the way she smiled and kicked her feet that she liked the music.'

John didn't question this. Most babies loved music, and they had their ways of letting you know.

'The book had all the hits – "Hey Jude", "Lady Madonna", "Let

It Be" – but the one Abra liked best was one of the minor songs, a B-side called "Not a Second Time". Do you know it?'

'Not offhand,' John said. 'I might if I heard it.'

'It's upbeat, but unlike most of the Beatles' fast stuff, it's built around a piano riff rather than the usual guitar sound. It isn't a boogie-woogie, but close. Abra loved it. She wouldn't just kick her feet when Lucy played that one, she'd actually bicycle them.' Dave smiled at the memory of Abra on her back in her bright purple onesie, not yet able to walk but crib-dancing like a disco queen. 'The instrumental break is almost all piano, and it's simple as pie. The left hand just picks out the notes. There are only twenty-nine – I counted. A kid could play it. And our kid did.'

John raised his eyebrows until they almost met his hairline.

'It started in the spring of 2002. Lucy and I were in bed, reading. The weather report was on TV, and that comes about halfway through the eleven p.m. newscast. Abra was in her room – fast asleep, as far as we knew. Lucy asked me to turn off the TV because she wanted to go to sleep. I clicked the remote, and that's when we heard it. The piano break of "Not a Second Time", those twenty-nine notes. Perfect. Not a single miss, and coming from downstairs.

'Doc, we were scared shitless. We thought we had an intruder in the house, only what kind of burglar stops to play a little Beatles before grabbing the silverware? I don't have a gun and my golf clubs were in the garage, so I just picked up the biggest book I could find and went down to confront whoever was there. Pretty stupid, I know. I told Lucy to grab the phone and dial 911 if I yelled. But there was no one, and all the doors were locked. Also, the cover was down over the piano keys.

'I went back upstairs and told Lucy I hadn't found anything or anyone. We went down the hall to check the baby. We didn't talk about it, we just did it. I think we knew it was Abra, but neither of us wanted to say it right out loud. She was awake, just lying there in her crib and looking at us. You know the wise little eyes that they have?'

John knew. As if they could tell you all the secrets of the universe, if they were only able to talk. There were times when he thought that might even be so, only God had arranged things in such a way so that by the time they *could* get beyond goo-goo-ga-ga, they had forgotten it all, the way we forget even our most vivid dreams a couple of hours after waking.

'She smiled when she saw us, closed her eyes, and dropped off. The next night it happened again. Same time. Those twenty-nine notes from the living room . . . then silence . . . then down to Abra's room and finding her awake. Not fussing, not even sucking her bink, just looking at us through the bars of her crib. Then off to sleep.'

'This is the truth,' John said. Not really questioning, only wanting to get it straight. 'You're not pulling my leg.'

David didn't smile. 'Not even twitching the cuff of your pants.'

John turned to Chetta. 'Have you heard it yourself?'

'No. Let David finish.'

'We got a couple of nights off, and . . . you know how you say that the secret of successful parenting is always make a plan?'

'Sure.' This was John Dalton's chief sermon to new parents. How are you going to handle night feedings? Draw up a schedule so someone's always on call and no one gets too ragged. How are you going to handle bathing and feeding and dressing and playtime so the kid has a regular – and hence comforting – routine? Draw up a schedule. Make a plan. Do you know how to handle an emergency? Anything from a collapsed crib to a choking incident? If you make a plan, you will, and nineteen times out of twenty, things will turn out fine.

'So that's what we did. For the next three nights I slept on the sofa right across from the piano. On the third night the music started just as I was snugging down for the night. The cover on the Vogel was closed, so I hustled over and raised it. The keys weren't moving. Which didn't surprise me much, because I could tell the music wasn't coming from the piano.'

'Beg pardon?'

'It was coming from *above* it. From thin air. By then, Lucy was in Abra's room. The other times we hadn't said anything, we were too stunned, but this time she was ready. She told Abra to play it again. There was a little pause . . . and then she did. I was standing so close I almost could have snatched those notes out of the air.'

Silence in John Dalton's office. He had stopped writing on the pad. Chetta was looking at him gravely. At last he said, 'Is this still going on?'

'No. Lucy took Abra on her lap and told her not to play anymore at night, because we couldn't sleep. And that was the end of it.' He paused to consider. '*Almost* the end. Once, about three weeks later, we heard the music again, but very soft and coming from upstairs this time. From her room.'

'She was playing to herself,' Concetta said. 'She woke up . . . she couldn't get back to sleep right away . . . so she played herself a little lullaby.'

6

One Monday afternoon just about a year after the fall of the Twin Towers, Abra – walking by now and with recognizable words beginning to emerge from her all-but-constant gabble – teetered her way to the front door and plopped down there with her favorite doll in her lap.

'Whatcha doon, sweetheart?' Lucy asked. She was sitting at the piano, playing a Scott Joplin rag.

'Dada!' Abra announced.

'Honey, Dada won't be home until supper,' Lucy said, but fifteen minutes later the Acura pulled up the drive and Dave got out, hauling his briefcase. There had been a water-main break in the building where he taught his Monday-Wednesday-Friday classes, and everything had been canceled.

'Lucy told me about that,' Concetta said, 'and of course I already knew about the 9/11 crying jag and the phantom piano. I took a run up there a week or two later. I told Lucy not to say a word to Abra about my visit. But Abra knew. She planted herself in front of the door ten minutes before I showed up. When Lucy asked who was coming, Abra said, "Momo."'

'She does that a lot,' David said. 'Not every time someone's coming, but if it's someone she knows and likes . . . almost always.'

In the late spring of 2003, Lucy found her daughter in their bedroom, tugging at the second drawer of Lucy's dresser.

'Mun!' she told her mother. 'Mun, mun!'

'I don't get you, sweetie,' Lucy said, 'but you can look in the drawer if you want to. It's just some old underwear and leftover cosmetics.'

But Abra had no interest in the drawer, it seemed; didn't even look in it when Lucy pulled it out to show her what was inside.

'Hind! Mun!' Then, drawing a deep breath. 'Mun hind, Mama!'

Parents never become absolutely fluent in Baby – there's not enough time – but most learn to speak it to some degree, and Lucy finally understood that her daughter's interest wasn't in the contents of the dresser but in something behind it.

Curious, she pulled it out. Abra darted into the space immediately. Lucy, thinking that it would be dusty in there even if there weren't bugs or mice, made a swipe for the back of the baby's shirt and missed. By the time she got the dresser out far enough to slip into the gap herself, Abra was holding up a twenty-dollar bill that had found its way through the hole between the dresser's surface and the bottom of the mirror. 'Look!' she said gleefully. 'Mun! *My* mun!'

'Nope,' Lucy said, plucking it out of the small fist, 'babies don't get mun because they don't need mun. But you did just earn yourself an ice cream cone.'

'I-keem!' Abra shouted. '*My* i-keem!'

'Now tell Doctor John about Mrs Judkins,' David said. 'You were there for that.'

'Indeed I was,' Concetta said. 'That was some Fourth of July weekend.'

By the summer of 2003, Abra had begun speaking in – more or less – full sentences. Concetta had come to spend the holiday weekend with the Stones. On the Sunday, which happened to be July sixth, Dave had gone to the 7-Eleven to buy a fresh canister of Blue Rhino for the backyard barbecue. Abra was playing with blocks in the living room. Lucy and Chetta were in the kitchen, one of them checking periodically on Abra to make sure she hadn't decided to pull out the plug on the TV and chew it or go climbing Mount Sofa. But Abra showed no interest in those things; she was busy constructing what looked like a Stonehenge made out of her plastic toddler blocks.

Lucy and Chetta were unloading the dishwasher when Abra began to scream.

'She sounded like she was dying,' Chetta said. 'You know how scary that is, right?'

John nodded. He knew.

'Running doesn't come naturally to me at my age, but I ran like Wilma Rudolph that day. Beat Lucy to the living room by half a length. I was so convinced the kid was hurt that for a second or two I actually *saw* blood. But she was okay. Physically, anyhow. She ran to me and threw her arms around my legs. I picked her up. Lucy was with me by then, and we managed to get her soothed a little. "Wannie!" she said. "Help Wannie, Momo! Wannie fall down!" I didn't know who Wannie was, but Lucy did — Wanda Judkins, the lady across the street.'

'She's Abra's favorite neighbor,' David said, 'because she makes cookies and usually brings one over for Abra with her name written on it. Sometimes in raisins, sometimes in frosting. She's a widow. Lives alone.'

'So we went across,' Chetta resumed, 'me in the lead and Lucy holding Abra. I knocked. No one answered. "Wannie in the dinner room!" Abra said. "Help Wannie, Momo! Help Wannie, Mama! She hurted herself and blood is coming out!"

'The door was unlocked. We went in. First thing I smelled was burning cookies. Mrs Judkins was lying on the dining room floor next to a stepladder. The rag she'd been using to dust out the moldings was still in her hand, and there was blood, all right — a puddle of it around her head in a kind of halo. I thought she was finished — I couldn't see her breathing — but Lucy found a pulse. The fall fractured her skull, and there was a small brain-bleed, but she woke up the next day. She'll be at Abra's birthday party. You can say hello to her, if you come.' She looked at Abra Stone's pediatrician unflinchingly. 'The doctor at the ER said that if she'd lain there much longer, she would have either died or ended up in a persistent vegetative state . . . far worse than death, in my humble opinion. Either way, the kid saved her life.'

John tossed his pen on top of the legal pad. 'I don't know what to say.'

'There's more,' Dave said, 'but the other stuff's hard to quantify. Maybe just because Lucy and I have gotten used to it. The way, I guess, you'd get used to living with a kid who was born blind. Except this is almost the opposite of that. I think we knew even before the 9/11 thing. I think we knew there was *something* almost from the time we brought her home from the hospital. It's like . . .'

He huffed out a breath and looked at the ceiling, as if for inspiration. Concetta squeezed his arm. 'Go on. At least he hasn't called for the men with the butterfly nets yet.'

'Okay, it's like there's always a wind blowing through the house, only you can't exactly feel it or see what it's doing. I keep thinking the curtains are going to billow and the pictures are going to fly off the walls, but they never do. Other stuff does happen, though. Two or three times a week – sometimes two or three times a *day* – the circuit breakers trip. We've had two different electricians out, on four different occasions. They check the circuits and tell us everything is hunky-dory. Some mornings we come downstairs and the cushions from the chairs and the sofa are on the floor. We tell Abra to put her toys away before bed and unless she's overtired and cranky, she's very good about it. But sometimes the toybox will be open the next morning and some of the toys will be back on the floor. Usually the blocks. They're her favorites.'

He paused for a moment, now looking at the eye chart on the far wall. John thought Concetta would prod him to go on, but she kept silent.

'Okay, this is totally weird, but I swear to you it happened. One night when we turned on the TV, *The Simpsons* were on every channel. Abra laughed like it was the biggest joke in the world. Lucy freaked out. She said, "Abra Rafaella Stone, if you're doing that, stop it right now!" Lucy hardly ever speaks sharply to her, and when she does, Abra just dissolves. Which is what happened that night. I turned off the TV, and when I turned it on again, everything was back to normal. I could give you half a dozen other things . . . incidents . . . phenomena . . . but most of it's so small you'd hardly even notice.' He shrugged. 'Like I say, you get used to it.'

John said, 'I'll come to the party. After all that, how can I resist?'

'Probably nothing will happen,' Dave said. 'You know the old joke about how to stop a leaky faucet, don't you? Call the plumber.'

Concetta snorted. 'If you really believe that, sonny-boy, I think you might get a surprise.' And, to Dalton: 'Just getting him here was like pulling teeth.'

'Give it a rest, Momo.' Color had begun to rise in Dave's cheeks.

John sighed. He had sensed the antagonism between these two before. He didn't know the cause of it – some kind of competition for Lucy, perhaps – but he didn't want it breaking out into the open now. Their bizarre errand had turned them into temporary allies, and that was the way he wanted to keep it.

'Save the sniping.' He spoke sharply enough so they looked away from each other and back at him, surprised. 'I believe you. I've never heard of anything remotely like this before . . .'

Or had he? He trailed off, thinking of his lost watch.

'Doc?' David said.

'Sorry. Brain cramp.'

At this they both smiled. Allies again. Good.

'Anyway, no one's going to send for the men in the white coats. I accept you both as level-headed folks, not prone to hysteria or hallucination. I might guess some bizarre form of Munchausen syndrome was at work if it was just one person claiming these . . . these psychic outbreaks . . . but it's not. It's all three of you. Which raises the question, what do you want me to do?'

Dave seemed at a loss, but his grandmother-in-law was not. 'Observe her, the way you would any child with a disease—'

The color had begun to leave David Stone's cheeks, but now it rushed back. *Slammed* back. 'Abra is not sick,' he snapped.

She turned to him. 'I know that! *Cristo!* Will you let me finish?'

Dave put on a longsuffering expression and raised his hands. 'Sorry, sorry, sorry.'

'Just don't jump down my throat, David.'

John said, 'If you insist on bickering, children, I'll have to send you to the Quiet Room.'

Concetta sighed. 'This is very stressful. For all of us. I'm sorry, Davey, I used the wrong word.'

'No prob, *cara*. We're in this together.'

She smiled briefly. 'Yes. Yes, we are. Observe her as you'd observe any child with an undiagnosed condition, Dr Dalton. That's all we can ask, and I think it's enough for now. You may have some ideas. I hope so. You see . . .'

She turned to David Stone with an expression of helplessness that John thought was probably rare on that firm face.

'We're afraid,' Dave said. 'Me, Lucy, Chetta – scared to death. Not of her, but for her. Because she's just *little*, do you see? What if this power of hers . . . I don't know what else to call it . . . what if it hasn't topped out yet? What if it's still growing? What do we do then? She could . . . I don't know . . .'

'He *does* know,' Chetta said. 'She could lose her temper and hurt herself or someone else. I don't know how likely that is, but just thinking it *could* happen . . .' She touched John's hand. 'It's awful.'

7

Dan Torrance knew he would be living in the turret room of the Helen Rivington House from the moment he had seen his old friend Tony waving to him from a window that on second look turned out to be boarded shut. He asked Mrs Clausen, the Rivington's chief supervisor, about the room six months or so after going to work at the hospice as janitor/orderly . . . and unofficial doctor in residence. Along with his faithful sidekick Azzie, of course.

'That room's junk from one end to the other,' Mrs Clausen had said. She was a sixtysomething with implausibly red hair. She was possessed of a sarcastic, often dirty mouth, but she was a smart and compassionate administrator. Even better, from the standpoint of HRH's board of directors, she was a tremendously effective fund-raiser. Dan wasn't sure he liked her, but he had come to respect her.

'I'll clean it out. On my own time. It would be better for me to be right here, don't you think? On call?'

'Danny, tell me something. How come you're so good at what you do?'

'I don't really know.' This was at least half true. Maybe even seventy percent. He had lived with the shining all his life and still didn't understand it.

'Junk aside, the turret's hot in the summer and cold enough to freeze the balls off a brass monkey in the winter.'

'That can be rectified,' Dan had said.

'Don't talk to *me* about your rectum.' Mrs Clausen peered sternly at him from above her half-glasses. 'If the board knew what I was letting you do, they'd probably have me weaving baskets in that assisted living home down in Nashua. The one with the pink walls and the piped-in Mantovani.' She snorted. 'Doctor Sleep, indeed.'

'I'm not the doctor,' Dan said mildly. He knew he was going to get what he wanted. 'Azzie's the doctor. I'm just his assistant.'

'Azreel's the fucking *cat*,' she said. 'A raggedy-ass stray that wandered in off the street and got adopted by guests who have now all gone to the Great Who Knows. All he cares about is his twice-daily bowl of Friskies.'

To this Dan hadn't responded. There was no need, because they both knew it wasn't true.

'I thought you had a perfectly good place on Eliot Street. Pauline Robertson thinks the sun shines out of your asshole. I know because I sing with her in the church choir.'

'What's your favorite hymn?' Dan asked. '"What a Fucking Friend We Have in Jesus"?'

She showed the Rebecca Clausen version of a smile. 'Oh, very well. Clean out the room. Move in. Have it wired for cable, put in quadraphonic sound, set up a wetbar. What the hell do I care, I'm only the boss.'

'Thanks, Mrs C.'

'Oh, and don't forget the space heater, okay? See if you can't find something from a yard sale with a nice frayed cord. Burn the fucking place down some cold February night. Then they can put up a brick monstrosity to match the abortions on either side of us.'

Dan stood up and raised the back of his hand to his forehead in a half-assed British salute. 'Whatever you say, boss.'

She waved a hand at him. 'Get outta here before I change my mind, doc.'

8

He *did* put in a space heater, but the cord wasn't frayed and it was the kind that shut off immediately if it tipped over. There was never going to be any air-conditioning in the third-floor turret room, but a couple of fans from Walmart placed in the open windows provided a nice cross-draft. It got plenty hot just the same on summer days, but Dan was almost never there in the daytime. And summer nights in New Hampshire were usually cool.

Most of the stuff that had been stashed up there was disposable junk, but he kept a big grammar school-style blackboard he found leaning against one wall. It had been hidden for fifty years or more behind an ironmongery of ancient and grievously wounded wheelchairs. The blackboard was useful. On it he listed the hospice's patients and their room numbers, erasing the names of the folks who passed away and adding names as new folks checked in. In the spring of 2004, there were thirty-two names on the board. Ten were in Rivington One and twelve in Rivington Two – these were the ugly brick buildings flanking the Victorian home where the famous Helen Rivington had once lived and written thrilling romance novels under the pulsating name of Jeannette Montparsse. The rest of the patients were housed on the two floors below Dan's cramped but serviceable turret apartment.

Was Mrs Rivington famous for anything besides writing bad novels? Dan had asked Claudette Albertson not long after starting work at the hospice. They were in the smoking area at the time, practicing their nasty habit. Claudette, a cheerful African American RN with the shoulders of an NFL left tackle, threw back her head and laughed.

'You bet! For leaving this town a shitload of money, honey! And giving away this house, of course. She thought old folks should have a place where they could die with dignity.'

And in Rivington House, most of them did. Dan – with Azzie to assist – was now a part of that. He thought he had found his calling. The hospice now felt like home.

9

On the morning of Abra's birthday party, Dan got out of bed and saw that all the names on his blackboard had been erased. Written where they had been, in large and straggling letters, was a single word:

hEll☺

Dan sat on the edge of the bed in his underwear for a long time, just looking. Then he got up and put one hand on the letters, smudging them a little, hoping for a shine. Even a little twinkle. At last he took his hand away, rubbing chalkdust on his bare thigh.

'Hello yourself,' he said . . . and then: 'Would your name be Abra, by any chance?'

Nothing. He put on his robe, got his soap and towel, and went down to the staff shower on two. When he came back, he picked up the eraser he'd found to go with the board and began erasing the word. Halfway through, a thought

(daddy says we'll have balloons)

came to him, and he stopped, waiting for more. But no more came, so he finished erasing the board and then began replacing the names and room numbers, working from that Monday's attendance memo. When he came back upstairs at noon, he half expected the board to be erased again, the names and numbers replaced by *hEll*☺, but all was as he had left it.

10

Abra's birthday party was in the Stones' backyard, a restful sweep of green grass with apple and dogwood trees that were just coming into blossom. At the foot of the yard was a chainlink fence and a gate secured by a combination padlock. The fence was decidedly unbeautiful, but neither David nor Lucy cared, because beyond it was the Saco River, which wound its way southeast, through Frazier, through North Conway, and across the border into Maine. Rivers and small children did not mix, in the Stones' opinion, especially in the spring, when this one was wide and turbulent with melting snows. Each year the local weekly reported at least one drowning.

Today the kids had enough to occupy them on the lawn. The only organized game they could manage was a brief round of follow-the-leader, but they weren't too young to run around (and sometimes roll around) on the grass, to climb like monkeys on Abra's playset, to crawl through the Fun Tunnels David and a couple of the other dads had set up, and to bat around the balloons now drifting everywhere. These were all yellow (Abra's professed favorite color), and there were at least six dozen, as John Dalton could attest. He had helped Lucy and her grandmother blow them up. For a woman in her eighties, Chetta had an awesome set of lungs.

There were nine kids, counting Abra, and because at least one of every parental set had come, there was plenty of adult supervision. Lawn chairs had been set up on the back deck, and as the party hit cruising speed, John sat in one of these next to Concetta, who was dolled up in designer jeans and her WORLD'S BEST GREAT-GRAMMA sweatshirt. She was working her way through a giant slice of birthday cake. John, who had taken on a few pounds of ballast during the winter, settled for a single scoop of strawberry ice cream.

'I don't know where you put it,' he said, nodding at the rapidly disappearing cake on her paper plate. 'There's nothing to you. You're a stuffed string.'

'Maybe so, *caro*, but I've got a hollow leg.' She surveyed the roistering children and fetched a deep sigh. 'I wish my daughter could have lived to see this. I don't have many regrets, but that's one of them.'

John decided not to venture out on this conversational limb. Lucy's mother had died in a car accident when Lucy was younger than Abra was now. This he knew from the family history the Stones had filled out jointly.

In any case, Chetta turned the conversation herself. 'Do you know what I like about em at this age?'

'Nope.' John liked them at all ages . . . at least until they turned fourteen. When they turned fourteen their glands went into hyperdrive, and most of them felt obliged to spend the next five years being boogersnots.

'Look at them, Johnny. It's the kiddie version of that Edward Hicks painting, *The Peaceable Kingdom*. You've got six white ones – of course you do, it's New Hampshire – but you've also got two black ones and one gorgeous Korean American baby who looks like she should be modeling clothes in the Hanna Andersson catalogue. You know the Sunday school song that goes "Red and yellow, black and white, they are precious in His sight"? That's what we have here. Two hours, and not one of them has raised a fist or given a push in anger.'

John – who had seen plenty of toddlers who kicked, pushed, punched, and bit – gave a smile in which cynicism and wistfulness were exactly balanced. 'I wouldn't expect anything different. They all go to L'il Chums. It's the smart-set daycare in these parts, and they charge smart-set prices. That means their parents are all at least upper-middle, they're all college grads, and they all practice the gospel of Go Along to Get Along. These kids are your basic domes-ticated social animals.'

John stopped there because she was frowning at him, but he could have gone farther. He could have said that, until the age of seven or thereabouts – the so-called age of reason – most children were emotional echo chambers. If they grew up around people who got along and didn't raise their voices, they did the same. If they were raised by biters and shouters . . . well . . .

Twenty years of treating little ones (not to mention raising two of his own, now away at good Go Along to Get Along prep schools) hadn't destroyed all the romantic notions he'd held when first deciding to specialize in pediatric medicine, but those years had tempered them. Perhaps kids really did come into the world trailing clouds of glory, as Wordsworth had so confidently proclaimed, but they also shit in their pants until they learned better.

11

A silvery run of bells – like those on an ice cream truck – sounded in the afternoon air. The kids turned to see what was up.

Riding onto the lawn from the Stones' driveway was an amiable apparition: a young man on a wildly oversize red tricycle. He was wearing white gloves and a zoot suit with comically wide shoulders. In one lapel was a boutonniere the size of a hothouse orchid. His pants (also oversize) were currently hiked up to his knees as he worked the pedals. The handlebars were hung with bells, which he rang with one finger. The trike rocked from side to side but never quite fell over. On the newcomer's head, beneath a huge brown derby, was a crazy blue wig. David Stone was walking behind him, carrying a large suitcase in one hand and a fold-up table in the other. He looked bemused.

'Hey, kids! Hey, kids!' the man on the trike shouted. 'Gather round, gather round, because the *show* is about to *start*!' He didn't need to ask them twice; they were already flocking toward the trike, laughing and shouting.

Lucy came over to John and Chetta, sat down, and blew hair out of her eyes with a comical *foof* of her lower lip. She had a smudge of chocolate frosting on her chin. 'Behold the magician. He's a street performer in Frazier and North Conway during the summer season. Dave saw an ad in one of those freebie newspapers, auditioned the guy, and hired him. His name is Reggie Pelletier, but he styles himself The Great Mysterio. Let's see how long he can hold their attention once they've all had a good close look at the fancy trike. I'm thinking three minutes, tops.'

John thought she might be wrong about that. The guy's entrance had been perfectly calculated to capture the imaginations of little ones, and his wig was funny rather than scary. His cheerful face was unmarked by greasepaint, and that was also good. Clowns, in John's opinion, were highly overrated. They scared the shit out of kids under six. Kids over that age merely found them boring.

My, you're in a bilious mood today.

Maybe because he'd come ready to observe some sort of freaky-deaky, and nothing had transpired. To him, Abra seemed like a perfectly ordinary little kid. Cheerier than most, maybe, but good cheer seemed to run in the family. Except when Chetta and Dave were sniping at each other, that was.

'Don't understimate the attention spans of the wee folk.' He leaned past Chetta and used his napkin to wipe the smudge of frosting from Lucy's chin. 'If he has an act, he'll hold them for fifteen minutes, at least. Maybe twenty.'

'*If* he does,' Lucy said skeptically.

It turned out that Reggie Pelletier, aka The Great Mysterio, *did* have an act, and a good one. While his faithful assistant, The Not-So-Great Dave, set up his table and opened the suitcase, Mysterio asked the birthday girl and her guests to admire his flower. When they drew close, it shot water into their faces: first red, then green, then blue. They screamed with sugar-fueled laughter.

'Now, boys and girls . . . *ooh! Ahh! Yike!* That tickles!'

He took off his derby and pulled out a white rabbit. The kids gasped. Mysterio passed the bunny to Abra, who stroked it and then passed it on without having to be told. The rabbit didn't seem to mind the attention. Maybe, John thought, it had snarked up a few Valium-laced pellets before the show. The last kid handed it back to Mysterio, who popped it into his hat, passed a hand over it, and then showed them the inside of the derby. Except for the American flag lining, it was empty.

'Where did the bunny go?' little Susie Soong-Bartlett asked.

'Into your dreams, darlin,' Mysterio said. 'It'll hop there tonight. Now who wants a magic scarf?'

There were cries of *I do, I do* from boys and girls alike. Mysterio produced them from his fists and passed them out. This was followed by more tricks in rapid-fire succession. By Dalton's watch, the kids stood around Mysterio in a bug-eyed semicircle for at least twenty-five minutes. And just as the first signs of restiveness began to appear in the audience, Mysterio wrapped things up. He produced five plates from his suitcase (which, when he showed it, had appeared to be as empty as his hat) and juggled them, singing 'Happy Birthday to You' as he did it. All the kids joined in, and Abra seemed almost to levitate with joy.

The plates went back into the suitcase. He showed it to them again so they could see it was empty, then produced half a dozen spoons from it. These he proceeded to hang on his face, finishing with one on the tip of his nose. The birthday girl liked that one; she sat down on the grass, laughing and hugging herself with glee.

'Abba can do that,' she said (she was currently fond of referring to herself in the third person – it was what David called her 'Rickey Henderson phase'). 'Abba can do spoongs.'

'Good for you, honey,' Mysterio said. He wasn't really paying attention, and John couldn't blame him for that; he had just put on one hell of a kiddie matinee, his face was red and damp with sweat in spite of the cool breeze blowing up from the river, and he still had his big exit to make, this time pedaling the oversize trike uphill.

He bent and patted Abra's head with one white-gloved hand. 'Happy birthday to you, and thank all you kids for being such a good aud—'

From inside the house came a large and musical jangling, not unlike the sound of the bells hanging from the Godzilla-trike's handlebars. The kids only glanced in that direction before turning to watch Mysterio pedal away, but Lucy got up to see what had fallen over in the kitchen.

Two minutes later she came back outside. 'John,' she said. 'You better look at this. I think it's what you came to see.'

12

John, Lucy, and Concetta stood in the kitchen, looking up at the ceiling and saying nothing. None of them turned when Dave joined them; they were hypnotized. 'What—' he began, then saw what. 'Holy shit.'

To this no one replied. David stared a little longer, trying to get the sense of what he was seeing, then left. A minute or two later he returned, leading his daughter by the hand. Abra was holding a balloon. Around her waist, worn like a sash, was the scarf she'd received from The Great Mysterio.

John Dalton dropped to one knee beside her. 'Did you do that, honey?' It was a question to which he felt sure he knew the answer, but he wanted to hear what she had to say. He wanted to know how much she was aware of.

Abra first looked at the floor, where the silverware drawer lay. Some of the knives and forks had bounced free when the drawer shot from its socket, but they were all there. Not the spoons, however. The spoons were hanging from the ceiling, as if drawn upward and held by some exotic magnetic attraction. A couple swung lazily from the overhead light fixtures. The biggest, a serving spoon, dangled from the exhaust hood of the stove.

All kids had their own self-comforting mechanisms. John knew from long experience that for most it was a thumb socked securely in the mouth. Abra's was a little different. She cupped her right hand over the lower half of her face and rubbed her lips with her palm. As a result, her words were muffled. John took the hand away – gently. 'What, honey?'

In a small voice she said, 'Am I in trouble? I . . . I . . .' Her small chest began to hitch. She tried to put her comfort-hand back, but John held it. 'I wanted to be like Minstrosio.' She began to weep. John let her hand go and it went to her mouth, rubbing furiously.

David picked her up and kissed her cheek. Lucy put her arms around them both and kissed the top of her daughter's head. 'No, honey, no. No trouble. You're fine.'

Abra buried her face against her mother's neck. As she did it, the spoons fell. The clatter made them all jump.

13

Two months later, with summer just beginning in the White Mountains of New Hampshire, David and Lucy Stone sat in John Dalton's office, where the walls were papered with smiling photographs of the children he had treated over the years – many now old enough to have kids of their own.

John said, 'I hired a computer-savvy nephew of mine – at my own expense, and don't worry about it, he works cheap – to see if there were any other documented cases like your daughter's, and to research them if there were. He restricted his search to the last thirty years and found over nine hundred.'

David whistled. 'That many!'

John shook his head. '*Not* that many. If it *were* a disease – and we don't need to revisit that discussion, because it's not – it would be as rare as elephantiasis. Or Blaschko's lines, which basically turns those who have it into human zebras. Blaschko's affects about one in every seven million. This thing of Abra's would be on that order.'

'What exactly *is* Abra's thing?' Lucy had taken her husband's hand and was holding it tightly. 'Telepathy? Telekinesis? Some other *tele*?'

'Those things clearly play a part. Is she telepathic? Since she knows when people are coming to visit, and knew Mrs Judkins had been hurt, the answer seems to be yes. Is she telekinetic? Based on what we saw in your kitchen on the day of her birthday party, the answer is a hard yes. Is she psychic? A precognate, if you want to fancy it up? We can't be so sure of that, although the 9/11 thing and the story of the twenty-dollar bill behind the dresser are both suggestive. But what about the night your television showed *The Simpsons* on all the channels? What do you call that? Or what about the phantom Beatles tune? It would be telekinesis if the notes came from the piano . . . but you say they didn't.'

'So what's next?' Lucy asked. 'What do we watch out for?'

'I don't know. There's no predictive path to follow. The trouble with the field of psychic phenomena is that it isn't a field at all. There's too much charlatanry and too many people who are just off their damn rockers.'

'So you can't tell us what to do,' Lucy said. 'That's the long and short of it.'

John smiled. 'I can tell you exactly what to do: keep on loving her. If my nephew is right – and you have to remember that A, he's only seventeen, and B, he's basing his conclusions on unstable data – you're apt to keep seeing weird stuff until she's a teenager. Some of it may be *gaudy* weird stuff. Around thirteen or fourteen, it'll plateau and then start to subside. By the time she's in her twenties, the various phenomena she's generating will probably be negligible.' He smiled. 'But she'll be a terrific poker player all her life.'

'What if she starts seeing dead people, like the little boy in that movie?' Lucy asked. 'What do we do then?'

'Then I guess you'd have proof of life after death. In the meantime, don't buy trouble. And keep your mouths shut, right?'

'Oh, you bet,' Lucy said. She managed a smile, but given the fact she'd nibbled most of her lipstick off, it didn't look very confident. 'The last thing we want is our daughter on the cover of *Inside View*.'

'Thank God none of the other parents saw that thing with the spoons,' David said.

'Here's a question,' John said. 'Do you think she knows how special she is?'

The Stones exchanged a look.

'I . . . don't think so,' Lucy said at last. 'Although after the spoons . . . we made sort of a big deal about it . . .'

'A big deal in *your* mind,' John said. 'Probably not hers. She cried a little, then went back out with a smile on her face. There was no shouting, scolding, spanking, or shaming. My advice is to let it ride for the time being. When she gets a little older, you can caution her about not doing any of her special tricks at school. Treat her as normal, because mostly she is. Right?'

'Right,' David said. 'And it's not like she's got spots, or swellings, or a third eye.'

'Oh yes she does,' Lucy said. She was thinking of the caul. 'She does so have a third eye. You can't see it — but it's there.'

John stood up. 'I'll get all my nephew's printouts and sent them to you, if you'd like that.'

'I would,' David said. 'Very much. I think dear old Momo would, too.' He wrinkled his nose a bit at this. Lucy saw it and frowned.

'In the meantime, enjoy your daughter,' John told them. 'From everything I've seen, she's a very enjoyable child. You're going to get through this.'

For a while, it seemed he was right.

CHAPTER FOUR
PAGING DOCTOR SLEEP

1

It was January of 2007. In the turret room of Rivington House, Dan's space heater was running full blast, but the room was still cold. A nor'easter, driven by a fifty-mile-an-hour gale, had blown down from the mountains, piling five inches of snow an hour on the sleeping town of Frazier. When the storm finally eased the following afternoon, some of the drifts against the north and east sides of the buildings on Cranmore Avenue would be twelve feet deep.

Dan wasn't bothered by the cold; nestled beneath two down comforters, he was warm as tea and toast. Yet the wind had found its way inside his head just as it found its way under the sashes and doorsills of the old Victorian he now called home. In his dream, he could hear it moaning around the hotel where he had spent one winter as a little boy. In his dream, he *was* that little boy.

He's on the second floor of the Overlook. Mommy is sleeping and Daddy's in the basement, looking at old papers. He's doing RESEARCH. The RESEARCH is for the book he's going to write. Danny isn't supposed to be up here, and he's not supposed to have the passkey that's clutched in one hand, but he hasn't been able to stay away. Right now he's staring at a firehose that's bolted to the wall. It's folded over and over on itself, and it looks like a snake with a brass head. A sleeping snake. Of course it's not a snake — that's canvas he's looking at, not scales — but it sure does look like a snake.

Sometimes it *is* a snake.

'Go on,' he whispers to it in this dream. He's trembling with terror, but something drives him on. And why? Because he's doing his own RESEARCH, that's why. 'Go on, bite me! You can't, can you? Because you're just a stupid HOSE!'

The nozzle of the stupid hose stirs, and all at once, instead of looking at it sideways, Danny is looking into its bore. Or maybe into its mouth. A single clear drop appears below the black hole, elongating. In it he can see his own wide eyes reflected back at him.

A drop of water or a drop of poison?

Is it a snake or a hose?

Who can say, my dear Redrum, Redrum my dear? Who can say?

It buzzes at him, and terror jumps up his throat from his rapidly beating heart. Rattlesnakes buzz like that.

Now the nozzle of the hose-snake rolls away from the stack of canvas it's lying on and drops to the carpet with a dull thud. It buzzes again and he knows he should step back before it can rush forward and bite him, but he's frozen he can't move and it's buzzing—

'Wake up, Danny!' Tony calls from somewhere. 'Wake up, wake up!'

But he can wake up no more than he can move, this is the Overlook, they are snowed in, and things are different now. Hoses become snakes, dead women open their eyes, and his father . . . oh dear God WE HAVE TO GET OUT OF HERE BECAUSE MY FATHER IS GOING CRAZY.

The rattlesnake buzzes. It buzzes. It

2

Dan heard the wind howling, but not outside the Overlook. No, outside the turret of Rivington House. He heard snow rattle against the north-facing window. It sounded like sand. And he heard the intercom giving off its low buzz.

He threw back the comforters and swung his legs out, wincing as his warm toes met the cold floor. He crossed the room, almost prancing on the balls of his feet. He turned on the desk lamp and blew out his breath. No visible vapor, but even with the space heater's element coils glowing a dull red, the room temperature tonight had to be in the mid-forties.

Buzz.

He pushed talk on the intercom and said, 'I'm here. Who's there?'

'Claudette. I think you've got one, doc.'

'Mrs Winnick?' He was pretty sure it was her, and that would mean putting on his parka, because Vera Winnick was in Rivington Two, and the walkway between here and there would be colder than a witch's belt buckle. Or a well-digger's tit. Or whatever the saying was. Vera had been hanging by a thread for a week now, comatose, in and out of Cheyne-Stokes respiration, and this was exactly the sort of night the frail ones picked to go out on. Usually at 4 a.m. He checked his watch. Only 3:20, but that was close enough for government work.

Claudette Albertson surprised him. 'No, it's Mr Hayes, right down here on the first floor with us.'

'Are you sure?' Dan had played a game of checkers with Charlie Hayes just that afternoon, and for a man with acute myelogenous leukemia, he'd seemed as lively as a cricket.

'Nope, but Azzie's in there. And you know what you say.'

What he said was Azzie was never wrong, and he had almost six years' worth of experience on which to base that conclusion. Azreel wandered freely around the three buildings that made up the Rivington complex, spending most of his afternoons curled up on a sofa in the rec room, although it wasn't unusual to see him draped across one of the card tables – with or without a half-completed jigsaw puzzle on it – like a carelessly thrown stole. All the residents seemed to like him (if there had been complaints about the House housecat, they hadn't reached Dan's ears), and Azzie liked them all right back. Sometimes he would jump up in some half-dead oldster's lap . . . but lightly, never seeming to hurt. Which was remarkable, given his size. Azzie was a twelve-pounder.

Other than during his afternoon naps, Az rarely stayed in one location for long; he always had places to go, people to see, things to do. ('That cat's a *playa*,' Claudette had once told Danny.) You might see him visiting the spa, licking a paw and taking a little heat. Relaxing on a stopped treadmill in the Health Suite. Sitting atop an abandoned gurney and staring into thin air at those things only cats can see. Sometimes he stalked the back lawn with his ears flattened against his skull, the very picture of feline predation, but if he caught birds and chipmunks, he took them into one of the neighboring yards or across to the town common and dismembered them there.

The rec room was open round-the-clock, but Azzie rarely visited there once the TV was off and the residents were gone. When evening gave way to night and the pulse of Rivington House slowed, Azzie became restless, patrolling the corridors like a sentry on the edge of enemy territory. Once the lights dimmed, you might not even see him unless you were looking right at him; his unremarkable mouse-colored fur blended in with the shadows.

He never went into the guest rooms unless one of the guests was dying.

Then he would either slip in (if the door was unlatched) or sit outside with his tail curled around his haunches, *waowing* in a low, polite voice to be admitted. When he was, he would jump up on the guest's bed (they were always guests at Rivington House, never patients) and settle there, purring. If the person so chosen happened to be awake, he or she might stroke the cat. To Dan's knowledge, no one had ever demanded that Azzie be evicted. They seemed to know he was there as a friend.

'Who's the doctor on call?' Dan asked.

'You,' Claudette promptly came back.

'You know what I mean. The real doctor.'

'Emerson, but when I phoned his service, the woman told me not to be silly. Everything's socked in from Berlin to Manchester. She said that except for the ones on the turnpikes, even the plows are waiting for daylight.'

'All right,' Dan said. 'I'm on my way.'

3

After working at the hospice for a while, Dan had come to realize there was a class system even for the dying. The guest accommodations in the main house were bigger and more expensive than those in Rivington One and Two. In the Victorian manse where Helen Rivington had once hung her hat and written her romances, the rooms were called suites and named after famous New Hampshire residents. Charlie Hayes was in Alan Shepard. To get there, Dan had to pass the snack alcove at the foot of the stairs, where there were vending machines and a few hard plastic chairs. Fred Carling was plopped down in one of these, munching peanut butter crackers and reading an old issue of *Popular Mechanics*. Carling was one of three orderlies on the midnight-to-eight shift. The other two rotated to days twice a month; Carling never did. A self-proclaimed night owl, he was a beefy time-server whose arms, sleeved out in a tangle of tats, suggested a biker past.

'Well lookit here,' he said. 'It's Danny-boy. Or are you in your secret identity tonight?'

Dan was still only half awake and in no mood for joshing. 'What do you know about Mr Hayes?'

'Nothing except the cat's in there, and that usually means they're going to go tits-up.'

'No bleeding?'

The big man shrugged. 'Well yeah, he had a little noser. I put the bloody towels in a plague-bag, just like I'm s'posed to. They're in Laundry A, if you want to check.'

Dan thought of asking how a nosebleed that took more than one towel to clean up could be characterized as little, and decided to let it go. Carling was an unfeeling dolt, and how he'd gotten a job here – even on the night shift, when most of the guests were either asleep or trying to be quiet so they wouldn't disturb anyone else – was beyond Dan. He suspected somebody might have pulled a wire or two. It was how the world worked. Hadn't his own father pulled a wire to get his final job, as caretaker at the Overlook Hotel? Maybe that wasn't proof positive that who you knew was a lousy way to get a job, but it certainly seemed suggestive.

'Enjoy your evening, Doctor *Sleeeep*,' Carling called after him, making no effort to keep his voice down.

At the nurses' station, Claudette was charting meds while Janice Barker watched a small TV with the sound turned down low. The current program was one of those endless ads for colon cleanser, but Jan was watching with her eyes wide and her mouth hung ajar. She started when Dan tapped his fingernails on the counter and he realized she hadn't been fascinated but half asleep.

'Can either of you tell me anything substantive about Charlie? Carling knows from nothing.'

Claudette glanced down the hall to make sure Fred Carling wasn't in view, then lowered her voice, anyway. 'That man's as useless as boobs on a bull. I keep hoping he'll get fired.'

Dan kept his similar opinion to himself. Constant sobriety, he had discovered, did wonders for one's powers of discretion.

'I checked him fifteen minutes ago,' Jan said. 'We check them a lot when Mr Pussycat comes to visit.'

'How long's Azzie been in there?'

'He was meowing outside the door when we came on duty at midnight,' Claudette said, 'so I opened it for him. He jumped right up on the bed. You know how he does. I almost called you then, but Charlie was awake and responsive. When I said hi, he hi'd me right back and started petting Azzie. So I decided to wait. About an hour later, he had a nosebleed. Fred cleaned him up. I had to tell him to put the towels in a plague-bag.'

Plague-bags were what the staff called the dissolvable plastic sacks in which clothing, linen, and towels contaminated with bodily fluids or tissue were stored. It was a state regulation that was supposed to minimize the spread of blood-borne pathogens.

'When I checked him forty or fifty minutes ago,' Jan said, 'he was asleep. I gave him a shake. He opened his eyes, and they were all bloodshot.'

'That's when I called Emerson,' Claudette said. 'And after I got the big no-way-Jose from the girl on service, I called you. Are you going down now?'

'Yes.'

'Good luck,' Jan said. 'Ring if you need something.'

'I will. Why are you watching an infomercial for colon cleanser, Jannie? Or is that too personal?'

She yawned. 'At this hour, the only other thing on is an info-mercial for the Ahh Bra. I already have one of those.'

4

The door of the Alan Shepard Suite was standing half open, but Dan knocked anyway. When there was no response, he pushed it all the way open. Someone (probably one of the nurses; it almost certainly hadn't been Fred Carling) had cranked up the bed a little. The sheet was pulled to Charlie Hayes's chest. He was ninety-one, painfully thin, and so pale he hardly seemed to be there at all. Dan had to stand still for thirty seconds before he could be absolutely sure the old man's pajama top was going up and down. Azzie was curled beside the scant bulge of one hip. When Dan came in, the cat surveyed him with those inscrutable eyes.

'Mr Hayes? Charlie?'

Charlie's eyes didn't open. The lids were bluish. The skin beneath them was darker, a purple-black. When Dan got to the side of the bed, he saw more color: a little crust of blood beneath each nostril and in one corner of the folded mouth.

Dan went into the bathroom, took a facecloth, wetted it in warm water, wrung it out. When he returned to Charlie's bedside, Azzie got to his feet and delicately stepped to the other side of the sleeping man, leaving Dan a place to sit down. The sheet was still warm from Azzie's body. Gently, Dan wiped the blood from beneath Charlie's nose. As he was doing the mouth, Charlie opened his eyes. 'Dan. It's you, isn't it? My eyes are a little blurry.'

Bloody was what they were.

'How are you feeling, Charlie? Any pain? If you're in pain, I can get Claudette to bring you a pill.'

'No pain,' Charlie said. His eyes shifted to Azzie, then went back to Dan. 'I know why he's here. And I know why *you're* here.'

'I'm here because the wind woke me up. Azzie was probably just looking for some company. Cats are nocturnal, you know.'

Dan pushed up the sleeve of Charlie's pajama top to take a pulse, and saw four purple bruises lined up on the old man's stick of a forearm. Late-stage leukemia patients bruised if you even breathed on them, but these were finger-bruises, and Dan knew perfectly well where they had come from. He had more control over his temper now that he was sober, but it was still there, just like the occasional strong urge to take a drink.

Carling, you bastard. Wouldn't he move quick enough for you? Or were you just mad to have to be cleaning up a nosebleed when all you wanted to do was read magazines and eat those fucking yellow crackers?

He tried not to show what he was feeling, but Azzie seemed to sense it; he gave a small, troubled meow. Under other circumstances,

Dan might have asked questions, but now he had more pressing matters to deal with. Azzie was right again. He only had to touch the old man to know.

'I'm pretty scared,' Charlie said. His voice was little more than a whisper. The low, steady moan of the wind outside was louder. 'I didn't think I would be, but I am.'

'There's nothing to be scared of.'

Instead of taking Charlie's pulse – there was really no point – he took one of the old man's hands in his. He saw Charlie's twin sons at four, on swings. He saw Charlie's wife pulling down a shade in the bedroom, wearing nothing but the slip of Belgian lace he'd bought her for their first anniversary; saw how her ponytail swung over one shoulder when she turned to look at him, her face lit in a smile that was all *yes*. He saw a Farmall tractor with a striped umbrella raised over the seat. He smelled bacon and heard Frank Sinatra singing 'Come Fly with Me' from a cracked Motorola radio sitting on a worktable littered with tools. He saw a hubcap full of rain reflecting a red barn. He tasted blueberries and gutted a deer and fished in some distant lake whose surface was dappled by steady autumn rain. He was sixty, dancing with his wife in the American Legion hall. He was thirty, splitting wood. He was five, wearing shorts and pulling a red wagon. Then the pictures blurred together, the way cards do when they're shuffled in the hands of an expert, and the wind was blowing big snow down from the mountains, and in here was the silence and Azzie's solemn watching eyes. At times like this, Dan knew what he was for. At times like this he regretted none of the pain and sorrow and anger and horror, because they had brought him here to this room while the wind whooped outside. Charlie Hayes had come to the border.

'I'm not scared of hell. I lived a decent life, and I don't think there is such a place, anyway. I'm scared there's *nothing*.' He struggled for breath. A pearl of blood was swelling in the corner of his right eye. 'There was nothing *before*, we all know that, so doesn't it stand to reason that there's nothing after?'

'But there is.' Dan wiped Charlie's face with the damp cloth. 'We never really end, Charlie. I don't know how that can be, or what it means, I only know that it is.'

'Can you help me get over? They say you can help people.'

'Yes. I can help.' He took Charlie's other hand, as well. 'It's just going to sleep. And when you wake up – you *will* wake up – everything is going to be better.'

'Heaven? Do you mean heaven?'

'I don't know, Charlie.'

The power was very strong tonight. He could feel it flowing through their clasped hands like an electric current and cautioned himself to be gentle. Part of him was inhabiting the faltering body that was shutting down and the failing senses

(*hurry up please*)

that were turning off. He was inhabiting a mind

(*hurry up please it's time*)

that was still as sharp as ever, and aware it was thinking its last thoughts . . . at least as Charlie Hayes.

The blood shot eyes closed, then opened again. Very slowly.

'Everything's all right,' Dan said. 'You only need sleep. Sleep will make you better.'

'Is that what you call it?'

'Yes. I call it sleep, and it's safe to sleep.'

'Don't go.'

'I won't. I'm with you.' So he was. It was his terrible privilege.

Charlie's eyes closed again. Dan closed his own and saw a slow blue pulse in the darkness. Once . . . twice . . . stop. Once . . . twice . . . stop. Outside the wind was blowing.

'Sleep, Charlie. You're doing fine, but you're tired and you need to sleep.'

'I see my wife.' The faintest of whispers.

'Do you?'

'She says . . .'

There was no more, just a final blue pulse behind Dan's eyes and a final exhalation from the man on the bed. Dan opened his eyes, listened to the wind, and waited for the last thing. It came a few seconds later: a dull red mist that rose from Charlie's nose, mouth, and eyes. This was what an old nurse in Tampa – one who had about the same twinkle as Billy Freeman – called 'the gasp'. She said she had seen it many times.

Dan saw it *every* time.

It rose and hung above the old man's body. Then it faded.

Dan slid up the right sleeve of Charlie's pajamas, and felt for a pulse. It was just a formality.

5

Azzie usually left before it was over, but not tonight. He was standing on the counterpane beside Charlie's hip, staring at the door. Dan turned, expecting to see Claudette or Jan, but no one was there.

Except there was.

'Hello?'

Nothing.

'Are you the little girl who writes on my blackboard sometimes?'

No response. But someone was there, all right.

'Is your name Abra?'

Faint, almost inaudible because of the wind, there came a ripple of piano notes. Dan might have believed it was his imagination (he could not always tell the difference between that and the shining) if not for Azzie, whose ears twitched and whose eyes never left the empty doorway. Someone was there, watching.

'Are you Abra?'

There was another ripple of notes, then silence again. Except this time it was absence. Whatever her name was, she was gone. Azzie stretched, leaped down from the bed, and left without a look back.

Dan sat where he was a little longer, listening to the wind. Then he lowered the bed, pulled the sheet up over Charlie's face, and went back to the nurses' station to tell them there had been a death on the floor.

6

When his part of the paperwork was complete, Dan walked down to the snack alcove. There was a time he would have gone there on the run, fists already clenched, but those days were gone. Now he walked, taking long slow breaths to calm his heart and mind. There was a saying in AA, 'Think before you drink,' but what Casey

K. told him during their once-a-week tête-à-têtes was to think before he did anything. *You didn't get sober to be stupid, Danny. Keep it in mind the next time you start listening to that itty-bitty shitty committee inside your head.*

But those goddam fingermarks.

Carling was rocked back in his chair, now eating Junior Mints. He had swapped *Popular Mechanics* for a photo mag with the latest bad-boy sitcom star on the cover.

'Mr Hayes has passed on,' Dan said mildly.

'Sorry to hear it.' Not looking up from the magazine. 'But that *is* what they're here for, isn't i—'

Dan lifted one foot, hooked it behind one of the tilted front legs of Carling's chair, and yanked. The chair spun away and Carling landed on the floor. The box of Junior Mints flew out of his hand. He stared up at Dan unbelievingly.

'Have I got your attention?'

'You sonofa—' Carling started to get up. Dan put his foot on the man's chest and pushed him back against the wall.

'I see I have. Good. It would be better right now if you didn't get up. Just sit there and listen to me.' Dan bent forward and clasped his knees with his hands. Tight, because all those hands wanted to do right now was hit. And hit. And hit. His temples were throbbing. *Slow*, he told himself. *Don't let it get the better of you.*

But it was hard.

'The next time I see your fingermarks on a patient, I'll photograph them and go to Mrs Clausen and you'll be out on the street no matter who you know. And once you're no longer a part of this institution, I'll find you and beat the living shit out of you.'

Carling got to his feet, using the wall to support his back and keeping a close eye on Dan as he did it. He was taller, and outweighed Dan by a hundred pounds at least. He balled his fists. 'I'd like to see you try. How about now?'

'Sure, but not here,' Dan said. 'Too many people trying to sleep, and we've got a dead man down the hall. One with your marks on him.'

'I didn't do nothing but go to take his pulse. You know how easy they bruise when they got the leukemia.'

'I do,' Dan agreed, 'but you hurt him on purpose. I don't know why, but I know you did.'

There was a flicker in Carling's muddy eyes. Not shame; Dan didn't think the man was capable of feeling that. Just unease at being seen through. And fear of being caught. 'Big man. Doctor *Sleeeep*. Think your shit don't stink?'

'Come on, Fred, let's go outside. More than happy to.' And this was true. There was a second Dan inside. He wasn't as close to the surface anymore, but he was still there and still the same ugly, irrational sonofabitch he'd always been. Out of the corner of his eye Dan could see Claudette and Jan standing halfway down the hall, their eyes wide and their arms around each other.

Carling thought it over. Yes, he was bigger, and yes, he had more reach. But he was also out of shape – too many overstuffed burritos, too many beers, much shorter wind than he'd had in his twenties – and there was something worrisome in the skinny guy's face. He'd seen it before, back in his Road Saints days. Some guys had lousy circuit breakers in their heads. They tripped easy, and once they did, those guys would burn on until they burned out. He had taken Torrance for some mousy little geek who wouldn't say shit if he had a mouthful, but he saw that he'd been wrong about that. His secret identity wasn't Doctor Sleep, it was Doctor Crazy.

After considering this carefully, Fred said, 'I wouldn't waste my time.'

Dan nodded. 'Good. Save us both getting frostbite. Just remember what I said. If you don't want to go to the hospital, keep your hands to yourself from now on.'

'Who died and left you in charge?'

'I don't know,' Dan said. 'I really don't.'

7

Dan went back to his room and back to bed, but he couldn't sleep. He had made roughly four dozen deathbed visits during his time at Rivington House, and usually they left him calm. Not tonight. He was still trembling with rage. His conscious mind hated that red storm, but some lower part of him loved it. Probably it went back to plain old genetics; nature triumphing over nurture. The longer

he stayed sober, the more old memories surfaced. Some of the
clearest were of his father's rages. He had been hoping that Carling
would take him up on it. Would go outside into the snow and wind,
where Dan Torrance, son of Jack, would give that worthless puppy
his medicine.

God knew he didn't want to be his father, whose bouts of sobriety
had been the white-knuckle kind. AA was supposed to help with
anger, and mostly it did, but there were times like tonight when
Dan realized what a flimsy barrier it was. Times when he felt worthless, and the booze seemed like all he deserved. At times like that
he felt very close to his father.

He thought: *Mama.*

He thought: *Canny.*

He thought: *Worthless pups need to take their medicine. And you
know where they sell it, don't you? Damn near everywhere.*

The wind rose in a furious gust, making the turret groan. When
it died, the blackboard girl was there. He could almost hear her
breathing.

He lifted one hand out from beneath the comforters. For a
moment it only hung there in the cold air, and then he felt hers
– small, warm – slip into it. 'Abra,' he said. 'Your name is Abra, but
sometimes people call you Abby. Isn't that right?'

No answer came, but he didn't really need one. All he needed
was the sensation of that warm hand in his. It only lasted for a few
seconds, but it was long enough to soothe him. He closed his eyes
and slept.

8

Twenty miles away, in the little town of Anniston, Abra Stone lay
awake. The hand that had enfolded hers held on for a moment or
two. Then it turned to mist and was gone. But it had been there.
He had been there. She had found him in a dream, but when she
woke, she had discovered the dream was real. She was standing in
the doorway of a room. What she had seen there was terrible and
wonderful at the same time. There was death, and death was scary,
but there had also been helping. The man who was helping hadn't

been able to see her, but the cat had. The cat had a name like hers, but not exactly.

He didn't see me but he felt me. And we were together just now. I think I helped him, like he helped the man who died.

That was a good thought. Holding onto it (as she had held the phantom hand), Abra rolled over on her side, hugged her stuffed rabbit to her chest, and went to sleep.

CHAPTER FIVE
THE TRUE KNOT

1

The True Knot wasn't incorporated, but if it had been, certain side o' the road communities in Maine, Florida, Colorado, and New Mexico would have been referred to as 'company towns'. These were places where all the major businesses and large plots of land could be traced back, through a tangle of holding companies, to them. The True's towns, with colorful names like Dry Bend, Jerusalem's Lot, Oree, and Sidewinder, were safe havens, but they never stayed in those places for long; mostly they were migratory. If you drive the turnpikes and main-traveled highways of America, you may have seen them. Maybe it was on I-95 in South Carolina, somewhere south of Dillon and north of Santee. Maybe it was on I-80 in Nevada, in the mountain country west of Draper. Or in Georgia, while negotiating – slowly, if you know what's good for you – that notorious Highway 41 speedtrap outside Tifton.

How many times have you found yourself behind a lumbering RV, eating exhaust and waiting impatiently for your chance to pass? Creeping along at forty when you could be doing a perfectly legal sixty-five or even seventy? And when there's finally a hole in the fast lane and you pull out, holy God, you see a long line of those damn things, gas hogs driven at exactly ten miles an hour below the legal speed limit by bespectacled golden oldies who hunch over their steering wheels, gripping them like they think they're going to fly away.

Or maybe you've encountered them in the turnpike rest areas, when you stop to stretch your legs and maybe drop a few quarters into one of the vending machines. The entrance ramps to those rest stops always divide in two, don't they? Cars in one parking lot, long-haul trucks and RVs in another. Usually the lot for the big rigs and RVs is a little farther away. You might have seen the True's rolling motorhomes parked in that lot, all in a cluster. You might have seen their owners walking up to the main building – slow, because many of them look old and some of them are pretty darn fat – always in a group, always keeping to themselves.

Sometimes they pull off at one of the exits loaded with gas stations, motels, and fast-food joints. And if you see those RVs parked at McDonald's or Burger King, you keep on going because you know they'll all be lined up at the counter, the men wearing floppy golf hats or long-billed fishing caps, the women in stretch pants (usually powder-blue) and shirts that say things like ASK ME ABOUT MY GRANDCHILDREN! or JESUS IS KING or HAPPY WANDERER. You'd rather go half a mile farther down the road, to the Waffle House or Shoney's, wouldn't you? Because you know they'll take forever to order, mooning over the menu, always wanting their Quarter Pounders without the pickles or their Whoppers without the sauce. Asking if there are any interesting tourist attractions in the area, even though anyone can see this is just another nothing three-stoplight burg where the kids leave as soon as they graduate from the nearest high school.

You hardly see them, right? Why would you? They're just the RV People, elderly retirees and a few younger compatriots living their rootless lives on the turnpikes and blue highways, staying at campgrounds where they sit around in their Walmart lawnchairs and cook on their hibachis while they talk about investments and fishing tournaments and hotpot recipes and God knows what. They're the ones who always stop at fleamarkets and yardsales, parking their damn dinosaurs nose-to-tail half on the shoulder and half on the road, so you have to slow to a crawl in order to creep by. They are the opposite of the motorcycle clubs you sometimes see on those same turnpikes and blue highways; the Mild Angels instead of the wild ones.

They're annoying as hell when they descend en masse on a rest area and fill up all the toilets, but once their balky, road-stunned bowels finally work and you're able to take a pew yourself, you put them out of your mind, don't you? They're no more remarkable than a flock of birds on a telephone wire or a herd of cows grazing in a field beside the road. Oh, you might wonder how they can afford to fill those fuel-guzzling monstrosities (because they *must* be on comfy fixed incomes, how else could they spend all their time driving around like they do), and you might puzzle over why anyone would want to spend their golden years cruising all those endless American miles between Hoot and Holler, but beyond that, you probably never spare them a thought.

And if you happen to be one of those unfortunate people who's ever lost a kid – nothing left but a bike in the vacant lot down the street, or a little cap lying in the bushes at the edge of a nearby stream – you probably never thought of *them*. Why would you? No, it was probably some hobo. Or (worse to consider, but horribly plausible) some sick fuck from your very own town, maybe your very own neighborhood, maybe even *your very own street*, some sick killer pervo who's very good at looking normal and will go on looking normal until someone finds a clatter of bones in the guy's basement or buried in his backyard. You'd never think of the RV People, those midlife pensioners and cheery older folks in their golf hats and sun visors with appliquéd flowers on them.

And mostly you'd be right. There are thousands of RV People, but by 2011 there was only one Knot left in America: the *True* Knot. They liked moving around, and that was good, because they had to. If they stayed in one place, they'd eventually attract attention, because they don't age like other people. Apron Annie or Dirty Phil (rube names Anne Lamont and Phil Caputo) might appear to grow twenty years older overnight. The Little twins (Pea and Pod) might snap back from twenty-two to twelve (or almost), the age at which they Turned, but their Turning was long ago. The only member of the True who's actually young is Andrea Steiner, now known as Snakebite Andi . . . and even she's not as young as she looks.

A tottery, grumpy old lady of eighty suddenly becomes sixty again. A leathery old gent of seventy is able to put away his cane; the skin-tumors on his arms and face disappear.

Black-Eyed Susie loses her hitching limp.

Diesel Doug goes from half blind with cataracts to sharp-eyed, his bald spot magically gone. All at once, hey presto, he's forty-five again.

Steamhead Steve's crooked back straightens. His wife, Baba the

Red, ditches those uncomfortable continence pants, puts on her rhinestone-studded Ariat boots, and says she wants to go out line dancing.

Given time to observe such changes, people would wonder and people would talk. Eventually some reporter would turn up, and the True Knot shied away from publicity the way vampires supposedly shy away from sunlight.

But since they *don't* live in one place (and when they stop for an extended period in one of their company towns, they keep to themselves), they fit right in. Why not? They wear the same clothes as the other RV People, they wear the same el cheapo sunglasses, they buy the same souvenir t-shirts and consult the same AAA roadmaps. They put the same decals on their Bounders and 'Bagos, touting all the peculiar places they've visited (I HELPED TRIM THE WORLD'S BIGGEST TREE IN CHRISTMASLAND!), and you find yourself looking at the same bumper stickers while you're stuck behind them (OLD BUT NOT DEAD, SAVE MEDICARE, I'M A CONSERVATIVE AND *I VOTE!!*), waiting for a chance to pass. They eat fried chicken from the Colonel and buy the occasional scratch ticket in those EZ-on, EZ-off convenience stores where they sell beer, bait, ammo, *Motor Trend* magazine, and ten thousand kinds of candybars. If there's a bingo hall in the town where they stop, a bunch of them are apt to go on over, take a table, and play until the last cover-all game is finished. At one of those games, Greedy G (rube name Greta Moore) won five hundred dollars. She gloated over that for *months*, and although the members of the True have all the money they need, it pissed off some of the other ladies to no end. Token Charlie wasn't too pleased, either. He said he'd been waiting on B7 for five pulls from the hopper when the G finally bingoed.

'Greedy, you're one lucky bitch,' he said.

'And you're one unlucky bastard,' she replied. 'One unlucky *black* bastard.' And went off chortling.

If one of them happens to get speed-trapped or stopped for some minor traffic offense – it's rare, but it does happen – the cop finds nothing but valid licenses, up-to-date insurance cards, and paperwork in apple-pie order. No voices are raised while the cop's standing there with his citation book, even if it's an obvious scam. The charges are never disputed, and all fines are paid promptly. America is a living body, the highways are its arteries, and the True Knot slips along them like a silent virus.

But there are no dogs.

Ordinary RV People travel with lots of canine company, usually those little shit-machines with white fur, gaudy collars, and nasty tempers. You know the kind; they have irritating barks that hurt your ears and ratty little eyes full of disturbing intelligence. You see them sniffing their way through the grass in the designated pet-walking areas of the turnpike rest stops, their owners trailing behind, pooper-scoopers at the ready. In addition to the usual decals and bumper stickers on the motorhomes of these ordinary RV People, you're apt to see yellow diamond-shaped signs reading POMERANIAN ON BOARD or I ♥ MY POODLE.

Not the True Knot. They don't like dogs, and dogs don't like them. You might say dogs see *through* them. To the sharp and watchful eyes behind the cut-rate sunglasses. To the strong and long-muscled hunters' legs beneath the polyester slacks from Walmart. To the sharp teeth beneath the dentures, waiting to come out.

They don't like dogs, but they like certain children.

Oh yes, they like certain children very much.

2

In May of 2011, not long after Abra Stone celebrated her tenth birthday and Dan Torrance his tenth year of AA sobriety, Crow Daddy knocked on the door of Rosie the Hat's EarthCruiser. The True was currently staying at the Kozy Kampground outside Lexington, Kentucky. They were on their way to Colorado, where they would spend most of the summer in one of their bespoke towns, this one a place Dan sometimes revisited in his dreams. Usually they were in no hurry to get anywhere, but there was some urgency this summer. All of them knew it but none of them talked about it.

Rose would take care of it. She always had.

'Come,' she said, and Crow Daddy stepped in.

When on a business errand, he always stepped out in good suits and expensive shoes polished to a mirror gloss. If he was feeling particularly old-school, he might even carry a walking stick. This morning he was wearing baggy pants held up by suspenders, a strappy t-shirt with a fish on it (KISS MY BASS printed beneath), and a flat workman's cap, which he swept off as he closed the door behind him. He was her sometime lover as well as her second-in-command, but he never failed to show respect. It was one of many things Rose liked about him. She had no doubt that the True could carry on under his leadership if she died. For a while, at least. But for another hundred years? Perhaps not. *Probably* not. He had a silver tongue and cleaned up well when he had to deal with the rubes, but Crow had only rudimentary planning skills, and no real vision.

This morning he looked troubled.

Rose was sitting on the sofa in capri pants and a plain white bra, smoking a cigarette and watching the third hour of *Today* on her big wall-mounted TV. That was the 'soft' hour, when they featured celebrity chefs and actors doing PR for their new movies. Her tophat was cocked back on her head. Crow Daddy had known her for more years than the rubes lived, and he still didn't know what magic held it at that gravity-defying angle.

She picked up the remote and muted the sound. 'Why, it's Henry Rothman, as I live and breathe. Looking remarkably tasty, too, although I doubt you came to be tasted. Not at quarter of ten in the morning, and not with that look on your face. Who died?'

She meant it as a joke, but the wincing frown that tightened his forehead told her it wasn't one. She turned the TV off and made a business of butting her cigarette, not wanting him to see the dismay she felt. Once the True had been over two hundred strong. As of yesterday, they numbered forty-one. If she was right about the meaning of that wince, they were one less today.

'Tommy the Truck,' he said. 'Went in his sleep. Cycled once, and then boom. Didn't suffer at all. Which is fucking rare, as you know.'

'Did Nut see him?' *While he was still there to be seen,* she thought but did not add. Walnut, whose rube driver's license and various rube credit cards identified him as Peter Wallis of Little Rock, Arkansas, was the True's sawbones.

'No, it was too quick. Heavy Mary was with him. Tommy woke her up, thrashing. She thought it was a bad dream and gave him an elbow . . . only by then there was nothing left to poke but his pajamas. It was probably a heart attack. Tommy had a bad cold. Nut thinks that might have been a contributing factor. And you know the sonofabitch always smoked like a chimney.'

'We don't *get* heart attacks.' Then, reluctantly: 'Of course, we usually don't get colds, either. He was really wheezing the last few days, wasn't he? Poor old TT.'

'Yeah, poor old TT. Nut says it'd be impossible to tell anything for sure without an autopsy.'

Which couldn't happen. By now there would be no body left to cut up.

'How's Mary taking it?'

'How do you think? She's broken-fucking-hearted. They go back to when Tommy the Truck was Tommy the Wagon. Almost ninety years. She was the one who took care of him after he Turned. Gave him his first steam when he woke up the next day. Now she says she wants to kill herself.'

Rose was rarely shocked, but this did the job. No one in the True had ever killed themselves. Life was – to coin a phrase – their only reason for living.

'Probably just talk,' Crow Daddy said. 'Only . . .'

'Only what?'

'You're right about us not usually getting colds, but there have been quite a few just lately. Mostly just sniffles that come and go. Nut says it may be malnutrition. Of course he's just guessing.'

Rose sat in thought, tapping her fingers against her bare midriff and staring at the blank rectangle of the TV. At last she said, 'Okay, I agree that nourishment's been a bit thin lately, but we took steam in Delaware just a month ago, and Tommy was fine then. Plumped right up.'

'Yeah, but Rosie – the kid from Delaware wasn't much. More hunchhead than steamhead.'

She'd never thought of it just that way, but it was true. Also, he'd been nineteen, according to his driver's license. Well past whatever stunted prime he might have had around puberty. In another ten years he'd have been just another rube. Maybe even five. He hadn't been much of a meal, point taken. But you couldn't always have steak. Sometimes you had to settle for bean sprouts and tofu. At least they kept body and soul together until you could butcher the next cow.

Except psychic tofu and bean sprouts hadn't kept Tommy the Truck's body and soul together, had they?

'There used to be more steam,' Crow said.

'Don't be daft. That's like the rubes saying that fifty years ago people were more neighborly. It's a myth, and I don't want you spreading it around. People are nervous enough already.'

'You know me better than that. And I don't think it *is* a myth, darlin. If you think about it, it stands to reason. Fifty years ago there was more of *everything* – oil, wildlife, arable land, clean air. There were even a few honest politicians.'

'Yes!' Rose cried. 'Richard Nixon, remember him? Prince of the Rubes?'

But he wouldn't go chasing up this false trail. Crow might be a bit lacking in the vision department, but he was rarely distracted. That was why he was her second. He might even have a point. Who was to say that humans capable of providing the nourishment the True needed weren't dwindling, just like schools of tuna in the Pacific?

'You better bust open one of the canisters, Rosie.' He saw her eyes widen and raised a hand to stop her from speaking. 'Nobody's saying that out loud, but the whole family's thinking about it.'

Rose had no doubt they were, and the idea that Tommy had died of complications resulting from malnutrition had a certain horrid plausibility. When steam was in short supply, life grew hard and lost its savor. They weren't vampires from one of those old Hammer horror pictures, but they still needed to eat.

'And how long since we've had a seventh wave?' Crow asked.

He knew the answer to that, and so did she. The True Knot had limited precognitive skills, but when a truly big rube disaster was approaching – a seventh wave – they all felt it. Although the details of the attack on the World Trade Center had only begun to clarify for them in the late summer of 2001, they had known *something* was going to happen in New York City for months in advance. She could still remember the joy and anticipation. She supposed hungry rubes felt the same way when they smelled a particularly savory meal cooking in the kitchen.

There had been plenty for everybody that day, and in the days following. There might only have been a couple of true steamheads among those who died when the Towers fell, but when the disaster was big enough, agony and violent death had an enriching quality. Which was why the True was drawn to such sites, like insects to a bright light. Locating single rube steamheads was far more difficult, and there were only three of them now with that specialized sonar in their heads: Grampa Flick, Barry the Chink, and Rose herself.

She got up, grabbed a neatly folded boatneck top from the counter, and pulled it over her head. As always, she looked gorgeous in a way that was a bit unearthly (those high cheekbones and slightly tipped eyes) but extremely sexy. She put her hat back on and gave it a tap for good luck. 'How many full canisters do you think are left, Crow?'

He shrugged. 'A dozen? Fifteen?'

'In that neighborhood,' she agreed. Better that none of them knew the truth, not even her second. The last thing she needed was for the current unease to become outright panic. When people panicked, they ran in all directions. If that happened, the True might disintegrate.

Meanwhile, Crow was looking at her, and closely. Before he could see too much, she said, 'Can you four-wall this place tonight?'

'You kidding? With the price of gas and diesel what it is, the guy who owns it can't fill half his spots, even on weekends. He'll jump at the chance.'

'Then do it. We're going to take canister steam. Spread the word.'

'You've got it.' He kissed her, caressing one of her breasts as he did so. 'This is my favorite top.'

She laughed and pushed him away. 'Any top with tits in it is your favorite top. Go on.'

But he lingered, a grin tipping one corner of his mouth. 'Is Rattlesnake Girl still sniffin around your door, beautiful?'

She reached down and briefly squeezed him below the belt. 'Oh my gosh. Is that your jealous bone I'm feeling?'

'Say it is.'

She doubted it, but was flattered, anyway. 'She's with Sarey now, and the two of them are perfectly happy. But since we're on the subject of Andi, she can help us. You know how. Spread the word but speak to her first.'

After he left, she locked the EarthCruiser, went to the cockpit, and dropped to her knees. She worked her fingers into the carpet between the driver's seat and the control pedals. A strip of it came up. Beneath was a square of metal with an embedded keypad. Rose ran the numbers, and the safe popped open an inch or two. She lifted the door the rest of the way and looked inside.

Fifteen or a dozen full canisters left. That had been Crow's guess, and although she couldn't read members of the Tribe the way she could read the rubes, Rose was sure he had been purposely lowballing to cheer her up.

If he only knew she thought.

The safe was lined with Styrofoam to protect the canisters in case of a road accident, and there were forty built-in cradles. On this fine May morning in Kentucky, thirty-seven of the canisters in those cradles were empty.

Rose took one of the remaining full ones and held it up. It was light; if you hefted it, you would have guessed it too was empty. She took the cap off, inspected the valve beneath to make sure the seal was still intact, then reclosed the safe and put the canister carefully – almost reverently – on the counter where her top had been folded.

After tonight there would only be two.

They had to find some big steam and refill at least a few of those empty canisters, and they had to do it soon. The True's back wasn't to the wall, not quite yet, but it was only inches away.

3

The Kozy Kampground owner and his wife had their own trailer, a permanent job set up on painted concrete blocks. April showers had brought lots of May flowers, and Mr and Mrs Kozy's front yard was full of them. Andrea Steiner paused a moment to admire the tulips and pansies before mounting the three steps to the door of the big Redman trailer, where she knocked.

Mr Kozy opened up eventually. He was a small man with a big belly currently encased in a bright red strappy undershirt. In one hand he held a can of Pabst Blue Ribbon. In the other was a mustard-smeared brat wrapped in a slice of spongy white bread. Because his wife was currently in the other room, he paused for a moment to do a visual inventory of the young woman before him, ponytail to sneakers. 'Yeah?'

Several in the Tribe had a bit of sleeper talent, but Andi was by far the best, and her Turning had proved of enormous benefit to the True. She still used the ability on occasion to lift cash from the wallets of certain older rube gentlemen who were attracted to her. Rose found this risky and childish, but knew from experience that in time, what Andi called her *issues* would fade away. For the True Knot, the only issue was survival.

'I just had a quick question,' Andi said.

'If it's about the toilets, darlin, the caca sucker don't come until Thursday.'

'It's not about that.'

'What, then?'

'Aren't you tired? Don't you want to go to sleep?'

Mr Kozy immediately closed his eyes. The beer and the brat tumbled out of his hands, leaving a mess on the rug. *Oh well*, Andi thought, *Crow fronted the guy twelve hundred. Mr Kozy can afford a bottle of carpet cleaner. Maybe even two.*

Andi took him by the arm and led him into the living room. Here was a pair of chintz-covered Kozy armchairs with TV trays set up in front of them.

'Sit,' she said.

Mr Kozy sat, eyes shut.

'You like to mess with young girls?' Andi asked him. 'You would if you could, wouldn't you? If you could run fast enough to catch them, anyway.' She surveyed him, hands on hips. 'You're disgusting. Can you say that?'

'I'm disgusting,' Mr Kozy agreed. Then he began to snore.

Mrs Kozy came in from the kitchen. She was gnawing on an ice cream sandwich. 'Here, now, who are you? What are you telling him? What do you want?'

'For you to sleep,' Andi told her.

Mrs Kozy dropped her ice cream. Then her knees unhinged and she sat on it.

'Ah, fuck,' Andi said. 'I didn't mean there. Get up.'

Mrs Kozy got up with the squashed ice cream sandwich sticking to the back of her dress. Snakebite Andi put her arm around the woman's mostly nonexistent waist and led her to the other Kozy chair, pausing long enough to pull the melting ice cream sandwich off her butt. Soon the two of them sat side by side, eyes shut.

'You'll sleep all night,' Andi instructed them. 'Mister can dream about chasing young girls. Missus, you can dream he died of a heart attack and left you a million-dollar insurance policy. How's that sound? Sound good?'

She snapped on the TV and turned it up loud. Pat Sajak was being embraced by a woman with enormous jahoobies who had just finished solving the puzzle, which was NEVER REST ON YOUR LAURELS. Andi took a moment to admire the mammoth mammaries, then turned back to the Kozys.

'When the eleven o'clock news is over, you can turn off the TV and go to bed. When you wake up tomorrow, you won't remember I was here. Any questions?'

They had none. Andi left them and hurried back to the cluster of RVs. She was hungry, had been for weeks, and tonight there would be plenty for everybody. As for tomorrow . . . it was Rose's job to worry about that, and as far as Snakebite Andi was concerned, she was welcome to it.

4

It was full dark by eight o'clock. At nine, the True gathered in the Kozy Kampground's picnic area. Rose the Hat came last, carrying the canister. A small, greedy murmur went up at the sight of it. Rose knew how they felt. She was plenty hungry herself.

She mounted one of the initial-scarred picnic tables and looked at them one by one. 'We are the True Knot.'

'*We are the True Knot,*' they responded. Their faces were solemn, their eyes avid and hungry. '*What is tied may never be untied.*'

'We are the True Knot, and we endure.'

'*We endure.*'

'We are the chosen ones. We are the fortunate ones.'

'*We are chosen and fortunate.*'

'They are the makers; we are the takers.'

'*We take what they make.*'

'Take this and use it well.'

'*We will use it well.*'

Once, early in the last decade of the twentieth century, there had been a boy from Enid, Oklahoma, named Richard Gaylesworthy. *I swear that child can read my mind*, his mother sometimes said. People smiled at this, but she wasn't kidding. And maybe not just *her* mind. Richard got A's on tests he hadn't even studied for. He knew when his father was going to come home in a good mood and when he was going to come home fuming about something at the plumbing supply company he owned. Once the boy begged his mother to play the Pick Six lottery because he swore he knew the winning numbers. Mrs Gaylesworthy refused – they were good Baptists – but later she was sorry. Not all six of the numbers Richard wrote down on the kitchen note-minder board came up, but five did. Her religious convictions had cost them seventy thousand dollars. She had begged the boy not to tell his father, and Richard had promised he wouldn't. He was a good boy, a lovely boy.

Two months or so after the lottery win that wasn't, Mrs Gaylesworthy was shot to death in her kitchen and the good and lovely boy disappeared. His body had long since rotted away beneath the gone-to-seed back field of an abandoned farm, but when Rose the Hat opened the valve on the silver canister, his essence – his *steam* – escaped in a cloud of sparkling silver mist. It rose to a height of about three feet above the canister, and spread out in a plane. The True stood looking up at it with expectant faces. Most were trembling. Several were actually weeping.

'Take nourishment and endure,' Rose said, and raised her hands until her spread fingers were just below the flat plane of mist. She beckoned. The mist immediately began to sink, taking on an umbrella shape as it descended toward those waiting below. When it enveloped their heads, they began to breathe deeply. This went on for five minutes, during which several of them hyperventilated and swooned to the ground.

Rose felt herself swelling physically and sharpening mentally. Every fragrant odor of this spring night declared itself. She knew that the faint lines around her eyes and mouth were disappearing. The white strands in her hair were turning dark again. Later tonight, Crow would come to her camper, and in her bed they would burn like torches.

They inhaled Richard Gaylesworthy until he was gone – really and truly gone. The white mist thinned and then disappeared. Those who had fainted sat up and looked around, smiling. Grampa Flick grabbed Petty the Chink, Barry's wife, and did a nimble little jig with her.

'Let go of me, you old donkey!' she snapped, but she was laughing.

Snakebite Andi and Silent Sarey were kissing deeply, Andi's hands plunged into Sarey's mouse-colored hair.

Rose leaped down from the picnic table and turned to Crow. He made a circle with his thumb and forefinger, grinning back at her.

Everything's cool, that grin said, and so it was. For now. But in spite of her euphoria, Rose thought of the canisters in her safe. Now there were thirty-eight empties instead of thirty-seven. Their backs were a step closer to the wall.

5

The True rolled out the next morning just after first light. They took Route 12 to I-64, the fourteen RVs in a nose-to-tail caravan. When they reached the interstate they would spread out so they weren't quite so obviously together, staying in touch by radio in case trouble arose.

Or if opportunity knocked.

Ernie and Maureen Salkowicz, fresh from a wonderful night's sleep, agreed those RV folks were just about the best they'd ever had. Not only did they pay cash and bus up their sites neat as a pin, someone left an apple bread pudding on the top step of their trailer, with a sweet thank-you note on top. With any luck, the

Salkowiczes told each other as they ate their gift dessert for breakfast, they'd come back next year.

'Do you know what?' Maureen said. 'I dreamed that lady on the insurance commercials – Flo – sold you a big insurance policy. Wasn't that a crazy dream?'

Ernie grunted and sploughed more whipped cream onto his bread pudding.

'Did you dream, honey?'

'Nope.'

But his eyes slid away from hers as he said it.

6

The True Knot's luck turned for the better on a hot July day in Iowa. Rose was leading the caravan, as she always did, and just west of Adair, the sonar in her head gave a ping. Not a head-blaster by any means, but moderately loud. She hopped on the CB at once to Barry the Chink, who was about as Asian as Tom Cruise.

'Barry, did you feel that? Come back.'

'Yuh.' Barry was not the garrulous type.

'Who's Grampa Flick riding with today?'

Before Barry could answer, there was a double break on the CB and Apron Annie said, 'He's with me and Long Paul, sweetie. Is it . . . is it a good one?' Annie sounded anxious, and Rose could understand that. Richard Gaylesworthy had been a *very* good one, but six weeks was a long time between meals, and he was beginning to wear off.

'Is the old feller *compos*, Annie?'

Before she could answer, a raspy voice came back. 'I'm fine, woman.' And for a guy who sometimes couldn't remember his own name, Grampa Flick did sound pretty much okay. Testy, sure, but testy was a lot better than befuddled.

A second ping hit her, this one not as strong. As if to underline a point that needed no underlining, Grampa said, 'We're going the wrong fuckin way.'

Rose didn't bother answering, just clicked another double break on her mike. 'Crow? Come back, honeybunch.'

'I'm here.' Prompt as always. Just waiting to be called.

'Pull em in at the next rest area. Except for me, Barry, and Flick. We'll take the next exit and double back.'

'Will you need a crew?'

'I won't know until we get closer, but . . . I don't think so.'

'Okay.' A pause, then he added: 'Shit.'

Rose racked the mike and looked out at the unending acres of corn on both sides of the fourlane. Crow was disappointed, of course. They all would be. Big steamheads presented problems because they were all but immune to suggestion. That meant taking them by force. Friends or family members often tried to interfere. They could sometimes be put to sleep, but not always; a kid with big steam could block even Snakebite Andi's best efforts in that regard. So sometimes people had to be killed. Not good, but the prize was always worth it: life and strength stored away in a steel canister. Stored for a rainy day. In many cases there was even a residual benefit. Steam was hereditary, and often everyone in the target's family had at least a little.

7

While most of the True Knot waited in a pleasantly shady rest area forty miles east of Council Bluffs, the RVs containing the three finders turned around, left the turnpike at Adair, and headed north. Once away from I–80 and out in the toolies, they spread apart and began working the grid of graveled, well-maintained farm roads that parceled this part of Iowa into big squares. Moving in on the ping from different directions. Triangulating.

It got stronger . . . a little stronger still . . . then leveled off. Good steam but not *great* steam. Ah, well. Beggars couldn't be choosers.

8

Bradley Trevor had been given the day off from his usual farm chores to practice with the local Little League All-Star team. If his pa had refused him this, the coach probably would have led the rest of the boys in a lynch party, because Brad was the team's best hitter.

You wouldn't think it to look at him – he was skinny as a rake handle, and only eleven – but he was able to tag even the District's best pitchers for singles and doubles. The meatballers he almost always took deep. Some of it was plain farmboy strength, but by no means all of it. Brad just seemed to know what pitch was coming next. It wasn't a case of stealing signs (a possibility upon which some of the other District coaches had speculated darkly). He just *knew*. The way he knew the best location for a new stock well, or where the occasional lost cow had gotten off to, or where Ma's engagement ring was the time she'd lost it. *Look under the floormat of the Suburban*, he'd said, and there it was.

That day's practice was an especially good one, but Brad seemed lost in the ozone during the debriefing afterward, and declined to take a soda from the tub filled with ice when it was offered. He said he thought he better get home and help his ma take in the clothes.

'Is it gonna rain?' Micah Johnson, the coach, asked. They'd all come to trust him on such things.

'Dunno,' Brad said listlessly.

'You feel okay, son? You look a little peaked.'

In fact, Brad *didn't* feel well, had gotten up that morning head-achey and a bit feverish. That wasn't why he wanted to go home now, though; he just had a strong sense that he no longer wanted to be at the baseball field. His mind didn't seem . . . quite his own. He wasn't sure if he was here or only dreaming he was – how crazy was that? He scratched absently at a red spot on his forearm. 'Same time tomorrow, right?'

Coach Johnson said that was the plan, and Brad walked off with his glove trailing from one hand. Usually he jogged – they all did – but today he didn't feel like it. His head still ached, and now his legs did, too. He disappeared into the corn behind the bleachers, meaning to take a shortcut back to the farm, two miles away. When he emerged onto Town Road D, brushing silk from his hair with a slow and dreamy hand, a midsize WanderKing was idling on the gravel. Standing beside it, smiling, was Barry the Chink.

'Well, there you are,' Barry said.

'Who are you?'

'A friend. Hop in. I'll take you home.'

'Sure,' Brad said. Feeling the way he did, a ride would be fine. He scratched at the red spot on his arm. 'You're Barry Smith. You're a friend. I'll hop in and you'll take me home.'

He stepped into the RV. The door closed. The WanderKing drove away.

By the next day the whole county would be mobilized in a hunt for the Adair All-Stars' centerfielder and best hitter. A State Police spokesman asked residents to report any strange cars or vans. There were many such reports, but they all came to nothing. And although the three RVs carrying the finders were much bigger than vans (and Rose the Hat's was truly huge), nobody reported them. They were the RV People, after all, and traveling together. Brad was just . . . gone.

Like thousands of other unfortunate children, he had been swallowed up, seemingly in a single bite.

9

They took him north to an abandoned ethanol-processing plant that was miles from the nearest farmhouse. Crow carried the boy out of Rose's EarthCruiser and laid him gently on the ground. Brad was bound with duct tape and weeping. As the True Knot gathered around him (like mourners over an open grave), he said, 'Please take me home. I'll never tell.'

Rose dropped to one knee beside him and sighed. 'I would if I could, son, but I can't.'

His eyes found Barry. 'You said you were one of the good guys! I heard you! You *said* so!'

'Sorry, pal.' Barry didn't look sorry. What he looked was hungry. 'It's not personal.'

Brad shifted his eyes back to Rose. 'Are you going to hurt me? Please don't hurt me.'

Of course they were going to hurt him. It was regrettable, but pain purified steam, and the True had to eat. Lobsters also felt pain when they were dropped into pots of boiling water, but that didn't stop the rubes from doing it. Food was food, and survival was survival.

Rose put her hands behind her back. Into one of these, Greedy G placed a knife. It was short but very sharp. Rose smiled down at the boy and said, 'As little as possible.'

The boy lasted a long time. He screamed until his vocal cords ruptured and his cries became husky barks. At one point, Rose paused and looked around. Her hands, long and strong, wore bloody red gloves.

'Something?' Crow asked.

'We'll talk later,' Rose said, and went back to work. The light of a dozen flashlights had turned a piece of ground behind the ethanol plant into a makeshift operating theater.

Brad Trevor whispered, 'Please kill me.'

Rose the Hat gave him a comforting smile. 'Soon.'

But it wasn't.

Those husky barks recommenced, and eventually they turned to steam.

At dawn, they buried the boy's body. Then they moved on.

CHAPTER SIX
WEIRD RADIO

1

It hadn't happened in at least three years, but some things you don't forget. Like when your child begins screaming in the middle of the night. Lucy was on her own because David was attending a two-day conference in Boston, but she knew if he'd been there, he would have raced her down the hall to Abra's room. He hadn't forgotten, either.

Their daughter was sitting up in bed, her face pale, her hair standing out in a sleep-scruff all around her head, her eyes wide and staring blankly into space. The sheet – all she needed to sleep under during warm weather – had been pulled free and was balled up around her like a crazy cocoon.

Lucy sat beside her and put an arm around Abra's shoulders. It was like hugging stone. This was the worst part, before she came all the way out of it. Being ripped from sleep by your daughter's scream was terrifying, but the nonresponsiveness was worse. Between the ages of five and seven, these night terrors had been fairly common, and Lucy was always afraid that sooner or later the child's mind would break under the strain. She would continue to breathe, but her eyes would never unlock from whatever world it was that she saw and they couldn't.

It won't happen, David had assured her, and John Dalton had doubled down on that. *Kids are resilient. If she's not showing any lingering after-effects – withdrawal, isolation, obsessional behavior, bedwetting – you're probably okay.*

But it wasn't okay for children to wake themselves, shrieking, from nightmares. It wasn't okay that sometimes wild piano chords sounded from downstairs in the aftermath, or that the faucets in the bathroom at the end of the hall might turn themselves on, or that the light over Abra's bed sometimes blew out when she or David flipped the switch.

Then her invisible friend had come, and intervals between night-mares had grown longer. Eventually they stopped. Until tonight. Not that it *was* night anymore, exactly; Lucy could see the first faint glow on the eastern horizon, and thank God for that.

'Abs? It's Mommy. Talk to me.'

There was still nothing for five or ten seconds. Then, at last, the statue Lucy had her arm around relaxed and became a little girl again. Abra took a long, shuddering breath.

'I had one of my bad dreams. Like in the old days.'

'I kind of figured that, honey.'

Abra could hardly ever remember more than a little, it seemed. Sometimes it was people yelling at each other or hitting with their fists. *He knocked the table over chasing after her,* she might say. Another time the dream had been of a one-eyed Raggedy Ann doll lying on a highway. Once, when Abra was only four, she told them she had seen ghostie people riding *The Helen Rivington,* which was a popular tourist attraction in Frazier. It ran a loop from Teenytown, out to Cloud Gap, and then back again. *I could see them because of the moonlight,* Abra told her parents that time. Lucy and David were sitting on either side of her, their arms around her. Lucy still remembered the dank feel of Abra's pajama top, which was soaked with sweat. *I knew they were ghostie people because they had faces like old apples and the moon shone right through.*

By the following afternoon Abra had been running and playing and laughing with her friends again, but Lucy had never forgotten the image: dead people riding that little train through the woods, their faces like transparent apples in the moonlight. She had asked Concetta if she had ever taken Abra on the train during one of their 'girl days'. Chetta said no. They had been to Teenytown, but the train had been under repairs that day so they rode the carousel instead.

Now Abra looked up at her mother and said, 'When will Daddy be back?'

'Day after tomorrow. He said he'd be in time for lunch.'

'That's not soon enough,' Abra said. A tear spilled from her eye, rolled down her cheek, and plopped onto her pajama top.

'Soon enough for what? What do you remember, Abba-Doo?'

'They were hurting the boy.'

Lucy didn't want to pursue this, but felt she had to. There had been too many correlations between Abra's earlier dreams and things that had actually happened. It was David who had spotted the picture of the one-eyed Raggedy Ann in the North Conway *Sun*, under the heading THREE KILLED IN OSSIPEE CRASH. It was Lucy who had hunted out police blotter items about domestic violence arrests in the days following two of Abra's *people were yelling and hitting* dreams. Even John Dalton agreed that Abra might be picking up transmissions on what he called 'the weird radio in her head.'

So now she said, 'What boy? Does he live around here? Do you know?'

Abra shook her head. 'Far away. I can't remember.' Then she brightened. The speed at which she came out of these fugues was to Lucy almost as eerie as the fugues themselves. 'But I think I told Tony. He might tell *his* daddy.'

Tony, her invisible friend. She hadn't mentioned him in a couple of years, and Lucy hoped this wasn't some sort of regression. Ten was a little old for invisible friends.

'Tony's daddy might be able to stop it.' Then Abra's face clouded. 'I think it's too late, though.'

'Tony hasn't been around in a while, has he?' Lucy got up and fluffed out the displaced sheet. Abra giggled when it floated against her face. The best sound in the world, as far as Lucy was concerned. A *sane* sound. And the room was brightening all the time. Soon the first birds would begin to sing.

'Mommy, that tickles!'

'Mommies like to tickle. It's part of their charm. Now, what about Tony?'

'He said he'd come any time I needed him,' Abra said, settling back under the sheet. She patted the bed beside her, and Lucy lay down, sharing the pillow. 'That was a bad dream and I needed him. I think he came, but I can't really remember. His daddy works in a hot spice.'

This was new. 'Is that like a chili factory?'

'No, silly, it's for people who are going to die.' Abra sounded indulgent, almost teacherly, but a shiver went up Lucy's back.

'Tony says that when people get so sick they can't get well, they go to the hot spice and his daddy tries to make them feel better. Tony's daddy has a cat with a name like mine. I'm Abra and the cat is Azzie. Isn't that *weird*, but in a funny way?'

'Yes. Weird but funny.'

John and David would both probably say, based on the similarity of the names, that the stuff about the cat was the confabulation of a very bright little ten-year-old girl. But they would only half believe it, and Lucy hardly believed it at all. How many ten-year-olds knew what a hospice was, even if they mispronounced it?

'Tell me about the boy in your dream.' Now that Abra was calmed down, this conversation seemed safer. 'Tell me who was hurting him, Abba-Doo.'

'I don't remember, except he thought Barney was supposed to be his friend. Or maybe it was Barry. Momma, can I have Hoppy?'

Her stuffed rabbit, now sitting in lop-eared exile on the highest shelf in her room. Abra hadn't slept with him in at least two years. Lucy got the Hopster and put him in her daughter's arms. Abra hugged the rabbit to her pink pajama top and was asleep almost at once. With luck, she'd be out for another hour, maybe even two. Lucy sat beside her, looking down.

Let this stop for good in another few years, just like John said it would. Better yet, let it stop today, this very morning. No more, please. No more hunting through the local papers to see if some little boy was killed by his stepfather or beaten to death by bullies who were high on glue, or something. Let it end.

'God,' she said in a very low voice, 'if you're there, would you do something for me? Would you break the radio in my little girl's head?'

2

When the True headed west again along I-80, rolling toward the town in the Colorado high country where they would spend the summer (always assuming the opportunity to collect some nearby big steam did not come up), Crow Daddy was riding in the shotgun seat of Rose's EarthCruiser. Jimmy Numbers, the Tribe's whizbang accountant, was piloting Crow's Affinity Country Coach for the time being. Rose's satellite radio was tuned to Outlaw Country and currently playing Hank Jr's 'Whiskey Bent and Hell Bound'. It was a good tune, and Crow let it run its course before pushing the OFF button.

'You said we'd talk later. This is later. What happened back there?'

'We had a looker,' Rose said.

'Really?' Crow raised his eyebrows. He had taken as much of the Trevor kid's steam as any of them, but he looked no younger. He rarely did after eating. On the other hand, he rarely looked older between meals, unless the gap was very long. Rose thought it was a good trade-off. Probably something in his genes. Assuming they still *had* genes. Nut said they almost certainly did. 'A steamhead, you mean.'

She nodded. Ahead of them, I-80 unrolled under a faded blue denim sky dotted with drifting cumulus clouds.

'Big steam?'

'Oh yeah. Huge.'

'How far away?'

'East Coast. I think.'

'You're saying someone looked in from what, almost fifteen hundred miles away?'

'Could have been even further. Could have been way the hell and gone up in Canada.'

'Boy or girl?'

'Probably a girl, but it was only a flash. Three seconds at most. Does it matter?'

It didn't. 'How many canisters could you fill from a kid with that much steam in the boiler?'

'Hard to say. Three, at least.' This time it was Rose who was lowballing. She guessed the unknown looker might fill ten canisters, maybe even a dozen. The presence had been brief but muscular. The looker had seen what they were doing, and her horror (if it *was* a her) had been strong enough to freeze Rose's hands and make her feel a momentary loathing. It wasn't her own feeling, of course – gutting a rube was no more loathsome than gutting a deer – but a kind of psychic ricochet.

'Maybe we ought to turn around,' Crow said. 'Get her while the getting's good.'

'No. I think this one's still getting stronger. We'll let her ripen a bit.'

'Is that something you know or just intuition?'

Rose waggled her hand in the air.

'An intuition strong enough to risk her getting killed by a hit-and-run driver or grabbed by some child-molesting perv?' Crow said this without irony. 'Or what about leukemia, or some other cancer? You know they're susceptible to stuff like that.'

'If you asked Jimmy Numbers, he'd say the actuarial tables are on our side.' Rose smiled and gave his thigh an affectionate pat. 'You worry too much, Daddy. We'll go on to Sidewinder, as planned, then head down to Florida in a couple of months. Both Barry and Grampa Flick think this might be a big year for hurricanes.'

Crow made a face. 'That's like scavenging out of Dumpsters.'

'Maybe, but the scraps in some of those Dumpsters are pretty tasty. And nourishing. I'm still kicking myself that we missed that tornado in Joplin. But of course we get less warning on sudden storms like that.'

'This kid. She *saw* us.'

'Yes.'

'And what we were doing.'

'Your point, Crow?'

'Could she nail us?'

'Honey, if she's more than eleven, I'll eat my hat.' Rose tapped it for emphasis. 'Her parents probably don't know what she is or what she can do. Even if they do, they're probably minimizing it like hell in their own minds so they don't have to think about it too much.'

'Or they'll send her to a psychiatrist who'll give her pills,' Crow said. 'Which will muffle her and make her harder to find.'

Rose smiled. 'If I got it right, and I'm pretty sure I did, giving Paxil to this kid would be like throwing a piece of Saran Wrap over a searchlight. We'll find her when it's time. Don't worry.'

'If you say so. You're the boss.'

'That's right, honeybunch.' This time instead of patting his thigh, she squeezed his basket. 'Omaha tonight?'

'It's a La Quinta Inn. I reserved the entire back end of the first floor.'

'Good. My intent is to ride you like a roller coaster.'

'We'll see who rides who,' Crow said. He was feeling frisky from the Trevor kid. So was Rose. So were they all. He turned the radio on again. Got Cross Canadian Ragweed singing about the boys from Oklahoma who rolled their joints all wrong.

The True rolled west.

3

There were easy AA sponsors, and hard AA sponsors, and then there were ones like Casey Kingsley, who took absolutely zero shit from their pigeons. At the beginning of their relationship, Casey ordered Dan to do ninety-in-ninety, and instructed him to telephone every morning at seven o'clock. When Dan completed his ninety consecutive meetings, he was allowed to drop the morning calls. Then they met three times a week for coffee at the Sunspot Café.

Casey was sitting in a booth when Dan came in on a July afternoon in 2011, and although Casey hadn't made it to retirement just yet, to Dan his longtime AA sponsor (and first New Hampshire employer) looked very old. Most of his hair was gone, and he walked with a pronounced limp. He needed a hip replacement, but kept putting it off.

Dan said hi, sat down, folded his hands, and waited for what Casey called The Catechism.

'You sober today, Danno?'

'Yes.'

'How did that miracle of restraint happen?'

He recited, 'Thanks to the program of Alcoholics Anonymous and the God of my understanding. My sponsor may also have played a small part.'

'Lovely compliment, but don't blow smoke up my dress and I won't blow any up yours.'

Patty Noyes came over with the coffeepot and poured Dan a cup, unasked. 'How are you, handsome?'

Dan grinned at her. 'I'm good.'

She ruffled his hair, then headed back to the counter, with a little extra swing in her stride. The men followed the sweet tick-tock of her hips, as men do, then Casey returned his gaze to Dan.

'Made any progress with that God-of-my-understanding stuff?'

'Not much,' Dan said. 'I've got an idea it may be a lifetime work.'

'But you ask for help to stay away from a drink in the morning?'

'Yes.'

'On your knees?'

'Yes.'

'Say thank you at night?'

'Yes, and on my knees.'

'Why?'

'Because I need to remember the drink put me there,' Dan said. It was the absolute truth.

Casey nodded. 'That's the first three steps. Give me the short form.'

'"I can't, God can, I think I'll let Him."' He added: 'The God of my understanding.'

'Which you *don't* understand.'

'Right.'

'Now tell me why you drank.'

'Because I'm a drunk.'

'Not because Mommy didn't give you no love?'

'No.' Wendy had had failings, but her love for him – and his for her – had never wavered.

'Because Daddy didn't give you no love?'

'No.' *Although once he broke my arm, and at the end he almost killed me.*

'Because it's hereditary?'

'No.' Dan sipped his coffee. 'But it is. You know that, right?'

'Sure. I also know it doesn't matter. We drank because we're drunks. We never get better. We get a daily reprieve based on our spiritual condition, and that's *it*.'

'Yes, boss. Are we through with this part?'

'Almost. Did you think about taking a drink today?'

'No. Did you?'

'No.' Casey grinned. It filled his face with light and made him young again. 'It's a miracle. Would you say it's a miracle, Danny?'

'Yes. I would.'

Patty came back with a big dish of vanilla pudding – not just one cherry on top but two – and stuck it in front of Dan. 'Eat that. On the house. You're too thin.'

'What about me, sweetheart?' Casey asked.

Patty sniffed. 'You're a horse. I'll bring you a pine tree float, if you want. That's a glass of water with a toothpick in it.' Having gotten the last word, she sashayed off.

'You still hitting that?' Casey asked as Dan began to eat his pudding.

'Charming,' Dan said. 'Very sensitive and New Age.'

'Thanks. Are you still hitting it?'

'We had a thing that lasted maybe four months, and that was three years ago, Case. Patty's engaged to a very nice boy from Grafton.'

'Grafton,' Casey said dismissively. 'Pretty views, shit town. She doesn't act so engaged when you're in the house.'

'Casey—'

'No, don't get me wrong. I'd never advise a pidge of mine to stick his nose – or his dick – into an ongoing relationship. That's a terrific setup for a drink. But . . . are you seeing *anybody*?'

'Is it your business?'

'Happens it is.'

'Not currently. There was a nurse from Rivington House – I told you about her . . .'

'Sarah something.'

'Olson. We talked a little about moving in together, then she got a great job down at Mass General. We email sometimes.'

'No relationships for the first year, that's the rule of thumb,' Casey said. 'Very few recovering alkies take it seriously. You did. But Danno . . . it's time you got regular with *somebody*.'

'Oh gee, my sponsor just turned into Dr Phil,' Dan said.

'Is your life better? Better than it was when you showed up here fresh off the bus with your ass dragging and your eyes bleeding?'

'You know it is. Better than I ever could have imagined.'

'Then think about sharing it with somebody. All I'm saying.'

'I'll make a note of it. Now can we discuss other things? The Red Sox, maybe?'

'I need to ask you something else as your sponsor first. Then we can just be friends again, having a coffee.'

'Okay . . .' Dan looked at him warily.

'We've never talked much about what you do at the hospice. How you help people.'

'No,' Dan said, 'and I'd just as soon keep it that way. You know what they say at the end of every meeting, right? "What you saw here, what you heard here, when you leave here, let it stay here." That's how I am about the other part of my life.'

'How many parts of your life were affected by your drinking?'

Dan sighed. 'You know the answer to that. All of them.'

'So?' And when Dan said nothing: 'The Rivington staff calls you Doctor Sleep. Word gets around, Danno.'

Dan was silent. Some of the pudding was left, and Patty would rag him about it if he didn't eat it, but his appetite had flown. He supposed he'd known this conversation had been coming, and he also knew that, after ten years without a drink (and with a pigeon or two of his own to watch over these days), Casey would respect his boundaries, but he still didn't want to have it.

'You help people to die. Not by putting pillows over their faces, or anything, nobody thinks that, but just by . . . I don't know. *Nobody* seems to know.'

'I sit with them, that's all. Talk to them a little. If it's what they want.'

'Do you work the Steps, Danno?'

If Dan had believed this was a new conversational tack he would have welcomed it, but he knew it was not. 'You know I do. You're my sponsor.'

'Yeah, you ask for help in the morning and say thanks at night. You do it on your knees. So that's the first three. Four is all that moral inventory shit. How about number five?'

There were twelve in all. After hearing them read aloud at the beginning of every meeting he'd attended, Dan knew them by heart. '"Admitted to God, ourselves, and another human being the exact nature of our wrongs."'

'Yuh.' Casey lifted his coffee cup, sipped, and looked at Dan over the rim. 'Have you done that one?'

'Most of it.' Dan found himself wishing he were somewhere else. Almost anywhere else. Also – for the first time in quite a while – he found himself wishing for a drink.

'Let me guess. You've told *yourself* all of your wrongs, and you've told the God of your not-understanding all of your wrongs, and you've told one other person – that would be me – *most* of your wrongs. Would that be a bingo?'

Dan said nothing.

'Here's what I think,' Casey said, 'and you're welcome to correct me if I'm wrong. Steps eight and nine are about cleaning up the wreckage we left behind when we were drunk on our asses pretty much twenty-four/seven. I think at least part of your work at the hospice, the *important* part, is about making those amends. And I think there's one wrong you can't quite get past because you're too fucking ashamed to talk about it. If that's the case, you wouldn't be the first, believe me.'

Dan thought: *Mama.*

Dan thought: *Canny.*

He saw the red wallet and the pathetic wad of food stamps. He also saw a little money. Seventy dollars, enough for a four-day drunk. Five if it was parceled out carefully and food was kept to a bare nutritional minimum. He saw the money first in his hand and then going into his pocket. He saw the kid in the Braves shirt and the sagging diaper.

He thought: *The kid's name was Tommy.*

He thought, not for the first time or the last: *I will never speak of this.*

'Danno? Is there anything you want to tell me? I think there is. I don't know how long you've been dragging the motherfucker around, but you can leave it with me and walk out of here a hundred pounds lighter. That's how it works.'

He thought of how the kid had trotted to his mother

(*Deenie her name was Deenie*)

and how, even deep in her drunken slumber, she had put an arm around him and hugged him close. They had been face-to-face in the morning sun shafting through the bedroom's dirty window.

'There's nothing,' he said.

'Let it go, Dan. I'm telling you that as your friend as well as your sponsor.'

Dan gazed at the other man steadily and said nothing.

Casey sighed. 'How many meetings have you been at where someone said you're only as sick as your secrets? A hundred? Probably a thousand. Of all the old AA chestnuts, that's just about the oldest.'

Dan said nothing.

'We all have a bottom,' Casey said. 'Someday you're going to have to tell somebody about yours. If you don't, somewhere down the line you're going to find yourself in a bar with a drink in your hand.'

'Message received,' Dan said. 'Now can we talk about the Red Sox?'

Casey looked at his watch. 'Another time. I've got to get home.'

Right, Dan thought. *To your dog and your goldfish.*

'Okay.' He grabbed the check before Casey could. 'Another time.'

4

When Dan got back to his turret room, he looked at his blackboard for a long time before slowly erasing what was written there:

They are killing the baseball boy!

When the board was blank again, he asked, 'What baseball boy would that be?'

No answer.

'Abra? Are you still here?'

No. But she had been; if he'd come back from his uncomfortable coffee meeting with Casey ten minutes earlier, he might have seen her phantom shape. But had she come for him? Dan didn't think so. It was undeniably crazy, but he thought she might have come for Tony. Who had been *his* invisible friend, once upon a time. The one who sometimes brought visions. The one who sometimes warned. The one who had turned out to be a deeper and wiser version of himself.

For the scared little boy trying to survive in the Overlook Hotel, Tony had been a protective older brother. The irony was that now, with the booze behind him, Daniel Anthony Torrance had become an authentic adult and Tony was still a kid. Maybe even the fabled inner child the New Age gurus were always going on about. Dan felt sure that inner-child stuff was brought into service to excuse a lot of selfish and destructive behavior (what Casey liked to call the Gotta-Have-It-Now Syndrome), but he also had no doubt that grown men and women held every stage of their development somewhere in their brains – not just the inner child, but the inner infant, the inner teenager, and the inner young adult. And if the mysterious Abra came to him, wasn't it natural that she'd hunt past his adult mind, looking for someone her own age?

A playmate?

A protector, even?

If so, it was a job Tony had done before. But did she need protection? Certainly there had been anguish

(*they are killing the baseball boy*)

in her message, but anguish went naturally with the shining, as Dan had found out long ago. Mere children were not meant to know and see so much. He could seek her out, maybe try to discover more, but what would he say to the parents? *Hi, you don't know me, but I know your daughter, she visits my room sometimes and we've gotten to be pretty good pals?*

Dan didn't think they'd sic the county sheriff on him, but he wouldn't blame them if they did, and given his checkered past, he had no urge to find out. Better to let Tony be her long-distance friend, if that was what was really going on. Tony might be invisible, but at least he was more or less age-appropriate.

Later, he could replace the names and room numbers that belonged on his blackboard. For now he picked the stub of chalk out of the ledge and wrote: **Tony and I wish you a happy summer day, Abra! Your OTHER friend, Dan.**

He studied this for a moment, nodded, and went to the window. A beautiful late summer afternoon, and still his day off. He decided to go for a walk and try to get the troubling conversation with Casey out of his mind. Yes, he supposed Deenie's apartment in Wilmington had been his bottom, but if keeping to himself what had happened there hadn't stopped him from piling up ten years of sobriety, he didn't see why keeping it to himself should stop him from getting another ten. Or twenty. And why think about years anyway, when the AA motto was one day at a time?

Wilmington was a long time ago. That part of his life was done.

He locked his room when he left, as he always did, but a lock wouldn't keep the mysterious Abra out if she wanted to visit. When he came back, there might be another message from her on the blackboard.

Maybe we can become pen pals.

Sure, and maybe a cabal of Victoria's Secret lingerie models would crack the secret of hydrogen fusion.

5

The Anniston Public Library was having its annual summer book sale, and when Abra asked to go, Lucy was delighted to put aside her afternoon chores and walk down to Main Street with her daughter. Card tables loaded with various donated volumes had been set up on the lawn, and while Lucy browsed the paperback table ($1 EACH, 6 FOR $5, YOU PICK 'EM), looking for Jodi Picoults she hadn't read, Abra checked out the selections on the tables marked YOUNG ADULTS. She was still a long way from adulthood of even the youngest sort, but she was a voracious (and precocious) reader with a particular love of fantasy and science fiction. Her favorite t-shirt had a huge, complicated machine on the front above the declaration STEAMPUNK RULES.

Just as Lucy was deciding she'd have to settle for an old Dean Koontz and a slightly newer Lisa Gardner, Abra came running over to her. She was smiling. 'Mom! Mommy! His name is Dan!'

'Whose name is Dan, sweetheart?'

'Tony's father! He told me to have a happy summer day!'

Lucy looked around, almost expecting to see a strange man with a boy Abra's age in tow. There were plenty of strangers – it was summer, after all – but no pairs like that.

Abra saw what she was doing and giggled. 'Oh, he's not here.'

'Then where is he?'

'I don't know, exactly. But close.'

'Well . . . I guess that's good, hon.'

Lucy had just enough time to tousle her daughter's hair before Abra ran back to renew her hunt for rocketeers, time travelers, and sorcerers. Lucy stood watching her, her own choices hanging forgotten in her hand. Tell David about this when he called from Boston, or not? She thought not.

Weird radio, that was all.

Better to let it pass.

6

Dan decided to pop into Java Express, buy a couple of coffees, and take one to Billy Freeman over in Teenytown. Although Dan's employment by the Frazier Municipal Department had been extremely short, the two men had remained friendly over the last ten years. Part of that was having Casey in common – Billy's boss, Dan's sponsor – but mostly it was simple liking. Dan enjoyed Billy's no-bullshit attitude.

He also enjoyed driving *The Helen Rivington*. Probably that inner-child thing again; he was sure a psychiatrist would say so. Billy was usually willing to turn over the controls, and during the summer season he often did so with relief. Between the Fourth of July and Labor Day, the *Riv* made the ten-mile loop out to Cloud Gap and back ten times a day, and Billy wasn't getting any younger.

As he crossed the lawn to Cranmore Avenue, Dan spied Fred Carling sitting on a shady bench in the walkway between Rivington House proper and Rivington Two. The orderly who had once left a set of fingermarks on poor old Charlie Hayes still worked the night shift, and was as lazy and ill-tempered as ever, but he had at least learned to stay clear of Doctor Sleep. That was fine with Dan.

Carling, soon to go on shift, had a grease-spotted McDonald's bag on his lap and was munching a Big Mac. The two men locked eyes for a moment. Neither said hello. Dan thought Fred Carling was a lazy bastard with a sadistic streak and Carling thought Dan was a holier-than-thou meddler, so *that* balanced. As long as they stayed out of each other's way, all would be well and all would be well and all manner of things would be well.

Dan got the coffees (Billy's with four sugars), then crossed to the common, which was busy in the golden early-evening light. Frisbees soared. Mothers and dads pushed toddlers on swings or caught them as they flew off the slides. A game was in progress on the softball field, kids from the Frazier YMCA against a team with ANNISTON REC DEPARTMENT on their orange shirts. He spied Billy in the train station, standing on a stool and polishing the *Riv*'s chrome. It all looked good. It looked like home.

If it isn't, Dan thought, *it's as close as I'm ever going to get. All I need now is a wife named Sally, a kid named Pete, and a dog named Rover.*

He strolled up the Teenytown version of Cranmore Avenue and into the shade of Teenytown Station. 'Hey Billy, I brought you some of that coffee-flavored sugar you like.'

At the sound of his voice, the first person to offer Dan a friendly word in the town of Frazier turned around. 'Why, ain't you the neighborly one. I was just thinking I could use – oh shitsky, there it goes.'

The cardboard tray had dropped from Danny's hands. He felt warmth as hot coffee splattered his tennis shoes, but it seemed faraway, unimportant.

There were flies crawling on Billy Freeman's face.

7

Billy didn't want to go see Casey Kingsley the following morning, didn't want to take the day off, and *certainly* didn't want to go see no doctor. He kept telling Dan he felt fine, in the pink, absolutely tip-top. He'd even missed the summer cold that usually hit him in June or July.

Dan, however, had lain sleepless most of the previous night, and wouldn't take no for an answer. He might have if he'd been convinced it was too late, but he didn't think it was. He had seen the flies before, and had learned to gauge their meaning. A swarm of them – enough to obscure the person's features behind a veil of nasty, jostling bodies – and you knew there was no hope. A dozen or so meant something *might* be done. Only a few, and there was time. There had only been three or four on Billy's face.

He never saw any at all on the faces of the terminal patients in the hospice.

Dan remembered visiting his mother nine months before her death, on a day when she had also claimed to feel fine, in the pink, absolutely tickety-boo. *What are you looking at, Danny?* Wendy Torrance had asked. *Have I got a smudge?* She had swiped comically at the tip of her nose, her fingers passing right through the hundreds of deathflies that were covering her from chin to hairline, like a caul.

8

Casey was used to mediating. Fond of irony, he liked to tell people it was why he made that enormous six-figure annual salary.

First he listened to Dan. Then he listened to Billy's protests about how there was no way he could leave, not at the height of the season with people already lining up to ride the *Riv* on its 8 a.m. run. Besides, no doctor would see him on such short notice. It was the height of the season for them, too.

'When's the last time you had a checkup?' Casey asked once Billy finally ran down. Dan and Billy were standing in front of his desk. Casey was rocked back in his office chair, head resting in its accustomed place just below the cross on the wall, fingers laced together across his belly.

Billy looked defensive. 'I guess back in oh-six. But I was fine then, Case. Doc said my blood pressure was ten points lower'n his.'

Casey's eyes shifted to Dan. They held speculation and curiosity but no disbelief. AA members mostly kept their lips zipped during their various interactions with the wider world, but inside the groups, people talked – and sometimes gossiped – quite freely. Casey therefore knew that Dan Torrance's talent for helping terminal patients die easily was not his *only* talent. According to the grapevine, Dan T. had certain helpful insights from time to time. The kind that can't exactly be explained.

'You're tight with Johnny Dalton, aren't you?' he asked Dan now. 'The pediatrician?'

'Yes. I see him most Thursday nights, in North Conway.'

'Got his number?'

'As a matter of fact, I do.' Dan had a whole list of AA contact numbers in the back of the little notebook Casey had given him, which he still carried.

'Call him. Tell him it's important this yobbo here sees someone right away. Don't suppose you know what kind of a doctor it is he needs, do you? Sure as hell isn't a pediatrician at his age.'

'Casey—' Billy began.

'Hush,' Casey said, and returned his attention to Dan. 'I think you do know, by God. Is it his lungs? That seems the most likely, the way he smokes.'

Dan decided he had come too far to turn back now. He sighed and said, 'No, I think it's something in his guts.'

'Except for a little indigestion, my guts are—'

'*Hush* I said.' Then, turning back to Dan: 'A gut doctor, then. Tell Johnny D. it's important.' He paused. 'Will he believe you?'

This was a question Dan was glad to hear. He had helped several AAs during his time in New Hampshire, and although he asked them all not to talk, he knew perfectly well that some had, and still did. He was happy to know John Dalton hadn't been one of them.

'I think so.'

'Okay.' Casey pointed at Billy. 'You got the day off, and with pay. Medical leave.'

'The *Riv*—'

'There's a dozen people in this town that can drive the *Riv*. I'll make some calls, then take the first two runs myself.'

'Your bad hip—'

'Balls to my bad hip. Do me good to get out of this office.'

'But Casey, I feel f—'

'I don't care if you feel good enough to run a footrace all the way to Lake Winnipesaukee. You're going to see the doctor and that's the end of it.'

Billy looked resentfully at Dan. 'See the trouble you got me in? I didn't even get my morning coffee.'

The flies were gone this morning – except they were still there. Dan knew that if he concentrated, he could see them again if he wanted to . . . but who in Christ's name would *want* to?

'I know,' Dan said. 'There is no gravity, life just sucks. Can I use your phone, Casey?'

'Be my guest.' Casey stood up. 'Guess I'll toddle on over to the train station and punch a few tickets. You got an engineer's cap that'll fit me, Billy?'

'No.'

'Mine will,' Dan said.

9

For an organization that didn't advertise its presence, sold no goods, and supported itself with crumpled dollar bills thrown into passed baskets or baseball caps, Alcoholics Anonymous exerted a quietly powerful influence that stretched far beyond the doors of the various rented halls and church basements where it did its business. It wasn't the old boys' network, Dan thought, but the old drunks' network.

He called John Dalton, and John called an internal medicine specialist named Greg Fellerton. Fellerton wasn't in the Program, but he owed Johnny D. a favor. Dan didn't know why, and didn't care. All that mattered was that later that day, Billy Freeman was on the examining table in Fellerton's Lewiston office. Said office was a seventy-mile drive from Frazier, and Billy bitched the whole way.

'Are you sure indigestion's all that's been bothering you?' Dan asked as they pulled into Fellerton's little parking area on Pine Street.

'Yuh,' Billy said. Then he reluctantly added, 'It's been a little worse lately, but nothin that keeps me up at night.'

Liar, Dan thought, but let it pass. He'd gotten the contrary old sonofabitch here, and that was the hard part.

Dan was sitting in the waiting room, leafing through a copy of *OK!* with Prince William and his pretty but skinny new bride on the cover, when he heard a lusty cry of pain from down the hall. Ten minutes later, Fellerton came out and sat down beside Dan. He looked at the cover of *OK!* and said, 'That guy may be heir to the British throne, but he's still going to be as bald as a nine ball by the time he's forty.'

'You're probably right.'

'Of course I'm right. In human affairs, the only real king is genetics. I'm sending your friend up to Central Maine General for a CT scan. I'm pretty sure what it'll show. If I'm right, I'll schedule Mr Freeman to see a vascular surgeon for a little cut-and-splice early tomorrow morning.'

'What's wrong with him?'

Billy was walking up the hall, buckling his belt. His tanned face was now sallow and wet with sweat. 'He says there's a bulge in my aorta. Like a bubble on a car tire. Only car tires don't yell when you poke em.'

'An aneurysm,' Fellerton said. 'Oh, there's a chance it's a tumor, but I don't think so. In any case, time's of the essence. Damn thing's the size of a Ping-Pong ball. It's good you got him in for a look-see. If it had burst without a hospital nearby . . .' Fellerton shook his head.

10

The CT scan confirmed Fellerton's aneurysm diagnosis, and by six that evening, Billy was in a hospital bed, where he looked considerably diminished. Dan sat beside him.

'I'd kill for a cigarette,' Billy said wistfully.

'Can't help you there.'

Billy sighed. 'High time I quit, anyway. Won't they be missin you at Rivington House?'

'Day off.'

'And ain't this one hell of a way to spend it. Tell you what, if they don't murder me with their knives and forks tomorrow morning, I guess I'm going to owe you my life. I don't know how you knew, but if there's anything I can ever do for you – I mean anything at all – you just have to ask.'

Dan thought of how he'd descended the steps of an interstate bus ten years ago, stepping into a snow flurry as fine as wedding lace. He thought of his delight when he had spotted the bright red locomotive that pulled *The Helen Rivington*. Also of how this man had asked him if he liked the little train instead of telling him to get the fuck away from what he had no business touching. Just a small kindness, but it had opened the door to all he had now.

'Billy-boy, I'm the one who owes you, and more than I could ever repay.'

11

He had noticed an odd fact during his years of sobriety. When things in his life weren't going so well – the morning in 2008 when he had discovered someone had smashed in the rear window of his car with a rock came to mind – he rarely thought of a drink. When they were going well, however, the old dry thirst had a way of coming back on him. That night after saying goodbye to Billy, on the way home from Lewiston with everything okey-doke, he spied a roadhouse bar called the Cowboy Boot and felt a nearly insurmountable urge to go in. To buy a pitcher of beer and get enough quarters to fill the jukebox for at least an hour. To sit there listening to Jennings and Jackson and Haggard, not talking to anyone, not causing any trouble, just getting high. Feeling the weight of sobriety – sometimes it was like wearing lead shoes – fall away. When he got down to his last five quarters, he'd play 'Whiskey Bent and Hell Bound' six times straight.

He passed the roadhouse, turned in at the gigantic Walmart parking lot just beyond, and opened his phone. He let his finger hover over Casey's number, then remembered their difficult conversation in the café. Casey might want to revisit that discussion, especially the subject of whatever Dan might be holding back. That was a nonstarter.

Feeling like a man having an out-of-body experience, he returned to the roadhouse and parked in the back of the dirt lot. He felt good about this. He also felt like a man who has just picked up a loaded gun and put it to his temple. His window was open and he could hear a live band playing an old Derailers tune: 'Lover's Lie'. They didn't sound too bad, and with a few drinks in him, they would sound great. There would be ladies in there who would want to dance. Ladies with curls, ladies with pearls, ladies in skirts, ladies in cowboy shirts. There always were. He wondered what kind of whiskey they had in the well, and God, God, great God, he was so thirsty. He opened the car door, put one foot out on the ground, then sat there with his head lowered.

Ten years. Ten *good* years, and he could toss them away in the next ten minutes. It would be easy enough to do. *Like honey to the bee.*

We all have a bottom. Someday you're going to have to tell somebody about yours. If you don't, somewhere down the line, you're going to find yourself in a bar with a drink in your hand.

And I can blame you, Casey, he thought coldly. *I can say you put the idea in my head while we were having coffee in the Sunspot.*

There was a flashing red arrow over the door, and a sign reading PITCHERS $2 UNTIL 9 PM MILLER LITE COME ON IN.

Dan closed the car door, opened his phone again, and called John Dalton.

'Is your buddy okay?' John asked.

'Tucked up and ready to go tomorrow morning at seven a.m. John, I feel like drinking.'

'*Oh, nooo!*' John cried in a trembling falsetto. 'Not *booooze!*'

And just like that the urge was gone. Dan laughed. 'Okay, I needed that. But if you ever do the Michael Jackson voice again, I *will* drink.'

'You should hear me on "Billie Jean". I'm a karaoke monster. Can I ask you something?'

'Sure.' Through the windshield, Dan could see the Cowboy Boot patrons come and go, probably not talking of Michelangelo.

'Whatever you've got, did drinking . . . I don't know . . . shut it up?'

'Muffled it. Put a pillow over its face and made it struggle for air.'

'And now?'

'Like Superman, I use my powers to promote truth, justice, and the American Way.'

'Meaning you don't want to talk about it.'

'No,' Dan said. 'I don't. But it's better now. Better than I ever thought it could be. When I was a teenager . . .' He trailed off. When he'd been a teenager, every day had been a struggle for sanity. The voices in his head were bad; the pictures were frequently worse. He had promised both his mother and himself that he would never drink like his father, but when he finally began, as a freshman in high school, it had been such a huge relief that he had – at first – only wished he'd started sooner. Morning hangovers were a thousand times better than nightmares all night long. All of which sort of led to a question: How much of his father's son *was* he? In how many ways?

'When you were a teenager, what?' John asked.

'Nothing. It doesn't matter. Listen, I better get moving. I'm sitting in a bar parking lot.'

'Really?' John sounded interested. 'Which bar?'

'Place called the Cowboy Boot. It's two-buck pitchers until nine o'clock.'

'Dan.'

'Yes, John.'

'I know that place from the old days. If you're going to flush your life down the toilet, don't start there. The ladies are skanks with meth-mouth and the men's room smells like moldy jockstraps. The Boot is strictly for when you hit your bottom.'

There it was, that phrase again.

'We all have a bottom,' Dan said. 'Don't we?'

'Get out of there, Dan.' John sounded dead serious now. 'Right this second. No more fucking around. And stay on the phone with me until that big neon cowboy boot on the roof is out of your rearview mirror.'

Dan started his car, pulled out of the lot, and back onto Route 11.

'It's going,' he said. 'It's going . . . annnd . . . it's gone.' He felt inexpressible relief. He also felt bitter regret – how many two-buck pitchers could he have gotten through before nine o'clock?

'Not going to pick up a six or a bottle of wine before you get back to Frazier, are you?'

'No. I'm good.'

'Then I'll see you Thursday night. Come early, I'm making the coffee. Folgers, from my special stash.'

'I'll be there,' Dan said.

12

When he got back to his turret room and flipped on the light, there was a new message on the blackboard.

I had a wonderful day!
Your friend,
ABRA

'That's good, honey,' Dan said. 'I'm glad.'

Buzz. The intercom. He went over and hit talk.

'Hey there, Doctor Sleep,' Loretta Ames said. 'I thought I saw you come in. I guess it's still technically your day off, but do you want to pay a house call?'

'On who? Mr Cameron or Mr Murray?'

'Cameron. Azzie's been visiting with him since just after dinner.'

Ben Cameron was in Rivington One. Second floor. An eighty-three-year-old retired accountant with congestive heart failure. Hell of a nice guy. Good Scrabble player and an absolute pest at Parcheesi, always setting up blockades that drove his opponents crazy.

'I'll be right over,' Dan said. On his way out, he paused for a single backward glance at the blackboard. 'Goodnight, hon,' he said.

He didn't hear from Abra Stone for another two years.

During those same two years, something slept in the True Knot's bloodstream. A little parting gift from Bradley Trevor, aka the baseball boy.

PART TWO
EMPTY DEVILS

CHAPTER SEVEN
'HAVE YOU SEEN ME?'

1

On an August morning in 2013, Concetta Reynolds awoke early in her Boston condo apartment. As always, the first thing she was aware of was that there was no dog curled up in the corner, by the dresser. Betty had been gone for years now, but Chetta still missed her. She put on her robe and headed for the kitchen, where she intended to make her morning coffee. This was a trip she had made thousands of times before, and she had no reason to believe this one would be any different. Certainly it never crossed her mind to think it would prove to be the first link in a chain of malignant events. She didn't stumble, she would tell her granddaughter, Lucy, later that day, nor did she bump into anything. She just heard an unimportant snapping sound from about halfway down her body on the right-hand side and then she was on the floor with warm agony rushing up and down her leg.

She lay there for three minutes or so, staring at her faint reflection in the polished hardwood floor, willing the pain to subside. At the same time she talked to herself. *Stupid old woman, not to have a companion. David's been telling you for the last five years that you're too old to live alone and now he'll never let you hear the end of it.*

But a live-in companion would have needed the room she'd set aside for Lucy and Abra, and Chetta lived for their visits. More than ever, now that Betty was gone and all the poetry seemed to be written out of her. And ninety-seven or not, she'd been getting around well and feeling fine. Good genes on the female side. Hadn't her own momo buried four husbands and seven children and lived to be a hundred and two?

Although, truth be told (if only to herself), she hadn't felt quite so fine this summer. This summer things had been . . . difficult.

When the pain finally did abate – a bit – she began crawling down the short hall toward the kitchen, which was now filling up with dawn. She found it was harder to appreciate that lovely rose light from floor level. Each time the pain became too great, she stopped with her head laid on one bony arm, panting. During these rest stops she reflected on the seven ages of man, and how they described a perfect (and perfectly stupid) circle. This had been her mode of locomotion long ago, during the fourth year of World War I, also known as – how funny – the War to End All Wars. Then she had been Concetta Abruzzi, crawling across the dooryard of her parents' farm in Davoli, intent on capturing chickens that easily outpaced her. From those dusty beginnings she had gone on to lead a fruitful and interesting life. She had published twenty books of poetry, taken tea with Graham Greene, dined with two presidents, and – best of all – had been gifted with a lovely, brilliant, and strangely talented great-granddaughter. And what did all those wonderful things lead to?

More crawling, that was what. Back to the beginning. *Dio mi benedica.*

She reached the kitchen and eeled her way through an oblong of sun to the little table where she took most of her meals. Her cell phone was on it. Chetta grabbed one leg of the table and shook it until her phone slid to the edge and dropped off. And, *meno male*, landed unbroken. She punched in the number they told you to call when shit like this happened, then waited while a recorded voice summed up all the absurdity of the twenty-first century by telling her that her call was being recorded.

And finally, praise Mary, an actual human voice.

'This is 911, what is your emergency?'

The woman on the floor who had once crawled after the chickens in southern Italy spoke clearly and coherently in spite of the pain. 'My name is Concetta Reynolds, and I live on the third floor of a condominium at Two nineteen Marlborough Street. I seem to have broken my hip. Can you send an ambulance?'

'Is there anyone with you, Mrs Reynolds?'

'For my sins, no. You're speaking to a stupid old lady who insisted she was fine to live alone. And by the way, these days I prefer *Ms.*'

2

Lucy got the call from her grandmother shortly before Concetta was wheeled into surgery. 'I've broken my hip, but they can fix it,' she told Lucy. 'I believe they put in pins and such.'

'Momo, did you fall?' Lucy's first thought was for Abra, who was away at summer camp for another week.

'Oh yes, but the break that *caused* the fall was completely spontaneous. Apparently this is quite common in people my age, and since there are ever so many more people my age than there used to be, the doctors see a lot of it. There's no need for you to come immediately, but I think you'll want to come quite soon. It seems that we'll need to have a talk about various arrangements.'

Lucy felt a coldness in the pit of her stomach. 'What sort of arrangements?'

Now that she was loaded with Valium or morphine or whatever it was they'd given her, Concetta felt quite serene. 'It seems that a broken hip is the least of my problems.' She explained. It didn't take long. She finished by saying, 'Don't tell Abra, *cara*. I've had dozens of emails from her, even an actual *letter*, and it sounds like she's enjoying her summer camp a great deal. Time enough later for her to find her old momo's circling the drain.'

Lucy thought, *If you really believe I'll have to tell her—*

'I can guess what you're thinking without being psychic, *amore*, but maybe this time bad news will give her a miss.'

'Maybe,' Lucy said.

She had barely hung up when the phone rang. 'Mom? Mommy?' It was Abra, and she was crying. 'I want to come home. Momo's got cancer and I want to come home.'

3

Following her early return from Camp Tapawingo in Maine, Abra got an idea of what it would be like to shuttle between divorced parents. She and her mother spent the last two weeks of August and the first week of September in Chetta's Marlborough Street condo. The old woman had come through her hip surgery quite nicely, and had decided against a longer hospital stay, or any sort of treatment for the pancreatic cancer the doctors had discovered.

'No pills, no chemotherapy. Ninety-seven years are enough. As for you, Lucia, I refuse to allow you to spend the next six months bringing me meals and pills and the bedpan. You have a family, and I can afford round-the-clock care.'

'You're not going to live the end of your life among strangers,' Lucy said, speaking in her she-who-must-be-obeyed voice. It was the one both Abra and her father knew not to argue with. Not even Concetta could do that.

There was no discussion about Abra staying; on September ninth, she was scheduled to start the eighth grade at Anniston Middle School. It was David Stone's sabbatical year, which he was using to write a book comparing the Roaring Twenties to the Go-Go Sixties, and so – like a good many of the girls with whom she'd gone to Camp Tap – Abra shuttled from one parent to the other. During the week, she was with her father. On the weekends, she shipped down to Boston, to be with her mom and Momo. She thought that things could not get worse . . . but they always can, and often do.

4

Although he was working at home now, David Stone never bothered to walk down the driveway and get the mail. He claimed the US Postal Service was a self-perpetuating bureaucracy that had ceased to have any relevance around the turn of the century. Every now and then a package turned up, sometimes books he'd ordered to help with his work, more often something Lucy had ordered from a catalogue, but otherwise he claimed it was all junkola.

When Lucy was home, she retrieved the post from the mailbox by the gate and looked the stuff over while she had her mid-morning coffee. It *was* mostly crap, and it went directly into what Dave called the Circular File. But she wasn't home that early September, so it was Abra – now the nominal woman of the house – who checked the box when she got off the school bus. She also washed the dishes, did a load of laundry for herself and her dad twice a week, and set the Roomba robo-vac going, if she remembered. She did these chores without complaint because she knew that her mother was helping Momo and that her father's book was very important. He said this one was POPULAR instead of ACADEMIC. If it was successful, he might be able to stop teaching and write full-time, at least for a while.

On this day, the seventeenth of September, the mailbox contained a Walmart circular, a postcard announcing the opening of a new dental office in town (WE GUARANTEE MILES OF SMILES!), and two glossy come-ons from local realtors selling time shares at the Mount Thunder ski resort.

There was also a local bulk-mail rag called *The Anniston Shopper*. This had a few wire-service stories on the front two pages and a few local stories (heavy on regional sports) in the middle. The rest was ads and coupons. If she had been home, Lucy would have saved a few of these latter and then tossed the rest of the *Shopper* into the recycling bin. Her daughter would never have seen it. On this day, with Lucy away in Boston, Abra did.

She thumbed through it as she idled her way up the driveway, then turned it over. On the back page there were forty or fifty photographs not much bigger than postage stamps, most in color, a few in black and white. Above them was this heading:

HAVE YOU SEEN ME?
A Weekly Service Of Your *Anniston Shopper*

For a moment Abra thought it was some sort of contest, like a scavenger hunt. Then she realized these were missing children, and it was as if a hand had grasped the soft lining of her stomach and squeezed it like a washcloth. She had bought a three-pack of Oreos in the caf at lunch, and had saved them for the bus ride home. Now she seemed to feel them being wadded up toward her throat by that clutching hand.

Don't look at it if it bothers you, she told herself. It was the stern and lecturely voice she often employed when she was upset or confused (a Momo-voice, although she had never consciously realized this). *Just toss it in the garage trashcan with the rest of this gluck*. Only she seemed unable *not* to look at it.

Here was Cynthia Abelard, DOB 9 June, 2005. After a moment's thought, Abra realized DOB stood for date of birth. So Cynthia would be eight now. If she was still alive, that was. She had been missing since 2009. *How does somebody lose track of a four-year-old?* Abra wondered. *She must have really crappy parents.* But of course, the parents probably *hadn't* lost her. Probably some weirdo had been cruising around the neighborhood, seen his chance, and stolen her.

Here was Merton Askew, DOB 4 September 1998. He had disappeared in 2010.

Here, halfway down the page, was a beautiful little Hispanic girl named Angel Barbera, who had disappeared from her Kansas City home at the age of seven and had already been gone for nine years. Abra wondered if her parents really thought this tiny picture would help them get her back. And if they did, would they still even know her? For that matter, would *she* know *them*?

Get rid of that thing, the Momo-voice said. *You've got enough to worry about without looking at a lot of missing ki—*

Her eyes found a picture in the very bottom row, and a little sound escaped her. Probably it was a moan. At first she didn't even know why, although she almost did; it was like how you sometimes knew the word you wanted to use in an English composition but you still couldn't quite get it, the damn thing just sat there on the tip of your tongue.

This photo was of a white kid with short hair and a great big goofy-ass grin. It looked like he had freckles on his cheeks. The picture was too small to tell for sure, but

(*they're freckles you know they are*)

Abra was somehow sure, anyway. Yes, they were freckles and his big brothers had teased him about them and his mother told him they would go away in time.

'She told him freckles are good luck,' Abra whispered.

Bradley Trevor, DOB 2 March 2000. Missing since 12 July 2011. Race: Caucasian. Location: Bankerton, Iowa. Current Age: 13. And below this – below all these pictures of mostly smiling children: *If you think you have seen Bradley Trevor, contact The National Center for Missing & Exploited Children.*

Only no one was going to contact them about Bradley, because no one was going to see him. His current age wasn't thirteen, either.

Bradley Trevor had stopped at eleven. He had stopped like a busted wristwatch that shows the same time twenty-four hours a day. Abra found herself wondering if freckles faded underground.

'The baseball boy,' she whispered.

There were flowers lining the driveway. Abra leaned over, hands on her knees, pack all at once far too heavy on her back, and threw up her Oreos and the undigested portion of her school lunch into her mother's asters. When she was sure she wasn't going to puke a second time, she went into the garage and tossed the mail into the trash. *All* the mail.

Her father was right, it was junkola.

5

The door of the little room her dad used as his study was open, and when Abra stopped at the kitchen sink for a glass of water to rinse the sour-chocolate taste of used Oreos out of her mouth, she heard the keyboard of his computer clicking steadily away. That was good. When it slowed down or stopped completely, he had a tendency to be grumpy. Also, he was more apt to notice her. Today she didn't want to be noticed.

'Abba-Doo, is that you?' her father half-sang.

Ordinarily she would have asked him to *please* stop using that baby name, but not today. 'Yup, it's me.'

'School go okay?'

The steady *click-click-click* had stopped. *Please don't come out here*, Abra prayed. *Don't come out and look at me and ask me why I'm so pale or something.*

'Fine. How's the book?'

'Having a great day,' he said. 'Writing about the Charleston and the Black Bottom. Vo-doe-dee-oh-doe.' Whatever *that* meant. The important thing was the *click-click-click* started up again. Thank God.

'Terrific,' she said, rinsing her glass and putting it in the drainer. 'I'm going upstairs to start my homework.'

'That's my girl. Think Harvard in '18.'

'Okay, Dad.' And maybe she would. Anything to keep herself from thinking about Bankerton, Iowa, in '11.

6

Only she couldn't stop.

Because.

Because what? Because why? Because . . . well . . .

Because there are things I can do.

She IM'ed with Jessica for a while, but then Jessica went to the mall in North Conway to have dinner at Panda Garden with her parents, so Abra opened her social studies book. She meant to go to chapter four, a majorly boresome twenty pages titled 'How Our Government Works', but instead the book had fallen open to chapter five: 'Your Responsibilities As a Citizen'.

Oh God, if there was a word she didn't want to see this afternoon, it was *responsibilities*. She went into the bathroom for another glass of water because her mouth still tasted blick and found herself staring at her own freckles in the mirror. There were exactly three, one on her left cheek and two on her schnozz. Not bad. She had lucked out in the freckles department. Nor did she have a birthmark, like Bethany Stevens, or a cocked eye like Norman McGinley, or a stutter like Ginny Whitlaw, or a horrible name like poor picked-on Pence Effersham. Abra was a little strange, of course, but Abra was fine, people thought it was interesting instead of just weird, like Pence, who was known among the boys (but girls always somehow found these things out) as Pence the Penis.

And the biggie, I didn't get cut apart by crazy people who paid no attention when I screamed and begged them to stop. I didn't have to see some of the crazy people licking my blood off the palms of their hands before I died. Abba-Doo is one lucky ducky.

But maybe not such a lucky ducky after all. Lucky duckies didn't know things they had no business knowing.

She closed the lid of the toilet, sat on it, and cried quietly with her hands over her face. Being forced to think of Bradley Trevor again and how he died was bad enough, but it wasn't just him. There were all those other kids to think about, so many pictures that they were crammed together on the last page of the *Shopper* like the school assembly from hell. All those gap-toothed smiles and all those eyes that knew even less of the world than Abra did herself, and what did *she* know? Not even 'How Our Government Works'.

What did the parents of those missing children think? How did they go on with their lives? Was Cynthia or Merton or Angel the first thing they thought about in the morning and the last thing they thought about at night? Did they keep their rooms ready for them in case they came home, or did they give all their clothes and toys away to the Goodwill? Abra had heard that was what Lennie O'Meara's parents did after Lennie fell out of a tree and hit his head on a rock and died. Lennie O'Meara, who got as far as the fifth grade and then just . . . stopped. But of course Lennie's parents *knew* he was dead, there was a grave where they could go and put flowers, and maybe that made it different. Maybe not, but Abra thought it would. Because otherwise you'd pretty much have to wonder, wouldn't you? Like when you were eating breakfast, you'd wonder if your missing

(*Cynthia Merton Angel*)

was also eating breakfast somewhere, or flying a kite, or picking oranges with a bunch of migrants, or whatever. In the back of your mind you'd have to be pretty sure he or she was dead, that's what happened to most of them (you only had to watch *Action News at Six* to know), but you couldn't be sure.

There was nothing she could do about that uncertainty for the parents of Cynthia Abelard or Merton Askew or Angel Barbera, she had no idea what had happened to them, but that wasn't true of Bradley Trevor.

She had almost forgotten him, then that stupid *newspaper* . . . those stupid *pictures* . . . and the stuff that had come back to her, stuff she didn't even know she knew, as if the pictures had been startled out of her subconscious . . .

And those things she could do. Things she had never told her parents about because it would worry them, the way she guessed it would worry them if they knew she had made out with Bobby Flannagan – just a little, no sucking face or anything gross like that – one day after school. That was something they wouldn't *want* to know. Abra guessed (and about this she wasn't entirely wrong, although there was no telepathy involved) that in her parents' minds, she was sort of frozen at eight and would probably stay that way at least until she got boobs, which she sure hadn't yet – not that you'd notice, anyway.

So far they hadn't even had THE TALK with her. Julie Vandover said it was almost always your mom who gave you the lowdown, but the only lowdown Abra had gotten lately was on how important it was for her to get the trash out on Thursday mornings before the bus came. 'We don't ask you to do many chores,' Lucy had said, 'and this fall it's especially important for all of us to pitch in.'

Momo had at least approached THE TALK. In the spring, she had taken Abra aside one day and said, 'Do you know what boys want from girls, once boys and girls get to be about your age?'

'Sex, I guess,' Abra had said . . . although all that humble, scurrying Pence Effersham ever seemed to want was one of her cookies, or to borrow a quarter for the vending machines, or to tell her how many times he'd seen *The Avengers*.

Momo had nodded. 'You can't blame human nature, it is what it is, but don't give it to them. Period. End of discussion. You can rethink things when you're nineteen, if you want.'

That had been a little embarrassing, but at least it was straight and clear. There was nothing clear about the thing in her head. That was *her* birthmark, invisible but real. Her parents no longer talked about the crazy shit that had happened when she was little. Maybe they thought the thing that had caused that stuff was almost gone. Sure, she'd known Momo was sick, but that wasn't the same as the crazy piano music, or turning on the water in the bathroom, or the birthday party (which she barely remembered) when she had hung spoons all over the kitchen ceiling. She had just learned to control it. Not completely, but mostly.

And it had changed. Now she rarely saw things before they happened. Or take moving stuff around. When she was six or seven, she could have concentrated on her pile of schoolbooks and lifted them all the way to the ceiling. Nothing to it. Easy as knitting kitten-britches, as Momo liked to say. Now, even if it was only a single book, she could concentrate until it felt like her brains were going to come splooshing out her ears, and she might only be able to shove it a few inches across her desk. That was on a good day. On many, she couldn't even flutter the pages.

But there were other things she *could* do, and in many cases far better than she'd been able to as a little kid. Looking into people's heads, for instance. She couldn't do it with everyone – some people were entirely enclosed, others only gave off intermittent flashes – but many people were like windows with the curtains pulled back. She could look in anytime she felt like it. Mostly she didn't want to, because the things she discovered were sometimes sad and often shocking. Finding out that Mrs Moran, her beloved sixth-grade teacher, was having AN AFFAIR had been the biggest mind-blower so far, and not in a good way.

These days she mostly kept the *seeing* part of her mind shut down. Learning to do that had been difficult at first, like learning to skate backwards or print with her left hand, but she *had* learned. Practice didn't make perfect (not yet, at least), but it sure helped. She still sometimes looked, but always tentatively, ready to pull back at the first sign of something weird or disgusting. And she *never* peeked into her parents' minds, or into Momo's. It would have been wrong. Probably it was wrong with everyone, but it was like Momo herself had said: You can't blame human nature, and there was nothing more human than curiosity.

Sometimes she could make people do things. Not everyone, not even *half* of everyone, but a lot of people were *very* open to suggestions. (Probably they were the same ones who thought the stuff they sold on TV really would take away their wrinkles or make their hair grow back.) Abra knew this was a talent that could grow if she exercised it like a muscle, but she didn't. It scared her.

There were other things, too, some for which she had no name, but the one she was thinking about now did have one. She called it far-seeing. Like the other aspects of her special talent, it came and went, but if she really wanted it – and if she had an object to fix upon – she could usually summon it.

I could do that now.

'Shut up, Abba-Doo,' she said in a low, strained voice. 'Shut up, Abba-Doo-Doo.'

She opened *Early Algebra* to tonight's homework page, which she had bookmarked with a sheet on which she had written the names Boyd, Steve, Cam, and Pete at least twenty times each. Collectively they were 'Round Here, her favorite boy band. *So* hot, especially Cam. Her best friend, Emma Deane, thought so, too. Those blue eyes, that careless tumble of blond hair.

Maybe I could help. His parents would be sad, but at least they'd know.

'Shut up, Abba-Doo. Shut up, Abba-Doo-Doo-For-Brains.'

If $5x - 4 = 26$, what does x equal?

'Sixty zillion!' she said. 'Who cares?'

Her eyes fell on the names of the cute boys in 'Round Here, written in the pudgy cursive she and Emma affected ('Writing looks more romantic that way,' Emma had decreed), and all at once they looked stupid and babyish and all wrong. *They cut him up and licked his blood and then they did something even worse to him.* In a world where something like that could happen, mooning over a boy band seemed worse than wrong.

Abra slammed her book shut, went downstairs (the *click-click-click* from her dad's study continued unabated) and out to the garage. She retrieved the *Shopper* from the trash, brought it up to her room, and smoothed it flat on her desk.

All those faces, but right now she cared about only one.

7

Her heart was thumping hard-hard-hard. She had been scared before when she consciously tried to far-see or thought-read, but never scared like this. Never even close.

What are you going to do if you find out?

That was a question for later, because she might not be able to. A sneaking, cowardly part of her mind hoped for that.

Abra put the first two fingers of her left hand on the picture of Bradley Trevor because her left hand was the one that saw better. She would have liked to get all her fingers on it (and if it had been an object, she would have held it), but the picture was too small. Once her fingers were on it she couldn't even see it anymore. Except she could. She saw it very well.

Blue eyes, like Cam Knowles's in 'Round Here. You couldn't tell from the picture, but they were that same deep shade. She *knew*.

Right-handed, like me. But left-handed like me, too. It was the left hand that knew what pitch was coming next, fastball or curveb—

Abra gave a little gasp. The baseball boy had *known* things.

The baseball boy really had been like her.

Yes, that's right. That's why they took him.

She closed her eyes and saw his face. Bradley Trevor. Brad, to his friends. The baseball boy. Sometimes he turned his cap around because that way it was a rally cap. His father was a farmer. His mother cooked pies and sold them at a local restaurant, also at the family farmstand. When his big brother went away to college, Brad took all his AC/DC discs. He and his best friend Al especially liked the song 'Big Balls'. They'd sit on Brad's bed and sing it together and laugh and laugh.

He walked through the corn and a man was waiting for him. Brad thought he was a nice man, one of the good guys, because the man—

'Barry,' Abra whispered in a low voice. Behind her closed lids, her eyes moved rapidly back and forth like those of a sleeper in the grip of a vivid dream. 'His name was Barry the Chunk. He fooled you, Brad. Didn't he?'

But not just Barry. If it had been just him, Brad might have known. It had to be all of the Flashlight People working together, sending the same thought: that it would be okay to get into Barry the Chunk's truck or camper-van or whatever it was, because Barry was good. One of the good guys. A friend.

And they took him . . .

Abra went deeper. She didn't bother with what Brad had seen because he hadn't seen anything but a gray rug. He was tied up with tape and lying facedown on the floor of whatever Barry the Chunk was driving. That was okay, though. Now that she was tuned in, she could see wider than him. She could see—

His glove. A Wilson baseball glove. And Barry the Chunk—

Then that part flew away. It might swoop back or it might not.

It was night. She could smell manure. There was a factory. Some kind of

(it's busted)

factory. There was a whole line of vehicles going there, some small, most big, a couple of them enormous. The headlights were off in case someone was looking, but there was a three-quarters moon in the sky. Enough light to see by. They went down a potholed and bumpy tar road, they went past a water tower, they went past a shed with a broken roof, they went through a rusty gate that was standing open, they went past a sign. It went by so fast she couldn't read it. Then the factory. A busted factory with busted smokestacks and busted windows. There was another sign and thanks to the moonlight this one she *could* read: NO TRESPASSING BY ORDER OF THE CANTON COUNTY SHERIFF'S DEPT.

They were going around the back, and when they got there they were going to hurt Brad the baseball boy and go on hurting him until he was dead. Abra didn't want to see that part so she made everything go backwards. That was a little hard, like opening a jar with a really tight cap, but she could do it. When she got back where she wanted, she let go.

Barry the Chunk liked that glove because it reminded him of when he was a little boy. That's why he tried it on. Tried it on and smelled the oil Brad used to keep it from getting stiff and bopped his fist in the pocket a few ti—

But now things were reeling forward and she forgot about Brad's baseball glove again.

Water tower. Shed with broken roof. Rusty gate. And then the first sign. What did it say?

Nope. Still too quick, even with the moonlight. She rewound again (now beads of sweat were standing out on her forehead) and let go. Water tower. Shed with broken roof. *Get ready, here it comes.* Rusty gate. Then the sign. This time she could read it, although she wasn't sure she understood it.

Abra grabbed the sheet of notepaper on which she had curlicued all those stupid boy names and turned it over. Quickly, before she forgot, she scrawled down everything she had seen on that sign: ORGANIC INDUSTRIES and ETHANOL PLANT #4 and FREEMAN, IOWA and CLOSED UNTIL FURTHER NOTICE.

Okay, now she knew where they had killed him, and where – she was sure – they had buried him, baseball glove and all. What next? If she called the number for Missing and Exploited Children, they would hear a little kid's voice and pay no attention . . . except maybe to give her telephone number to the police, who would probably have her arrested for trying to prank on people who were already sad and unhappy. She thought of her mother next, but with Momo sick and getting ready to die, it was out of the question. Mom had enough to worry about without this.

Abra got up, went to the window, and stared out at her street, at the Lickety-Split convenience store on the corner (which the older kids called the Lickety-Spliff, because of all the dope that got smoked behind it, where the Dumpsters were), and the White Mountains poking up at a clear blue late summer sky. She had begun to rub her mouth, an anxiety tic her parents were trying to break her of, but they weren't here, so boo on that. Boo all *over* that.

Dad's right downstairs.

She didn't want to tell him, either. Not because he had to finish his book, but because he wouldn't want to get involved in something like this even if he believed her. Abra didn't have to read his mind to know that.

So who?

Before she could think of the logical answer, the world beyond her window began to turn, as if it were mounted on a gigantic disc. A low cry escaped her and she clutched at the sides of the window, bunching the curtains in her fists. This had happened before, always without warning, and she was terrified each time it did, because it was like having a seizure. She was no longer in her own body, she was far-*being* instead of far-*seeing*, and what if she couldn't get back?

The turntable slowed, then stopped. Now instead of being in her bedroom, she was in a supermarket. She knew because ahead of her was the meat counter. Over it (this sign easy to read, thanks to bright fluorescents) was a promise: AT SAM'S, EVERY CUT IS A BLUE RIBBON **COWBOY** CUT! For a moment or two the meat counter drew closer because the turntable had slid her into someone who was walking. Walking and *shopping*. Barry the Chunk? No, not him, although Barry was near; Barry was how she had *gotten* here. Only she had been drawn away from him by someone much more powerful. Abra could see a cart loaded with groceries at the bottom of her vision. Then the forward movement stopped and there was this sensation, this

(*rummaging prying*)

crazy feeling of someone INSIDE HER, and Abra suddenly understood that for once she wasn't alone on the turntable. She was looking toward a meat counter at the end of a supermarket aisle, and the other person was looking out her window at Richland Court and the White Mountains beyond.

Panic exploded inside her; it was as if gasoline had been poured on a fire. Not a sound escaped her lips, which were pressed together so tightly that her mouth was only a stitch, but inside her head she produced a scream louder than anything of which she would ever have believed herself capable:

(*NO! GET OUT OF MY HEAD!*)

8

When David felt the house rumble and saw the overhead light fixture in his study swaying on its chain, his first thought was

(*Abra*)

that his daughter had had one of her psychic outbursts, though there hadn't been any of that telekinetic crap in years, and never anything like this. As things settled back to normal, his second – and, to his mind, far more reasonable – thought was that he had just experienced his first New Hampshire earthquake. He knew they happened from time to time, but . . . wow!

He got up from his desk (not neglecting to hit Save before he did), and ran into the hall. From the foot of the stairs he called, 'Abra! Did you feel that?'

She came out of her room, looking pale and a little scared. 'Yeah, sorta. I . . . I think I . . .'

'It was an earthquake!' David told her, beaming. 'Your first earthquake! Isn't that neat?'

'Yes,' Abra said, not sounding very thrilled. 'Neat.'

He looked out the living room window and saw people standing on their stoops and lawns. His good friend Matt Renfrew was among them. 'I'm gonna go across the street and talk to Matt, hon. You want to come with?'

'I guess I better finish my math.'

David started toward the front door, then turned to look up at her. 'You're not scared, are you? You don't have to be. It's over.'

Abra only wished it was.

9

Rose the Hat was doing a double shop, because Grampa Flick was feeling poorly again. She saw a few other members of the True in Sam's, and nodded to them. She stopped awhile in canned goods to talk to Barry the Chink, who had his wife's list in one hand. Barry was concerned about Flick.

'He'll bounce back,' Rose said. 'You know Grampa.'

Barry grinned. 'Tougher'n a boiled owl.'

Rose nodded and got her cart rolling again. 'You bet he is.'

Just an ordinary weekday afternoon at the supermarket, and as she took her leave of Barry, she at first mistook what was happening to her for something mundane, maybe low sugar. She was prone to sugar crashes, and usually kept a candybar in her purse. Then she realized someone was inside her head. Someone was *looking*.

Rose had not risen to her position as head of the True Knot by being indecisive. She halted with her cart pointed toward the meat counter (her planned next stop) and immediately leaped into the conduit some nosy and potentially dangerous person had established. Not a member of the True, she would have known any one of them immediately, but not an ordinary rube, either.

No, this was far from ordinary.

The market swung away and suddenly she was looking out at a mountain range. Not the Rockies, she would have recognized those. These were smaller. The Catskills? The Adirondacks? It could have been either, or some other. As for the looker . . . Rose thought it was a child. Almost certainly a girl, and one she had encountered before.

I have to see what she looks like, then I can find her anytime I want to. I have to get her to look in a mir—

But then a thought as loud as a shotgun blast in a closed room

(*NO! GET OUT OF MY HEAD!*)

wiped her mind clean and sent her staggering against shelves of canned soups and vegetables. They went cascading to the floor, rolling everywhere. For a moment or two Rose thought she was going to follow them, swooning like the dewy heroine of a romance novel. Then she was back. The girl had broken the connection, and in rather spectacular fashion.

Was her nose bleeding? She wiped it with her fingers and checked. No. Good.

One of the stockboys came rushing up. 'Are you okay, ma'am?'

'Fine. Just felt a little faint for a second or two. Probably from the tooth extraction I had yesterday. It's passed off now. I've made a mess, haven't I? Sorry. Good thing it was cans instead of bottles.'

'No problem, no problem at all. Would you like to come up front and sit down on the taxi bench?'

'That won't be necessary,' Rose said. And it wasn't, but she was done shopping for the day. She rolled her cart two aisles over and left it there.

10

She had brought her Tacoma (old but reliable) down from the high-country campground west of Sidewinder, and once she was in the cab, she pulled her phone out of her purse and hit speed dial. It rang at the other end just a single time.

'What's up, Rosie-girl?' Crow Daddy.

'We've got a problem.'

Of course it was also an opportunity. A kid with enough in her boiler to set off a blast like that – to not only detect Rose but send her reeling – wasn't just a steamhead but the find of the century. She felt like Captain Ahab, for the first time sighting his great white whale.

'Talk to me.' All business now.

'A little over two years ago. The kid in Iowa. Remember him?'

'Sure.'

'You also remember me telling you we had a looker?'

'Yeah. East Coast. You thought it was probably a girl.'

'It was a girl, all right. She just found me again. I was in Sam's, minding my own business, and then all at once there she was.'

'Why, after all this time?'.

'I don't know and I don't care. But we have to have her, Crow. We *have* to have her.'

'Does she know who you are? Where *we* are?'

Rose had thought about this while walking to the truck. The intruder hadn't seen her, of that much she was sure. The kid had been on the inside looking out. As to what she *had* seen? A supermarket aisle. How many of those were there in America? Probably a million.

'I don't think so, but that's not the important part.'

'Then what is?'

'Remember me telling you she was big steam? *Huge* steam? Well, she's even bigger than that. When I tried to turn it around on her, she blew me out of her head like I was a piece of milkweed fluff. Nothing like that's ever happened to me before. I would have said it was impossible.'

'Is she potential True or potential food?'

'I don't know.' But she did. They needed steam – *stored* steam – a lot more than they needed fresh recruits. Besides, Rose wanted no one in the True with that much power.

'Okay, how do we find her? Any ideas?'

Rose thought of what she'd seen through the girl's eyes before she had been so unceremoniously booted back to Sam's Supermarket in Sidewinder. Not much, but there had been a store . . .

She said, 'The kids call it the Lickety-Spliff.'

'Huh?'

'Nothing, never mind. I need to think about it. But we're going to have her, Crow. We've *got* to have her.'

There was a pause. When he spoke again, Crow sounded cautious. 'The way you're talking, there might be enough to fill a dozen canisters. If, that is, you really don't want to try Turning her.'

Rose gave a distracted, yapping laugh. 'If I'm right, we don't *have* enough canisters to store the steam from this one. If she was a mountain, she'd be Everest.' He made no reply. Rose didn't need to see him or poke into his mind to know he was flabbergasted. 'Maybe we don't have to do either one.'

'I don't follow.'

Of course he didn't. Long-think had never been Crow's specialty. 'Maybe we don't have to Turn her *or* kill her. Think cows.'

'Cows.'

'You can butcher one and get a couple of months' worth of steaks and hamburgers. But if you keep it alive and take care of it, it will give milk for six years. Maybe even eight.'

Silence. Long. She let it stretch. When he replied, he sounded more cautious than ever. 'I've never heard of anything like that. We kill em once we've got the steam or if they've got something we need and they're strong enough to survive the Turn, we Turn em. The way we Turned Andi back in the eighties. Grampa Flick might say different, if you believe him he remembers all the way back to when Henry the Eighth was killing his wives, but I don't think the True has ever tried just holding onto a steamhead. If she's as strong as you say, it could be dangerous.'

Tell me something I don't know. If you'd felt what I did, you'd call me crazy to even think about it. And maybe I am. But . . .

But she was tired of spending so much of her time – the whole family's time – scrambling for nourishment. Of living like tenth-century Gypsies when they should have been living like the kings and queens of creation. Which was what they were.

'Talk to Grampa, if he's feeling better. And Heavy Mary, she's been around almost as long as Flick. Snakebite Andi. She's new, but she's got a good head on her shoulders. Anyone else you think might have valuable input.'

'Jesus, Rosie. I don't know—'

'Neither do I, not yet. I'm still reeling. All I'm asking right now is for you to do some spadework. You are the advance man, after all.'

'Okay . . .'

'Oh, and make sure you talk to Walnut. Ask him what drugs might keep a rube child nice and docile for a long period of time.'

'This girl doesn't sound like much of a rube to me.'

'Oh, she is. A big old fat rube milk-cow.'

Not exactly true. A great big white whale, that's what she is.

Rose ended the call without waiting to see if Crow Daddy had anything else to say. She was the boss, and as far as she was concerned, the discussion was over.

She's a white whale, and I want her.

But Ahab hadn't wanted *his* whale just because Moby would

provide tons of blubber and almost endless barrels of oil, and Rose didn't want the girl because she might – given the right drug cocktails and a lot of powerful psychic soothing – provide a nearly endless supply of steam. It was more personal than that. Turn her? Make her part of the True Knot? Never. The kid had kicked Rose the Hat out of her head as if she were some annoying religious goofball going door-to-door and handing out end-of-the-world tracts. No one had ever given her that kind of bum's rush before. No matter how powerful she was, she had to be taught a lesson.

And I'm just the woman for the job.

Rose the Hat started her truck, pulled out of the supermarket parking lot, and headed for the family-owned Bluebell Campground. It was a really beautiful location, and why not? One of the world's great resort hotels had once stood there.

But of course, the Overlook had burned to the ground long ago.

11

The Renfrews, Matt and Cassie, were the neighborhood's party people, and they decided on the spur of the moment to have an Earthquake Barbecue. They invited everyone on Richland Court, and almost everyone came. Matt got a case of soda, a few bottles of cheap wine, and a beer-ball from the Lickety-Split up the street. It was a lot of fun, and David Stone enjoyed himself tremendously. As far as he could tell, Abra did, too. She hung with her friends Julie and Emma, and he made sure that she ate a hamburger and some salad. Lucy had told him they had to be vigilant about their daughter's eating habits, because she'd reached the age when girls started to be very conscious about their weight and looks – the age at which anorexia or bulimia were apt to show their skinny, starveling faces.

What he didn't notice (although Lucy might have, had she been there) was that Abra wasn't joining in her friends' apparently nonstop gigglefest. And, after eating a bowl of ice cream (a *small* bowl), she asked her father if she could go back across the street and finish her homework.

'Okay,' David said, 'but thank Mr and Mrs Renfrew first.'

This Abra would have done without having to be reminded, but she agreed without saying so.

'You're very welcome, Abby,' Mrs Renfrew said. Her eyes were almost preternaturally bright from three glasses of white wine. 'Isn't this cool? We should have earthquakes more often. Although I was talking to Vicky Fenton – you know the Fentons, on Pond Street? That's just a block over and she said they didn't feel anything. Isn't that *weird*?'

'Sure is,' Abra agreed, thinking that when it came to weird, Mrs Renfrew didn't know the half of it.

12

She finished her homework and was downstairs watching TV with her dad when Mom called. Abra talked to her awhile, then turned the phone over to her father. Lucy said something, and Abra knew what it had been even before Dave glanced at her and said, 'Yeah, she's fine, just blitzed from homework, I think. They give the kids so much now. Did she tell you we had a little earthquake?'

'Going upstairs, Dad,' Abra said, and he gave her an absent wave.

She sat at her desk, turned on her computer, then turned it off again. She didn't want to play Fruit Ninja and she certainly didn't want to IM with anyone. She had to think about what to do, because she had to do *something*.

She put her schoolbooks in her backpack, then looked up and the woman from the supermarket was staring in at her from the window. That was impossible because the window was on the second floor, but she was there. Her skin was unblemished and purest white, her cheekbones high, her dark eyes wide-set and slightly tilted at the corners. Abra thought she might be the most beautiful woman she had ever seen. Also, she realized at once, and without a shadow of a doubt, she was insane. Masses of black hair framed her perfect, somehow arrogant face, and streamed down over her shoulders. Staying in place on this wealth of hair, in spite of the crazy angle at which it was cocked, was a jaunty tophat of scuffed velvet.

She's not really there, and she's not in my head, either. I don't know how I can be seeing her but I am and I don't think she kn—

The madwoman in the darkening window grinned, and when her lips spread apart, Abra saw she only had one tooth on top, a monstrous discolored tusk. She understood it had been the last thing Bradley Trevor had ever seen, and she screamed, screamed as loudly as she could . . . but only inside, because her throat was locked and her vocal cords were frozen.

Abra shut her eyes. When she opened them again, the grinning white-faced woman was gone.

Not there. But she could come. She knows about me and she could come.

In that moment, she realized what she should have known as soon as she saw the abandoned factory. There was really only one person she could call on. Only one who could help her. She closed her eyes again, this time not to hide from a horrible vision looking in at her from the window, but to summon help.

(*TONY, I NEED YOUR DAD! PLEASE, TONY, PLEASE!*)

Still with her eyes shut – but now feeling the warmth of tears on her lashes and cheeks – she whispered, 'Help me, Tony. I'm scared.'

CHAPTER EIGHT
ABRA'S THEORY OF RELATIVITY

1

The last run of the day on *The Helen Rivington* was called the Sunset Cruise, and many evenings when Dan wasn't on shift at the hospice, he took the controls. Billy Freeman, who had made the run roughly twenty-five thousand times during his years as a town employee, was delighted to turn them over.

'You never get tired of it, do you?' he asked Dan once.

'Put it down to a deprived childhood.'

It hadn't been, not really, but he and his mother had moved around a lot after the settlement money ran out, and she had worked a lot of jobs. With no college degree, most of them had been low-paying. She'd kept a roof over their heads and food on the table, but there had never been much extra.

Once – he'd been in high school, the two of them living in Bradenton, not far from Tampa – he'd asked her why she never dated. By then he was old enough to know she was still a very good-looking woman. Wendy Torrance had given him a crooked smile and said, 'One man was enough for me, Danny. Besides, now I've got you.'

'How much did she know about your drinking?' Casey K. had asked him during one of their meetings at the Sunspot. 'You started pretty young, right?'

Dan had needed to give that one some thought. 'Probably more than I knew at the time, but we never talked about it. I think she was afraid to bring it up. Besides, I never got in trouble with the law – not then, anyway – and I graduated high school with honors.' He had smiled grimly at Casey over his coffee cup. 'And of course I never beat her up. I suppose that made a difference.'

Never got that train set, either, but the basic tenet AAs lived by was don't drink and things will get better. They did, too. Now he had the biggest little choo-choo a boy could wish for, and Billy was right, it never got old. He supposed it might in another ten or twenty years, but even then Dan thought he'd probably still offer to drive the last circuit of the day, just to pilot the *Riv* at sunset, out to the turnaround at Cloud Gap. The view was spectacular, and when the Saco was calm (which it usually was once its spring convulsions had subsided), you could see all the colors twice, once above and once below. Everything was silence at the far end of the *Riv*'s run; it was as if God was holding His breath.

The trips between Labor Day and Columbus Day, when the *Riv* shut down for the winter, were the best of all. The tourists were gone, and the few riders were locals, many of whom Dan could now call by name. On weeknights like tonight, there were less than a dozen paying customers. Which was fine by him.

It was fully dark when he eased the *Riv* back into its dock at Teenytown Station. He leaned against the side of the first passenger car with his cap (ENGINEER DAN stitched in red above the bill) tipped back on his head, wishing his handful of riders a very good night. Billy was sitting on a bench, the glowing tip of his cigarette intermittently lighting his face. He had to be nearly seventy, but he looked good, had made a complete recovery from his abdominal surgery two years before, and said he had no plans to retire.

'What would I do?' he'd asked on the single occasion Dan had brought the subject up. 'Retire to that deathfarm where you work? Wait for your pet cat to pay me a visit? Thanks but no thanks.'

When the last two or three riders had ambled on their way, probably in search of dinner, Billy butted his cigarette and joined him. 'I'll put er in the barn. Unless you want to do that, too.'

'No, go right ahead. You've been sitting on your ass long enough. When are you going to give up the smokes, Billy? You know the doctor said they contributed to your little gut problem.'

'I've cut down to almost nothing,' Billy said, but with a telltale downward shift in his gaze. Dan could have found out just how much Billy had cut down – he probably wouldn't even need to touch the guy in order to get that much info – but he didn't. One day in the summer just past, he'd seen a kid wearing a t-shirt with an octagonal road sign printed on it. Instead of STOP, the sign said

TMI. When Danny asked him what it meant, the kid had given him a sympathetic smile he probably reserved strictly for gentlemen of a fortyish persuasion. 'Too much information,' he'd said. Dan thanked him, thinking: *Story of my life, young fellow.*

Everyone had secrets. This he had known from earliest childhood. Decent people deserved to keep theirs, and Billy Freeman was decency personified.

'Want to go for a coffee, Danno? You got time? Won't take me ten minutes to put this bitch to bed.'

Dan touched the side of the engine lovingly. 'Sure, but watch your mouth. This is no bitch, this is a la—'

That was when his head exploded.

2

When he came back to himself, he was sprawled on the bench where Billy had been smoking. Billy was sitting beside him, looking worried. Hell, looking scared half to death. He had his phone in one hand, with his finger poised over the buttons.

'Put it away,' Dan said. The words came out in a dusty croak. He cleared his throat and tried again. 'I'm okay.'

'You sure? Jesus Christ, I thought you was havin a stroke. I thought it for sure.'

That's what it felt like.

For the first time in years Dan thought of Dick Hallorann, the Overlook Hotel's chef extraordinaire back in the day. Dick had known almost at once that Jack Torrance's little boy shared his own talent. Dan wondered now if Dick might still be alive. Almost certainly not; he'd been pushing sixty back then.

'Who's Tony?' Billy asked.

'Huh?'

'You said "Please, Tony, please." Who's Tony?'

'A guy I used to know back in my drinking days.' As an improvisation it wasn't much, but it was the first thing to come into his still-dazed mind. 'A good friend.'

Billy looked at the lighted rectangle of his cell a few seconds longer, then slowly folded the phone and put it away. 'You know, I don't believe that for a minute. I think you had one of your flashes. Like on the day you found out about my . . .' He tapped his stomach.

'Well . . .'

Billy raised a hand. 'Say nummore. As long as you're okay, that is. And as long as it isn't somethin bad about me. Because I'd want to know if it was. I don't s'pose that's true of everyone, but it is with me.'

'Nothing about you.' Dan stood up and was pleased to discover his legs held him just fine. 'But I'm going to take a raincheck on that coffee, if you don't mind.'

'Not a bit. You need to go back to your place and lie down. You're still pale. Whatever it was, it hit you hard.' Billy glanced at the *Riv*. 'Glad it didn't happen while you were up there in the peak-seat, rolling along at forty.'

'Tell me about it,' Dan said.

3

He crossed Cranmore Avenue to the Rivington House side, meaning to take Billy's advice and lie down, but instead of turning in at the gate giving on the big old Victorian's flower-bordered walk, he decided to stroll a little while. He was getting his wind back now – getting *himself* back – and the night air was sweet. Besides, he needed to consider what had just happened, and very carefully.

Whatever it was, it hit you hard.

That made him think again of Dick Hallorann, and of all the things he had never told Casey Kingsley. Nor would he. The harm he had done to Deenie – and to her son, he supposed, simply by doing nothing – was lodged deep inside, like an impacted wisdom tooth, and there it would stay. But at five, Danny Torrance had been the one harmed – along with his mother, of course – and his father had not been the only culprit. About that Dick *had* done something. If not, Dan and his mother would have died in the Overlook. Those old things were still painful to think about, still bright with the childish primary colors of fear and horror. He would have preferred never to think of them again, but now he had to. Because . . . well . . .

Because everything that goes around comes around. Maybe it's luck or maybe it's fate, but either way, it comes back around. What was it Dick said that day he gave me the lockbox? When the pupil is ready, the teacher will appear. Not that I'm equipped to teach anyone anything, except maybe that if you don't take a drink, you won't get drunk.

He'd reached the end of the block; now he turned around and headed back. He had the sidewalk entirely to himself. It was eerie how fast Frazier emptied out once the summer was over, and that made him think of the way the Overlook had emptied out. How quickly the little Torrance family had had the place entirely to themselves.

Except for the ghosts, of course. *They* never left.

4

Halloran had told Danny he was headed to Denver, and from there he'd fly south to Florida. He had asked if Danny would like to help him down to the Overlook's parking lot with his bags, and Danny had carried one to the cook's rental car. Just a little thing, hardly more than a briefcase, but he'd needed to use both hands to tote it. When the bags were safely stowed in the trunk and they were sitting in the car, Halloran had put a name to the thing in Danny Torrance's head, the thing his parents only half believed in.

You got a knack. Me, I've always called it the shining. That's what my grandmother called it, too. Get you kinda lonely, thinkin you were the only one?

Yes, he had been lonely, and yes, he had believed he was the only one. Halloran had disabused him of that notion. In the years since, Dan had run across a lot of people who had, in the cook's words, 'a little bit of shine to them'. Billy, for one.

But never anyone like the girl who had screamed into his head tonight. It had felt like that cry might tear him apart.

Had *he* been that strong? He thought he had been, or almost. On closing day at the Overlook, Halloran had told the troubled little boy sitting beside him to . . . what had he said?

He said to give him a blast.

Dan had arrived back at Rivington House and was standing outside the gate. The first leaves had begun to fall, and an evening breeze whisked them around his feet.

And when I asked him what I should think about, he told me anything. 'Just think it hard,' he said. So I did, but at the last second I softened it, at least a little. If I hadn't, I think I might have killed him. He jerked back – no, he slammed back – and bit his lip. I remember the blood. He called me a pistol. And later, he asked about Tony. My invisible friend. So I told him.

Tony was back, it seemed, but he was no longer Dan's friend. Now he was the friend of a little girl named Abra. She was in trouble just as Dan had been, but grown men who sought out little girls attracted attention and suspicion. He had a good life here in Frazier, and he felt it was one he deserved after all the lost years.

But . . .

But when he needed Dick – at the Overlook, and later, in Florida, when Mrs Massey had come back – Dick had come. In AA, people called that kind of thing a Twelfth Step call. Because when the pupil was ready, the teacher would appear.

On several occasions, Dan had gone with Casey Kingsley and some other guys in the Program to pay Twelfth Step calls on men who were over their heads in drugs or booze. Sometimes it was friends or bosses who asked for this service; more often it was relatives who had exhausted every other resource and were at their wits' end. They'd had a few successes over the years, but most visits ended with slammed doors or an invitation for Casey and his friends to stick their sanctimonious, quasireligious bullshit up their asses. One fellow, a meth-addled veteran of George Bush's splendid Iraq adventure, had actually waved a pistol at them. Heading back from the Chocura hole-in-the-wall shack where the vet was denned up with his terrified wife, Dan had said, '*That* was a waste of time.'

'It would be if we did it for them,' Casey said, 'but we don't. We do it for us. You like the life you're living, Danny-boy?' It wasn't the first time he had asked this question, and it wouldn't be the last.

'Yes.' No hesitation on that score. Maybe he wasn't the president of General Motors or doing nude love scenes with Kate Winslet, but in Dan's mind, he had it all.

'Think you earned it?'

'No,' Dan said, smiling. 'Not really. Can't earn this.'

'So what was it that got you back to a place where you like getting up in the morning? Was it luck or grace?'

He'd believed that Casey wanted him to say it was grace, but during the sober years he had learned the sometimes uncomfortable habit of honesty. 'I don't know.'

'That's okay, because when your back's against the wall, there's no difference.'

5

'Abra, Abra, Abra,' he said as he walked up the path to Rivington House. 'What have you gotten yourself into, girl? And what are you getting *me* into?'

He was thinking he'd have to try to get in touch with her by using the shining, which was never completely reliable, but when he stepped into his turret room, he saw that wouldn't be necessary. Written neatly on his blackboard was this:

cadabra@nhml.com

He puzzled over her screen name for a few seconds, then got it and laughed. 'Good one, kid, good one.'

He powered up his laptop. A moment later, he was looking at a blank email form. He typed in her address and then sat watching the blinking cursor. How old was she? As far as he could calculate by their few previous communications, somewhere between a wise twelve and a slightly naïve sixteen. Probably closer to the former. And here he was, a man old enough to have salt speckles in his stubble if he skipped shaving. Here he was, getting ready to start compu-chatting with her. *To Catch a Predator*, anyone?

Maybe it's nothing. It could be; she's just a kid, after all.

Yes, but one who was damn scared. Plus, he was curious about her. Had been for some time. The same way, he supposed, that Hallorann had been curious about him.

I could use a little bit of grace right now. And a whole lot of luck.

In the SUBJECT box at the top of the email form, Dan wrote *Hello Abra*. He dropped the cursor, took a deep breath, and typed four words: *Tell me what's wrong.*

6

On the following Saturday afternoon, Dan was sitting in bright sunshine on one of the benches outside the ivy-covered stone building that housed the Anniston Public Library. He had a copy of the *Union-Leader* open in front of him, and there were words on the page, but he had no idea what they said. He was too nervous.

Promptly at two o'clock, a girl in jeans rode up on her bike and lodged it in the rack at the foot of the lawn. She gave him a wave and a big smile.

So. Abra. As in Cadabra.

She was tall for her age, most of that height in her legs. Masses of curly blond hair were held back in a thick ponytail that looked ready to rebel and spray everywhere. The day was a bit chilly, and she was wearing a light jacket with ANNISTON CYCLONES screen-printed on the back. She grabbed a couple of books that were bungee-corded to the rear bumper of her bike, then ran up to him, still with that open smile. Pretty but not beautiful. Except for her wide-set blue eyes. *They* were beautiful.

'Uncle Dan! Gee, it's good to see you!' And she gave him a hearty smack on the cheek. That hadn't been in the script. Her confidence in his basic okayness was terrifying.

'Good to see you, too, Abra. Sit down.'

He had told her they would have to be careful, and Abra – a child of her culture – understood at once. They had agreed that the best thing would be to meet in the open, and there were few places in Anniston more open than the front lawn of the library, which was situated near the middle of the small downtown district.

She was looking at him with frank interest, perhaps even hunger.

He could feel something like tiny fingers patting lightly at the inside of his head.

(*where's Tony?*)

Dan touched a finger to his temple.

Abra smiled, and that completed her beauty, turned her into a girl who would break hearts in another four or five years.

(*HI TONY!*)

That was loud enough to make him wince, and he thought again of how Dick Halloran had recoiled behind the wheel of his rental car, his eyes going momentarily blank.

(*we need to talk out loud*)

(*okay yes*)

'I'm your father's cousin, okay? Not really an uncle, but that's what you call me.'

'Right, right, you're Uncle Dan. We'll be fine as long as my mother's best friend doesn't come along. Her name's Gretchen Silverlake. I think she knows our whole family tree, and there isn't very much of it.'

Oh, great, Dan thought. *The nosy best friend.*

'It's okay,' Abra said. 'Her older son's on the football team, and she never misses a Cyclones game. Almost *everyone* goes to the game, so stop worrying that someone will think you're—'

She finished the sentence with a mental picture – a cartoon, really. It blossomed in an instant, crude but clear. A little girl in a dark alley was being menaced by a hulking man in a trenchcoat. The little girl's knees were knocking together, and just before the picture faded, Dan saw a word balloon form over her head: *Eeek, a freak!*

'Actually not that funny.'

He made his own picture and sent it back to her: Dan Torrance in jail-stripes, being led away by two big policemen. He had never tried anything like this, and it wasn't as good as hers, but he was delighted to find he could do it at all. Then, almost before he knew what was happening, she appropriated his picture and made it her own. Dan pulled a gun from his waistband, pointed it at one of the cops, and pulled the trigger. A handkerchief with the word POW! on it shot from the barrel of the gun.

Dan stared at her, mouth open.

Abra put fisted hands to her mouth and giggled. 'Sorry. Couldn't resist. We could do this all afternoon, couldn't we? And it would be fun.'

He guessed it would also be a relief. She had spent years with a splendid ball but no one to play catch with. And of course it was the same with him. For the first time since childhood – since Hallorann – he was sending as well as receiving.

'You're right, it would be, but now's not the time. You need to run through this whole thing again. The email you sent only hit the high spots.'

'Where should I start?'

'How about with your last name? Since I'm your honorary uncle, I probably should know.'

That made her laugh. Dan tried to keep a straight face and couldn't. God help him, he liked her already.

'I'm Abra Rafaella Stone,' she said. Suddenly the laughter was gone. 'I just hope the lady in the hat never finds that out.'

7

They sat together on the bench outside the library for forty-five minutes, with the autumn sun warm on their faces. For the first time in her life Abra felt unconditional pleasure – joy, even – in the talent that had always puzzled and sometimes terrified her. Thanks to this man, she even had a name for it: the shining. It was a good name, a comforting name, because she had always thought of it as a dark thing.

There was plenty to talk about – volumes of notes to compare – and they had hardly gotten started when a stout fiftyish woman in a tweed skirt came over to say hello. She looked at Dan with curiosity, but not *untoward* curiosity.

'Hi, Mrs Gerard. This is my uncle Dan. I had Mrs Gerard for Language Arts last year.'

'Pleased to meet you, ma'am. Dan Torrance.'

Mrs Gerard took his offered hand and gave it a single no-nonsense pump. Abra could feel Dan – *Uncle* Dan – relaxing. That was good.

'Are you in the area, Mr Torrance?'

'Just down the road, in Frazier. I work in the hospice there. Helen Rivington House?'

'Ah. That's good work you do. Abra, have you read *The Fixer* yet? The Malamud novel I recommended?'

Abra looked glum. 'It's on my Nook – I got a gift card for my birthday – but I haven't started it yet. It looks hard.'

'You're ready for hard things,' Mrs Gerard said. 'More than ready. High school will be here sooner than you think, and then college. I suggest you get started today. Nice to have met you, Mr Torrance. You have an extremely smart niece. But Abra – with brains comes responsibility.' She tapped Abra's temple to emphasize this point, then mounted the library steps and went inside.

She turned to Dan. 'That wasn't so bad, was it?'

'So far, so good,' Dan agreed. 'Of course, if she talks to your parents . . .'

'She won't. Mom's in Boston, helping with my momo. She's got cancer.'

'I'm very sorry to hear it. Is Momo your'

(*grandmother*)

(*great-grandmother*)

'Besides,' Abra said, 'we're not really lying about you being my uncle. In science last year, Mr Staley told us that all humans share the same genetic plan. He said that the things that make us different are very small things. Did you know that we share something like ninety-nine percent of our genetic makeup with *dogs*?'

'No,' Dan said, 'but it explains why Alpo has always looked so good to me.'

She laughed. 'So you *could* be my uncle or cousin or whatever. All I'm saying.'

'That's Abra's theory of relativity, is it?'

'I guess so. And do we need the same color eyes or hairline to be related? We've got something else in common that hardly anyone has. That makes us a special kind of relatives. Do you think it's a gene, like the one for blue eyes or red hair? And by the way, did you know that Scotland has the highest ratio of people with red hair?'

'I didn't,' Dan said. 'You're a font of information.'

Her smile faded a little. 'Is that a put-down?'

'Not at all. I guess the shining might be a gene, but I really don't think so. I think it's unquantifiable.'

'Does that mean you can't figure it out? Like God and heaven and stuff like that?'

'Yes.' He found himself thinking of Charlie Hayes, and all those before and after Charlie whom he'd seen out of this world in his Doctor Sleep persona. Some people called the moment of death *passing on*. Dan liked that, because it seemed just about right. When you saw men and women pass on before your eyes – leaving the Teenytown people called reality for some Cloud Gap of an afterlife – it changed your way of thinking. For those in mortal extremis, it was the world that was passing on. In those gateway moments, Dan had always felt in the presence of some not-quite-seen enormity. They slept, they woke, they went *somewhere*. They went on. He'd had reason to believe that, even as a child.

'What are you thinking?' Abra asked. 'I can see it, but I don't understand it. And I want to.'

'I don't know how to explain it,' he said.

'It was partly about the ghostie people, wasn't it? I saw them once, on the little train in Frazier. It was a dream, but I think it was real.'

His eyes widened. 'Did you really?'

'Yes. I don't think they wanted to hurt me – they just looked at me – but they were kind of scary. I think maybe they were people who rode the train in olden days. Have you seen ghostie people? You have, haven't you?'

'Yes, but not for a very long time.' And some that were a lot more than ghosts. Ghosts didn't leave residue on toilet seats and shower curtains. 'Abra, how much do your parents know about your shine?'

'My dad thinks it's gone except for a few things – like me calling from camp because I knew Momo was sick – and he's glad. My mom knows it's still there, because sometimes she'll ask me to help her find something she's lost – last month it was her car keys, she left them on Dad's worktable in the garage – but she doesn't know how *much* is still there. They don't talk about it anymore.' She paused. 'Momo knows. She's not scared of it like Mom and Dad, but she told me I have to be careful. Because if people found out—' She made a comic face, rolling her eyes and poking her tongue out the corner of her mouth. 'Eeek, a freak. You know?'

(*yes*)

She smiled gratefully. 'Sure you do.'

'Nobody else?'

'Well . . . Momo said I should talk to Dr John, because he already knew about some of the stuff. He, um, saw something I did with spoons when I was just a little kid. I kind of hung them on the ceiling.'

'This wouldn't by chance be John Dalton, would it?'

Her face lit up. 'You know him?'

'As a matter of fact, I do. I found something once for *him*. Something he lost.'

(*a watch!*)

(*that's right*)

'I don't tell him everything,' Abra said. She looked uneasy. 'I sure didn't tell him about the baseball boy, and I'd *never* tell him about the woman in the hat. Because he'd tell my folks, and they've got a lot on their minds already. Besides, what could they do?'

'Let's just file that away for now. Who's the baseball boy?'

'Bradley Trevor. Brad. Sometimes he used to turn his hat around and call it a rally cap. Do you know what that is?'

Dan nodded.

'He's dead. *They* killed him. But they hurt him first. They hurt him so *bad*.' Her lower lip began to tremble, and all at once she looked closer to nine than almost thirteen.

(*don't cry Abra we can't afford to attract*)

(*I know, I know*)

She lowered her head, took several deep breaths, and looked up at him again. Her eyes were overbright, but her mouth had stopped trembling. 'I'm okay,' she said. 'Really. I'm just glad not to be alone with this inside my head.'

8

He listened carefully as she described what she remembered of her initial encounter with Bradley Trevor two years ago. It wasn't much.

The clearest image she retained was of many crisscrossing flashlight beams illuminating him as he lay on the ground. And his screams. She remembered those.

'They had to light him up because they were doing some kind of operation,' Abra said. 'That's what they called it, anyway, but all they were really doing was torturing him.'

She told him about finding Bradley again on the back page of *The Anniston Shopper*, with all the other missing children. How she had touched his picture to see if she could find out about him.

'Can you do that?' she asked. 'Touch things and get pictures in your head? Find things out?'

'Sometimes. Not always. I used to be able to do it more – and more reliably – when I was a kid.'

'Do you think I'll grow out of it? I wouldn't mind that.' She paused, thinking. 'Except I sort of would. It's hard to explain.'

'I know what you mean. It's our thing, isn't it? What we can do.'

Abra smiled.

'You're pretty sure you know where they killed this boy?'

'Yes, and they buried him there. They even buried his baseball glove.' Abra handed him a piece of notebook paper. It was a copy, not the original. She would have been embarrassed for anyone to see how she had written the names of the boys in 'Round Here, not just once but over and over again. Even the *way* they had been written now seemed all wrong, those big fat letters that were supposed to express not love but *luv*.

'Don't get bent out of shape about it,' Dan said absently, studying what she'd printed on the sheet. 'I had a thing for Stevie Nicks when I was your age. Also for Ann Wilson, of Heart. You've probably never even heard of her, she's old-school, but I used to daydream about inviting her to one of the Friday night dances at Glenwood Junior High. How's that for stupid?'

She was staring at him, openmouthed.

'Stupid but normal. Most normal thing in the world, so cut yourself some slack. And I wasn't peeking, Abra. It was just there. Kind of jumped out in my face.'

'Oh God.' Abra's cheeks had gone bright red. 'This is going to take some getting used to, isn't it?'

'For both of us, kiddo.' He looked back down at the sheet.

NO TRESPASSING BY ORDER OF THE CANTON COUNTY
SHERIFF'S DEPARTMENT

ORGANIC INDUSTRIES
ETHANOL PLANT #4
FREEMAN, IOWA

CLOSED UNTIL FURTHER NOTICE

'You got this by . . . what? Watching it over and over? Rerunning
it like a movie?'

'The NO TRESPASSING sign was easy, but the stuff about
Organic Industries and the ethanol plant, yeah. Can't you do that?'

'I never tried. Maybe once, but probably not anymore.'

'I found Freeman, Iowa, on the computer,' she said. 'And when
I ran Google Earth, I could see the factory. Those places are really
there.'

Dan's thoughts returned to John Dalton. Others in the Program
had talked about Dan's peculiar ability to find things; John never
had. Not surprising, really. Doctors took a vow of confidentiality
similar to the one in AA, didn't they? Which in John's case made
it a kind of double coverage.

Abra was saying, 'You could call Bradley Trevor's parents, couldn't
you? Or the sheriff's office in Canton County? They wouldn't
believe me, but they'd believe a grown-up.'

'I suppose I could.' But of course a man who knew where the
body was buried would automatically go to the head of the suspect
list, so if he did it, he would have to be very, very careful about the
way he did it.

Abra, the trouble you're getting me into.

'Sorry,' she whispered.

He put his hand over hers and gave it a gentle squeeze. 'Don't
be. That's one *you* weren't supposed to hear.'

She straightened. 'Oh God, here comes Yvonne Stroud. She's in
my class.'

Dan pulled his hand back in a hurry. He saw a plump, brown-haired girl about Abra's age coming up the sidewalk. She was wearing a backpack and carrying a looseleaf notebook curled against her chest. Her eyes were bright and inquisitive.

'She'll want to know everything about you,' Abra said. 'I mean *everything*. And she *talks*.'

Uh-oh.

Dan looked at the oncoming girl.

(*we're not interesting*)

'Help me, Abra,' he said, and felt her join in. Once they were together, the thought instantly gained depth and strength.

(*WE'RE NOT A BIT INTERESTING*)

'That's good,' Abra said. 'A little more. Do it with me. Like singing.'

(*YOU HARDLY SEE US WE'RE NOT INTERESTING AND BESIDES YOU HAVE BETTER THINGS TO DO*)

Yvonne Stroud hurried along the walk, flipping one hand to Abra in a vague hello gesture but not slowing down. She ran up the library steps and disappeared inside.

'I'll be a monkey's uncle,' Dan said.

She looked at him seriously. 'According to Abra's theory of relativity, you really could be. Very similar—' She sent a picture of pants flapping on a clothesline.

(*jeans*)

Then they were both laughing.

9

Dan made her go over the turntable thing three times, wanting to make sure he was getting it right.

'You never did that, either?' Abra asked. 'The far-seeing thing?'

'Astral projection? No. Does it happen to you a lot?'

'Only once or twice.' She considered. 'Maybe three times. Once I went into a girl who was swimming in the river. I was looking at her from the bottom of our backyard. I was nine or ten. I don't know why it happened, she wasn't in trouble or anything, just swimming with her friends. That one lasted the longest. It went on for at least three minutes. Is astral projection what you call it? Like outer space?'

'It's an old term, from séances back a hundred years ago, and probably not a very good one. All it means is an out-of-body experience.' If you could label anything like that at all. 'But – I want to make sure I've got this straight – the swimming girl didn't go into you?'

Abra shook her head emphatically, making her ponytail fly. 'She didn't even know I was there. The only time it worked both ways was with that woman. The one who wears the hat. Only I didn't see the hat *then*, because I was inside her.'

Dan used one finger to describe a circle. 'You went into her, she went into you.'

'Yes.' Abra shivered. 'She was the one who cut Bradley Trevor until he was dead. When she smiles she has one big long tooth on top.'

Something about the hat struck a chord, something that made him think of Deenie from Wilmington. Because Deenie had worn a hat? Nope, at least not that he remembered; he'd been pretty blitzed. It probably meant nothing – sometimes the brain made phantom associations, that was all, especially when it was under stress, and the truth (little as he liked to admit it) was that Deenie was never far from his thoughts. Something as random as a display of cork-soled sandals in a store window could bring her to mind.

'Who's Deenie?' Abra asked. Then she blinked rapidly and drew back a little, as if Dan had suddenly flapped a hand in front of her eyes. 'Oops. Not supposed to go there, I guess. Sorry.'

'It's okay,' he said. 'Let's go back to your hat woman. When you saw her later – in your window – that wasn't the same?'

'No. I'm not even sure that was a shining. I think it was a *remembering*, from when I saw her hurting the boy.'

'So she didn't see you then, either. She's *never* seen you.' If the woman was as dangerous as Abra believed, this was important.

'No. I'm sure she hasn't. But she wants to.' She looked at him, her eyes wide, her mouth trembling again. 'When the turntable thing happened, she was thinking *mirror*. She wanted me to look at myself. She wanted to use my eyes to see me.'

'What *did* she see through your eyes? Could she find you that way?'

(turn, world)

As it did, she felt the maddening flutter in her head first diminish and then cease as the little girl was rotated back to wherever she came from.

Except that's not right, and this is far too serious for you to indulge in the luxury of lying to yourself. You *came to* her. *And walked right into a trap. Why? Because in spite of all you knew, you underestimated.*

Rose opened her eyes, sat up, and swung her feet onto the carpet. One of them struck the empty canister and she kicked it away. The Sidewinder t-shirt she had pulled on before lying down was damp; she reeked of sweat. It was a piggy smell, entirely unattractive. She looked unbelievingly at her hand, which was scraped and bruised and swelling. Her fingernails were going from purple to black, and she guessed she might lose at least two of them.

'But I *didn't* know,' she said. 'There was no way I could.' She hated the whine she heard in her voice. It was the voice of a querulous old woman. 'No way at all.'

She had to get out of this goddam camper. It might be the biggest, luxiest one in the world, but right now it felt the size of a coffin. She made her way to the door, holding onto things to keep her balance. She glanced at the clock on the dashboard before she went out. Ten to two. Everything had happened in just twenty minutes. Incredible.

How much did she find out before I got free of her? How much does she know?

No way of telling for sure, but even a little could be dangerous. The brat had to be taken care of, and soon.

Rose stepped out into the pale early moonlight and took half a dozen long, steadying breaths of fresh air. She began to feel a little better, a little more herself, but she couldn't let go of that *fluttering* sensation. The feeling of having someone else inside her – a rube, no less – looking at her private things. The pain had been bad, and the surprise of being trapped that way was worse, but the worst thing of all was the humiliation and sense of violation. She had been *stolen* from.

You are going to pay for that, princess. You just messed in with the wrong bitch.

A shape was moving toward her. Rose had settled on the top step of her RV, but now she stood up, tense, ready for anything. Then the shape got closer and she saw it was Crow. He was dressed in pajama bottoms and slippers.

'Rose, I think you better—' He stopped. 'What the hell happened to your hand?'

'Never mind my fucking hand,' she snapped. 'What are you doing here at two in the morning? Especially when you knew I was apt to be busy?'

'It's Grampa Flick,' Crow said. 'Apron Annie says he's dying.'

CHAPTER ELEVEN
THOME 25

1

Instead of pine-scented air freshener and Alcazar cigars, Grampa Flick's Fleetwood this morning smelled of shit, disease, and death. It was also crowded. There were at least a dozen members of the True Knot present, some gathered around the old man's bed, many more sitting or standing in the living room, drinking coffee. The rest were outside. Everyone looked stunned and uneasy. The True wasn't used to death among their own.

'Clear out,' Rose said. 'Crow and Nut — you stay.'

'Look at him,' Petty the Chink said in a trembling voice. 'Them spots! And 'e's cycling like crazy, Rose! Oh, this is 'orrible!'

'Go on,' Rose said. She spoke gently and gave Petty a comforting squeeze on the shoulder when what she felt like doing was kicking her fat Cockney ass right out the door. She was a lazy gossip, good for nothing but warming Barry's bed, and probably not very good at that. Rose guessed that nagging was more Petty's specialty. When she wasn't scared out of her mind, that is.

'Come on, folks,' Crow said. 'If he *is* going to die, he doesn't need to do it with an audience.'

'He'll pull through,' Harpman Sam said. 'Tougher'n a boiled owl, that's Grampa Flick.' But he put his arm around Baba the Russian, who looked devastated, and hugged her tight against him for a moment.

They got moving, some taking a last look back over their shoulders before going down the steps to join the others. When it was just the three of them, Rose approached the bed.

Grampa Flick stared up at her without seeing her. His lips had pulled back from his gums. Great patches of his fine white hair had fallen out on the pillowcase, giving him the look of a distempered dog. His eyes were huge and wet and filled with pain. He was naked except for a pair of boxer shorts, and his scrawny body was stippled with red marks that looked like pimples or insect bites.

She turned to Walnut and said, 'What in hell are those?'

'Koplik's spots,' he said. 'That's what they look like to me, anyway. Although Koplik's are usually just inside the mouth.'

'Talk English.'

Nut ran his hands through his thinning hair. 'I think he's got the measles.'

Rose gaped in shock, then barked laughter. She didn't want to stand here listening to this shit; she wanted some aspirin for her hand, which sent out a pain-pulse with every beat of her heart. She kept thinking about how the hands of cartoon characters looked when they got whopped with a mallet. 'We don't catch rube diseases!'

'Well . . . we never used to.'

She stared at him furiously. She wanted her hat, she felt naked without it, but it was back in the EarthCruiser.

Nut said, 'I can only tell you what I see, which is red measles, also known as rubeola.'

A rube disease called rubeola. How too fucking perfect.

'That is just . . . *horseshit!*'

He flinched, and why not? She sounded strident even to herself, but . . . ah, Jesus God, *measles*? The oldest member of the True Knot dying of a childhood disease even children didn't catch anymore?

'That baseball-playing kid from Iowa had a few spots on him, but I never thought . . . because yeah, it's like you say. We don't catch their diseases.'

'He was *years* ago!'

'I know. All I can think is that it was in the steam, and it kind of hibernated. There are diseases that do that, you know. Lie passive, sometimes for years, then break out.'

'Maybe with rubes!' She kept coming back to that.

Walnut only shook his head.

'If Gramp's got it, why don't we all have it? Because those childhood diseases – chicken pox, measles, mumps – run through rube kids like shit through a goose. It doesn't make sense.' Then she turned to Crow Daddy and promptly contradicted herself. 'What the fuck were you thinking when you let a bunch of them in to stand around and breathe his air?'

Crow just shrugged, his eyes never leaving the shivering old man on the bed. Crow's narrow, handsome face was pensive.

'Things change,' Nut said. 'Just because we had immunity to rube diseases fifty or a hundred years ago doesn't mean we have it now. For all we know, this could be part of a natural process.'

'Are you telling me there's anything natural about *that*?' She pointed to Grampa Flick.

'A single case doesn't make an epidemic,' Nut said, 'and it *could* be something else. But if this happens again, we'll have to put whoever it happens to in complete quarantine.'

'Would it help?'

He hesitated a long time. 'I don't know. Maybe we do have it, all of us. Maybe it's like an alarm clock set to go off or dynamite on a timer. According to the latest scientific thinking, that's sort of how rubes age. They go along and go along, pretty much the same, and then something turns off in their genes. The wrinkles start showing up and all at once they need canes to walk with.'

Crow had been watching Grampa. 'There he goes. *Fuck*.'

Grampa Flick's skin was turning milky. Then translucent. As it moved toward complete transparency, Rose could see his liver, the shriveled gray-black bags of his lungs, the pulsing red knot of his heart. She could see his veins and arteries like the highways and turnpikes on her in-dash GPS. She could see the optic nerves that connected his eyes to his brain. They looked like ghostly strings.

Then he came back. His eyes moved, caught Rosie's, held them. He reached out and took her unhurt hand. Her first impulse was to pull away – if he had what Nut said he had, he was contagious – but what the hell. If Nut was right, they had all been exposed.

'Rose,' he whispered. 'Don't leave me.'

'I won't.' She sat down beside him on the bed, her fingers entwined in his. 'Crow?'

'Yes, Rose.'

'The package you had sent to Sturbridge – they'll hold it, won't they?'

'Sure.'

'All right, we'll see this through. But we can't afford to wait too long. The little girl is a lot more dangerous than I thought.' She sighed. 'Why do problems always come in bunches?'

'Did she do that to your hand, somehow?'

That was a question she didn't want to answer directly. 'I won't be able to go with you, because she knows me now.' *Also*, she thought but didn't say, *because if this is what Walnut thinks it is, the rest will need me here to play Mother Courage.* 'But we have to have her. It's more important than ever.'

'Because?'

'If she's had the measles, she'll have the rube immunity to catching it again. That might make her steam useful in all sorts of ways.'

'The kids get vaccinated against all that crap now,' Crow said.

Rose nodded. 'That could work, too.'

Grampa Flick once more began to cycle. It was hard to watch, but Rose made herself do it. When she could no longer see the old fellow's organs through his fragile skin, she looked at Crow and held up her bruised and scraped hand.

'Also . . . she needs to be taught a lesson.'

2

When Dan woke up in his turret room on Monday, the schedule had once more been wiped from his blackboard and replaced with a message from Abra. At the top was a smiley-face. All the teeth were showing, which gave it a gleeful look.

> She came! I was ready and I hurt her!
> I REALLY DID!!
> She deserves it, so HOORAY!!!
> I need to talk to you, not this way or 'Net.
> Same place as before 3PM

Dan lay back on his bed, covered his eyes, and went looking for her. He found her walking to school with three of her friends, which struck him as dangerous in itself. For the friends as well as

for Abra. He hoped Billy was there and on the job. He also hoped
Billy would be discreet and not get tagged by some zealous
Neighborhood Watch type as a suspicious character.

(*I can come John and I don't leave until tomorrow but it has to be fast
and we have to be careful*)

(*yes okay good*)

3

Dan was once more seated on a bench outside the ivy-covered
Anniston Library when Abra emerged, dressed for school in a red
jumper and snazzy red sneakers. She held a knapsack by one strap.
To Dan she looked as if she'd grown an inch since the last time
he'd seen her.

She waved. 'Hi, Uncle Dan!'

'Hello, Abra. How was school?'

'Great! I got an A on my biology report!'

'Sit down a minute and tell me about it.'

She crossed to the bench, so filled with grace and energy she
almost seemed to dance. Eyes bright, color high: a healthy after-
school teenager with all systems showing green. Everything about
her said ready-steady-go. There was no reason for this to make Dan
feel uneasy, but it did. One very good thing: a nondescript Ford
pickup was parked half a block down, the old guy behind the wheel
sipping a take-out coffee and reading a magazine. Appearing to read
a magazine, at least.

(*Billy?*)

No answer, but he looked up from his magazine for a moment,
and that was enough.

'Okay,' Dan said in a lower voice. 'I want to hear exactly what
happened.'

She told him about the trap she had set, and how well it had
worked. Dan listened with amazement, admiration . . . and that
growing sense of unease. Her confidence in her abilities worried
him. It was a kid's confidence, and the people they were dealing
with weren't kids.

'I just told you to set an alarm,' he said when she had finished.

'This was better. I don't know if I could have gone at her that way if I wasn't pretending to be Daenerys in the *Game of Thrones* books, but I think so. Because she killed the baseball boy and lots of others. Also because . . .' For the first time her smile faltered a little. As she was telling her story, Dan had seen what she would look like at eighteen. Now he saw what she had looked like at nine.

'Because what?'

'She's not human. None of them are. Maybe they were once, but not anymore.' She straightened her shoulders and tossed her hair back. 'But I'm stronger. She knew it, too.'

(*I thought she pushed you away*)

She frowned at him, annoyed, wiped at her mouth, then caught her hand doing it and returned it to her lap. Once it was there, the other one clasped it to keep it still. There was something familiar about this gesture, but why wouldn't there be? He'd seen her do it before. Right now he had bigger things to worry about.

(*next time I'll be ready if there is a next time*)

That might be true. But if there was a next time, the woman in the hat would be ready, too.

(*I only want you to be careful*)

'I will. For sure.' This, of course, was what all kids said in order to placate the adults in their lives, but it still made Dan feel better. A little, anyway. Besides, there was Billy in his F-150 with the faded red paint.

Her eyes were dancing again. 'I found lots of stuff out. That's why I needed to see you.'

'What stuff?'

'Not where she is, I didn't get that far, but I did find . . . see, when she was in my head, I was in hers. Like swapsies, you know? It was full of drawers, like being in the world's biggest library reference room, although maybe I only saw it that way because *she* did. If she had been looking at computer screens in my head, *I* might have seen computer screens.'

'How many of her drawers did you get into?'

'Three. Maybe four. They call themselves the True Knot. Most of them are old, and they really are like vampires. They look for kids like me. And like you were, I guess. Only they don't drink blood, they breathe in the stuff that comes out when the special kids die.' She winced in disgust. 'The more they hurt them before, the stronger that stuff is. They call it steam.'

'It's red, right? Red or reddish-pink?'

He felt sure of this, but Abra frowned and shook her head. 'No, white. A bright white cloud. Nothing red about it. And listen: they can store it! What they don't use they put it in these thermos bottle thingies. But they never have enough. I saw this show once, about sharks? It said they're always on the move, because they never have enough to eat. I think the True Knot is like that.' She grimaced. 'They're naughty, all right.'

White stuff. Not red but white. It still had to be what the old nurse had called the gasp, but a different kind. Because it came from healthy young people instead of old ones dying of almost every disease the flesh was heir to? Because they were what Abra called 'the special kids'? Both?

She was nodding. 'Both, probably.'

'Okay. But the thing that matters most is that they know about you. *She* knows.'

'They're a little scared I might tell someone about them, but not too scared.'

'Because you're just a kid, and no one believes kids.'

'Right.' She blew her bangs off her forehead. 'Momo would believe me, but she's going to die. She's going to your hot spice, Dan. Hospice, I mean. You'll help her, won't you? If you're not in Iowa?'

'All I can. Abra — are they coming for you?'

'Maybe, but if they do it won't be because of what I know. It will be because of what I *am*.' Her happiness was gone now that she was facing this head-on. She rubbed at her mouth again, and when she dropped her hand, her lips were parted in an angry smile. *This girl has a temper*, Dan thought. He could relate to that. He had a temper himself. It had gotten him in trouble more than once.

'*She* won't come, though. That bitch. She knows I know her now, and I'll sense her if she gets close, because we're sort of tied together. But there are others. If they come for me, they'll hurt anyone who gets in their way.'

Abra took his hands in hers, squeezing hard. This worried Dan, but he didn't make her let go. Right now she needed to touch someone she trusted.

'We have to stop them so they can't hurt my daddy, or my mom, or any of my friends. And so they won't kill any more kids.'

For a moment Dan caught a clear picture from her thoughts – not sent, just there in the foreground. It was a collage of photos. Children, dozens of them, under the heading HAVE YOU SEEN ME? She was wondering how many of them had been taken by the True Knot, murdered for their final psychic gasp – the obscene delicacy this bunch lived on – and left in unmarked graves.

'*You have to get that baseball glove.* If I have it, I'll be able to find out where Barry the Chunk is. I know I will. And the rest of them will be where he is. If you can't kill them, at least you can report them to the police. Get me that glove, Dan, *please.*'

'If it's where you say it is, we'll get it. But in the meantime, Abra, you have to watch yourself.'

'I will, but I don't think she'll try sneaking into my head again.' Abra's smile reemerged. In it, Dan saw the take-no-prisoners warrior woman she sometimes pretended to be – Daenerys, or whoever. 'If she does, she'll be sorry.'

Dan decided to let this go. They had been together on this bench as long as he dared. Longer, really. 'I've set up my own security system on your behalf. If you looked into me, I imagine you could find out what it is, but I don't want you to do that. If someone else from this Knot tries to go prospecting in your head – not the woman in the hat, but someone else – they can't find out what you don't know.'

'Oh. Okay.' He could see her thinking that anyone else who tried that would be sorry, too, and this increased his sense of unease.

'Just . . . if you get in a tight place, yell *Billy* with all your might. Got that?'

(*yes the way you once called for your friend Dick*)

He jumped a little. Abra smiled. 'I wasn't peeking; I just—'

'I understand. Now tell me one thing before you go.'

'What?'

'Did you really get an A on your bio report?'

4

At quarter to eight on that Monday evening, Rose got a double break on her walkie. It was Crow. 'Better get over here,' he said. 'It's happening.'

The True was standing around Grampa's RV in a silent circle. Rose (now wearing her hat at its accustomed gravity-defying angle) cut through them, pausing to give Andi a hug, then went up the steps, rapped once, and let herself in. Nut was standing with Big Mo and Apron Annie, Grampa's two reluctant nurses. Crow was sitting on the end of the bed. He stood up when Rose came in. He was showing his age this evening. Lines bracketed his mouth, and there were a few threads of white silk in his black hair.

We need to take steam, Rose thought. *And when this is over, we will.*

Grampa Flick was cycling rapidly now: first transparent, then solid again, then transparent. But each transparency was longer, and more of him disappeared. He knew what was happening, Rose saw. His eyes were wide and terrified; his body writhed with the pain of the changes it was going through. She had always allowed herself to believe, on some deep level of her mind, in the True Knot's immortality. Yes, every fifty or a hundred years or so, someone died – like that big dumb Dutchman, Hands-Off Hans, who had been electrocuted by a falling powerline in an Arkansas windstorm not long after World War II ended, or Katie Patches, who had drowned, or Tommy the Truck – but those were exceptions. Usually the ones who fell were taken down by their own carelessness. So she had always believed. Now she saw she had been as foolish as rube children clinging to their belief in Santa Claus and the Easter Bunny.

He cycled back to solidity, moaning and crying and shivering. 'Make it stop, Rosie-girl, make it stop. It *hurts*—'

Before she could answer – and really, what could she have said? – he was fading again until there was nothing left of him but a sketch of bones and his staring, floating eyes. They were the worst.

Rose tried to contact him with her mind and comfort him that way, but there was nothing to hold onto. Where Grampa Flick had always been – often grumpy, sometimes sweet – there was now only a roaring windstorm of broken images. Rose withdrew from him, shaken. Again she thought, *This can't be happening.*

'Maybe we should put him out of his miz'y,' Big Mo said. She was digging her fingernails into Annie's forearm, but Annie didn't seem to feel it. 'Give him a shot, or something. You got something in your bag, don't you, Nut? You must.'

'What good would it do?' Walnut's voice was hoarse. 'Maybe earlier, but it's going too fast now. He's got no system for any drug to circulate in. If I gave him a hypo in the arm, we'd see it soaking into the bed five seconds later. Best to just let it happen. It won't be long.'

Nor was it. Rose counted four more full cycles. On the fifth, even his bones disappeared. For a moment the eyeballs remained, staring first at her and then rolling to look at Crow Daddy. They hung above the pillow, which was still indented by the weight of his head and stained with Wildroot Cream-Oil hair tonic, of which he seemed to have an endless supply. She thought she remembered Greedy G telling her once that he bought it on eBay. eBay, for fuck's sweet sake!

Then, slowly, the eyes disappeared, too. Except of course they weren't really gone; Rose knew she'd be seeing them in her dreams later tonight. So would the others in attendance at Grampa Flick's deathbed. If they got any sleep at all.

They waited, none of them entirely convinced that the old man wouldn't appear before them again like the ghost of Hamlet's father or Jacob Marley or some other, but there was only the shape of his disappeared head, the stains left by his hair tonic, and the deflated pee- and shit-stained boxers he had been wearing.

Mo burst into wild sobs and buried her head in Apron Annie's generous bosom. Those waiting outside heard, and one voice (Rose would never know whose) began to speak. Another joined in, then a third and a fourth. Soon they were all chanting under the stars, and Rose felt a wild chill go zigzagging up her back. She reached out, found Crow's hand, and squeezed it.

Annie joined in. Mo next, her words muffled. Nut. Then Crow.

Rose the Hat took a deep breath and added her voice to theirs.

Lodsam hanti, *we are the chosen ones.*

Cahanna risone hanti, *we are the fortunate ones.*

Sabbatha hanti, sabbatha hanti, sabbatha hanti.

We are the True Knot, and we endure.

5

Later, Crow joined her in her EarthCruiser. 'You won't be going east, will you?'

'No. You'll be in charge.'

'What do we do now?'

'Mourn him, of course. Unfortunately, we can only give him two days.'

The traditional period was seven: no fucking, no idle talk, no steam. Just meditation. Then a circle of farewell where everyone would step forward and say one memory of Grampa Jonas Flick and give up one object they had from him, or that they associated with him (Rose had already picked hers, a ring with a Celtic design Grampa had given her when this part of America had still been Indian country and she had been known as the Irish Rose). There was never a body when a member of the Tribe died, so the objects of remembrance had to serve the purpose. Those things were wrapped in white linen and buried.

'So my group leaves when? Wednesday night or Thursday morning?'

'Wednesday night.' Rose wanted the girl as soon as possible. 'Drive straight through. And you're positive they'll hold the knockout stuff at the mail drop in Sturbridge?'

'Yes. Set your mind at ease on that.'

My mind won't be at ease until I can look at that little bitch lying in the room right across from mine, drugged to the gills, handcuffed, and full of tasty, suckable steam.

'Who are you taking? Name them off.'

'Me, Nut, Jimmy Numbers, if you can spare him—'

'I can spare him. Who else?'

'Snakebite Andi. If we need to put someone to sleep, she can get it done. And the Chink. Him for sure. He's the best locator we've got now that Grampa's gone. Other than you, that is.'

'By all means take him, but you won't need a locator to find this one,' Rose said. 'That's not going to be the problem. And just one vehicle will be enough. Take Steamhead Steve's Winnebago.'

'Already spoke to him about it.'

She nodded, pleased. 'One other thing. There's a little hole-in-the-wall store in Sidewinder called District X.'

Crow raised his eyebrows. 'The porno palace with the inflatable nurse doll in the window?'

'You know it, I see.' Rose's tone was dry. 'Now listen to me, Daddy.'

Crow listened.

6

Dan and John Dalton flew out of Logan on Tuesday morning just as the sun was rising. They changed planes in Memphis and touched down in Des Moines at 11:15 CDT on a day that felt more like mid-July than late September.

Dan spent the first part of the Boston-to-Memphis leg pretending to sleep so he wouldn't have to deal with the doubts and second thoughts he felt sprouting like weeds in John's mind. Somewhere over upstate New York, pretending ceased and he fell asleep for real. It was John who slept between Memphis and Des Moines, so *that* was all right. And once they were actually in Iowa, rolling toward the town of Freeman in a totally unobtrusive Ford Focus from Hertz, Dan sensed that John had put his doubts to bed. For the time being, at least. What had replaced them was curiosity and uneasy excitement.

'Boys on a treasure hunt,' Dan said. He'd had the longer nap, and so he was behind the wheel. High corn, now more yellow than green, flowed past them on either side.

John jumped a little. 'Huh?'

Dan smiled. 'Isn't that what you were thinking? That we're like boys on a treasure hunt?'

'You're pretty goddam spooky, Daniel.'

'I suppose. I've gotten used to it.' This was not precisely true.

'When did you find out you could read minds?'

'It isn't just mind-reading. The shining's a uniquely variable talent. If it *is* a talent. Sometimes – lots of times – it feels more like a disfiguring birthmark. I'm sure Abra would say the same. As for when I found out . . . I never did. I just always had it. It came with the original equipment.'

'And you drank to blot it out.'

A fat woodchuck trundled with leisurely fearlessness across Route 150. Dan swerved to avoid it and the chuck disappeared into the corn, still not hurrying. It was nice out here, the sky looking a thousand miles deep and nary a mountain in sight. New Hampshire was fine, and he'd come to think of it as home, but Dan thought he was always going to feel more comfortable in the flatlands. Safer.

'You know better than that, Johnny. Why does any alcoholic drink?'

'Because he's an alcoholic?'

'Bingo. Simple as can be. Cut through the psychobabble and you're left with the stark truth. We drank because we're drunks.'

John laughed. 'Casey K. has truly indoctrinated you.'

'Well, there's also the heredity thing,' Dan said. 'Casey always kicks that part to the curb, but it's there. Did your father drink?'

'Him and mother dearest both. They could have kept the Nineteenth Hole at the country club in business all by themselves. I remember the day my mother took off her tennis dress and jumped into the pool with us kids. The men applauded. My dad thought it was a scream. Me, not so much. I was nine, and until I went to college I was the boy with the Striptease Mommy. Yours?'

'My mother could take it or leave it alone. Sometimes she used to call herself Two Beers Wendy. My dad, however . . . one glass of wine or can of Bud and he was off to the races.' Dan glanced at the odometer and saw they still had forty miles to go. 'You want to hear a story? One I've never told anybody? I should warn you, it's a weird one. If you think the shining begins and ends with paltry shit like telepathy, you're way short.' He paused. 'There are other worlds than these.'

'You've . . . um . . . seen these other worlds?' Dan had lost track of John's mind, but DJ suddenly looked a little nervous. As if he thought the guy sitting next to him might suddenly stick his hand in his shirt and declare himself the reincarnation of Napoleon Bonaparte.

'No, just some of the people who live there. Abra calls them the ghostie people. Do you want to hear, or not?'

'I'm not sure I do, but maybe I better.'

Dan didn't know how much this New England pediatrician would believe about the winter the Torrance family had spent at the Overlook Hotel, but found he didn't particularly care. Telling it in this nondescript car, under this bright Midwestern sky, would be good enough. There was one person who would have believed it all, but Abra was too young, and the story was too scary. John Dalton would have to do. But how to begin? With Jack Torrance, he supposed. A deeply unhappy man who had failed at teaching, writing, and husbanding. What did the baseball players call three strikeouts in a row? The Golden Sombrero? Dan's father had had only one notable success: when the moment finally came – the one the Overlook had been pushing him toward from their first day in the hotel – he had refused to kill his little boy. If there was a fitting epitaph for him, it would be . . .

'Dan?'

'My father tried,' he said. 'That's the best I can say for him. The most malevolent spirits in his life came in bottles. If he'd tried AA, things might have been a lot different. But he didn't. I don't think my mother even knew there was such a thing, or she would have suggested he give it a shot. By the time we went up to the Overlook Hotel, where a friend of his got him a job as the winter caretaker, his picture could have been next to *dry drunk* in the dictionary.'

'That's where the ghosts were?'

'Yes. I saw them. He didn't, but he felt them. Maybe he had his own shining. Probably he did. Lots of things are hereditary, after all, not just a tendency toward alcoholism. And they worked on him. He thought they – the ghostie people – wanted him, but that was just another lie. What they wanted was the little boy with the great big shine. The same way this True Knot bunch wants Abra.'

He stopped, remembering how Dick, speaking through Eleanor

Ouellette's dead mouth, had answered when Dan had asked where the empty devils were. *In your childhood, where every devil comes from.*

'Dan? Are you okay?'

'Yes,' Dan said. 'Anyway, I knew something was wrong in that goddam hotel even before I stepped through the door. I knew when the three of us were still living pretty much hand-to-mouth down in Boulder, on the Eastern Slope. But my father needed a job so he could finish a play he was working on . . .'

7

By the time they reached Adair, he was telling John how the Overlook's boiler had exploded, and how the old hotel had burned to the ground in a driving blizzard. Adair was a two-stoplight town, but there was a Holiday Inn Express, and Dan noted the location.

'That's where we'll be checking in a couple of hours from now,' he told John. 'We can't go digging for treasure in broad daylight, and besides, I'm dead for sleep. Haven't been getting much lately.'

'All that really happened to you?' John asked in a subdued voice.

'It really did.' Dan smiled. 'Think you can believe it?'

'If we find the baseball glove where she says it is, I'll have to believe a lot of things. Why did you tell me?'

'Because part of you thinks we're crazy to be here, in spite of what you know about Abra. Also because you deserve to know that there are . . . forces. I've encountered them before; you haven't. All you've seen is a little girl who can do assorted psychic parlor tricks like hanging spoons on the ceiling. This isn't a boys' treasure hunt game, John. If the True Knot finds out what we're up to, we'll be pinned to the target right along with Abra Stone. If you decided to bail on this business, I'd make the sign of the cross in front of you and say go with God.'

'And continue on by yourself.'

Dan tipped him a grin. 'Well . . . there's Billy.'

'Billy's seventy-three if he's a day.'

'He'd say that's a plus. Billy likes to tell people that the good thing about being old is that you don't have to worry about dying young.'

John pointed. 'Freeman town line.' He gave Dan a small, tight smile. 'I can't completely believe I'm doing this. What are you going to think if that ethanol plant is gone? If it's been torn down since Google Earth snapped its picture, and planted over with corn?'

'It'll still be there,' Dan said.

8

And so it was: a series of soot-gray concrete blocks roofed in rusty corrugated metal. One smokestack still stood; two others had fallen and lay on the ground like broken snakes. The windows had been smashed and the walls were covered in blotchy spray-paint graffiti that would have been laughed at by the pro taggers in any big city. A potholed service road split off from the two-lane, ending in a parking lot that had sprouted with errant seed corn. The water tower Abra had seen stood nearby, rearing against the horizon like an H. G. Wells Martian war machine. FREEMAN, IOWA was printed on the side. The shed with the broken roof was also present and accounted for.

'Satisfied?' Dan asked. They had slowed to a crawl. 'Factory, water tower, shed, No Trespassing sign. All just like she said it would be.'

John pointed to the rusty gate at the end of the service road. 'What if that's locked? I haven't climbed a chainlink fence since I was in junior high.'

'It wasn't locked when the killers brought that kid here, or Abra would have said.'

'Are you sure of that?'

A farm truck was coming the other way. Dan sped up a little and lifted a hand as they passed. The guy behind the wheel – green John Deere cap, sunglasses, bib overalls – raised his in return but hardly glanced at them. That was a good thing.

'I asked if—'

'I know what you asked,' Dan said. 'If it's locked, we'll deal with it. Somehow. Now let's go back to that motel and check in. I'm whipped.'

9

While John got adjoining rooms at the Holiday Inn – paying cash – Dan sought out the Adair True Value Hardware. He bought a spade, a rake, two hoes, a garden trowel, two pairs of gloves, and a duffel to hold his new purchases. The only tool he actually wanted was the spade, but it seemed best to buy in bulk.

'What brings you to Adair, may I ask?' the clerk asked as he rang up Dan's stuff.

'Just passing through. My sister's in Des Moines, and she's got quite the garden patch. She probably owns most of this stuff, but presents always seem to improve her hospitality.'

'I hear *that*, brother. And she'll thank you for this short-handle hoe. No tool comes in handier, and most amateur gardeners never think to get one. We take MasterCard, Visa—'

'I think I'll give the plastic a rest,' Dan said, taking out his wallet. 'Just give me a receipt for Uncle Sugar.'

'You bet. And if you give me your name and address – or your sister's – we'll send our catalogue.'

'You know what, I'm going to pass on that today,' Dan said, and put a little fan of twenties on the counter.

10

At eleven o'clock that night, there came a soft rap on Dan's door. He opened it and let John inside. Abra's pediatrician was pale and keyed-up. 'Did you sleep?'

'Some,' Dan said. 'You?'

'In and out. Mostly out. I'm nervous as a goddam cat. If a cop stops us, what are we going to say?'

'That we heard there was a juke joint in Freeman and decided to go looking for it.'

'There's nothing in Freeman but corn. About nine billion acres of it.'

'*We* don't know that,' Dan said mildly. 'We're just passing through. Besides, no cop's going to stop us, John. Nobody's even going to notice us. But if you want to stay here—'

'I didn't come halfway across the country to sit in a motel watching Jay Leno. Just let me use the toilet. I used mine before I left the room, but now I need to go again. *Christ*, am I nervous.'

The drive to Freeman seemed very long to Dan, but once they left Adair behind, they didn't meet a single car. Farmers went to bed early, and they were off the trucking routes.

When they reached the ethanol plant, Dan doused the rental car's lights, turned in to the service road, and rolled slowly up to the closed gate. The two men got out. John cursed when the Ford's dome light came on. 'I should have turned that thing off before we left the motel. Or smashed the bulb, if it doesn't have a switch.'

'Relax,' Dan said. 'There's no one out here but us chickens.' Still, his heart was beating hard in his chest as they walked to the gate. If Abra was right, a little boy had been murdered and buried out here after being miserably tortured. If ever a place should be haunted—

John tried the gate, and when pushing didn't work, he tried pulling. 'Nothing. What now? Climb, I guess. I'm willing to try, but I'll probably break my fucking—'

'Wait.' Dan took a penlight from his jacket pocket and shone it on the gate, first noting the broken padlock, then the heavy twists of wire above and below it. He went back to the car, and it was his turn to wince when the trunk light came on. Well, shit. You couldn't think of everything. He yanked out the new duffel, and slammed the trunk lid down. Dark returned.

'Here,' he told John, holding out a pair of gloves. 'Put these on.' Dan put on his own, untwisted the wire, and hung both pieces in one of the chainlink diamonds for later reference. 'Okay, let's go.'

'I have to pee again.'

'Oh, man. Hold it.'

11

Dan drove the Hertz Ford slowly and carefully around to the loading dock. There were plenty of potholes, some deep, all hard to see with the headlights off. The last thing in the world he wanted was to drop the Focus into one and smash an axle. Behind the plant, the surface was a mixture of bare earth and crumbling asphalt. Fifty feet away was another chainlink fence, and beyond that, endless leagues of corn. The dock area wasn't as big as the parking lot, but it was plenty big.

'Dan? How will we know where—'

'Be quiet.' Dan bent his head until his brow touched the steering wheel and closed his eyes.

(*Abra*)

Nothing. She was asleep, of course. Back in Anniston it was already Wednesday morning. John sat beside him, chewing his lips.

(*Abra*)

A faint stirring. It could have been his imagination. Dan hoped it was more.

(*ABRA!*)

Eyes opened in his head. There was a moment of disorientation, a kind of double vision, and then Abra was looking with him. The loading dock and the crumbled remains of the smokestacks were suddenly clearer, even though there was only starlight to see by.

Her vision's a hell of a lot better than mine.

Dan got out of the car. So did John, but Dan barely noticed. He had ceded control to the girl who was now lying awake in her bed eleven hundred miles away. He felt like a human metal detector. Only it wasn't metal that he – *they* – were looking for.

(*walk over to that concrete thing*)

Dan walked to the loading dock and stood with his back to it.

(*now start going back and forth*)

A pause as she hunted for a way to clarify what she wanted.

(*like on* CSI)

He coursed fifty feet or so to the left, then turned right, moving out from the dock on opposing diagonals. John had gotten the spade out of the duffel bag and stood by the rental car, watching.

(*here is where they parked their RVs*)

Dan cut back left again, walking slowly, occasionally kicking a loose brick or chunk of concrete out of his way.

(*you're close*)

Dan stopped. He smelled something unpleasant. A gassy whiff of decay.

(*Abra? do you*)

(*yes oh God Dan*)

(*take it easy hon*)

(*you went too far turn around go slow*)

Dan turned on one heel, like a soldier doing a sloppy about-face. He started back toward the loading dock.

(*left a little to your left slower*)

He went that way, now pausing after each small step. Here was that smell again, a little stronger. Suddenly the preternaturally sharp nighttime world began to blur as his eyes filled with Abra's tears.

(*there the baseball boy you're standing right on top of him*)

Dan took a deep breath and wiped at his cheeks. He was shivering. Not because he was cold, but because she was. Sitting up in her bed, clutching her lumpy stuffed rabbit, and shaking like an old leaf on a dead tree.

(*get out of here Abra*)

(*Dan are you*)

(*yes fine but you don't need to see this*)

Suddenly that absolute clarity of vision was gone. Abra had broken the connection, and that was good.

'Dan?' John called, low. 'All right?'

'Yes.' His voice was still clogged with Abra's tears. 'Bring that spade.'

12

It took them twenty minutes. Dan dug for the first ten, then passed the spade to John, who actually found Brad Trevor. He turned away from the hole, covering his mouth and nose. His words were muffled but understandable. 'Okay, there's a body. *Jesus!*'

'You didn't smell it before?'

'Buried that deep, and after two years? Are you saying that you did?'

Dan didn't reply, so John addressed the hole again, but without conviction this time. He stood for a few seconds with his back bent as if he still meant to use the spade, then straightened and drew back when Dan shone the penlight into the little excavation they had made. 'I can't,' he said. 'I thought I could, but I can't. Not with . . . that. My arms feel like rubber.'

Dan handed him the light. John shone it into the hole, centering the beam on what had freaked him out: a dirt-clotted sneaker. Working slowly, not wanting to disturb the earthly remains of Abra's baseball boy any more than necessary, Dan scraped dirt away from the sides of the body. Little by little, an earth-covered shape emerged. It reminded him of the carvings on sarcophagi he had seen in *National Geographic*.

The smell of decay was now very strong.

Dan stepped away and hyperventilated, ending with the deepest breath he could manage. Then he dropped into the end of the shallow grave, where both of Brad Trevor's sneakers now protruded in a v. He knee-walked up to about where he thought the boy's waist must be, then held up a hand for the penlight. John handed it over and turned away. He was sobbing audibly.

Dan clamped the slim flashlight between his lips and began brushing away more dirt. A child's t-shirt came into view, clinging to a sunken chest. Then hands. The fingers, now little more than bones wrapped in yellow skin, were clasped over something. Dan's chest was starting to pound for air now, but he pried the Trevor boy's fingers apart as gently as he could. Still, one of them snapped with a dry crunching sound.

They had buried him holding his baseball glove to his chest. Its lovingly oiled pocket was full of squirming bugs.

The air escaped Dan's lungs in a shocked *whoosh*, and the breath he inhaled to replace it was rich with rot. He lunged out of the grave to his right, managing to vomit on the dirt they'd taken out of the hole instead of on the wasted remains of Bradley Trevor, whose only crime had been to be born with something a tribe of monsters wanted. And had stolen from him on the very wind of his dying shrieks.

13

They reburied the body, John doing most of the work this time, and covered the spot with a makeshift crypt of broken asphalt chunks. Neither of them wanted to think of foxes or stray dogs feasting on what scant meat was left.

When they were done, they got back into the car and sat without speaking. At last John said, 'What are we going to do about him, Danno? We can't just leave him. He's got parents. Grandparents. Probably brothers and sisters. All of them still wondering.'

'He has to stay awhile. Long enough so nobody's going to say, "Gee, that anonymous call came in just after some stranger bought a spade in the Adair hardware store." That probably wouldn't happen, but we can't take the chance.'

'How long's awhile?'

'Maybe a month.'

John considered this, then sighed. 'Maybe even two. Give his folks that long to go on thinking he might just have run off. Give them that long before we break their hearts.' He shook his head. 'If I'd had to look at his face, I don't think I ever could have slept again.'

'You'd be surprised what a person can live with,' Dan said. He was thinking of Mrs Massey, now safely stored away in the back of his head, her haunting days over. He started the car, powered down his window, and beat the baseball glove several times against the door to dislodge the dirt. Then he put it on, sliding his fingers into the places where the child's had been on so many sunlit afternoons. He closed his eyes. After thirty seconds or so, he opened them again.

'Anything?'

'"You're Barry. You're one of the good guys."'

'What does that mean?'

'I don't know, except I'm betting he's the one Abra calls Barry the Chunk.'

'Nothing else?'

'Abra will be able to get more.'

'Are you sure of that?'

Dan thought of the way his vision had sharpened when Abra opened her eyes inside his head. 'I am. Shine your light on the pocket of the glove for a sec, will you? There's something written there.'

John did it, revealing a child's careful printing: **THOME 25**.

'What does that mean?' John asked. 'I thought his name was Trevor.'

'Jim Thome's a baseball player. His number is twenty-five.' He stared into the pocket of the glove for a moment, then laid it gently on the seat between them. 'He was that kid's favorite Major Leaguer. He named his glove after him. I'm going to get these fuckers. I swear before God Almighty, I'm going to get them and make them sorry.'

14

Rose the Hat shone – the entire True shone – but not in the way Dan or Billy did. Neither Rose nor Crow had any sense, as they said their goodbyes, that the child they had taken years ago in Iowa was at that moment being uncovered by two men who knew far too much about them already. Rose could have caught the communications flying between Dan and Abra if she had been in a state of deep meditation, but of course then the little girl would have noticed her presence immediately. Besides, the goodbyes going on in Rose's EarthCruiser that night were of an especially intimate sort.

She lay with her fingers laced together behind her head and watched Crow dress. 'You visited that store, right? District X?'

'Not me personally, I have a reputation to protect. I sent Jimmy Numbers.' Crow grinned as he buckled his belt. 'He could've gotten what we needed in fifteen minutes, but he was gone for two hours. I think Jimmy's found a new home.'

'Well, that's good. I hope you boys enjoy yourselves.' Trying to keep it light, but after two days of mourning Grampa Flick, climaxed by the circle of farewell, keeping anything light was an effort.

'He didn't get anything that compares to you.'

She raised her eyebrows. 'Had a preview, did you, Henry?'

'Didn't need one.' He eyed her as she lay naked with her hair spread out in a dark fan. She was tall, even lying down. He had ever liked tall women. 'You're the feature attraction in my home theater and always will be.'

Overblown – just a bit of Crow's patented razzle-dazzle – but it pleased her just the same. She got up and pressed against him, her hands in his hair. 'Be careful. Bring everyone back. And bring *her*.'

'We will.'

'Then you better get a wiggle on.'

'Relax. We'll be in Sturbridge when EZ Mail Services opens on Friday morning. In New Hampshire by noon. By then, Barry will have located her.'

'As long as *she* doesn't locate *him*.'

'I'm not worried about that.'

Fine, Rose thought. *I'll worry for both of us. I'll worry until I'm looking at her wearing cuffs on her wrists and clamps on her ankles.*

'The beauty of it,' Crow said, 'is that if she *does* sense us and tries to put up an interference wall, Barry will key on that.'

'If she's scared enough, she might go to the police.'

He flashed a grin. 'You think? "Yes, little girl," they'd say, "we're sure these awful people are after you. So tell us if they're from outer space or just your ordinary garden variety zombies. That way we'll know what to look for."'

'Don't joke, and don't take this lightly. Get in clean and get out the same way, that's how it has to be. No outsiders involved. No innocent bystanders. Kill the parents if you need to, kill *anyone* who tries to interfere, but keep it quiet.'

Crow snapped off a comic salute. 'Yes, my captain.'

'Get out of here, idiot. But give me another kiss first. Maybe a little of that educated tongue, for good measure.'

He gave her what she asked for. Rose held him tight, and for a long time.

15

Dan and John rode in silence most of the way back to the motel in Adair. The spade was in the trunk. The baseball glove was in the backseat, wrapped in a Holiday Inn towel. At last John said, 'We've got to bring Abra's folks into this now. She's going to hate it and Lucy and David won't want to believe it, but it has to be done.'

Dan looked at him, straight-faced, and said: 'What are you, a mind-reader?'

John wasn't, but Abra was, and her sudden loud voice in Dan's head made him glad that this time John was driving. If he had been behind the wheel, they very likely would have ended up in some farmer's cornpatch.

(*NOOOOO!*)

'Abra.' He spoke aloud so that John could hear at least his half of the conversation. 'Abra, listen to me.'

(*NO, DAN! THEY THINK I'M ALL RIGHT! THEY THINK I'M ALMOST NORMAL NOW!*)

'Honey, if these people had to kill your mom and dad to get to you, do you think they'd hesitate? I sure don't. Not after what we found back there.'

There was no counterargument she could make to this, and Abra didn't try . . . but suddenly Dan's head was filled with her sorrow and her fear. His eyes welled up again and spilled tears down his cheeks.

Shit.

Shit, shit, *shit.*

16

Early Thursday morning.

Steamhead Steve's Winnebago, with Snakebite Andi currently behind the wheel, was cruising eastbound on I-80 in western Nebraska at a perfectly legal sixty-five miles an hour. The first streaks of dawn had just begun to show on the horizon. In Anniston it was two hours later. Dave Stone was in his bathrobe making coffee when the phone rang. It was Lucy, calling from Concetta's Marlborough Street condo. She sounded like a woman who had nearly reached the end of her resources.

'If nothing changes for the worse − although I guess that's the only way things *can* change now − they'll be releasing Momo from the hospital first thing next week. I talked with the two doctors on her case last night.'

'Why didn't you call me, sweetheart?'

'Too tired. And too depressed. I thought I'd feel better after a night's sleep, but I didn't get much. Honey, this place is just so full of her. Not just her work, her *vitality* . . .'

Her voice wavered. David waited. They had been together for

over fifteen years, and he knew that when Lucy was upset, waiting was sometimes better than talking.

'I don't know what we're going to *do* with it all. Just looking at the books makes me tired. There are thousands on the shelves and stacked in her study, and the super says there are thousands more in storage.'

'We don't have to decide right now.'

'He says there's also a trunk marked *Alessandra*. That was my mother's real name, you know, although I guess she always called herself Sandra or Sandy. I never knew Momo had her stuff.'

'For someone who let it all hang out in her poetry, Chetta could be one closemouthed lady when she wanted to.'

Lucy seemed not to hear him, only continued in the same dull, slightly nagging, tired-to-death tone. 'Everything's arranged, although I'll have to reschedule the private ambulance if they decide to let her go Sunday. They said they might. Thank God she's got good insurance. That goes back to her teaching days at Tufts, you know. She never made a dime from poetry. Who in this fucked-up country would pay a dime to *read* it anymore?'

'Lucy—'

'She's got a good place in the main building at Rivington House – a little suite. I took the online tour. Not that she'll be using it long. I made friends with the head nurse on her floor here, and she says Momo's just about at the end of her—'

'Chia, I love you, honey.'

That – Concetta's old nickname for her – finally stopped her.

'With all my admittedly non-Italian heart and soul.'

'I know, and thank God you do. This has been so hard, but it's almost over. I'll be there Monday at the very latest.'

'We can't wait to see you.'

'How are you? How's Abra?'

'We're both fine.' David would be allowed to go on believing this for another sixty seconds or so.

He heard Lucy yawn. 'I might go back to bed for an hour or two. I think I can sleep now.'

'You do that. I've got to get Abs up for school.'

They said their goodbyes, and when Dave turned away from the kitchen wall phone, he saw that Abra was already up. She was still in her pajamas. Her hair was every which way, her eyes were red, and her face was pale. She was clutching Hoppy, her old stuffed rabbit.

'Abba-Doo? Honey? Are you sick?'

Yes. No. I don't know. But you will be, when you hear what I'm going to tell you.

'I need to talk to you, Daddy. And I don't want to go to school today. Tomorrow, either. Maybe not for a while.' She hesitated. 'I'm in trouble.'

The first thing that phrase brought to mind was so awful that he pushed it away at once, but not before Abra caught it.

She smiled wanly. 'No, I'm not pregnant.'

He stopped on his way to her, halfway across the kitchen, his mouth falling open. 'You . . . did you just—'

'Yes,' she said. 'I just read your mind. Although anyone could have guessed what you were thinking that time, Daddy – it was all over your face. And it's called shining, not mind-reading. I can still do most of the things that used to scare you when I was little. Not all, but most.'

He spoke very slowly. 'I know you still sometimes have premonitions. Your mom and I both know.'

'It's a lot more than that. I have a friend. His name is Dan. He and Dr John have been in Iowa—'

'John Dalton?'

'Yes—'

'Who's this Dan? Is he a kid Dr John treats?'

'No, he's a grown-up.' She took his hand and led him to the kitchen table. There they sat down, Abra still holding Hoppy. 'But when he was a kid, he was like me.'

'Abs, I'm not understanding any of this.'

'There are bad people, Daddy.' She knew she couldn't tell him they were more than people, *worse* than people, until Dan and John were here to help her explain. 'They might want to hurt me.'

'Why would anyone want to hurt you? You're not making sense. As for all those things you used to do, if you could still do them, we'd kn—'

The drawer below the hanging pots flew open, then shut, then opened again. She could no longer lift the spoons, but the drawer was enough to get his attention.

'Once I understood how much it worried you guys – how much it scared you – I hid it. But I can't hide it anymore. Dan says I have to tell.'

She pressed her face against Hoppy's threadbare fur and began to cry.

CHAPTER TWELVE
THEY CALL IT STEAM

1

John turned on his cell as soon as he and Dan emerged from the jetway at Logan Airport late Thursday afternoon. He had no more than registered the fact that he had well over a dozen missed calls when the phone rang in his hand. He glanced down at the window.

'Stone?' Dan asked.

'I've got a lot of missed calls from the same number, so I'd say it has to be.'

'Don't answer. Call him back when we're on the expressway north and tell him we'll be there by—' Dan glanced at his watch, which he had never changed from eastern time. 'By six. When we get there, we'll tell him everything.'

John reluctantly pocketed his cell. 'I spent the flight back hoping I'm not going to lose my license to practice over this. Now I'm just hoping the cops don't grab us as soon as we park in front of Dave Stone's house.'

Dan, who had consulted several times with Abra on their way back across the country, shook his head. 'She's convinced him to wait, but there's a lot going on in that family just now, and Mr Stone is one confused American.'

To this, John offered a smile of singular bleakness. 'He's not the only one.'

2

Abra was sitting on the front step with her father when Dan swung into the Stones' driveway. They had made good time; it was only five thirty.

Abra was up before Dave could grab her and came running down the walk with her hair flying out behind her. Dan saw she was heading for him, and handed the towel-wrapped fielder's mitt to John. She threw herself into his arms. She was trembling all over.

(*you found him you found him and you found the glove give it to me*)

'Not yet,' Dan said, setting her down. 'We need to thrash this out with your dad first.'

'Thrash what out?' Dave asked. He took Abra by the wrist and pulled her away from Dan. 'Who are these bad people she's talking about? And who the hell are you?' His gaze shifted to John, and there was nothing friendly in his eyes. 'What in the name of sweet Jesus is going on here?'

'This is Dan, Daddy. He's like me. I *told* you.'

John said, 'Where's Lucy? Does she know about this?'

'I'm not telling you anything until I find out what's going on.'

Abra said, 'She's still in Boston, with Momo. Daddy wanted to call her, but I persuaded him to wait until you got here.' Her eyes remained pinned on the towel-wrapped glove.

'Dan Torrance,' Dave said. 'That your name?'

'Yes.'

'You work at the hospice in Frazier?'

'That's right.'

'How long have you been meeting my daughter?' His hands were clenching and unclenching. 'Did you meet her on the internet? I'm betting that's it.' He switched his gaze to John. 'If you hadn't been Abra's pediatrician from the day she was born, I would have called the police six hours ago, when you didn't answer your phone.'

'I was in an airplane,' John said. 'I couldn't.'

'Mr Stone,' Dan said. 'I haven't known your daughter as long as John has, but almost. The first time I met her, she was just a baby. And it was she who reached out to me.'

Dave shook his head. He looked perplexed, angry, and little inclined to believe anything Dan told him.

'Let's go in the house,' John said. 'I think we can explain everything – *almost* everything – and if that's the case, you'll be very happy that we're here, and that we went to Iowa to do what we did.'

'I damn well hope so, John, but I've got my doubts.'

They went inside, Dave with his arm around Abra's shoulders – at that moment they looked more like jailer and prisoner than father and daughter – John Dalton next, Dan last. He looked across the street at the rusty red pickup parked there. Billy gave him a quick thumbs-up . . . then crossed his fingers. Dan returned the gesture, and followed the others through the front door.

3

As Dave was sitting down in his Richland Court living room with his puzzling daughter and his even more puzzling guests, the Winnebago containing the True raiding party was southeast of Toledo. Walnut was at the wheel. Andi Steiner and Barry were sleeping – Andi like the dead, Barry rolling from side to side and muttering. Crow was in the parlor area, paging through *The New Yorker*. The only things he really liked were the cartoons and the tiny ads for weird items like yak-fur sweaters, Vietnamese coolie hats, and faux Cuban cigars.

Jimmy Numbers plunked down next to him with his laptop in hand. 'I've been combing the 'net. Had to hack and back with a couple of sites, but . . . can I show you something?'

'How can you surf the 'net from an interstate highway?'

Jimmy gave him a patronizing smile. '4G connection, baby. This is the modern age.'

'If you say so.' Crow put his magazine aside. 'What've you got?'

'School pictures from Anniston Middle School.' Jimmy tapped the touchpad and a photo appeared. No grainy newsprint job, but a high-res school portrait of a girl in a red dress with puffed sleeves. Her braided hair was chestnut brown, her smile wide and confident.

'Julianne Cross,' Jimmy said. He tapped the touchpad again and a redhead with a mischievous grin popped up. 'Emma Deane.' Another tap, and an even prettier girl appeared. Blue eyes, blond hair framing her face and spilling over her shoulders. Serious expression, but dimples hinting at a smile. 'This one's Abra Stone.'

'Abra?'

'Yeah, they name em anything these days. Remember when Jane and Mabel used to be good enough for the rubes? I read somewhere that Sly Stallone named his kid Sage Moonblood, how fucked up is that?'

'You think one of these three is Rose's girl.'

'If she's right about the girl being a young teenager, it just about has to be. Probably Deane or Stone, they're the two who actually live on the street where the little earthquake was, but you can't count the Cross girl out completely. She's just around the corner.' Jimmy Numbers made a swirling gesture on the touchpad and the three pictures zipped into a row. Written below each in curly script was *MY SCHOOL MEMORIES.*

Crow studied them. 'Is anyone going to trip to the fact that you've been filching pictures of little girls off of Facebook, or something? Because that sets off all kinds of warning bells in Rubeland.'

Jimmy looked offended. 'Facebook, my ass. These came from the Frazier Middle School files, pipelined direct from their computer to mine.' He made an unlovely sucking sound. 'And guess what, a guy with access to a whole bank of NSA computers couldn't follow my tracks on this one. Who rocks?'

'You do,' Crow said. 'I guess.'

'Which one do you think it is?'

'If I had to pick . . .' Crow tapped Abra's picture. 'She's got a certain look in her eyes. A *steamy* look.'

Jimmy puzzled over this for a moment, decided it was dirty, and guffawed. 'Does it help?'

'Yes. Can you print these pictures and make sure the others have copies? Particularly Barry. He's Locator in Chief on this one.'

'I'll do it right now. I'm packing a Fujitsu ScanSnap. Great little on-the-go machine. I used to have the S1100, but I swapped it when I read in *Computerworld*—'

'Just do it, okay?'

'Sure.'

Crow picked up the magazine again and turned to the cartoon on the last page, the one where you were supposed to fill in the caption. This week's showed an elderly woman walking into a bar with a bear on a chain. She had her mouth open, so the caption had to be her dialogue. Crow considered carefully, then printed: '*Okay, which one of you assholes called me a cunt?*'

Probably not a winner.

The Winnebago rolled on through the deepening evening. In the

She trailed off with a sigh. Crow said nothing. There was really nothing to say. Andi Steiner had been with a lot of women during her early years with the True – not a surprise, steam always made newbies especially randy – but she and Sarah Carter had been a couple for the last ten years, and devoted to each other. In some ways, Andi had seemed more like Silent Sarey's daughter than her lover.

'Sarey's inconsolable,' Rose said, 'and Black-Eyed Susie's not much better about Nut. That little girl is going to answer for taking those three from us. One way or the other, her rube life is over. Any more questions?'

Crow had none.

10

No one paid any particular attention to Crow Daddy and his snoozing passengers as they left Anniston on the old Granite State Highway, headed west. With a few notable exceptions (sharp-eyed old ladies and little kids were the worst), Rube America was staggeringly unobservant even twelve years into the Dark Age of Terrorism. *If you see something, say something* was a hell of a slogan, but first you had to see something.

By the time they crossed into Vermont it was growing dark, and cars passing by in the other direction saw only Crow's headlights, which he purposely left on hi-beam. Toady Slim had called three times already, feeding him route information. Most were byroads, many unmarked. Toady had also told Crow that Diesel Doug, Dirty Phil, and Apron Annie were on their way. They were riding in an '06 Caprice that looked like a dog but had four hundred horses under the hood. Speeding would not be a problem; they were also carrying Homeland Security creds that would check out all the way up the line, thanks to the late Jimmy Numbers.

The Little twins, Pea and Pod, were using the True's sophisticated satellite communications gear to monitor police chatter in the Northeast, and so far there had been nothing about the possible kidnapping of a young girl. This was good news, but not unexpected. Friends smart enough to set up an ambush were probably smart enough to know what could happen to their chickadee if they went public.

Another phone rang, this one muffled. Without taking his eyes off the road, Crow leaned across his sleeping passengers, reached into the glove compartment, and found a cell. The geezer's, no doubt. He held it up to his eyes. There was no name, so the caller wasn't in the phone's memory, but the number had a New Hampshire area code. One of the ambushers, wanting to know if Billy and the girl were all right? Very likely. Crow considered answering it and decided not to. He would check later to see if the caller had left a message, though. Information was power.

When he leaned over again to return the cell to the glove compartment, his fingers touched metal. He stowed the phone and brought out an automatic pistol. A nice bonus, and a lucky find. If the geezer had awakened a little sooner than expected, he might have gotten to it before Crow could read his intentions. Crow slid the Glock under his seat, then flipped the glove compartment closed.

Guns were also power.

11

It was full dark and they were deep into the Green Mountains on Highway 108 when Abra began to stir. Crow, still feeling brilliantly alive and aware, wasn't sorry. For one thing, he was curious about her. For another, the old truck's gas gauge was touching empty, and someone was going to have to fill the tank.

But it wouldn't do to take chances.

With his right hand he removed one of the two remaining hypos from his pocket and held it on his thigh. He waited until the girl's eyes – still soft and muzzy – opened. Then he said, 'Good evening, little lady. I'm Henry Rothman. Do you understand me?'

'You're . . .' Abra cleared her throat, wet her lips, tried again. 'You're not Henry anything. You're the Crow.'

'So you do understand. That's good. You feel woolly-headed just now, I imagine, and you're going to stay that way, because that's just how I like you. But there will be no need to knock you all the way out again as long as you mind your Ps and Qs. Have you got that?'

'Where are we going?'

'Hogwarts, to watch the International Quidditch Tourney. I'll buy you a magic hotdog and a cone of magic cotton candy. Answer my question. Are you going to mind your Ps and Qs?'

'Yes.'

'Such instant agreement is pleasing to the ear, but you'll have to pardon me if I don't completely trust it. I need to give you some vital information before you try something foolish that you might regret. Do you see the needle I have?'

'Yes.' Abra's head was still resting against the window, but she looked down at the hypo. Her eyes drifted shut then opened again, very slowly. 'I'm thirsty.'

'From the drug, no doubt. I don't have anything to drink with me, we left in a bit of a hurry—'

'I think there's a juice box in my pack.' Husky. Low and slow. The eyes still opening with great effort after every blink.

'Afraid that's back in your garage. You may get something to drink in the next town we come to – if you're a good little Goldilocks. If you're a bad little Goldilocks, you can spend the night swallowing your own spit. Clear?'

'Yes . . .'

'If I feel you fiddling around inside my head – yes, I know you can do it – or if you try attracting attention when we stop, I'll inject this old gentleman. On top of what I already gave him, it will kill him as dead as Amy Winehouse. Are we clear on that, as well?'

'Yes.' She licked her lips again, then rubbed them with her hand. 'Don't hurt him.'

'That's up to you.'

'Where are you taking me?'

'Goldilocks? Dear?'

'What?' She blinked at him dazedly.

'Just shut up and enjoy the ride.'

'Hogwarts,' she said. 'Cotton . . . candy.' This time when her eyes closed, the lids stayed down. She began to snore lightly. It was a breezy sound, sort of pleasant. Crow didn't think she was shamming, but he continued to hold the hypo next to the geezer's leg just to be sure. As Gollum had once said about Frodo Baggins, it was tricksy, precious. It was very tricksy.

12

Abra didn't go under completely; she still heard the truck's motor, but it was far away. It seemed to be above her. It made her remember when she and her parents went to Lake Winnipesaukee on hot summer afternoons, and how you could hear the distant drone of the motorboats if you ducked your head underwater. She knew she was being kidnapped, and she knew this should concern her, but she felt serene, content to float between sleep and waking. The dryness in her mouth and throat was horrible, though. Her tongue felt like a strip of dusty carpet.

I have to do something. He's taking me to the hat woman and I have to do something. If I don't, they'll kill me like they killed the baseball boy. Or something even worse.

She *would* do something. After she got something to drink. And after she slept a little more . . .

The engine sound had faded from a drone to a distant hum when light penetrated her closed eyelids. Then the sound stopped completely and the Crow was poking her in the leg. Easy at first, then harder. Hard enough to hurt.

'Wake up, Goldilocks. You can go back to sleep later.'

She struggled her eyes open, wincing at the brightness. They were parked beside some gas pumps. There were fluorescents over them. She shielded her eyes from the glare. Now she had a headache to go with her thirst. It was like . . .

'What's funny, Goldilocks?'

'Huh?'

'You're smiling.'

'I just figured out what's wrong with me. I'm hungover.'

Crow considered this, and grinned. 'I suppose you are at that, and you didn't even get to prance around with a lampshade on your head. Are you awake enough to understand me?'

'Yes.' At least she thought she was. Oh, but the thudding in her head. Awful.

'Take this.'

He was holding something in front of her face, reaching across his body with his left hand to do it. His right one still held the hypodermic, the needle resting next to Mr Freeman's leg.

She squinted. It was a credit card. She reached up with a hand that felt too heavy and took it. Her eyes started to close and he slapped her face. Her eyes flew open, wide and shocked. She had never been hit in her life, not by an adult, anyway. Of course she had never been kidnapped, either.

'Ow! *Ow!*'

'Get out of the truck. Follow the instructions on the pump – you're a bright kid, I'm sure you can do that – and fill the tank. Then replace the nozzle and get back in. If you do all that like a good little Goldilocks, we'll drive over to yonder Coke machine.' He pointed to the far corner of the store. 'You can get a nice big twenty-ounce soda. Or a water, if that's what you want; I spy with my little eye that they have Dasani. If you're a *bad* little Goldilocks, I'll kill the old man, then go into the store and kill the kid at the register. No problem there. Your friend had a gun, which is now in my possession. I'll take you with me and you can watch the kid's head go splat. It's up to you, okay? You get it?'

'Yes,' Abra said. A little more awake now. 'Can I have a Coke *and* a water?'

His grin this time was high, wide, and handsome. In spite of her situation, in spite of the headache, even in spite of the slap he'd administered, Abra found it charming. She guessed lots of people found it charming, especially women. 'A little greedy, but that's not always a bad thing. Let's see how you mind those Ps and Qs.'

She unbuckled her belt – it took three tries, but she finally managed – and grabbed the doorhandle. Before she got out, she said: 'Stop calling me Goldilocks. You know my name, and I know yours.'

She slammed the door and headed for the gas island (weaving a little) before he could reply. She had spunk as well as steam. He could almost admire her. But, given what had happened to Snake, Nut, and Jimmy, almost was as far as it went.

13

At first Abra couldn't read the instructions because the words kept doubling and sliding around. She squinted and they came into focus.

The Crow was watching her. She could feel his eyes like tiny warm weights on the back of her neck.

(*Dan?*)

Nothing, and she wasn't surprised. How could she hope to reach Dan when she could barely figure out how to run this stupid pump? She had never felt less shiny in her life.

Eventually she managed to start the gas, although the first time she tried his credit card, she put it in upside-down and had to begin all over again. The pumping seemed to go on forever, but there was a rubber sleeve over the nozzle to keep the stench of the fumes down, and the night air was clearing her head a little. There were billions of stars. Usually they awed her with their beauty and profusion, but tonight looking at them only made her feel scared. They were far away. They didn't see Abra Stone.

When the tank was full, she squinted at the new message in the pump's window and turned to Crow. 'Do you want a receipt?'

'I think we can crutch along without that, don't you?' Again came his dazzling grin, the kind that made you happy if you were the one who caused it to break out. Abra bet he had lots of girlfriends.

No. He just has one. The hat woman is his girlfriend. Rose. If he had another one, Rose would kill her. Probably with her teeth and fingernails.

She trudged back to the truck and got in.

'That was very good,' Crow said. 'You win the grand prize – a Coke *and* a water. So . . . what do you say to your Daddy?'

'Thank you,' Abra said listlessly. 'But you're not my daddy.'

'I could be, though. I can be a very good daddy to little girls who are good to me. The ones who mind their Ps and Qs.' He drove to the machine and gave her a five-dollar bill. 'Get me a Fanta if they have it. A Coke if they don't.'

'You drink sodas, like anyone else?'

He made a comical wounded face. 'If you prick us, do we not bleed? If you tickle us, do we not laugh?'

'Shakespeare, right?' She wiped her mouth again. '*Romeo and Juliet.*'

'*Merchant of Venice*, dummocks,' Crow said . . . but with a smile. 'Don't know the rest of it, I bet.'

She shook her head. A mistake. It refreshed the throbbing, which had begun to diminish.

'If you poison us, do we not die?' He tapped the needle against Mr Freeman's leg. 'Meditate on that while you get our drinks.'

14

He watched closely as she operated the machine. This gas stop was on the wooded outskirts of some little town, and there was always a chance she might decide to hell with the geezer and run for the trees. He thought of the gun, but left it where it was. Chasing her down would be no great task, given her current soupy condition. But she didn't even look in that direction. She slid the five-spot into the machine and got the drinks, one after the other, pausing only to drink deeply from the water. She came back and gave him his Fanta, but didn't get in. Instead she pointed farther down the side of the building.

'I need to pee.'

Crow was flummoxed. This was something he hadn't foreseen, although he should have. She had been drugged, and her body needed to purge itself of toxins. 'Can't you hold it awhile?' He was thinking that a few more miles down the road, he could find a turnout and pull in. Let her go behind a bush. As long as he could see the top of her head, they'd be fine.

But she shook her head. Of course she did.

He thought it over. 'Okay, listen up. You can use the ladies' toilet if the door's unlocked. If it's not, you'll have to take your leak around back. There's no way I'm letting you go inside and ask the counterboy for the key.'

'And if I have to go in back, you'll watch me, I suppose. Pervo.'

'There'll be a Dumpster or something you can squat behind. It would break my heart not to get a look at your precious little buns, but I'd try to survive. Now get in the truck.'

'But you said—'

'Get in, or I'll start calling you Goldilocks again.'

She got in, and he pulled the truck up next to the bathroom doors, not quite blocking them. 'Now hold out your hand.'

'Why?'

'Just do it.'

Very reluctantly, she held out her hand. He took it. When she saw the needle, she tried to pull back.

'Don't worry, just a drop. We can't have you thinking bad thoughts, now can we? Or broadcasting them. This is going to happen one way or the other, so why make a production of it?'

She stopped trying to pull away. It was easier just to let it happen. There was a brief sting on the back of her hand, then he released her. 'Go on, now. Make wee-wee and make it quick. As the old song says, sand is a-runnin through the hourglass back home.'

'I don't know any song like that.'

'Not surprised. You don't even know *The Merchant of Venice* from *Romeo and Juliet*.'

'You're mean.'

'I don't have to be,' he said.

She got out and just stood beside the truck for a moment, taking deep breaths.

'Abra?'

She looked at him.

'Don't try locking yourself in. You know who'd pay for that, don't you?' He patted Billy Freeman's leg.

She knew.

Her head, which had begun to clear, was fogging in again. Horrible man – horrible *thing* – behind that charming grin. And smart. He thought of everything. She tried the bathroom door and it opened. At least she wouldn't have to whizz out back in the weeds, and that was something. She went inside, shut the door, and took care of her business. Then she simply sat there on the toilet with her swimming head hung down. She thought of being in the bathroom at Emma's house, when she had foolishly believed everything was going to turn out all right. How long ago that seemed.

I have to do something.

But she was doped up, woozy.

(*Dan*)

She sent this with all the force she could muster . . . which wasn't much. And how much time would the Crow give her? She felt despair wash over her, undermining what little will to resist was left.

All she wanted to do was button her pants, get into the truck again, and go back to sleep. Yet she tried one more time.

(*Dan! Dan, please!*)

And waited for a miracle.

What she got instead was a single brief tap of the pickup truck's horn. The message was clear: *time's up.*

CHAPTER FIFTEEN
SWAPSIES

1

You will remember what was forgotten.

In the aftermath of the pyrrhic victory at Cloud Gap, the phrase haunted Dan, like a snatch of irritating and nonsensical music that gets in your head and won't let go, the kind you find yourself humming even as you stumble to the bathroom in the middle of the night. This one was plenty irritating, but not quite nonsensical. For some reason he associated it with Tony.

You will remember what was forgotten.

There was no question of taking the True Knot's Winnebago back to their cars, which were parked at Teenytown Station on the Frazier town common. Even if they hadn't been afraid of being observed getting out of it or leaving forensic evidence inside it, they would have refused without needing to take a vote on the matter. It smelled of more than sickness and death; it smelled of evil. Dan had another reason. He didn't know if members of the True Knot came back as ghostie people or not, but he didn't want to find out.

So they threw the abandoned clothes and the drug paraphernalia into the Saco, where the stuff that didn't sink would float downstream to Maine, and went back as they had come, in *The Helen Rivington*.

David Stone dropped into the conductor's seat, saw that Dan was still holding Abra's stuffed rabbit, and held out his hand for it. Dan passed it over willingly enough, taking note of what Abra's father held in his other hand: his BlackBerry.

'What are you going to do with that?'

Dave looked at the woods flowing by on both sides of the narrow-gauge tracks, then back at Dan. 'As soon as we get to where there's cell coverage, I'm going to call the Deanes' house. If there's no answer, I'm going to call the police. If there *is* an answer, and either Emma or her mother tells me that Abra's gone, I'm going to call the police. Assuming they haven't already.' His gaze was cool and measuring and far from friendly, but at least he was keeping his fear for his daughter – his terror, more likely – at bay, and Dan respected him for that. Also, it would make him easier to reason with.

'I hold you responsible for this, Mr Torrance. It was your plan. Your crazy plan.'

No use pointing out that they had all signed on to the crazy plan. Or that he and John were almost as sick about Abra's continued silence as her father. Basically, the man was right.

You will remember what was forgotten.

Was that another Overlook memory? Dan thought it was. But why now? Why here?

'Dave, she's almost *certainly* been taken.' That was John Dalton. He had moved up to the car just behind them. The last of the lowering sun came through the trees and flickered on his face. 'If that's the case and you tell the police, what do you think will happen to Abra?'

God bless you, Dan thought. *If I'd been the one to say it, I doubt if he would have listened. Because, at bottom, I'm the stranger who was conspiring with his daughter. He'll never be completely convinced that I'm not the one who got her into this mess.*

'What else can we do?' Dave asked, and then his fragile calm broke. He began to weep, and held Abra's stuffed rabbit to his face. 'What am I going to tell my wife? That I was shooting people in Cloud Gap while some bogeyman was stealing our daughter?'

'First things first,' Dan said. He didn't think AA slogans like *Let go and let God* or *Take it easy* would fly with Abra's dad right now. 'You *should* call the Deanes when you get cell coverage. I think you'll reach them, and they'll be fine.'

'You think this why?'

'In my last communication with Abra, I told her to have her friend's mom call the police.'

Dave blinked. 'You really did? Or are you just saying that now to cover your ass?'

'I really did. Abra started to answer. She said "I'm not," and then I lost her. I think she was going to tell me she wasn't at the Deanes' anymore.'

'Is she alive?' Dave grasped Dan's elbow with a hand that was dead cold. 'Is my daughter still alive?'

'I haven't heard from her, but I'm sure she is.'

'Of course you'd say that,' Dave whispered. 'CYA, right?'

Dan bit back a retort. If they started squabbling, any thin chance of getting Abra back would become no chance.

'It makes sense,' John said. Although he was still pale and his hands weren't quite steady, he was using his calm bedside manner voice. 'Dead, she's no good to the one who's left. The one who grabbed her. Alive, she's a hostage. Also, they want her for . . . well . . .'

'They want her for her essence,' Dan said. 'The steam.'

'Another thing,' John said. 'What are you going to tell the cops about the men we killed? That they started cycling in and out of invisibility until they disappeared completely? And then we got rid of their . . . their leavings?'

'I can't believe I let you get me into this.' Dave was twisting the rabbit from side to side. Soon the old toy would split open and spill its stuffing. Dan wasn't sure he could bear to see that.

John said, 'Listen, Dave. For your daughter's sake, you have to clear your mind. She's been in this ever since she saw that boy's picture in the *Shopper* and tried to find out about him. As soon as the one Abra calls the hat woman was aware of her, she almost had to come after her. I don't know about steam, and I know very little about what Dan calls the shining, but I know people like the ones we're dealing with don't leave witnesses. And when it comes to the Iowa boy, that's what your daughter was.'

'Call the Deanes but keep it light,' Dan said.

'Light? *Light?*' He looked like a man trying out a word in Swedish.

'Say you want to ask Abra if there's anything you should pick up at the store – bread or milk or something like that. If they say she went home, just say fine, you'll reach her there.'

'Then what?'

Dan didn't know. All he knew was that he needed to think. He needed to think about what was forgotten.

John *did* know. 'Then you try to reach Billy Freeman.'

It was dusk, with the *Riv*'s headlight cutting a visible cone up the aisle of the tracks, before Dave got bars on his phone. He called the Deanes', and although he was clutching the now-deformed Hoppy in a mighty grip and large beads of sweat were trickling down his face, Dan thought he did a pretty good job. Could Abby come to the phone for a minute and tell him if they needed anything at the Stop & Shop? Oh? She did? Then he'd try her at home. He listened a moment longer, said he'd be sure to do that, and ended the call. He looked at Dan, his eyes white-rimmed holes in his face.

'Mrs Deane wanted me to find out how Abra's feeling. Apparently she went home complaining of menstrual cramps.' He hung his head. 'I didn't even know she'd started having periods. Lucy never said.'

'There are things dads don't need to know,' John said. 'Now try Billy.'

'I don't have his number.' He gave a single chop of a laugh – *HA*! 'We're one fucked-up posse.'

Dan recited it from memory. Up ahead the trees were thinning, and he could see the glow of the streetlights along Frazier's main drag.

Dave punched in the number and listened. Listened some more, then killed the call. 'Voice mail.'

The three men were silent as the *Riv* broke out of the trees and rolled the last two miles toward Teenytown. Dan tried again to reach Abra, throwing his mental voice with all the energy he could muster, and got nothing back. The one she called the Crow had probably knocked her out somehow. The tattoo woman had been carrying a needle. Probably the Crow had another one.

You will remember what was forgotten.

The origin of that thought arose from the very back of his mind, where he kept the lockboxes containing all the terrible memories of the Overlook Hotel and the ghosts who had infested it.

'It was the boiler.'

In the conductor's seat, Dave glanced at him. 'Huh?'

'Nothing.'

The Overlook's heating system had been ancient. The steam pressure had to be dumped at regular intervals or it crept up and up to the point where the boiler could explode and send the whole hotel sky-high. In his steepening descent into dementia, Jack

Torrance had forgotten this, but his young son had been warned. By Tony.

Was this another warning, or just a maddening mnemonic brought on by stress and guilt? Because he *did* feel guilty. John was right, Abra was going to be a True target no matter what, but feelings were invulnerable to rational thought. It had been his plan, the plan had gone wrong, and he was on the hook.

You will remember what was forgotten.

Was it the voice of his old friend, trying to tell him something about their current situation, or just the gramophone?

2

Dave and John went back to the Stone house together. Dan followed in his own car, delighted to be alone with his thoughts. Not that it seemed to help. He was almost positive there was something there, something *real*, but it wouldn't come. He even tried to summon Tony, a thing he hadn't attempted since his teenage years, and had no luck.

Billy's truck was no longer parked on Richland Court. To Dan, that made sense. The True Knot raiding party had come in the Winnebago. If they dropped the Crow off in Anniston, he would have been on foot and in need of a vehicle.

The garage was open. Dave got out of John's car before it pulled completely to a stop and ran inside, calling Abra's name. Then, spotlighted in the headlights of John's Suburban like an actor on a stage, he lifted something up and uttered a sound somewhere between a groan and a scream. As Dan pulled up next to the Suburban, he saw what it was: Abra's backpack.

The urge to drink came on Dan then, even stronger than the night he'd called John from the parking lot of the cowboy-boogie bar, stronger than in all the years since he'd picked up a white chip at his first meeting. The urge to simply reverse down the driveway, ignoring their shouts, and drive back to Frazier. There was a bar there called the Bull Moose. He'd been past it many times, always with the recovered drunk's reflexive speculations – what was it like inside? What was on draft? What kind of music was on the juke?

What whiskey was on the shelf and what kind in the well? Were there any good-looking ladies? And what would that first drink taste like? Would it taste like home? Like finally coming home? He could answer at least some of those questions before Dave Stone called the cops and the cops took him in for questioning in the matter of a certain little girl's disappearance.

A time will come, Casey had told him in those early white-knuckle days, *when your mental defenses will fail and the only thing left standing between you and a drink will be your Higher Power.*

Dan had no problem with the Higher Power thing, because he had a bit of inside information. God remained an unproven hypothesis, but he knew there really was another plane of existence. Like Abra, Dan had seen the ghostie people. So sure, God was possible. Given his glimpses of the world beyond the world, Dan thought it even likely . . . although what kind of God only sat by while shit like this played out?

As if you're the first one to ask that question, he thought.

Casey Kingsley had told him to get down on his knees twice a day, asking for help in the morning and saying thanks at night. *It's the first three steps: I can't, God can, I think I'll let Him. Don't think too much about it.*

To newcomers reluctant to take this advice, Casey was wont to offer a story about the film director John Waters. In one of his early movies, *Pink Flamingos,* Waters's drag-queen star, Divine, had eaten a bit of dog excrement off a suburban lawn. Years later, Waters was still being asked about that glorious moment of cinematic history. Finally he snapped. 'It was just a *little* piece of dogshit,' he told a reporter, 'and it made her a star.'

So get down on your knees and ask for help even if you don't like it, Casey always finished. *After all, it's just a little piece of dogshit.*

Dan couldn't very well get on his knees behind the steering wheel of his car, but he assumed the automatic default position of his morning and nightly prayers – eyes closed and one palm pressed against his lips, as if to keep out even a trickle of the seductive poison that had scarred twenty years of his life.

God, help me not to dri—

He got that far and the light broke.

It was what Dave had said on their way to Cloud Gap. It was Abra's angry smile (Dan wondered if the Crow had seen that smile yet, and what he made of it, if so). Most of all, it was the feel of his own skin, pressing his lips back against his teeth.

'Oh my God,' he whispered. He got out of the car and his legs gave way. He fell on his knees after all, but got up and ran into the garage, where the two men were standing and looking at Abra's abandoned pack.

He grabbed Dave Stone's shoulder. 'Call your wife. Tell her you're coming to see her.'

'She'll want to know what it's about,' Dave said. It was clear from his quivering mouth and downcast eyes how little he wanted to have that conversation. 'She's staying at Chetta's apartment. I'll tell her . . . Christ, I don't know what I'll tell her.'

Dan gripped tighter, increasing the pressure until the lowered eyes came up and met his. 'We're all going to Boston, but John and I have other business to take care of there.'

'What other business? I don't understand.'

Dan did. Not everything, but a lot.

3

They took John's Suburban. Dave rode shotgun. Dan lay in the back with his head on an armrest and his feet on the floor.

'Lucy kept trying to get me to tell her what it was about,' Dave said. 'She told me I was scaring her. And of course she thought it was Abra, because she's got a little of what Abra's got. I've always known it. I told her Abby was staying the night at Emma's house. Do you know how many times I've lied to my wife in the years we've been married? I could count them on one hand, and three of them would be about how much I lost in the Thursday night poker games the head of my department runs. Nothing like this. And in just three hours, I'm going to have to eat it.'

Of course Dan and John knew what he'd said about Abra, and how upset Lucy had been at her husband's continued insistence that the matter was too important and complex to go into on the telephone. They had both been in the kitchen when he made the call. But he needed to talk. To *share*, in AA-speak. John took care of any responses that needed to be made, saying *uh-huh* and *I know* and *I understand*.

At some point, Dave broke off and looked into the backseat. 'Jesus God, are you *sleeping*?'

'No,' Dan said without opening his eyes. 'I'm trying to get in touch with your daughter.'

That ended Dave's monologue. Now there was only the hum of the tires as the Suburban ran south on Route 16 through a dozen little towns. Traffic was light and John kept the speedometer pegged at a steady sixty miles an hour once the two lanes broadened to four.

Dan made no effort to call Abra; he wasn't sure that would work. Instead he tried to open his mind completely. To turn himself into a listening post. He had never attempted anything like this before, and the result was eerie. It was like wearing the world's most powerful set of headphones. He seemed to hear a steady low rushing sound, and believed it was the hum of human thoughts. He held himself ready to hear her voice somewhere in that steady surf, not really expecting it, but what else could he do?

It was shortly after they went through the first tolls on the Spaulding Turnpike, now only sixty miles from Boston, that he finally picked her up.

(*Dan*)

Low. Barely there. At first he thought it was just imagination – wish fulfillment – but he turned in that direction anyway, trying to narrow his concentration down to a single searchlight beam. And it came again, a bit louder this time. It was real. It was *her*.

(*Dan, please!*)

She was drugged, all right, and he'd never tried anything remotely like what had to be done next . . . but Abra had. She would have to show him the way, doped up or not.

(*Abra push you have to help me*)

(*help what help how*)

(*swapsies*)

(*???*)

(*help me turn the world*)

4

Dave was in the passenger seat, going through the change in the cup holder for the next toll, when Dan spoke from behind him. Only it most certainly wasn't Dan.

'Just give me another minute, I have to change my tampon!'

The Suburban swerved as John sat up straight and jerked the wheel. 'What the *hell*?'

Dave unsnapped his seatbelt and got on his knees, twisting around to peer at the man lying on the backseat. Dan's eyes were half-lidded, but when Dave spoke Abra's name, they opened.

'No, Daddy, not now, I have to help . . . I have to try . . .' Dan's body twisted. One hand came up, wiped his mouth in a gesture Dave had seen a thousand times, then fell away. 'Tell him I said not to call me that. Tell him—'

Dan's head cocked sideways until it was lying on his shoulder. He groaned. His hands twitched aimlessly.

'What's going on?' John shouted. 'What do I do?'

'I don't know,' Dave said. He reached between the seats, took one of the twitching hands, and held it tight.

'Drive,' Dan said. 'Just drive.'

Then the body on the backseat began to buck and twist. Abra began to scream with Dan's voice.

5

He found the conduit between them by following the sluggish current of her thoughts. He saw the stone wheel because Abra was visualizing it, but she was far too weak and disoriented to turn it. She was using all the mental force she could muster just to keep her end of the link open. So he could enter her mind and she could enter his. But he was still mostly in the Suburban, with the lights of the cars headed in the other direction running across the padded roof. Light . . . dark . . . light . . . dark.

The wheel was so heavy.

There was a sudden hammering from somewhere, and a voice. 'Come out, Abra. Time's up. We have to roll.'

That frightened her, and she found a little extra strength. The wheel began to move, pulling him deeper into the umbilicus that connected them. It was the strangest sensation Dan had ever had in his life, exhilarating even in the horror of the situation.

Somewhere, distant, he heard Abra say, 'Just give me another minute, I have to change my tampon!'

The roof of John's Suburban was sliding away. *Turning* away. There was darkness, the sense of being in a tunnel, and he had time to think, *If I get lost in here, I'll never be able to get back. I'll wind up in a mental hospital somewhere, labeled a hopeless catatonic.*

But then the world was sliding back into place, only it wasn't the same place. The Suburban was gone. He was in a smelly bathroom with dingy blue tiles on the floor and a sign beside the washbasin reading SORRY COLD WATER ONLY. He was sitting on the toilet.

Before he could even think about getting up, the door bammed open hard enough to crack some of the old tiles, and a man strode in. He looked about thirty-five, his hair dead black and combed away from his forehead, his face angular but handsome in a rough-hewn, bony way. In one hand he held a pistol.

'Change your tampon, sure,' he said. 'Where'd you have it, Goldilocks, in your pants pocket? Must have been, because your backpack's a long way from here.'

(*tell him I said not to call me that*)

Dan said, 'I told you not to call me that.'

Crow paused, looking at the girl sitting on the toilet seat, swaying a little from side to side. Swaying because of the dope. Sure. But what about the way she sounded? Was *that* because of the dope?

'What happened to your voice? You don't sound like yourself.'

Dan tried to shrug the girl's shoulders and only succeeded in twitching one of them. Crow grabbed Abra's arm and yanked Dan to Abra's feet. It hurt, and he cried out.

Somewhere – miles from here – a faint voice shouted, *What's going on? What do I do?*

'Drive,' he told John as Crow pulled him out the door. 'Just drive.'

'Oh, I'll drive, all right,' Crow said, and muscled Abra into the truck next to the snoring Billy Freeman. Then he grabbed a sheaf of her hair, wound it in his fist, and pulled. Dan screamed with Abra's voice, knowing it wasn't *quite* her voice. Almost, but not quite. Crow heard the difference, but didn't know what it was. The hat woman would have; it was the hat woman who had unwittingly shown Abra this mindswap trick.

'But before we get rolling, we're going to have an understanding. No more lies, that's the understanding. The next time you lie to your Daddy, this old geezer snoring beside me is dead meat. I won't use the dope, either. I'll pull in at a camp road and put a bullet in his belly. That way it takes awhile. You'll get to listen to him scream. Do you understand?'

'Yes,' Dan whispered.

'Little girl, I fucking hope so, because I don't chew my cabbage twice.'

Crow slammed the door and walked quickly around to the driver's side. Dan closed Abra's eyes. He was thinking about the spoons at the birthday party. About opening and shutting drawers – that, too. Abra was too physically weak to grapple with the man now getting behind the wheel and starting the engine, but part of her was strong. If he could find that part . . . the part that had moved the spoons and opened drawers and played air-music . . . the part that had written on his blackboard from miles away . . . if he could find it and then take control of it . . .

As Abra had visualized a female warrior's lance and a stallion, Dan now visualized a bank of switches on a control room wall. Some worked her hands, some her legs, some the shrug of her shoulders. Others, though, were more important. He should be able to pull them; he had at least some of the same circuits.

The truck was moving, first reversing, then turning. A moment later they were back on the road.

'That's right,' Crow said grimly. 'Go to sleep. What the hell did you think you were going to do back there? Jump in the toilet and flush yourself away to . . .'

His words faded, because here were the switches Dan was looking for. The special switches, the ones with the red handles. He didn't know if they were really there, and actually connected to Abra's powers, or if this was just some mental game of solitaire he was playing. He only knew that he had to try.

Shine on, he thought, and pulled them all.

6

Billy Freeman's pickup was six or eight miles west of the gas station and rolling through rural Vermont darkness on 108 when Crow first felt the pain. It was like a small silver band circling his left eye. It was cold, pressing. He reached up to touch it, but before he could, it slithered right, freezing the bridge of his nose like a shot of novocaine. Then it circled his other eye as well. It was like wearing metal binoculars.

Or eyecuffs.

Now his left ear began to ring, and suddenly his left cheek was numb. He turned his head and saw the little girl looking at him. Her eyes were wide and unblinking. They didn't look doped in the slightest. For that matter, they didn't look like her eyes. They looked older. Wiser. And as cold as his face now felt.

(stop the truck)

Crow had capped the hypo and put it away, but he was still holding the gun he'd taken from beneath the seat when he decided she was spending way too much time in the crapper. He raised it, meaning to threaten the geezer and make her stop whatever it was she was doing, but all at once his hand felt as if it had been plunged into freezing water. The gun put on weight: five pounds, ten pounds, what felt like twenty-five. Twenty-five at least. And while he was struggling to raise it, his right foot came off the F-150's gas pedal and his left hand turned the wheel so that the truck veered off the road and rolled along the soft shoulder – gently, slowing – with the right-side wheels tilting toward the ditch.

'What are you doing to me?'

'What you deserve. *Daddy*.'

The truck bumped a downed birch tree, snapped it in two, and stopped. The girl and the geezer were seatbelted in, but Crow had forgotten his. He jolted forward into the steering wheel, honking the horn. When he looked down, he saw the geezer's automatic turning in his fist. Very slowly turning toward him. This shouldn't be happening. The dope was supposed to stop it. Hell, the dope *had* stopped it. But something had changed in that bathroom. Whoever was behind those eyes now was cold fucking sober.

And horribly strong.

Rose! Rose, I need you!

'I don't think she can hear,' the voice that wasn't Abra's said. 'You may have some talents, you son of a bitch, but I don't think you have much in the way of telepathy. I think when you want to talk to your girlfriend, you use the phone.'

Exerting all his strength, Crow began to turn the Glock back toward the girl. Now it seemed to weigh fifty pounds. The tendons of his neck stood out like cables. Drops of perspiration beaded on his forehead. One ran into his eye, stinging, and Crow blinked it away.

'I'll . . . shoot . . . your friend,' he said.

'No,' the person inside Abra said. 'I won't let you.'

But Crow could see she was straining now, and that gave him hope. He put everything he had into pointing the muzzle at Rip Van Winkle's midsection, and had almost gotten there when the gun started to rotate back again. Now he could hear the little bitch panting. Hell, he was, too. They sounded like marathoners approaching the end of a race side by side.

A car went by, not slowing. Neither of them noticed. They were looking at each other.

Crow brought his left hand down to join his right on the gun. Now it turned a little more easily. He was beating her, by God. But his eyes! Jesus!

'Billy!' Abra shouted. 'Billy, little help here!'

Billy snorted. His eyes opened. 'Wha—'

For a moment Crow was distracted. The force he was exerting slackened, and the gun immediately began to turn back toward him. His hands were cold, cold. Those metal rings were pressing into his eyes, threatening to turn them to jelly.

The gun went off for the first time when it was between them, blowing a hole in the dashboard just above the radio. Billy jerked awake, arms flailing to either side like a man pulling himself out of a nightmare. One of them struck Abra's temple, the other Crow's chest. The cab of the truck was filled with blue haze and the smell of burnt gunpowder.

'What was that? What the hell was tha—'

Crow snarled, '*No, you bitch! No!*'

He swung the gun back toward Abra, and as he did it, he felt her control slip. It was the blow to the head. Crow could see dismay and terror in her eyes, and was savagely glad.

Have to kill her. Can't give her another chance. But not a headshot. In the gut. Then I'll suck the stea—

Billy slammed his shoulder into Crow's side. The gun jerked up and went off again, this time putting a hole in the roof just above Abra's head. Before Crow could bring it down again, huge hands laid themselves over his. He had time to realize that his adversary had only been tapping a fraction of the force at its command. Panic had unlocked a great, perhaps even unknowable, reserve. This time when the gun turned toward him, Crow's wrists snapped like bundles of twigs. For a moment he saw a single black eye staring up at him, and there was time for half a thought:

(*Rose I love y*)

There was a brilliant flash of white, then darkness. Four seconds later, there was nothing left of Crow Daddy but his clothes.

7

Steamhead Steve, Baba the Red, Bent Dick, and Greedy G were playing a desultory game of canasta in the Bounder that Greedy and Dirty Phil shared when the shrieks began. All four of them had been on edge – the whole True was on edge – and they dropped their cards immediately and ran for the door.

Everyone was emerging from their campers and RVs to see what the matter was, but they stopped when they saw Rose the Hat standing in the brilliant yellow-white glare of the security lights surrounding the Overlook Lodge. Her eyes were wild. She was pulling at her hair like an Old Testament prophet in the throes of a violent vision.

'*That fucking little bitch killed my Crow!*' she shrieked. '*I'll kill her! I'LL KILL HER AND EAT HER HEART!*'

At last she sank to her knees, sobbing into her hands.

The True Knot stood, stunned. No one knew what to say or do. At last Silent Sarey went to her. Rose shoved her violently away. Sarey landed on her back, got up, and returned to Rose without hesitation. This time Rose looked up and saw her would-be comforter, a woman who had also lost someone dear on this unbelievable night. She embraced Sarey, hugging so hard that the watching True heard bones crack. But Sarey didn't struggle, and after a few moments, the two women helped each other to their feet. Rose looked from Silent Sarey to Big Mo, then to Heavy Mary and Token Charlie. It was as if she had never seen any of them.

'Come on, Rosie,' Mo said. 'You've had a shock. You need to lie d—'

'*NO!*'

She stepped away from Silent Sarey and clapped her hands to the sides of her face in a huge double slap that knocked off her hat. She bent down to pick it up, and when she looked around at the gathered True again, some sanity had come back into her eyes. She was thinking of Diesel Doug and the crew she had sent to meet Daddy and the girl.

'I need to get hold of Deez. Tell him and Phil and Annie to turn around. We need to be together. We need to take steam. A lot of it. Once we're loaded, *we're going to get that bitch.*'

They only looked at her, their faces worried and unsure. The sight of those frightened eyes and stupid gaping mouths infuriated her.

'Do you doubt me?' Silent Sarey had crept back to her side. Rose pushed her away from her so hard Sarey almost fell down again. 'Whoever doubts me, let him step forward.'

'No one doubts you, Rose,' Steamhead Steve said, 'but maybe we ought to let her alone.' He spoke carefully, and couldn't quite meet Rose's eyes. 'If Crow's really gone, that's five dead. We've never lost five in one day. We've never even lost t—'

Rose stepped forward and Steve immediately stepped back, hunching his shoulders up around his ears like a child expecting a blow. 'You want to run away from one little steamhead girl? After all these years, you want to turn tail and run from a *rube*?'

No one answered her, least of all Steve, but Rose saw the truth in their eyes. They did. They actually did. They'd had a lot of good years. Fat years. Easy-hunting years. Now they had run across someone who not only had extraordinary steam but knew them for who they were and what they did. Instead of avenging Crow Daddy – who had, along with Rose, seen them through good times and bad – they wanted to put their tails between their legs and go yipping away. In that moment she wanted to kill them all. They felt it and shuffled further back, giving her room.

All but Silent Sarey, who was staring at Rose as if hypnotized, her mouth hung on a hinge. Rose seized her by her scrawny shoulders.

'No, Rosie!' Mo squealed. 'Don't hurt her!'

'What about you, Sarey? That little girl was responsible for murdering the woman you loved. Do you want to run away?'

'Nup,' Sarey said. Her eyes looked up into Rose's. Even now, with everyone looking at her, Sarey seemed little more than a shadow.

'Do you want payback?'

'Lup,' Sarey said. Then: '*Levenge.*'

She had a low voice (almost a no-voice) and a speech impediment, but they all heard her, and they all knew what she was saying.

Rose looked around at the others. 'For those of you who don't want what Sarey wants, who just want to get down on your bellies and squirm away . . .'

She turned to Big Mo and seized the woman's flabby arm. Mo screeched in fear and surprise and tried to draw away. Rose held her in place and lifted her arm so the others could see it. It was covered with red spots. 'Can you squirm away from this?'

They muttered and took another step or two back.

Rose said, 'It's in us.'

'Most of us are fine!' Sweet Terri Pickford shouted. '*I'm* fine! Not a mark on me!' She held her smooth arms out for inspection.

Rose turned her burning, tear-filled eyes on Terri. '*Now.* But for how long?' Sweet Terri made no reply, but turned her face away.

Rose put her arm around Silent Sarey and surveyed the others. 'Nut said that girl may be our only chance of getting rid of the sickness before it infects us all. Does anyone here know better? If you do, speak up.'

No one did.

'We're going to wait until Deez, Annie, and Dirty Phil get back, then we'll take steam. Biggest steam ever. We're going to empty the canisters.'

Looks of surprise and more uneasy mutters greeted this. Did they think she was crazy? Let them. It wasn't just measles eating into the True Knot; it was terror, and that was far worse.

'When we're all together, we're going to circle. We're going to grow strong. *Lodsam hanti*, we are the chosen ones – have you forgotten that? *Sabbatha hanti*, we are the True Knot, and we endure. Say it with me.' Her eyes raked them. '*Say it.*'

They said it, joining hands, making a ring. *We are the True Knot, and we endure.* A little resolution came into their eyes. A little belief. Only half a dozen of them were showing the spots, after all; there was still time.

Rose and Silent Sarey stepped to the circle. Terri and Baba let go of each other to make a place for them, but Rose escorted Sarey to the center. Under the security lights, the bodies of the two women radiated multiple shadows, like the spokes of a wheel. 'When we're strong – when we're one again – we're going to find her and take her. I tell you that as your leader. And even if her steam doesn't cure the sickness that's eating us, it'll be the end of the rotten—'

That was when the girl spoke inside her head. Rose could not see Abra Stone's angry smile, but she could feel it.

(*don't bother coming to me, Rose*)

8

In the back of John Dalton's Suburban, Dan Torrance spoke four clear words in Abra's voice.

'I'll come to you.'

9

'Billy? *Billy!*'

Billy Freeman looked at the girl who didn't exactly *sound* like a girl. She doubled, came together, and doubled again. He passed a hand over his face. His eyelids felt heavy and his thoughts seemed somehow glued together. He couldn't make sense of this. It wasn't daylight anymore, and they sure as hell weren't on Abra's street anymore. 'Who's shooting? And who took a shit in my mouth? *Christ*.'

'Billy, you have to wake up. You have to . . .'

You have to drive was what Dan meant to say, but Billy Freeman wasn't going to be driving anywhere. Not for a while. His eyes were drifting shut again, the lids out of sync. Dan threw one of Abra's elbows into the old guy's side and got his attention again. For the time being, at least.

Headlights flooded the cab of the truck as another car approached. Dan held Abra's breath, but this one also went by without slowing. Maybe a woman on her own, maybe a salesman in a hurry to get home. A bad Samaritan, whoever it was, and bad was good for them, but they might not be lucky a third time. Rural people tended to be neighborly. Not to mention nosy.

'Stay awake,' he said.

'Who *are* you?' Billy tried to focus on the kid, but it was impossible. 'Because you sure don't sound like Abra.'

'It's complicated. For now, just concentrate on staying awake.'

Dan got out and walked around to the driver's side of the truck, stumbling several times. Her legs, which had seemed so long on the day he met her, were too damned short. He only hoped he wouldn't have enough time to get used to them.

Crow's clothes were lying on the seat. His canvas shoes were on the dirty floormat with the socks trailing out of them. The blood and brains that had splattered his shirt and jacket had cycled out of existence, but they had left damp spots. Dan gathered everything up and, after a moment's consideration, added the gun. He didn't want to give it up, but if they were stopped . . .

He took the bundle to the front of the truck and buried it beneath a drift of old leaves. Then he grabbed a piece of the downed birch the F-150 had struck and dragged it over the burial site. It was hard work with Abra's arms, but he managed.

He found he couldn't just step into the cab; he had to pull himself up by the steering wheel. And once he was finally behind the wheel, her feet barely reached the pedals. *Fuck*.

Billy gave a galumphing snore, and Dan threw another elbow. Billy opened his eyes and looked around. 'Where are we? Did that guy drug me?' Then: 'I think I have to go back to sleep.'

At some point during the final life-or-death struggle for the gun, Crow's unopened bottle of Fanta had fallen to the floor. Dan bent over, grabbed it, then paused with Abra's hand on the cap, remembering what happens to soda when it takes a hard thump. From somewhere, Abra spoke to him

(*oh dear*)

and she was smiling, but it wasn't the angry smile. Dan thought that was good.

10

You can't let me go to sleep, the voice coming from Dan's mouth said, so John took the Fox Run exit and parked in the lot farthest from Kohl's. There he and Dave walked Dan's body up and down, one on each side. He was like a drunk at the end of a hard night – every now and then his head sagged to his chest before snapping back up again. Both men took a turn at asking what had happened, what was happening now, and *where* it was happening, but Abra only shook Dan's head. 'The Crow shot me in my hand before he let me go in the bathroom. The rest is all fuzzy. Now shh, I have to concentrate.'

On the third wide circle of John's Suburban, Dan's mouth broke into a grin, and a very Abra-like giggle issued from him. Dave looked a question at John across the body of their shambling, stumbling charge. John shrugged and shook his head.

'Oh, dear,' Abra said. 'Soda.'

11

Dan tilted the soda and removed the cap. A high-pressure spray of orange pop hit Billy full in the face. He coughed and spluttered, for the time being wide awake.

'Jesus, kid! Why'd you do that?'

'It worked, didn't it?' Dan handed him the still-fizzing soda. 'Put the rest inside you. I'm sorry, but you can't go back to sleep, no matter how much you want to.'

While Billy tilted the bottle and chugged soda, Dan leaned over and found the seat adjustment lever. He pulled it with one hand and yanked on the steering wheel with the other. The seat jolted forward. It caused Billy to spill Fanta down his chin (and to utter a phrase not generally used by adults around young girls from New Hampshire), but now Abra's feet could reach the pedals. Barely. Dan put the truck in reverse and backed up slowly, angling toward the road as he went. When they were on the pavement, he breathed a sigh of relief. Getting stuck in a ditch beside a little-used Vermont highway would not have advanced their cause much.

'Do you know what you're doing?' Billy asked.

'Yes. Been doing it for years . . . although there was a little lag time when the state of Florida took away my license. I was in another state at the time, but there's a little thing called reciprocity. The bane of traveling drunks all across this great country of ours.'

'You're Dan.'

'Guilty as charged,' he said, peering over the top of the steering wheel. He wished he had a book to sit on, but since he didn't, he would just have to do the best he could. He dropped the transmission into drive and got rolling.

'How'd you get inside her?'

'Don't ask.'

The Crow had said something (or only thought it, Dan didn't know which) about camp roads, and about four miles up Route 108, they came to a lane with a rustic wooden sign nailed to a pine tree: BOB AND DOT'S HAPPY PLACE. If that wasn't a camp road, nothing was. Dan turned in, Abra's arms glad for the power steering, and flicked on the high beams. A quarter of a mile up, the lane was barred by a heavy chain with another sign hanging from it, this one less rustic: NO TRESPASSING. The chain was good. It meant Bob and Dot hadn't decided on a getaway weekend at their happy place, and a quarter of a mile from the highway was enough to assure them of some privacy. There was another bonus: a culvert with water trickling out of it.

He killed the lights and engine, then turned to Billy. 'See that culvert? Go wash the soda off your face. Splash up good. You need to be as wide awake as you can get.'

'I'm awake,' Billy said.

'Not enough. Try to keep your shirt dry. And when you're done, comb your hair. You're going to have to meet the public.'

'Where are we?'

'Vermont.'

'Where's the guy who hijacked me?'

'Dead.'

'Good goddam riddance!' Billy exclaimed. Then, after a moment's thought: 'How about the body? Where's that?'

An excellent question, but not one Dan wanted to answer. What he wanted was for this to be over. It was exhausting, and disorienting in a thousand ways. 'Gone. That's really all you need to know.'

'But—'

'Not now. Wash your face, then walk up and down this road a few times. Swing your arms, take deep breaths, and get as clear as you can.'

'I've got one *bitch* of a headache.'

Dan wasn't surprised. 'When you come back, the girl is probably going to be the girl again, which means you'll have to drive. If you feel sober enough to be plausible, go to the next town that has a motel and check in. You're traveling with your granddaughter, got it?'

'Yeah,' Billy said. 'My granddaughter. Abby Freeman.'

'Once you're in, call me on my cell.'

'Because you'll be wherever . . . wherever the rest of you is.'

'Right.'

'This is fucked to the sky, buddy.'

'Yes,' Dan said. 'It certainly is. Our job now is to unfuck it.'

'Okay. What *is* the next town?'

'No idea. I don't want you having an accident, Billy. If you can't get clear enough to drive twenty or thirty miles and then check into a motel without having the guy on the counter call the cops, you and Abra will have to spend the night in the cab of this truck. It won't be comfortable, but it should be safe.'

Billy opened the passenger-side door. 'Give me ten minutes. I'll be able to pass for sober. Done it before.' He gave the girl behind the steering wheel a wink. 'I work for Casey Kingsley. Death on drinkin, remember?'

Dan watched him go to the culvert and kneel there, then closed Abra's eyes.

In a parking lot outside the Newington Mall, Abra closed Dan's.
(*Abra*)
(*I'm here*)
(*are you awake*)
(*yes sort of*)
(*we need to turn the wheel again can you help me*)
This time, she could.

12

'Let go of me, you guys,' Dan said. His voice was his own again. 'I'm all right. I think.'

John and Dave let go, ready to grab him again if he staggered, but he didn't. What he did was touch himself: hair, face, chest, legs. Then he nodded. 'Yeah,' he said. 'I'm here.' He looked around. 'Which is where?'

'Newington Mall,' John said. 'Sixty miles or so from Boston.'

'Okay, let's get back on the road.'

'Abra,' Dave said. 'What about Abra?'

'Abra's fine. Back where she belongs.'

'She *belongs* at home,' Dave said, and with more than a touch of resentment. 'In her room. IM'ing with her friends or listening to those stupid 'Round Here kids on her iPod.'

She is *at home*, Dan thought. *If a person's body is their home, she's there.*

'She's with Billy. Billy will take care of her.'

'What about the one who kidnapped her? This Crow?'

Dan paused beside the back door of John's Suburban. 'You don't have to worry about him anymore. The one we have to worry about now is Rose.'

13

The Crown Motel was actually over the state line, in Crownville, New York. It was a rattletrap place with a flickering sign out front reading VAC NCY and M NY CAB E CHAN ELS! Only four cars were parked in the thirty or so slots. The man behind the counter was a descending mountain of fat, with a ponytail that trickled to a stop halfway down his back. He ran Billy's Visa and gave him the keys to two rooms without taking his eyes from the TV, where two women on a red velvet sofa were engaged in strenuous osculation.

'Do they connect?' Billy asked. And, looking at the women: 'The rooms, I mean.'

'Yeah, yeah, they all connect, just open the doors.'

'Thanks.'

He drove down the rank of units to twenty-three and twenty-four, and parked the truck. Abra was curled up on the seat with her head pillowed on one arm, fast asleep. Billy unlocked the rooms, turned on the lights, and opened the connecting doors. He judged the accommodations shabby but not quite desperate. All he wanted now was to get the two of them inside and go to sleep himself. Preferably for about ten hours. He rarely felt old, but tonight he felt ancient.

Abra woke up a little as he laid her on the bed. 'Where are we?'

'Crownville, New York. We're safe. I'll be in the next room.'

'I want my dad. And I want Dan.'

'Soon.' Hoping he was right about that.

Her eyes closed, then slowly opened again. 'I talked to that woman. That *bitch*.'

'Did you?' Billy had no idea what she meant.

'She knows what we did. She felt it. And it *hurt*.' A harsh light gleamed momentarily in Abra's eyes. Billy thought it was like seeing a peek of sun at the end of a cold, overcast day in February. 'I'm glad.'

'Go to sleep, hon.'

That cold winter light still shone out of the pale and tired face. 'She knows I'm coming for her.'

Billy thought of brushing her hair out of her eyes, but what if she bit? Probably that was silly, but . . . the light in her eyes. His mother had looked like that sometimes, just before she lost her temper and whopped one of the kids. 'You'll feel better in the morning. I'd like it if we could go back tonight – I'm sure your dad feels that way, too – but I'm in no shape to drive. I was lucky to get this far without running off the road.'

'I wish I could talk to my mom and dad.'

Billy's own mother and father – never candidates for Parents of the Year, even at their best – were long dead and he wished only for sleep. He looked longingly through the open door at the bed in the other room. Soon, but not quite yet. He took out his cell phone and flipped it open. It rang twice, and then he was talking to Dan. After a few moments, he handed the phone to Abra. 'Your father. Knock yourself out.'

Abra seized the phone. 'Dad? *Dad*?' Tears began to fill her eyes. 'Yes, I'm . . . stop, Dad, I'm *all right*. Just so sleepy I can hardly—' Her eyes widened as a thought struck her. 'Are *you* okay?'

She listened. Billy's eyes drifted shut and he snapped them open with an effort. The girl was crying hard now, and he was sort of glad. The tears had doused that light in her eyes.

She handed the phone back. 'It's Dan. He wants to talk to you again.'

He took the phone and listened. Then he said, 'Abra, Dan wants to know if you think there are any other bad guys. Ones close enough to get here tonight.'

'No. I think the Crow was going to meet some others, but they're still a long way away. And they can't figure out where we are' – she broke off for a huge yawn – 'without him to tell them. Tell Dan we're safe. And tell him to make sure my dad gets that.'

Billy relayed this message. When he ended the call, Abra was curled up on the bed, knees to chest, snoring softly. Billy covered her with a blanket from the closet, then went to the door and ran the chain. He considered, then propped the desk chair under the knob for good measure. *Always safe, never sorry*, his father had liked to say.

14

Rose opened the compartment under the floor and took out one of the canisters. Still on her knees between the EarthCruiser's front seats, she cracked it and put her mouth over the hissing lid. Her jaw unhinged all the way to her chest, and the bottom of her head became a dark hole in which a single tooth jutted. Her eyes, ordinarily uptilted, bled downward and darkened. Her face became a doleful deathmask with the skull standing out clear beneath.

She took steam.

When she was done, she replaced the canister and sat behind the wheel of her RV, looking straight ahead. *Don't bother coming to me, Rose — I'll come to you.* That was what she had said. What she had *dared* to say to her, Rose O'Hara, Rose the Hat. Not just strong, then; strong and *vengeful*. Angry.

'Come ahead, darling,' she said. 'And stay angry. The angrier you are, the more foolhardy you'll be. Come and see your auntie Rose.'

There was a snap. She looked down and saw she had broken off the lower half of the EarthCruiser's steering wheel. Steam conveyed strength. Her hands were bleeding. Rose threw the jagged arc of plastic aside, raised her palms to her face, and began to lick them.

CHAPTER SIXTEEN
THAT WHICH WAS FORGOTTEN

1

The moment Dan closed his phone, Dave said, 'Let's pick up Lucy and go get her.'

Dan shook his head. 'She says they're okay, and I believe her.'

'She's been drugged, though,' John said. 'Her judgment might not be the best right now.'

'She was clear enough to help me take care of the one she calls the Crow,' Dan said, 'and I trust her on this. Let them sleep off whatever the bastard drugged them with. We have other things to do. Important things. You've got to trust me a little here. You'll be with your daughter soon enough, David. For the moment, though, listen to me carefully. We're going to drop you off at your grand-mother-in-law's place. You're going to bring your wife to the hospital.'

'I don't know if she'll believe me when I tell her what happened today. I don't know how convincing I can be when I hardly believe it myself.'

'Tell her the story has to wait until we're all together. And that includes Abra's momo.'

'I doubt if they'll let you in to see her.' Dave glanced at his watch. 'Visiting hours are long over, and she's very ill.'

'Floor staff doesn't pay much attention to the visiting rules when patients are near the end,' Dan said.

Dave looked at John, who shrugged. 'The man works in a hospice. I think you can trust him on that.'

'She may not even be conscious,' Dave said.

'Let's worry about one thing at a time.'

'What does Chetta have to do with this, anyway? She doesn't know anything about it!'

Dan said, 'I'm pretty sure she knows more than you think.'

2

They dropped Dave off at the condo on Marlborough Street and watched from the curb as he mounted the steps and rang one of the bells.

'He looks like a little kid who knows he's going to the woodshed for a pants-down butt whippin,' John said. 'This is going to strain the hell out of his marriage, no matter how it turns out.'

'When a natural disaster happens, no one's to blame.'

'Try to make Lucy Stone see that. She's going to think, "You left your daughter alone and a crazy guy snatched her." On some level, she's always going to think it.'

'Abra might change her mind about that. As for today, we did what we could, and so far we're not doing too badly.'

'But it's not over.'

'Not by a long shot.'

Dave was ringing the bell again and peering into the little lobby when the elevator opened and Lucy Stone came rushing out. Her face was strained and pale. Dave started to talk as soon as she opened the door. So did she. Lucy pulled him in – *yanked* him in – by both arms.

'Ah, man,' John said softly. 'That reminds me of too many nights when I rolled in drunk at three in the morning.'

'Either he'll convince her or he won't,' Dan said. 'We've got other business.'

3

Dan Torrance and John Dalton arrived at Massachusetts General Hospital shortly after ten thirty. It was slack tide on the intensive care floor. A deflating helium balloon with FEEL BETTER SOON printed on it in particolored letters drifted halfheartedly along the hallway ceiling, casting a jellyfish shadow. Dan approached the nurses' station, identified himself as a staffer at the hospice to which Ms Reynolds was scheduled to be moved, showed his Helen Rivington House ID, and introduced John Dalton as the family doctor (a stretch, but not an actual lie).

'We need to assess her condition prior to the transfer,' Dan said, 'and two family members have asked to be present. They are Ms Reynolds's granddaughter and her granddaughter's husband. I'm sorry about the lateness of the hour, but it was unavoidable. They'll be here shortly.'

'I've met the Stones,' the head nurse said. 'They're lovely people. Lucy in particular has been very attentive to her gran. Concetta's special. I've been reading her poems, and they're wonderful. But if you're expecting any input from her, gentlemen, you're going to be disappointed. She's slipped into a coma.'

We'll see about that, Dan thought.

'And . . .' The nurse looked at John doubtfully. 'Well . . . it's really not my place to say . . .'

'Go on,' John said. 'I've never met a head nurse who didn't know what the score was.'

She smiled at him, then turned her attention back to Dan. 'I've heard wonderful things about the Rivington hospice, but I doubt very much if Concetta will be going there. Even if she lasts until Monday, I'm not sure there's any point in moving her. It might be kinder to let her finish her journey here. If I'm stepping out of line, I'm sorry.'

'You're not,' Dan said, 'and we'll take that into consideration. John, would you go down to the lobby and escort the Stones up when they arrive? I can start without you.'

'Are you sure—'

'Yes,' Dan said, holding his eyes. 'I am.'

'She's in Room Nine,' the head nurse said. 'It's the single at the end of the hall. If you need me, ring her call bell.'

4

Concetta's name was on the Room 9 door, but the slot for medical orders was empty and the vitals monitor overhead showed nothing hopeful. Dan stepped into aromas he knew well: air freshener, antiseptic, and mortal illness. The last was a high smell that sang in his head like a violin that knows only one note. The walls were covered with photographs, many featuring Abra at various ages. One showed a gapemouthed cluster of little folks watching a magician pull a white rabbit from a hat. Dan was sure it had been taken at the famous birthday party, the Day of the Spoons.

Surrounded by these pictures, a skeleton woman slept with her mouth open and a pearl rosary twined in her fingers. Her remaining hair was so fine it almost disappeared against the pillow. Her skin, once olive-toned, was now yellow. The rise and fall of her thin bosom was hardly there. One look was enough to tell Dan that the head nurse had indeed known what the score was. If Azzie were here, he would have been curled up next to the woman in this room, waiting for Doctor Sleep to arrive so he could resume his late-night patrol of corridors empty save for the things only cats could see.

Dan sat down on the side of the bed, noting that the single IV going into her was a saline drip. There was only one medicine that could help her now, and the hospital pharmacy didn't stock it. Her cannula had come askew. He straightened it. Then he took her hand and looked into the sleeping face.

(*Concetta*)

There was a slight hitch in her breathing.

(*Concetta come back*)

Beneath the thin, bruised lids, the eyes moved. She might have been listening; she might have been dreaming her last dreams. Of Italy, perhaps. Bending over the household well and hauling up a bucket of cool water. Bending over in the hot summer sun.

(*Abra needs you to come back and so do I*)

It was all he could do, and he wasn't sure it would be enough until, slowly, her eyes opened. They were vacant at first, but they gained perception. Dan had seen this before. The miracle of returning consciousness. Not for the first time he wondered where it came from, and where it went when it departed. Death was no less a miracle than birth.

The hand he was holding tightened. The eyes remained on Dan's, and Concetta smiled. It was a timid smile, but it was there.

'*Oh mio caro! Sei tu? Sei tu? Come e possibile? Sei morto? Sono morta anch'io? . . . Siamo fantasmi?*'

Dan didn't speak Italian, and didn't have to. He heard what she was saying with perfect clarity in his head.

Oh my dear one, is it you? How can it be you? Are you dead? Am I?
Then, after a pause:
Are we ghosts?
Dan leaned toward her until his cheek lay against hers.
In her ear, he whispered.
In time, she whispered back.

5

Their conversation was short but illuminating. Concetta spoke mostly in Italian. At last she lifted a hand – it took great effort, but she managed – and caressed his stubbly cheek. She smiled.

'Are you ready?' he asked.

'*Sì*. Ready.'

'There's nothing to be afraid of.'

'*Sì*, I know that. I'm so glad you come. Tell me again your name, *signor*.'

'Daniel Torrance.'

'*Sì*. You are a gift from God, Daniel Torrance. *Sei un dono di Dio.*'

Dan hoped it was true. 'Will you give to me?'

'*Sì*, of course. What you need *per* Abra.'

'And I'll give to you, Chetta. We'll drink from the well together.'

She closed her eyes.

(*I know*)

'You'll go to sleep, and when you wake up—'

(*everything will be better*)

The power was even stronger than it had been on the night Charlie Hayes passed; he could feel it between them as he gently clasped her hands in his and felt the smooth pebbles of her rosary against his palms. Somewhere, lights were being turned off, one by one. It was all right. In Italy a little girl in a brown dress and sandals was drawing water from the cool throat of a well. She looked like Abra, that little girl. The dog was barking. *Il cane. Ginata. Il cane si rotolava sull'erba.* Barking and rolling in the grass. Funny Ginata!

Concetta was sixteen and in love, or thirty and writing a poem at the kitchen table of a hot apartment in Queens while children shouted on the street below; she was sixty and standing in the rain and looking up at a hundred thousand lines of purest falling silver. She was her mother and her great-granddaughter and it was time for her great change, her great voyage. Ginata was rolling in the grass and the lights

(*hurry up please*)

were going out one by one. A door was opening

(*hurry up please it's time*)

and beyond it they could both smell all the mysterious, fragrant respiration of the night. Above were all the stars that ever were.

He kissed her cool forehead. 'Everything's all right, *cara*. You only need to sleep. Sleep will make you better.'

Then he waited for her final breath.

It came.

6

He was still sitting there, holding her hands in his, when the door burst open and Lucy Stone came striding in. Her husband and her daughter's pediatrician followed, but not too closely; it was as if they feared being burned by the fear, fury, and confused outrage that surrounded her in a crackling aura so strong it was almost visible.

She seized Dan by the shoulder, her fingernails digging like claws into the shoulder beneath his shirt. 'Get away from her. You don't know her. You have no more business with my grandmother than you do with my daugh—'

'Lower your voice,' Dan said without turning. 'You're in the presence of death.'

The rage that had stiffened her ran out all at once, loosening her joints. She sagged to the bed beside Dan and looked at the waxen image that was now her grandmother's face. Then she looked at the haggard, beard-scruffy man who sat holding the dead hands, in which the rosary was still entwined. Unnoticed tears began rolling down Lucy's cheeks in big clear drops.

'I can't make out half of what they've been trying to tell me. Just that Abra was kidnapped, but now she's all right – supposedly – and she's in a motel with some man named Billy and they're both sleeping.'

'All that's true,' Dan said.

'Then spare me your holier-than-thou pronouncements, if you please. I'll mourn my momo after I see Abra. When I've got my arms around her. For now, I want to know . . . I want . . .' She trailed off, looking from Dan to her dead grandmother and back to Dan again. Her husband stood behind her. John had closed the door of Room 9 and was leaning against it. 'Your name is Torrance? Daniel Torrance?'

'Yes.'

Again that slow look from her grandmother's still profile to the man who had been present when she died. 'Who are you, Mr Torrance?'

Dan let go of Chetta's hands and took Lucy's. 'Walk with me. Not far. Just across the room.'

She stood up without protest, still looking into his face. He led her to the bathroom door, which was standing open. He turned on the light and pointed to the mirror above the washbasin, where they were framed as if in a photograph. Seen that way, there could be little doubt. None, really.

He said, 'My father was your father, Lucy. I'm your half brother.'

7

After notifying the head nurse that there had been a death on the floor, they went to the hospital's small nondenominational chapel. Lucy knew the way; although not much of a believer, she had spent a good many hours there, thinking and remembering. It was a comforting place to do those things, which are necessary when a loved one nears the end. At this hour, they had it all to themselves.

'First things first,' Dan said. 'I have to ask if you believe me. We can do the DNA test when there's time, but . . . do we need to?'

Lucy shook her head dazedly, never taking her eyes from his face. She seemed to be trying to memorize it. 'Dear Jesus. I can hardly get my breath.'

'I thought you looked familiar the first time I saw you,' Dave said to Dan. 'Now I know why. I would have gotten it sooner, I think, if it hadn't been . . . you know . . .'

'So right in front of you,' John said. 'Dan, does Abra know?'

'Sure.' Dan smiled, remembering Abra's theory of relativity.

'She got it from your mind?' Lucy asked. 'Using her telepathy thing?'

'No, because *I* didn't know. Even someone as talented as Abra can't read something that isn't there. But on a deeper level, we both knew. Hell, we even said it out loud. If anyone asked what we were doing together, we were going to say I was her uncle. Which I am. I should have realized consciously sooner than I did.'

'This is coincidence beyond coincidence,' Dave said, shaking his head.

'It's not. It's the farthest thing in the world from coincidence. Lucy, I understand that you're confused and angry. I'll tell you everything I know, but it will take some time. Thanks to John and your husband and Abra — her most of all — we've got some.'

'On the way,' Lucy said. 'You can tell me on the way to Abra.'

'All right,' Dan said, 'on the way. But three hours' sleep first.'

She was shaking her head before he finished. 'No, now. I have to see her as soon as I possibly can. Don't you understand? She's my daughter, she's been kidnapped, and *I have to see her!*'

'She's been kidnapped, but now she's safe,' Dan said.

'You say that, of course you do, but you don't know.'

'*Abra* says it,' he replied. 'And she *does* know. Listen, Mrs Stone — Lucy — she's asleep right now, and she needs her sleep.' *I do, too. I've got a long trip ahead of me, and I think it's going to be a hard one. Very hard.*

Lucy was looking at him closely. 'Are you all right?'

'Just tired.'

'We all are,' John said. 'It's been . . . a stressful day.' He uttered a brief yap of laughter, then pressed both hands over his mouth like a child who's said a naughty word.

'I can't even call her and hear her voice,' Lucy said. She spoke slowly, as if trying to articulate a difficult precept. 'Because they're sleeping off the drugs this man . . . the one you say she calls the Crow . . . put into her.'

'Soon,' Dave said. 'You'll see her soon.' He put his hand over hers. For a moment Lucy looked as if she would shake it off. She clasped it instead.

'I can start on the way back to your grandmother's,' Dan said. He got up. It was an effort. 'Come on.'

8

He had time to tell her how a lost man had ridden a northbound bus out of Massachusetts, and how – just over the New Hampshire state line – he'd tossed what would turn out to be his last bottle of booze into a trash can with IF YOU NO LONGER NEED IT, LEAVE IT HERE stenciled on the side. He told them how his childhood friend Tony had spoken up for the first time in years when the bus had rolled into Frazier. *This is the place*, Tony had said.

From there he doubled back to a time when he had been Danny instead of Dan (and sometimes doc, as in *what's up, doc*), and his invisible friend Tony had been an absolute necessity. The shining was only one of the burdens that Tony helped him bear, and not the major one. The major one was his alcoholic father, a troubled and ultimately dangerous man whom both Danny and his mother had loved deeply – perhaps as much because of his flaws as in spite of them.

'He had a terrible temper, and you didn't have to be a telepath to know when it was getting the best of him. For one thing, he was usually drunk when it happened. I know he was loaded on the night he caught me in his study, messing with his papers. He broke my arm.'

'How old were you?' Dave asked. He was riding in the backseat with his wife.

'Four, I think. Maybe even younger. When he was on the warpath, he had this habit of rubbing his mouth.' Danny demonstrated. 'Do you know anyone else who does that when she's upset?'

'Abra,' Lucy said. 'I thought she got it from me.' She raised her right hand toward her mouth, then captured it with her left and returned it to her lap. Dan had seen Abra do exactly the same thing on the bench outside the Anniston Public Library, on the day they'd met in person for the first time. 'I thought she got her temper from me, too. I can be . . . pretty ragged sometimes.'

'I thought of my father the first time I saw her do the mouth-rubbing thing,' Dan said, 'but I had other things on my mind. So I forgot.' This made him think of Watson, the caretaker at the

Overlook, who had first shown the hotel's untrustworthy furnace boiler to his father. *You have to watch it*, Watson had said. *Because she creeps*. But in the end, Jack Torrance had forgotten. It was the reason Dan was still alive.

'Are you telling me you figured out this family relationship from one little habit? That's quite a deductive leap, especially when it's you and I who look alike, not you and Abra – she gets most of her looks from her father.' Lucy paused, thinking. 'But of course you share another family trait – Dave says you call it the shining. *That's* how you knew, isn't it?'

Dan shook his head. 'I made a friend the year my father died. His name was Dick Hallorann, and he was the cook at the Overlook Hotel. He also had the shining, and he told me lots of people had a little bit of it. He was right. I've met plenty of people along the way who shine to a greater or lesser degree. Billy Freeman, for one. Which is why he's with Abra right now.'

John swung the Suburban into the little parking area behind Concetta's condo, but for the time being, none of them got out. In spite of her worry about her daughter, Lucy was fascinated by this history lesson. Dan didn't have to look at her to know it.

'If it wasn't the shining, what was it?'

'When we were going out to Cloud Gap on the *Riv*, Dave mentioned that you found a trunk in storage at Concetta's building.'

'Yes. My mother's. I had no idea Momo had saved some of her things.'

'Dave told John and me that she was quite the party girl, back in the day.' It was actually Abra that Dave had been talking to, via telepathic link, but this was something Dan felt it might be better for his newly discovered half sister not to know, at least for the time being.

Lucy flashed Dave the reproachful look reserved for spouses who have been telling tales out of school, but said nothing.

'He also said that when Alessandra dropped out of SUNY Albany, she was doing her student teaching at a prep school in Vermont or Massachusetts. My father taught English – until he lost his job for hurting a student, that is – in Vermont. At a school called Stovington Prep. And according to my mother, he was quite the party *boy* in those days. Once I knew that Abra and Billy were safe, I ran some numbers in my head. They seemed to add up, but I felt if anyone knew for sure, it would be Alessandra Anderson's mother.'

'*Did* she?' Lucy asked. She was leaning forward now, her hands on the console between the front seats.

'Not everything, and we didn't have long together, but she knew enough. She didn't remember the name of the school where your mother student-taught, but she knew it was in Vermont. And that she'd had a brief affair with her supervising teacher. Who was, she said, a published writer.' Dan paused. 'My father was a published writer. Only a few stories, but some of them were in very good magazines, like the *Atlantic Monthly*. Concetta never asked her for the man's name, and Alessandra never volunteered it, but if her college transcript is in that trunk, I'm pretty sure you'll find that her supervisor was John Daniel Torrance.' He yawned and looked at his watch. 'That's all I can do right now. Let's go upstairs. Three hours' sleep for all of us, then on to upstate New York. The roads will be empty, and we should be able to make great time.'

'Do you swear she's safe?' Lucy asked.

Dan nodded.

'All right, I'll wait. But only for three hours. As for sleeping . . .' She laughed. The sound had no humor in it.

9

When they entered Concetta's condo, Lucy strode directly to the microwave in the kitchen, set the timer, and showed it to Dan. He nodded, then yawned again. 'Three thirty a.m., we're out of here.'

She studied him gravely. 'I'd like to go without you, you know. Right this minute.'

He smiled a little. 'I think you better hear the rest of the story first.'

She nodded grimly.

'That and the fact that my daughter needs to sleep off whatever is in her system are the only things holding me here. Now go lie down before you fall down.'

Dan and John took the guest room. The wallpaper and furnishings made it clear that it had been mostly kept for one special little girl, but Chetta must have had other guests from time to time, because there were twin beds.

As they lay in the dark, John said: 'It's not a coincidence that this hotel you stayed in as a child is also in Colorado, is it?'

'No.'

'This True Knot is in the same town?'

'They are.'

'And the hotel was haunted?'

The ghostie people, Dan thought. 'Yes.'

Then John said something that surprised Dan and temporarily brought him back from the edge of sleep. Dave had been right – the easiest things to miss were the ones right in front of you. 'It makes sense, I suppose . . . once you accept the idea there could be supernatural beings among us and feeding on us. An evil place would call evil creatures. They'd feel right at home there. Do you suppose this Knot has other places like that, in other parts of the country? Other . . . I don't know . . . cold spots?'

'I'm sure they do.' Dan put an arm over his eyes. His body ached and his head was pounding. 'Johnny, I'd love to do the boys-having-a-sleepover thing with you, but I have to get some shuteye.'

'Okay, but . . .' John got up on one elbow. 'All things being equal, you would have gone right from the hospital, like Lucy wanted. Because you care almost as much about Abra as they do. You think she's safe, but you could be wrong.'

'I'm not.' Hoping that was the truth. He had to hope so, because the simple fact was that he couldn't go, not now. If it had only been to New York, maybe. But it wasn't, and he had to sleep. His whole body cried for it.

'What's wrong with you, Dan? Because you look terrible.'

'Nothing. Just tired.'

Then he was gone, first into darkness and then into a confused nightmare of running down endless halls while some Shape followed him, swinging a mallet from side to side, splitting wallpaper and driving up puffs of plaster dust. *Come out, you little shit!* the Shape yelled. *Come out, you worthless pup, and take your medicine!*

Then Abra was with him. They were sitting on the bench in front of the Anniston Public Library, in the late-summer sun. She was holding his hand. *It's all right, Uncle Dan. It's all right. Before he died, your father turned that Shape out. You don't have to*—

The library door banged open and a woman stepped into the sunlight. Great clouds of dark hair billowed around her head, yet her jauntily cocked tophat stayed on. It stayed on like magic.

'Oh, look,' she said. 'It's Dan Torrance, the man who stole a woman's money while she was sleeping one off and then left her kid to be beaten to death.'

She smiled at Abra, revealing a single tooth. It looked as long and sharp as a bayonet.

'What will he do to you, little sweetie? What will he do to *you*?'

10

Lucy woke him promptly at three thirty, but shook her head when Dan moved to wake John. 'Let him sleep a bit longer. And my husband is snoring on the couch.' She actually smiled. 'It makes me think of the Garden of Gethsemane, you know. Jesus reproaching Peter, saying, "So you could not watch with me even one hour?" Or something like that. But I have no reason to reproach David, I guess – he saw it, too. Come on. I've made scrambled eggs. You look like you could use some. You're skinny as a rail.' She paused and added: 'Brother.'

Dan wasn't particularly hungry, but he followed her into the kitchen. 'Saw what, too?'

'I was going through Momo's papers – anything to keep my hands busy and pass the time – and I heard a clunk from the kitchen.'

She took his hand and led him to the counter between the stove and the fridge. There was a row of old-fashioned apothecary jars here, and the one containing sugar had been overturned. A message had been written in the spill.

I'm OK

Going back to sleep

Love U

☺

In spite of how he felt, Dan thought of his blackboard and had to smile. It was so perfectly Abra.

'She must have woken up just enough to do that,' Lucy said.

'Don't think so,' Dan said.

She looked at him from the stove, where she was dishing up scrambled eggs.

'*You* woke her up. She heard your worry.'

'Do you really believe that?'

'Yes.'

'Sit down.' She paused. 'Sit down, *Dan*. I guess I better get used to calling you that. Sit down and eat.'

Dan wasn't hungry, but he needed the fuel. He did as she said.

11

She sat across from him, sipping a glass of juice from the last carafe Concetta Reynolds would ever have delivered from Dean & DeLuca. 'Older man with booze issues, starstruck younger woman. That's the picture I'm getting.'

'It's the one I got, too.' Dan shoveled the eggs in steadily and methodically, not tasting them.

'Coffee, Mr . . . Dan?'

'Please.'

She went past the spilled sugar to the Bunn. 'He's married, but his job takes him to a lot of faculty parties where there are a lot of pretty young gals. Not to mention a fair amount of blooming libido when the hour gets late and the music gets loud.'

'Sounds about right,' Dan said. 'Maybe my mom used to go along to those parties, but then there was a kid to take care of at home and no money for babysitters.' She passed him a cup of coffee. He sipped it black before she could ask what he took in it. 'Thanks. Anyway, they had a thing. Probably at one of the local motels. It sure wasn't in the back of his car – we had a VW Bug. Even a couple of horny acrobats couldn't have managed that.'

'Blackout screwing,' John said, coming into the room. His hair was standing up in sleep-quills at the back of his head. 'That's what the oldtimers call it. Are there any more of those eggs?'

'Plenty,' Lucy said. 'Abra left a message on the counter.'

'Really?' John went to look at it. 'That was her?'

'Yes. I'd know her printing anywhere.'

'Holy shit, this could put Verizon out of business.'

She didn't smile. 'Sit down and eat, John. You've got ten minutes, then I'm going to wake up Sleeping Beauty in there on the couch.' She sat down. 'Go on, Dan.'

'I don't know if she thought my dad would leave my mom for her or not, and I doubt if you'll find the answer to that one in her trunk. Unless maybe she left a diary. All I know – based on what Dave said and what Concetta told me later – is that she hung around for a while. Maybe hoping, maybe just partying, maybe both. But by the time she found out she was pregnant, she must have given up. For all I know, we might have been in Colorado by then.'

'Do you suppose your mother ever found out?'

'I don't know, but she must have wondered how faithful he was, especially on the nights when he came in late and shitfaced. I'm sure she knew that drunks don't limit their bad behavior to betting the ponies or tucking five-spots into the cleavages of the waitresses down at the Twist and Shout.'

She put a hand on his arm. 'Are you all right? You look exhausted.'

'I'm okay. But you're not the only one who's trying to process all this.'

'She died in a car accident,' Lucy said. She had turned from Dan and was looking fixedly at the bulletin board on the fridge. In the middle was a photograph of Concetta and Abra, who looked about four, walking hand in hand through a field of daisies. 'The man with her was a lot older. And drunk. They were going fast. Momo didn't want to tell me, but around the time I turned eighteen, I got curious and nagged her into giving me at least some of the details. When I asked if my mother was drunk, too, Chetta said she didn't know. She said the police have no reason to test passengers who are killed in fatal accidents, only the driver.' She sighed. 'It doesn't matter. We'll leave the family stories for another day. Tell me what's happened to my daughter.'

He did. At some point, he turned around and saw Dave Stone standing in the doorway, tucking his shirt into his pants and watching him.

12

Dan started with how Abra had gotten in touch with him, first using Tony as a kind of intermediary. Then how Abra had come in contact with the True Knot: a nightmare vision of the one she called 'the baseball boy'.

'I remember that nightmare,' Lucy said. 'She woke me up, screaming. It had happened before, but it was the first time in two or three years.'

Dave frowned. 'I don't remember that at all.'

'You were in Boston, at a conference.' She turned to Dan. 'Let me see if I've got this. These people aren't people, they're . . . what? Some kind of vampires?'

'In a way, I suppose. They don't sleep in coffins during the day or turn into bats by moonlight, and I doubt if crosses and garlic bother them, but they're parasites, and they're certainly not human.'

'Human beings don't disappear when they die,' John said flatly. 'You really saw that happen?'

'We did. All three of us.'

'In any case,' Dan said, 'the True Knot isn't interested in ordinary children, only those who have the shining.'

'Children like Abra,' Lucy said.

'Yes. They torture them before killing them – to purify the steam, Abra says. I keep picturing moonshiners making white lightning.'

'They want to . . . inhale her,' Lucy said. Still trying to get it straight in her head. 'Because she has the shining.'

'Not just the shining, but a *great* shining. I'm a flashlight. She's a lighthouse. And she *knows* about them. She knows what they are.'

'There's more,' John said. 'What we did to those men at Cloud Gap . . . as far as this Rose is concerned, that's down to Abra, no matter who actually did the killing.'

'What else could she expect?' Lucy asked indignantly. 'Don't they understand self-defense? *Survival?*'

'What Rose understands,' Dan said, 'is that there's a little girl who has challenged her.'

'Challenged—?'

'Abra got in touch telepathically. She told Rose that she was coming after her.'

'She *what?*'

'That temper of hers,' Dave said quietly. 'I've told her a hundred times it would get her in trouble.'

'She's not going anywhere *near* that woman, or her child-killing friends,' Lucy said.

Dan thought: *Yes . . . and no.* He took Lucy's hand. She started to pull away, then didn't.

'The thing you have to understand is really quite simple,' he said. '*They will never stop.*'

'But—'

'No buts, Lucy. Under other circumstances, Rose still might have decided to disengage – this is one crafty old she-wolf – but there's one other factor.'

'Which is?'

'They're sick,' John said. 'Abra says it's the measles. They might even have caught it from the Trevor boy. I don't know if you'd call that divine retribution or just irony.'

'*Measles?*'

'I know it doesn't sound like much, but believe me, it is. You know how, in the old days, measles could run through a whole family of kids? If that's happening to this True Knot, it could wipe them out.'

'Good!' Lucy cried. The angry smile on her face was one Dan knew well.

'Not if they think Abra's supersteam will cure them,' Dave said. 'That's what you need to understand, hon. This isn't just a skirmish. To this bitch it's a fight to the death.' He struggled and then brought out the rest of it. Because it had to be said. 'If Rose gets the chance, she'll eat our daughter alive.'

13

Lucy asked, 'Where are they? This True Knot, where are they?'

'Colorado,' Dan said. 'At a place called the Bluebell Campground in the town of Sidewinder.' That the site of the campground was the very place where he had once almost died at his father's hands was a thing he didn't want to say, because it would lead to more

questions and more cries of coincidence. The one thing of which
Dan was sure was that there were no coincidences.

'This Sidewinder must have a police department,' Lucy said. 'We'll
call them and get them on this.'

'By telling them what?' John's tone was gentle, nonargumentative.

'Well . . . that . . .'

'If you actually got the cops to go up there to the campground,'
Dan said, 'they'd find nothing but a bunch of middle-aged-going-
on-older Americans. Harmless RV folks, the kind who always want
to show you pictures of their grandkids. Their papers would all be
in apple-pie order, from dog licenses to land deeds. The police
wouldn't find guns if they managed to get a search warrant – which
they wouldn't, no probable cause – because the True Knot doesn't
need guns. Their weapons are up here.' Dan tapped his forehead.
'You'd be the crazy lady from New Hampshire, Abra would be your
crazy daughter who ran away from home, and we'd be your crazy
friends.'

Lucy pressed her palms to her temples. 'I can't believe this is
happening.'

'If you did a search of records, I think you'd find that the True
Knot – under whatever name they might be incorporated – has
been very generous to that particular Colorado town. You don't shit
in your nest, you feather it. Then, if bad times come, you have lots
of friends.'

'These bastards have been around a long time,' John said. 'Haven't
they? Because the main thing they take from this steam is longevity.'

'I'm pretty sure that's right,' Dan said. 'And as good Americans,
I'm sure they've been busy making money the whole time. Enough
to grease wheels a lot bigger than the ones that turn in Sidewinder.
State wheels. Federal wheels.'

'And this Rose . . . she'll never stop.'

'No.' Dan was thinking of the precognitive vision he'd had of
her. The cocked hat. The yawning mouth. The single tooth. 'Her
heart is set on your daughter.'

'A woman who stays alive by killing children *has* no heart,' Dave
said.

'Oh, she has one,' Dan said. 'But it's black.'

Lucy stood up. 'No more talking. I want to go to her *now*. Everybody use the bathroom, because once we leave, we're not stopping until we get to that motel.'

Dan said, 'Does Concetta have a computer? If she does, I need to take a quick peek at something before we go.'

Lucy sighed. 'It's in her study, and I think you can guess the password. But if you take more than five minutes, we're going without you.'

14

Rose lay awake in her bed, stiff as a poker, trembling with steam and fury.

When an engine started up at quarter past two, she heard it. Steamhead Steve and Baba the Russian. When another started at twenty till four, she heard that one, too. This time it was the Little twins, Pea and Pod. Sweet Terri Pickford was with them, no doubt looking nervously through the back window for any sign of Rose. Big Mo had asked to go along – *begged* to go along – but they had turned her down because Mo was carrying the disease.

Rose could have stopped them, but why bother? Let them discover what life was like in America on their own, with no True Knot to protect them in camp or watch their backs while they were on the road. *Especially when I tell Toady Sam to kill their credit cards and empty their rich bank accounts*, she thought.

Toady was no Jimmy Numbers, but he could still take care of it, and at the touch of a button. And he'd be there to do it. Toady would stick. So would all the good ones . . . or *almost* all the good ones. Dirty Phil, Apron Annie, and Diesel Doug were no longer on their way back. They had taken a vote and decided to head south instead. Deez had told them Rose was no longer to be trusted, and besides, it was long past time to cut the Knot.

Good luck with that, darling boy, she thought, clenching and unclenching her fists.

Splitting the True was a *terrible* idea, but thinning the herd was a good one. So let the weaklings run and the sicklings die. When the bitchgirl was also dead and they had swallowed her steam (Rose had no more illusions of keeping her prisoner), the twenty-five or so who were left would be stronger than ever. She mourned Crow, and knew she had no one who could step into his shoes, but Token Charlie would do the best he could. So would Harpman Sam . . . Bent Dick . . . Fat Fannie and Long Paul . . . Greedy G, not the brightest bulb, but loyal and unquestioning.

Besides, with the others gone, the steam she still had in storage would go farther and make them stronger. They would need to be strong.

Come to me, little bitchgirl, Rose thought. *See how strong you are when there are two dozen against you. See how you like it when it's just you against the True. We'll eat your steam and lap up your blood. But first, we'll drink your screams.*

Rose stared up into the darkness, hearing the fading voices of the runners, the faithless ones.

At the door came a soft, timid knock. Rose lay silent for a moment or two, considering, then swung her legs out of bed.

'Come.'

She was naked but made no attempt to cover herself when Silent Sarey crept in, shapeless inside one of her flannel nightgowns, her mouse-colored bangs covering her brows and almost hanging in her eyes. As always, Sarey seemed hardly there even when she was.

'I'm sad, Loze.'

'I know you are. I'm sad, too.'

She wasn't – she was furious – but it sounded good.

'I miss Andi.'

Andi, yes – rube name Andrea Steiner, whose father had fucked the humanity out of her long before the True Knot had found her. Rose remembered watching her that day in the movie theater, and how, later, she had fought her way through the Turning with sheer guts and willpower. Snakebite Andi would have stuck. Snake would have walked through fire, if Rose said the True Knot needed her to.

She held out her arms. Sarey scurried to her and laid her head against Rose's breast.

'Wivvout her I lunt to die.'

'No, honey, I don't think so.' Rose pulled the little thing into bed and hugged her tight. She was nothing but a rack of bones held together by scant meat. 'Tell me what you really want.'

Beneath the shaggy bangs, two eyes gleamed, feral. '*Levenge*.'

Rose kissed one cheek, then the other, then the thin dry lips. She drew back a little and said, 'Yes. And you'll have it. Open your mouth, Sarey.'

Sarey obediently did so. Their lips came together again. Rose the Hat, still full of steam, breathed down Silent Sarey's throat.

15

The walls of Concetta's study were papered with memos, fragments of poems, and correspondence that would never be answered. Dan typed in the four-letter password, launched Firefox, and googled the Bluebell Campground. They had a website that wasn't terribly informative, probably because the owners didn't care that much about attracting visitors; the place was your basic front. But there were photos of the property, and these Dan studied with the fascination people reserve for recently discovered old family albums.

The Overlook was long gone, but he recognized the terrain. Once, just before the first of the snowstorms that closed them in for the winter, he and his mother and father had stood together on the hotel's broad front porch (seeming even broader with the lawn gliders and wicker furniture in storage), looking down the long, smooth slope of the front lawn. At the bottom, where the deer and the antelope often came out to play, there was now a long rustic building called the Overlook Lodge. Here, the caption said, visitors could dine, play bingo, and dance to live music on Friday and Saturday nights. On Sundays there were church services, overseen by a rotating cadre of Sidewinder's men and women of the cloth.

Until the snow came, my father mowed that lawn and trimmed the topiary that used to be there. He said he'd trimmed lots of ladies' topiaries in his time. I didn't get the joke, but it used to make Mom laugh.

'Some joke,' he said, low.

He saw rows of sparkling RV hookups, lux mod cons that supplied LP gas as well as electricity. There were men's and women's shower buildings big enough to service mega-truckstops like Little America or Pedro's South of the Border. There was a playground for the wee folks. (Dan wondered if the kiddies who played there ever saw or sensed unsettling things, as Danny 'Doc' Torrance once had in the Overlook's playground.) There was a softball field, a shuffleboard area, a couple of tennis courts, even bocce.

No roque, though – not that. Not anymore.

Halfway up the slope – where the Overlook's hedge animals had once congregated – there was a row of clean white satellite dishes. At the crest of the hill, where the hotel itself had stood, was a wooden platform with a long flight of steps leading up to it. This site, now owned and administered by the State of Colorado, was identified as Roof O' the World. Visitors to the Bluebell Campground were welcome to use it, or to hike the trails beyond, free of charge. *The trails are recommended only for the more experienced hiker,* the caption read, *but Roof O' the World is for everyone. The views are spectacular!*

Dan was sure they were. Certainly they had been spectacular from the dining room and ballroom of the Overlook . . . at least until the steadily mounting snow blocked off the windows. To the west were the highest peaks of the Rocky Mountains, sawing at the sky like spears. To the east, you could see all the way to Boulder. Hell, all the way to Denver and Arvada on rare days when the pollution wasn't too bad.

The state had taken that particular piece of land, and Dan wasn't surprised. Who would have wanted to build there? The ground was rotten, and he doubted if you had to be telepathic to sense it. But the True had gotten as close as it could, and Dan had an idea that their wandering guests – the normal ones – rarely came back for a second visit, or recommended the Bluebell to their friends. *An evil place would call evil creatures,* John had said. If so, the converse would also be true: it would tend to repel good ones.

'Dan?' Dave called. 'Bus is leaving.'

'I need another minute!'

He closed his eyes and propped the heel of his palm against his forehead.

(*Abra*)

His voice awoke her at once.

CHAPTER SEVENTEEN
BITCHGIRL

1

It was dark outside the Crown Motel, dawn still an hour or more away, when the door of unit 24 opened and a girl stepped out. Heavy fog had moved in, and the world was hardly there at all. The girl was wearing black pants and a white shirt. She had put her hair up in pigtails, and the face they framed looked very young. She breathed deeply, the coolness and the hanging moisture in the air doing wonders for her lingering headache but not much for her unhappy heart. Momo was dead.

Yet, if Uncle Dan was right, not really dead; just somewhere else. Perhaps a ghostie person; perhaps not. In any case, it wasn't a thing she could spend time thinking about. Later, perhaps, she would meditate on these matters.

Dan had asked if Billy was asleep. Yes, she had told him, still fast asleep. Through the open door she could see Mr Freeman's feet and legs under the blankets and hear his steady snoring. He sounded like an idling motorboat.

Dan had asked if Rose or any of the others had tried to touch her mind. No. She would have known. Her traps were set. Rose would guess that. She wasn't stupid.

He had asked if there was a telephone in her room. Yes, there was a phone. Uncle Dan told her what he wanted her to do. It was pretty simple. The scary part was what she had to say to the strange woman in Colorado. And yet she wanted to. Part of her had wanted that ever since she'd heard the baseball boy's dying screams.

(*you understand the word you have to keep saying?*)

Yes, of course.

(*because you have to goad her do you know what that*)

(*yes I know what it means*)

Make her mad. Infuriate her.

Abra stood breathing into the fog. The road they'd driven in on was nothing but a scratch, the trees on the other side completely gone. So was the motel office. Sometimes she wished *she* was like that, all white on the inside. But only sometimes. In her deepest heart, she had never regretted what she was.

When she felt ready – as ready as she could be – Abra went back into her room and closed the door on her side so she wouldn't disturb Mr Freeman if she had to talk loud. She examined the instructions on the phone, pushed 9 to get an outside line, then dialed directory assistance and asked for the number of the Overlook Lodge at the Bluebell Campground, in Sidewinder, Colorado. *I could give you the main number,* Dan had said, *but you'd only get an answering machine.*

In the place where the guests ate meals and played games, the telephone rang for a long time. Dan said it probably would, and that she should just wait it out. It was, after all, two hours earlier there.

At last a grumpy voice said, 'Hello? If you want the office, you called the wrong num—'

'I don't want the office,' Abra said. She hoped the rapid heavy beating of her heart wasn't audible in her voice. 'I want Rose. Rose the Hat.'

A pause. Then: 'Who is this?'

'Abra Stone. You know my name, don't you? I'm the girl she's looking for. Tell her I'll call back in five minutes. If she's there, we'll talk. If she's not, tell her she can go fuck herself. I won't call back again.'

Abra hung up, then lowered her head, cupped her burning face in her palms, and took long deep breaths.

2

Rose was drinking coffee behind the wheel of her EarthCruiser, her feet on the secret compartment with the stored canisters of steam inside, when the knock came at her door. A knock this early could only mean more trouble.

'Yes,' she said. 'Come in.'

It was Long Paul, wearing a robe over childish pajamas with racing cars on them.' The pay phone in the Lodge started ringing. At first I let it go, thought it was a wrong number, and besides, I was making coffee in the kitchen. But it kept on, so I answered. It was that girl. She wanted to talk to you. She said she'd call back in five minutes.'

Silent Sarey sat up in bed, blinking through her bangs, the covers clutched around her shoulders like a shawl.

'Go,' Rose told her.

Sarey did so, without a word. Rose watched through the EarthCruiser's wide windshield as Sarey trudged barefooted back to the Bounder she had shared with Snake.

That girl.

Instead of running and hiding, the bitchgirl was making telephone calls. Talk about brassbound nerve. Her own idea? That was a little hard to believe, wasn't it?

'What were you doing up and bustling in the kitchen so early?'

'I couldn't sleep.'

She turned toward him. Just a tall, elderly fellow with thinning hair and bifocals sitting at the end of his nose. A rube could pass him on the street every day for a year without seeing him, but he wasn't without certain abilities. Paul didn't have Snake's sleeper talent, or the late Grampa Flick's locator talent, but he was a decent persuader. If he happened to suggest that a rube slap his wife's face – or a stranger's, for that matter – that face would be slapped, and briskly. Everyone in the True had their little skills; it was how they got along.

'Let me see your arms, Paulie.'

He sighed and brushed the sleeves of his robe and pajamas up to his wrinkly elbows. The red spots were there.

'When did they break?'

'Saw the first couple yesterday afternoon.'

'Fever?'

'Yuh. Some.'

She gazed into his honest, trusting eyes and felt like hugging him. Some had run, but Long Paul was still here. So were most of the others. Surely enough to take care of the bitchgirl if she were really foolish enough to show her face. And she might be. What girl of thirteen *wasn't* foolish?

'You're going to be all right,' she said.

He sighed again. 'Hope so. If not, it's been a damn good run.'

'None of that talk. Everyone who sticks is going to be all right. It's my promise, and I keep my promises. Now let's see what our little friend from New Hampshire has to say for herself.'

3

Less than a minute after Rose settled into a chair next to the big plastic bingo drum (with her cooling mug of coffee beside it), the Lodge's pay telephone exploded with a twentieth-century clatter that made her jump. She let it ring twice before lifting the receiver from the cradle and speaking in her most modulated voice. 'Hello, dear. You could have reached out to my mind, you know. It would have saved you long-distance charges.'

A thing the bitchgirl would have been very unwise to try. Abra Stone wasn't the only one who could lay traps.

'I'm coming for you,' the girl said. The voice was so young, so fresh! Rose thought of all the useful steam that would come with that freshness and felt greed rise in her like an unslaked thirst.

'So you've said. Are you sure you really want to do that, dear?'

'Will you be there if I do? Or only your trained rats?'

Rose felt a trill of anger. Not helpful, but of course she had never been much of a morning person.

'Why would I not be, dear?' She kept her voice calm and slightly indulgent – the voice of a mother (or so she imagined; she had never been one) speaking to a tantrum-prone toddler.

'Because you're a coward.'

'I'm curious to know what you base that assumption on,' Rose said. Her tone was the same – indulgent, slightly amused – but her hand had tightened on the phone, and pressed it harder against her ear. 'Never having met me.'

'Sure I have. Inside my head, and I sent you running with your tail between your legs. And you kill kids. Only cowards kill kids.'

You don't need to justify yourself to a child, she told herself. *Especially not a rube.* But she heard herself saying, 'You know nothing about us. What we are, or what we have to do in order to survive.'

'A tribe of cowards is what you are,' the bitchgirl said. 'You think you're so talented and so strong, but the only thing you're really good at is eating and living long lives. You're like hyenas. You kill the weak and then run away. Cowards.'

The contempt in her voice was like acid in Rose's ear. 'That's not true!'

'And you're the chief coward. You wouldn't come after me, would you? No, not you. You sent those others, instead.'

'Are we going to have a reasonable conversation, or—'

'What's reasonable about killing kids so you can steal the stuff in their minds? What's reasonable about that, you cowardly old whore? You sent your friends to do your work, you hid behind them, and I guess that was smart, because now they're all dead.'

'You stupid little bitch, you don't know anything!' Rose leaped to her feet. Her thighs bumped the table and her coffee spilled, running beneath the bingo drum. Long Paul peeked through the kitchen doorway, took one look at her face, and pulled back. 'Who's the coward? Who's the real coward? You can say such things over the phone, but you could never say them looking into my face!'

'How many will you have to have with you when I come?' Abra taunted. 'How many, you yellow bitch?'

Rose said nothing. She had to get herself under control, she knew it, but to be talked to this way by a rube girl with a mouthful of filthy schoolyard language . . . and she knew too much. *Much* too much.

'Would you even dare to face me alone?' the bitchgirl asked.

'Try me,' Rose spat.

There was a pause on the other end, and when the bitchgirl next spoke, she sounded thoughtful. 'One-on-one? No, you wouldn't dare. A coward like you would never dare. Not even against a kid. You're a cheater and a liar. You look pretty sometimes, but I've seen your real face. You're nothing but an old chickenshit whore.'

'You . . . you . . .' But she could say no more. Her rage was so great it felt like it was strangling her. Some of it was shock at finding herself – Rose the Hat – dressed down by a kid whose idea of transportation was a bicycle and whose major concern before these last weeks had probably been when she might get breasts bigger than mosquito bumps.

'But maybe I'll give you a chance,' the bitchgirl said. Her confidence and breezy temerity were unbelievable. 'Of course, if you take me up on it, I'll wipe the floor with you. I won't bother with the others, they're dying already.' She actually laughed. 'Choking on the baseball boy, and good for him.'

'If you come, I'll kill you,' Rose said. One hand found her throat, closed on it, and began to squeeze rhythmically. Later there would be bruises. 'If you run, I'll find you. And when I do, you'll scream for hours before you die.'

'I won't run,' the girl said. 'And we'll see who does the screaming.'

'How many will *you* have to back you up? *Dear?*'

'I'll be alone.'

'I don't believe you.'

'Read my mind,' the girl said. 'Or are you afraid to do that, too?'

Rose said nothing.

'Sure you are. You remember what happened last time you tried it. I gave you a taste of your own medicine, and you didn't like it, did you? Hyena. Child-killer. *Coward.*'

'Stop . . . calling . . . me that.'

'There's a place up the hill from where you are. A lookout. It's called Roof O' the World. I found it on the internet. Be there at five o'clock Monday afternoon. Be there alone. If you're not, if the rest of your pack of hyenas doesn't stay in that meeting-hall place while we do our business, I'll know. And I'll go away.'

'I'd find you,' Rose repeated.

'You think?' Actually *jeering* at her.

Rose shut her eyes and saw the girl. She saw her writhing on the ground, her mouth stuffed with stinging hornets and hot sticks jutting out of her eyes. *No one talks to me like this. Not ever.*

'I suppose you *might* find me. But by the time you did, how many of your stinking True Knot would be left to back you up? A dozen? Ten? Maybe only three or four?'

This idea had already occurred to Rose. For a child she'd never even seen face-to-face to reach the same conclusion was, in many ways, the most infuriating thing of all.

'The Crow knew Shakespeare,' the bitchgirl said. 'He quoted some to me not too long before I killed him. I know a little, too, because we had a Shakespeare unit in school. We only read one play, *Romeo and Juliet*, but Ms Franklin gave us a printout with a whole list of famous lines from his other plays. Things like "To be or not to be" and "It was Greek to me". Did you know those were from Shakespeare? I didn't. Don't you think it's interesting?'

Rose said nothing.

'You're not thinking about Shakespeare at all,' the bitchgirl said. 'You're thinking about how much you'd like to kill me. I don't have to read your mind to know that.'

'If I were you, I'd run,' Rose said thoughtfully. 'As fast and as far as your baby legs can carry you. It wouldn't do you any good, but you'd live a little longer.'

The bitchgirl was not to be turned. 'There was another saying. I can't remember it exactly, but it was something like "Hoisted on your own petard". Ms Franklin said a petard was a bomb on a stick. I think that's sort of what's happening to your tribe of cowards. You sucked the wrong kind of steam, and got stuck on a petard, and now the bomb is going off.' She paused. 'Are you still there, Rose? Or did you run away?'

'Come to me, dear,' Rose said. She had regained her calm. 'If you want to meet me on the lookout, that's where I'll be. We'll take in the view together, shall we? And see who's the stronger.'

She hung up before the bitchgirl could say anything else. She'd lost the temper she had vowed to keep, but she had at least gotten the last word.

Or maybe not, because the one the bitchgirl kept using played over and over in her head, like a gramophone record stuck in a bad groove. *Coward. Coward. Coward.*

4

Abra replaced the telephone receiver carefully in its cradle. She looked at it; she even stroked its plastic surface, which was hot from her hand and wet with her sweat. Then, before she realized it was going to happen, she burst into loud, braying sobs. They stormed through her, cramping her stomach and shaking her body. She rushed to the bathroom, still crying, knelt in front of the toilet, and threw up.

When she came out, Mr Freeman was standing in the connecting doorway with his shirttail hanging down and his gray hair in corkscrews. 'What's wrong? Are you sick from the dope he gave you?'

'It wasn't that.'

He went to the window and peered out into the pressing fog. 'Is it *them*? Are they coming for us?'

Temporarily incapable of speech, she could only shake her head so vehemently her pigtails flew. It was *she* who was coming for *them*, and that was what terrified her.

And not just for herself.

5

Rose sat still, taking long steadying breaths. When she had herself under control again, she called for Long Paul. After a moment or two, he poked his head cautiously through the swing door that gave on the kitchen. The look on his face brought a ghost of a smile to her lips. 'It's safe. You can come in. I won't bite you.'

He stepped in and saw the spilled coffee. 'I'll clean that up.'

'Leave it. Who's the best locator we've got left?'

'You, Rose.' No hesitation.

Rose had no intention of approaching the bitchgirl mentally, not even in a touch-and-go. 'Aside from me.'

'Well . . . with Grampa Flick gone . . . and Barry . . .' He considered. 'Sue's got a touch of locator, and so does Greedy G. But I think Token Charlie's got a bit more.'

'Is he sick?'

'He wasn't yesterday.'

'Send him to me. I'll wipe up the coffee while I'm waiting. Because – this is important, Paulie – the person who makes the mess is the one who should have to clean it up.'

After he left, Rose sat where she was for a while, fingers steepled under her chin. Clear thinking had returned, and with it the ability to plan. They wouldn't be taking steam today after all, it seemed. That could wait until Monday morning.

At last she went into the galley for a wad of paper towels. And cleaned up her mess.

6

'Dan!' This time it was John. 'Gotta go!'

'Right there,' he said. 'I just want to splash some cold water on my face.'

He went down the hall listening to Abra, nodding his head slightly as if she were there.

(*Mr Freeman wants to know why I was crying why I threw up what should I tell him*)

(*for now just that when we get there I'll want to borrow his truck*)

(*because we're going on going west*)

(*. . . well . . .*)

It was complicated, but she understood. The understanding wasn't in words and didn't need to be.

Beside the bathroom washbasin was a rack holding several wrapped toothbrushes. The smallest – not wrapped – had **ABRA** printed on the handle in rainbow letters. On one wall was a small plaque reading A LIFE WITHOUT LOVE IS LIKE A TREE WITHOUT FRUIT. He looked at it for a few seconds, wondering if there was anything in the AA program to that effect. The only thing he could think of was *If you can't love anybody today, at least try not to hurt anybody*. Didn't really compare.

He turned on the cold water and splashed his face several times, hard. Then he grabbed a towel, and raised his head. No Lucy in the portrait with him this time; just Dan Torrance, son of Jack and Wendy, who had always believed himself to be an only child.

His face was covered with flies.

PART FOUR
ROOF O' THE WORLD

CHAPTER EIGHTEEN
GOING WEST

1

What Dan remembered best about that Saturday wasn't the ride from Boston to the Crown Motel, because the four people in John Dalton's SUV said very little. The silence wasn't uncomfortable or hostile but exhausted – the quiet of people who have a great deal to think about but not a hell of a lot to say. What he remembered best was what happened when they reached their destination.

Dan knew she was waiting, because he had been in touch with her for most of the trip, talking in a way that had become comfortable for them – half words and half pictures. When they pulled in, she was sitting on the back bumper of Billy's old truck. She saw them and jumped to her feet, waving. At that moment the cloud cover, which had been thinning, broke apart and a ray of sun spotlighted her. It was as if God had given her a high five.

Lucy gave a cry that was not quite a scream. She had her seatbelt unbuckled and her door open before John could bring his Suburban to a complete stop. Five seconds later she had her daughter in her arms and was kissing the top of her head – the best she could do, with Abra's face crushed between her breasts. Now the sun spotlighted them both.

Mother and child reunion, Dan thought. The smile that brought felt strange on his face. It had been a long time between smiles.

2

Lucy and David wanted to take Abra back to New Hampshire. Dan had no problem with that, but now that they were together, the six of them needed to talk. The fat man with the ponytail was back on duty, today watching a cage-fighting match instead of porn. He was happy to re-rent them Room 24; it was nothing to him whether they spent the night or not. Billy went into Crownville proper to pick up a couple of pizzas. Then they settled in, Dan and Abra talking turn and turn about, filling in the others on everything that had happened and everything that was going to happen. If things went as they hoped, that was.

'No,' Lucy said at once. 'It's far too dangerous. For both of you.'

John offered a bleak grin. 'The most dangerous thing would be to ignore these . . . these *things*. Rose says that if Abra doesn't come to her, she'll come to Abra.'

'She's, like, fixated on her,' Billy said, and selected a slice of pepperoni-and-mushroom. 'Happens lots of times with crazy people. All you have to do to know that is watch *Dr Phil*.'

Lucy fixed her daughter with a reproachful glance. 'You goaded her. That was a dangerous thing to do, but when she has a chance to settle down . . .'

Although no one interrupted, she trailed off. Maybe, Dan thought, she heard how implausible that sounded when it was actually articulated.

'They won't stop, Mom,' Abra said. '*She* won't stop.'

'Abra will be safe enough,' Dan said. 'There's a wheel. I don't know how to explain it any better than that. If things get bad – if they go wrong – Abra will use the wheel to get away. To pull out. She's promised me that.'

'That's right,' Abra said. 'I promised.'

Dan fixed her with a hard look. 'And you'll keep it, won't you?'

'Yes,' Abra said. She spoke firmly enough, although with obvious reluctance. 'I will.'

'There's all those kids to consider, too,' John said. 'We'll never know how many this True Knot has taken over the years. Hundreds, maybe.'

Dan thought that if they lived as long as Abra believed, the number was probably in the thousands. He said, 'Or how many they *will* take, even if they leave Abra alone.'

'That's assuming the measles doesn't kill them all,' Dave said hopefully. He turned to John. 'You said that really might happen.'

'They want me because they think I can *cure* the measles,' Abra said. '*Duh*.'

'Keep a civil tongue, miss,' Lucy said, but she spoke absently. She picked up the last slice of pizza, looked at it, then threw it back in the box. 'I don't care about the other kids. I care about Abra. I know how horrible that sounds, but it's the truth.'

'You wouldn't feel that way if you'd seen all those little pictures in the *Shopper*,' Abra said. 'I can't get them out of my head. I dream about them sometimes.'

'If this crazy woman has half a brain, she'll know Abra isn't coming alone,' Dave said. 'What's she going to do, fly to Denver and then rent a car? A thirteen-year-old?' And, with a half-humorous look at his daughter: '*Duh.*'

Dan said, 'Rose already knows from what happened at Cloud Gap that Abra's got friends. What she doesn't know is that she has at least one with the shining.' He looked at Abra for confirmation. She nodded. 'Listen, Lucy. Dave. Together, I think that Abra and I can put an end to this' – he searched for the right word and found only one that fit – 'plague. Either of us alone . . .' He shook his head.

'Besides,' Abra said, 'you and Dad can't really stop me. You can lock me in my room, but you can't lock up my head.'

Lucy gave her the Death Stare, the one mothers save especially for rebellious young daughters. It had always worked with Abra, even when she was in one of her furies, but it didn't this time. She looked back at her mother calmly. And with a sadness that made Lucy's heart feel cold.

Dave took Lucy's hand. 'I think this has to be done.'

There was silence in the room. Abra was the one who broke it. 'If nobody's going to eat that last slice, I am. I'm *starving*.'

3

They went over it several more times, and at a couple of points voices were raised, but essentially, everything had been said. Except, it turned out, for one thing. When they left the room, Billy refused to get into John's Suburban.

'I'm goin,' he told Dan.

'Billy, I appreciate the thought, but it's not a good idea.'

'My truck, my rules. Besides, are you really gonna make the Colorado high country by Monday afternoon on your own? Don't make me laugh. You look like shit on a stick.'

Dan said, 'Several people have told me that lately, but none have put it so elegantly.'

Billy didn't smile. 'I can help you. I'm old, but I ain't dead.'

'Take him,' Abra said. 'He's right.'

Dan looked at her closely.

(*do you know something Abra*)

The reply was quick.

(*no* feel *something*)

That was good enough for Dan. He held out his arms and Abra hugged him hard, the side of her face pressed against his chest. Dan could have held her like that for a long time, but he let her go and stepped back.

(*let me know when you get close Uncle Dan I'll come*)

(*just little touches remember*)

She sent an image instead of a thought in words: a smoke detector beeping the way they did when they wanted a battery change. She remembered perfectly.

As she went to the car, Abra said to her father, 'We need to stop on the way back for a get-well card. Julie Cross broke her wrist yesterday in soccer practice.'

He frowned at her. 'How do you know that?'

'I know,' she said.

He gently pulled one of her pigtails. 'You really could do it all along, couldn't you? I don't understand why you didn't just tell us, Abba-Doo.'

Dan, who had grown up with the shining, could have answered that question.

Sometimes parents needed to be protected.

4

So they parted. John's SUV went east and Billy's pickup truck went west, with Billy behind the wheel. Dan said, 'Are you really okay to drive, Billy?'

'After all the sleep I got last night? Sweetheart, I could drive to California.'

'Do you know where we're going?'

'I bought a road atlas in town while I was waitin for the pizza.'

'So you'd made up your mind even then. And you knew what Abra and I were planning.'

'Well . . . sorta.'

'When you need me to take over, just yell,' Dan said, and promptly fell asleep with his head against the passenger window. He descended through a deepening depth of unpleasant images. First the hedge animals at the Overlook, the ones that moved when you weren't looking. This was followed by Mrs Massey from Room 217, who now wore a cocked tophat. Still descending, he revisited the battle at Cloud Gap. Only this time when he burst into the Winnebago, he found Abra lying on the floor with her throat cut and Rose standing over her with a dripping straight razor. Rose saw Dan and the bottom half of her face dropped away in an obscene grin where one long tooth gleamed. *I told her it would end this way but she wouldn't listen*, she said. *Children so rarely do.*

Below this there was only darkness.

When he woke it was to twilight with a broken white line running down the middle of it. They were on an interstate highway.

'How long did I sleep?'

Billy glanced at his watch. 'A good long while. Feel better?'

'Yes.' He did and didn't. His head was clear, but his stomach hurt like hell. Considering what he had seen that morning in the mirror, he wasn't surprised. 'Where are we?'

'Hunnert-n-fifty miles east of Cincinnati, give or take. You slept through two gas stops. And you snore.'

Dan sat up straight. 'We're in *Ohio*? Christ! What time is it?'

Billy glanced at his watch. 'Quarter past six. Wasn't no big thing; light traffic and no rain. I think we got an angel ridin with us.'

'Well, let's find a motel. You need to sleep and I have to piss like a racehorse.'

'Not surprised.'

Billy pulled off at the next exit showing signs for gas, food, and motels. He pulled into a Wendy's and got a bag of burgers while Dan used the men's. When they got back into the truck, Dan took one bite of his double, put it back in the bag, and sipped cautiously at a coffee milkshake. That his stomach seemed willing to take.

Billy looked shocked. 'Man, you gotta eat! What's wrong with you?'

'I guess pizza for breakfast was a bad idea.' And because Billy was still looking at him: 'The shake's fine. All I need. Eyes on the road, Billy. We can't help Abra if we're getting patched up in some emergency room.'

Five minutes later, Billy pulled the truck under the canopy of a Fairfield Inn with a blinking ROOMS AVAILABLE sign over the door. He turned off the engine but didn't get out. 'Since I'm riskin my life with you, chief, I want to know what ails you.'

Dan almost pointed out that taking the risk had been Billy's idea, not his, but that wasn't fair. He explained. Billy listened in round-eyed silence.

'Jesus jumped-up Christ,' he said when Dan had finished.

'Unless I missed it,' Dan said, 'there's nothing in the New Testament about Jesus jumping. Although I guess He might've, as a child. Most of them do. You want to check us in, or should I do it?'

Billy continued to sit where he was. 'Does Abra know?'

Dan shook his head.

'But she could find out.'

'Could but won't. She knows it's wrong to peek, especially when it's someone you care about. She'd no more do it than she'd spy on her parents when they were making love.'

'You know that from when you were a kid?'

'Yes. Sometimes you see a little – you can't help it – but then you turn away.'

'Are you gonna be all right, Danny?'

'For a while.' He thought of the sluggish flies on his lips and cheeks and forehead. 'Long enough.'

'What about after?'

'I'll worry about after after. One day at a time. Let's check in. We need to get an early start.'

'Have you heard from Abra?'

Dan smiled. 'She's fine.'

At least so far.

5

But she wasn't, not really.

She sat at her desk with *The Fixer* in her hand, trying not to look at her bedroom window, lest she should see a certain someone looking in at her. She knew something was wrong with Dan, and she knew he didn't want her to know what it was, but had been tempted to look anyway, in spite of all the years she'd taught herself to steer clear of APB: adult private business. Two things held her back. One was the knowledge that, like it or not, she couldn't help him with it now. The other (this was stronger) was knowing he might sense her in his head. If so, he would be disappointed in her.

It's probably locked up, anyway, she thought. *He can do that. He's pretty strong.*

Not as strong as she was, though . . . or, if you put it in terms of the shining, as bright. She could open his mental lockboxes and peer at the things inside, but she thought doing so might be dangerous for both of them. There was no concrete reason for this, it was just a feeling – like the one she'd had about how it would be a good idea for Mr Freeman to go with Dan – but she trusted it. Besides, maybe it was something that could help them. She could hope for that. *True hope is swift, and flies on swallow's wings* – that was another line from Shakespeare.

Don't you look at that window, either. Don't you dare.

No. Absolutely not. Never. So she did, and there was Rose, grinning in at her from below her rakishly tilted hat. All billowing hair and pale porcelain skin and dark mad eyes and rich red lips masking that one snaggle tooth. That *tusk*.

You're going to die screaming, bitchgirl.

Abra closed her eyes and thought hard

(*not there not there not there*)

and opened them again. The grinning face at the window was gone. But not really. Somewhere high in the mountains – at the roof of the world – Rose was thinking about her. And waiting.

6

The motel had a breakfast buffet. Because his traveling companion was watching him, Dan made a point of eating some cereal and yogurt. Billy looked relieved. While he checked them out, Dan strolled to the lobby men's room. Once inside, he turned the lock, fell to his knees, and vomited up everything he'd eaten. The undigested cereal and yogurt floated in a red foam.

'All right?' Billy asked when Dan rejoined him at the desk.

'Fine,' Dan said. 'Let's roll.'

7

According to Billy's road atlas, it was about twelve hundred miles from Cincinnati to Denver. Sidewinder lay roughly seventy-five miles further west, along roads full of switchbacks and lined with steep drops. Dan tried driving for a while on that Sunday afternoon, but tired quickly and turned the wheel over to Billy again. He fell asleep, and when he woke up, the sun was going down. They were in Iowa – home of the late Brad Trevor.

(*Abra?*)

He had been afraid distance would make mental communication difficult or even impossible, but she came back promptly, and as strong as ever; if she'd been a radio station, she would have been broadcasting at 100,000 watts. She was in her room, pecking away on her computer at some homework assignment or other. He was both amused and saddened to realize she had Hoppy, her stuffed rabbit, on her lap. The strain of what they were doing had regressed her to a younger Abra, at least on the emotional side.

With the line between them wide open, she caught this.

(*don't worry about me I'm all right*)

(*good because you have a call to make*)

(*yes okay are you all right*)

(*fine*)

She knew better but didn't ask, and that was just the way he wanted it.

(*have you got the*)

She made a picture.

(*not yet it's Sunday stores not open*)

Another picture, one that made him smile. A Walmart . . . except the sign out front read ABRA'S SUPERSTORE.

(*they wouldn't sell us what we need we'll find one that will*)

(*okay I guess*)

(*you know what to say to her?*)

(*yes*)

(*she'll try to suck you into a long conversation try to snoop don't let her*)

(*I won't*)

(*let me hear from you after so I won't worry*)

Of course he would worry plenty.

(*I will I love you Uncle Dan*)

(*love you too*)

He made a kiss. Abra made one back: big red cartoon lips. He could almost feel them on his cheek. Then she was gone.

Billy was staring at him. 'You were just talkin to her, weren't you?'

'Indeed I was. Eyes on the road, Billy.'

'Yeah, yeah. You sound like my ex-wife.'

Billy put on his blinker, switched to the passing lane, and rolled past a huge and lumbering Fleetwood Pace Arrow motorhome. Dan stared at it, wondering who was inside and if they were looking out the tinted windows.

'I want to make another hundred or so miles before we quit for the night,' Billy said. 'Way I got tomorrow figured, that should give us an hour to do your errand and still put us in the high country about the time you and Abra set for the showdown. But we'll want to get on the road before daybreak.'

'Fine. You understand how this will go?'

'I get how it's *supposed* to go.' Billy glanced at him. 'You better hope that if they have binoculars, they don't use them. Do you think we might come back alive? Tell me the truth. If the answer's no, I'm gonna order me the biggest steak dinner you ever saw when we stop for the night. MasterCard can chase my relatives for the last credit card bill, and guess what? I ain't *got* any relatives. Unless you count the ex, and if I was on fire she wouldn't piss on me to put me out.'

'We'll come back,' Dan said, but it sounded pale. He felt too sick to put up much of a front.

'Yeah? Well, maybe I'll have that steak dinner, anyway. What about you?'

'I think I could manage a little soup. As long as it's clear.' The thought of eating anything too thick to read a newspaper through – tomato bisque, cream of mushroom – made his stomach cringe.

'Okay. Why don't you close your eyes again?'

Dan knew he couldn't sleep deeply, no matter how tired and sick he felt – not while Abra was dealing with the ancient horror that looked like a woman – but he managed a doze. It was thin but rich enough to grow more dreams, first of the Overlook (today's version featured the elevator that ran by itself in the middle of the night), then of his niece. This time Abra had been strangled with a length of electrical cord. She stared at Dan with bulging, accusing eyes. It was all too easy to read what was in them. *You said you'd help me. You said you'd save me. Where were you?*

8

Abra kept putting off the thing she had to do until she realized her mother would soon be pestering her to go to bed. She wasn't going to school in the morning, but it was still going to be a big day. And, perhaps, a very long night.

Putting things off only makes them worse, cara mia.

That was the gospel according to Momo. Abra looked toward her window, wishing she could see her great-grandma there instead of Rose. That would be good.

'Momes, I'm so scared,' she said. But after two long and steadying breaths, she picked up her iPhone and dialed the Overlook Lodge at Bluebell Campground. A man answered, and when Abra said she wanted to talk to Rose, he asked who she was.

'You know who I am,' she said. And – with what she hoped was irritating inquisitiveness: 'Are you sick yet, mister?'

The man on the other end (it was Toady Sam) didn't answer that, but she heard him murmur to someone. A moment later, Rose was on, her composure once more firmly in place.

'Hello, dear. Where are you?'

'On my way,' Abra said.

'Are you really? That's nice, dear. So I don't suppose that I'd find this call came from a New Hampshire area code if I star-sixty-nined it?'

'Of course you would,' Abra said. 'I'm using my cell. You need to get with the twenty-first century, bitch.'

'What do you want?' The voice on the other end was now curt.

'To make sure you know the rules,' Abra said. 'I'll be there at five tomorrow. I'll be in an old red truck.'

'Driven by whom?'

'My uncle Billy,' Abra said.

'Was he one of the ones from the ambush?'

'He's the one who was with me and the Crow. Stop asking questions. Just shut up and listen.'

'So rude,' Rose said sadly.

'He'll park way at the end of the lot, by the sign that says KIDS EAT FREE WHEN COLORADO PRO TEAMS WIN.'

'I see you've been on our website. That's sweet. Or was it your uncle, perhaps? He's very brave to act as your chauffeur. Is he your father's brother or your mother's? Rube families are a hobby of mine. I make family trees.'

She'll try to snoop, Dan had told her, and how right he was.

'What part of "shut up and listen" don't you understand? Do you want this to happen or not?'

No reply, just waiting silence. *Creepy* waiting silence.

'From the parking lot, we'll be able to see everything: the campground, the Lodge, and Roof O' the World on top of the hill. My uncle and me better see you up there, and we better not see the people from your True Knot *anywhere*. They're going to stay in that meeting-hall thingy while we do our business. In the big room, got it? Uncle Billy won't know if they're not where they're supposed to be, but I will. If I pick up a single one somewhere else, we'll be gone.'

'Your uncle will stay in his truck?'

'No. *I'll* stay in the truck, until we're sure. Then he'll get back in and I'll come to you. I don't want him anywhere near you.'

'All right, dear. It will be as you say.'

No, it won't. You're lying.

But so was Abra, which kind of made them even.

'I have one really important question, dear,' Rose said pleasantly.

Abra almost asked what it was, then remembered her uncle's advice. Her *real* uncle. One question, right. Which would lead to another . . . and another . . . and another.

'Choke on it,' she said, and hung up. Her hands began to tremble. Then her legs and arms and shoulders.

'Abra?' Mom. Calling from the foot of the stairs. *She feels it. Just a little, but she does feel it. Is that a mom thing or a shining thing?* 'Honey, are you okay?'

'Fine, Mom! Getting ready for bed!'

'Ten minutes, then we're coming up for kisses. Be in your PJs.'

'I will.'

If they knew who I was just talking to, Abra thought. But they didn't. They only thought they knew what was going on. She was here in her bedroom, every door and window in the house was locked, and they believed that made her safe. Even her father, who had seen the True Knot in action.

But Dan knew. She closed her eyes and reached out to him.

9

Dan and Billy were under another motel canopy. And still nothing from Abra. That was bad.

'Come on, chief,' Billy said. 'Let's get you inside and—'

Then she was there. Thank God.

'Hush a minute,' Dan said, and listened. Two minutes later he turned to Billy, who thought the smile on his face finally made him look like Dan Torrance again.

'Was it her?'

'Yes.'

'How'd it go?'

'Abra says it went fine. We're in business.'

'No questions about me?'

'Just which side of the family you were on. Listen, Billy, the uncle thing was a bit of a mistake. You're *way* too old to be Lucy's or David's brother. When we stop tomorrow to do our errand, you need to buy sunglasses. Big ones. And keep that ball cap of yours jammed down all the way to your ears, so your hair doesn't show.'

'Maybe I should get some Just For Men, while I'm at it.'

'Don't sass me, you old fart.'

That made Billy grin. 'Let's get registered and get some food. You look better. Like you could actually eat.'

'Soup,' Dan said. 'No sense pressing my luck.'

'Soup. Right.'

He ate it all. Slowly. And – reminding himself that this would be over one way or the other in less than twenty-four hours – he managed to keep it down. They dined in Billy's room and when he was finally finished, Dan stretched out on the carpet. It eased the pain in his gut a little.

'What's that?' Billy asked. 'Some kind of yogi shit?'

'Exactly. I learned it watching Yogi Bear cartoons. Run it down for me again.'

'I got it, chief, don't worry. Now you're starting to sound like Casey Kingsley.'

'A scary thought. Now run it down again.'

'Abra starts pinging around Denver. If they have someone who can listen, they'll know she's coming. And that she's in the neighborhood. We get to Sidewinder early – say four instead of five – and drive right past the road to the campground. They won't see the truck. Unless they post a sentry down by the highway, that is.'

'I don't think they will.' Dan thought of another AA aphorism: *We're powerless over people, places, and things.* Like most alkie nuggets, it was seventy percent true and thirty percent rah-rah bullshit. 'In any case, we can't control everything. Carry on.'

'There's a picnic area about a mile further up the road. You went there a couple of times with your mom, before you guys got snowed in for the winter.' Billy paused. 'Just her and you? Never your dad?'

'He was writing. Working on a play. Go on.'

Billy did. Dan listened closely, then nodded. 'Okay. You've got it.'

'Didn't I say? Now can I ask a question?'

'Sure.'

'By tomorrow afternoon, will you still be able to walk a mile?'

'I'll be able to.'

I better be.

10

Thanks to an early start – 4 a.m., long before first light – Dan Torrance and Billy Freeman began to see a horizon-spanning cloud shortly after 9 a.m. An hour later, by which time the blue-gray cloud had resolved itself into a mountain range, they stopped in the town of Martenville, Colorado. There, on the short (and mostly deserted) main street, Dan saw not what he was hoping for, but something even better: a children's clothing store called Kids' Stuff. Half a block down was a drugstore flanked by a dusty-looking hockshop and a Video Express with CLOSING MUST SELL ALL STOCK AT BARGAIN PRICES soaped in the window. He sent Billy to Martenville Drugs & Sundries to get sunglasses and stepped through the door of Kids' Stuff.

The place had an unhappy, losing-hope vibe. He was the only customer. Here was somebody's good idea going bad, probably thanks to the big-box mall stores in Sterling or Fort Morgan. Why buy local when you could drive a little and get cheaper pants and dresses for back-to-school? So what if they were made in Mexico or Costa Rica? A tired-looking woman with a tired-looking hairdo came out from behind the counter and gave Dan a tired-looking smile. She asked if she could help him. Dan said she could. When he told her what he wanted, her eyes went round.

'I know it's unusual,' Dan said, 'but get with me on this a little. I'll pay cash.'

He got what he wanted. In little losing-hope stores off the turnpike, the C-word went a long way.

11

As they neared Denver, Dan got in touch with Abra. He closed his eyes and visualized the wheel they both now knew about. In the town of Anniston, Abra did the same. It was easier this time. When he opened his eyes again, he was looking down the slope of the Stones' back lawn at the Saco River, gleaming in the afternoon sun. Abra opened hers on a view of the Rockies.

'Wow, Uncle Billy, they're beautiful, aren't they?'

Billy glanced at the man sitting beside him. Dan had crossed his legs in a way that was utterly unlike him, and was bouncing one foot. Color had come back into his cheeks, and there was a bright clarity in his eyes that had been missing on their run west.

'They sure are, honey,' he said.

Dan smiled and closed his eyes. When he opened them again, the health Abra had brought to his face was fading. *Like a rose without water*, Billy thought.

'Anything?'

'Ping,' Dan said. He smiled again, but this one was weary. 'Like a smoke detector that needs a battery change.'

'Do you think they heard it?'

'I sure hope so,' Dan said.

12

Rose was pacing back and forth near her EarthCruiser when Token Charlie came running up. The True had taken steam that morning, all but one of the canisters she had in storage, and on top of what Rose had taken on her own over the last couple of days, she was too wired even to think about sitting down.

'What?' she asked. 'Tell me something good.'

'I got her, how's that for good?' Wired himself, Charlie grabbed Rose by the arms and whirled her around, making her hair fly. 'I *got* her! Just for a few seconds, but it was her!'

'Did you see the uncle?'

'No, she was looking out the windshield at the mountains. She said they were beautiful—'

'They are,' Rose said. A grin was spreading on her lips. 'Don't you agree, Charlie?'

'—and he said they sure were. They're coming, Rosie! They really are!'

'Did she know you were there?'

He let go of her, frowning. 'I can't say for sure . . . Grampa Flick probably could . . .'

'Just tell me what you think.'

'Probably not.'

'That's good enough for me. Go someplace quiet. Someplace where you can concentrate without being disturbed. Sit and listen. If – *when* – you pick her up again, let me know. I don't want to lose track of her if I can help it. If you need more steam, ask for it. I saved a little.'

'No, no, I'm fine. I'll listen. I'll listen *hard*!' Token Charlie gave a rather wild laugh and rushed off. Rose didn't think he had any idea where he was going, and she didn't care. As long as he kept listening.

13

Dan and Billy were at the foot of the Flatirons by noon. As he watched the Rockies draw closer, Dan thought of all the wandering years he had avoided them. That in turn made him think of some poem or other, one about how you could spend years running, but in the end you always wound up facing yourself in a hotel room, with a naked bulb hanging overhead and a revolver on the table.

Because they had time, they left the freeway and drove into Boulder. Billy was hungry. Dan wasn't . . . but he was curious. Billy pulled the truck into a sandwich shop parking lot, but when he asked Dan what he could get him, Dan only shook his head.

'Sure? You got a lot ahead of you.'

'I'll eat when this is over.'

'Well . . .'

Billy went into the Subway for a Buffalo Chicken. Dan got in touch with Abra. The wheel turned.

Ping.

When Billy came out, Dan nodded to his wrapped footlong. 'Save that a couple of minutes. As long as we're in Boulder, there's something I want to check out.'

Five minutes later, they were on Arapahoe Street. Two blocks from the seedy little bar-and-café district, he told Billy to pull over. 'Go on and chow that chicken. I won't be long.'

Dan got out of the truck and stood on the cracked sidewalk, looking at a slumped three-story building with a sign in the window reading EFFICIENCY APTS GOOD STUDENT VALUE. The lawn was balding. Weeds grew up through the cracks in the sidewalk. He had doubted that this place would still be here, had believed that Arapahoe would now be a street of condos populated by well-to-do slackers who drank lattes from Starbucks, checked their Facebook pages half a dozen times a day, and Twittered like mad bastards. But here it was, and looking – so far as he could tell – exactly as it had back in the day.

Billy joined him, sandwich in one hand. 'We've still got seventy-five miles ahead of us, Danno. Best we get our asses up the pass.'

'Right,' Dan said, then went on looking at the building with the peeling green paint. Once a little boy had lived here; once he had sat on the very piece of curbing where Billy Freeman now stood munching his chicken footlong. A little boy waiting for his daddy to come home from his job interview at the Overlook Hotel. He had a balsa glider, that little boy, but the wing was busted. It was okay, though. When his daddy came home, he would fix it with tape and glue. Then maybe they would fly it together. His daddy had been a scary man, and how that little boy had loved him.

Dan said, 'I lived here with my mother and father before we moved up to the Overlook. Not much, is it?'

Billy shrugged. 'I seen worse.'

In his wandering years, Dan had, too. Deenie's apartment in Wilmington, for instance.

He pointed left. 'There were a bunch of bars down that way. One was called the Broken Drum. Looks like urban renewal missed this side of town, so maybe it's still there. When my father and I walked past it, he'd always stop and look in the window, and I could feel how thirsty he was to go inside. So thirsty it made *me* thirsty. I drank a lot of years to quench that thirst, but it never really goes away. My dad knew that, even then.'

'But you loved him, I guess.'

'I did.' Still looking at that shambling, rundown apartment house. Not much, but Dan couldn't help wondering how different their lives might have been if they had stayed there. If the Overlook had not ensnared them. 'He was good and bad and I loved both sides of him. God help me, I guess I still do.'

'You and most kids,' Billy said. 'You love your folks and hope for the best. What else can you do? Come on, Dan. If we're gonna do this, we have to go.'

Half an hour later, Boulder was behind them and they were climbing into the Rockies.

CHAPTER NINETEEN
GHOSTIE PEOPLE

1

Although sunset was approaching – in New Hampshire, at least – Abra was still on the back stoop, looking down at the river. Hoppy was sitting nearby, on the lid of the composter. Lucy and David came out and sat on either side of her. John Dalton watched them from the kitchen, holding a cold cup of coffee. His black bag was on the counter, but there was nothing in it he could use this evening.

'You should come in and have some supper,' Lucy said, knowing that Abra wouldn't – probably couldn't – until this was over. But you clung to the known. Because everything looked normal, and because the danger was over a thousand miles away, that was easier for her than for her daughter. Although Abra's complexion had previously been clear – as unblemished as when she was an infant – she now had nests of acne around the wings of her nose and an ugly cluster of pimples on her chin. Just hormones kicking in, heralding the onset of true adolescence: so Lucy would have liked to believe, because that was normal. But stress caused acne, too. Then there was the pallor of her daughter's skin and the dark circles beneath her eyes. She looked almost as ill as Dan did when Lucy had last seen him, climbing with painful slowness into Mr Freeman's pickup truck.

'Can't eat now, Mom. No time. I probably couldn't keep it down, anyway.'

'How soon before this happens, Abby?' David asked.

She looked at neither of them. She looked fixedly down at the river, but Lucy knew she wasn't really looking at that, either. She was far away, in a place where none of them could help her. 'Not long. You should each give me a kiss and then go inside.'

'But—' Lucy began, then saw David shake his head at her. Only once, but very firmly. She sighed, took one of Abra's hands (how cold it was), and planted a kiss on her left cheek. David put one on her right.

Lucy: 'Remember what Dan said. If things go wrong—'

'You should go in now, guys. When it starts, I'm going to take Hoppy and put him in my lap. When you see that, you can't interrupt me. Not for *anything*. You could get Uncle Dan killed, and maybe Billy, too. I might fall over, like in a faint, but it won't be a faint, so don't move me and don't let Dr John move me, either. Just let me be until it's over. I think Dan knows a place where we can be together.'

David said, 'I don't understand how this can possibly work. That woman, Rose, will see there's no little girl—'

'You need to go in *now*,' Abra said.

They did as she said. Lucy looked pleadingly at John; he could only shrug and shake his head. The three of them stood at the kitchen window, arms around one another, looking out at the little girl sitting on the stoop with her arms clasped around her knees. There was no danger to be seen; all was placid. But when Lucy saw Abra – her little girl – reach for Hoppy and take the old stuffed rabbit on her lap, she groaned. John squeezed her shoulder. David tightened the arm around her waist, and she gripped his hand with panicky tightness.

Please let my daughter be all right. If something has to happen . . . something bad . . . let it happen to the half brother I never knew. Not to her.

'It'll be okay,' Dave said.

She nodded. 'Of course it will. Of course it will.'

They watched the girl on the stoop. Lucy understood that if she *did* call to Abra, she wouldn't answer. Abra was gone.

2

Billy and Dan reached the turnoff to the True's Colorado base of operations at twenty to four, Mountain Time, which put them comfortably ahead of schedule. There was a wooden ranch-style arch over the paved road with WELCOME TO THE BLUEBELL CAMPGROUND! STAY AWHILE, PARTNER! carved into it.

The sign beside the road was a lot less welcoming: **CLOSED UNTIL FURTHER NOTICE**.

Billy drove past without slowing, but his eyes were busy. 'Don't see nobody. Not even on the lawns, although I suppose they coulda stashed someone in that welcome-hut doohickey. Jesus, Danny, you look just awful.'

'Lucky for me the Mr America competition isn't until later this year,' Dan said. 'One mile up, maybe a little less. The sign says Scenic Turnout and Picnic Area.'

'What if they posted someone there?'

'They haven't.'

'How can you be sure?'

'Because neither Abra nor her uncle Billy could possibly know about it, never having been here. And the True doesn't know about me.'

'You better hope they don't.'

'Abra says everyone's where they're supposed to be. She's been checking. Now be quiet a minute, Billy. I need to think.'

It was Hallorann he wanted to think about. For several years following their haunted winter at the Overlook, Danny Torrance and Dick Hallorann had talked a lot. Sometimes face-to-face, more often mind-to-mind. Danny loved his mother, but there were things she didn't – couldn't – understand. About the lockboxes, for instance. The ones where you put the dangerous things that the shining sometimes attracted. Not that the lockbox thing always worked. On several occasions he had tried to make one for the drinking, but that effort had been an abject failure (perhaps because he had *wanted* it to be a failure). Mrs Massey, though . . . and Horace Derwent . . .

There was a third lockbox in storage now, but it wasn't as good as the ones he'd made as a kid. Because he wasn't as strong? Because what it held was different from the revenants that had been unwise enough to seek him out? Both? He didn't know. He only knew that it was leaky. When he opened it, what was inside might kill him. But—

'What do you mean?' Billy asked.

'Huh?' Dan looked around. One hand was pressed to his stomach. It hurt very badly now.

'You just said, "There isn't any choice." What did you mean?'

'Never mind.' They had reached the picnic area, and Billy was turning in. Up ahead was a clearing with picnic benches and barbecue pits. To Dan, it looked like Cloud Gap without the river. 'Just . . . if things go wrong, get in your truck and drive like hell.'

'You think that would help?'

Dan didn't reply. His gut was burning, burning.

3

Shortly before four o'clock on that Monday afternoon in late September, Rose walked up to Roof O' the World with Silent Sarey.

Rose was dressed in form-fitting jeans that accentuated her long and shapely legs. Although it was chilly, Silent Sarey wore only a housedress of unremarkable light blue that fluttered around stout calves clad in Jobst support stockings. Rose stopped to look at a plaque which had been bolted to a granite post at the base of the three dozen or so stairs leading up to the lookout platform. It announced that this was the site of the historic Overlook Hotel, which had burned to the ground some thirty-five years ago.

'Very strong feelings here, Sarey.'

Sarey nodded.

'You know there are hot springs where steam comes right out of the ground, don't you?'

'Lup.'

'This is like that.' Rose bent down to sniff at the grass and wild-flowers. Below their aromas was the iron smell of ancient blood. 'Strong emotions – hatred, fear, prejudice, lust. The echo of murder. Not food – too old – but refreshing, all the same. A heady bouquet.'

Sarey said nothing, but watched Rose closely.

'And *this* thing.' Rose waved a hand at the steep wooden stairs leading up to the platform. 'Looks like a gallows, don't you think? All it needs is a trapdoor.'

Nothing from Sarey. Out loud, at least. Her thought

(*no rope*)

was clear enough.

'That's true, my love, but one of us is going to hang here, just the same. Either me or the little bitch with her nose in our business. See that?' Rose pointed to a small green shed about twenty feet away.

Sarey nodded.

Rose was wearing a zipper pack on her belt. She opened it, rummaged, brought out a key, and handed it to the other woman. Sarey walked to the shed, grass whickering against her thick flesh-colored hose. The key fitted a padlock on the door. When she pulled the door open, late-day sunshine illuminated an enclosure not much bigger than a privy. There was a Lawn-Boy and a plastic bucket holding a hand-sickle and a rake. A spade and a pickax leaned against the back wall. There was nothing else, and nothing to hide behind.

'Go on in,' Rose said. 'Let's see what you can do.' *And with all that steam inside you, you should be able to amaze me.*

Like other members of the True Knot, Silent Sarey had her little talent.

She stepped into the little shed, sniffed, and said: 'Dusty.'

'Never mind the dust. Let's see you do your thing. Or rather, let's *not* see you.'

For that was Sarey's talent. She wasn't capable of invisibility (none of them was), but she could create a kind of *dimness* that went very well with her unremarkable face and figure. She turned to Rose, then looked down at her shadow. She moved – not much, only half a step – and her shadow merged with the one thrown by the handle of the Lawn-Boy. Then she became perfectly still, and the shed was empty.

Rose squeezed her eyes shut, then popped them wide open, and there was Sarey, standing beside the mower with her hands folded demurely at her waist like a shy girl hoping some boy at the party will ask her to dance. Rose looked away at the mountains, and when she looked back again the shed was empty – just a tiny storage room with nowhere to hide. In the strong sunlight there wasn't even a shadow. Except for the one thrown by the mower's handle, that was. Only . . .

'Pull your elbow in,' Rose said. 'I see it. Just a little.'

Silent Sarey did as she was told and for a moment she was truly gone, at least until Rose concentrated. When she did that, Sarey was there again. But of course she knew Sarey was there. When the time came – and it wouldn't be long – the bitchgirl wouldn't.

'Good, Sarey!' she said warmly (or as warmly as she could manage).
'Perhaps I won't need you. If I do, you'll use the sickle. And think
of Andi when you do. All right?'

At the mention of Andi's name, Sarey's lips turned down in a
moue of unhappiness. She stared at the sickle in the plastic bucket
and nodded.

Rose walked over and took the padlock. 'I'm going to lock you
in now. The bitchgirl will read the ones in the Lodge, but she won't
read you. I'm sure of it. Because you're the quiet one, aren't you?'

Sarey nodded again. She was the quiet one, always had been.

(*what about the*)

Rose smiled. 'The lock? Don't you worry about that. Just worry
about being still. Still and silent. Do you understand me?'

'Lup.'

'And you understand about the sickle?' Rose would not have
trusted Sarey with a gun even if the True had one.

'Sicka. Lup.'

'If I get the better of her – and as full of steam as I am right
now, that should be no problem – you'll stay right where you are
until I let you out. But if you hear me shout . . . let's see . . . if you
hear me shout *don't make me punish you*, that means I need help. I'll
make sure that her back is turned. You know what happens then,
don't you?'

(*I'll climb the stairs and*)

But Rose was shaking her head. 'No, Sarey. You won't need to.
She's never going to get near the platform up there.'

She would hate to lose the steam even more than she would hate
losing the opportunity to kill the bitchgirl herself . . . after making
her suffer, and at length. But she mustn't throw caution to the winds.
The girl *was* very strong.

'What will you listen for, Sarey?'

'Don't make me punish lu.'

'And what will you be thinking of?'

The eyes, half-hidden by the shaggy bangs, gleamed. 'Levenge.'

'That's right. Revenge for Andi, murdered by that bitchgirl's
friends. But not unless I need you, because I want to do this myself.'
Rose's hands clenched, her nails digging into deep, blood-crusted

crescents they had already made in her palms. 'But if I need you, *you come*. Don't hesitate or stop for anything. Don't stop until you've put that sickle blade in her neck and see the end of it come out of her fucking throat.'

Sarey's eyes gleamed. 'Lup.'

'Good.' Rose kissed her, then shut the door and snapped the padlock closed. She put the key in her zipper pack and leaned against the door. 'Listen to me, sweetheart. If all goes well, you'll get the first steam. I promise. And it will be the best you ever had.'

Rose walked back to the lookout platform, took several long and steadying breaths, and then began to climb the steps.

4

Dan stood with his hands propped against one of the picnic tables, head down, eyes closed.

'Doing it this way is crazy,' Billy said. 'I should stay with you.'

'You can't. You've got your own fish to fry.'

'What if you faint halfway down that path? Even if you don't, how are you going to take on the whole bunch of them? The way you look now, you couldn't go two rounds with a five-year-old.'

'I think pretty soon I'm going to feel a whole lot better. Stronger, too. Go on, Billy. You remember where to park?'

'Far end of the lot, by the sign that says kids eat for free when the Colorado teams win.'

'Right.' Dan raised his head and noted the oversize sunglasses Billy was now wearing. 'Pull your cap down hard. All the way to your ears. Look young.'

'I might have a trick that'll make me look even younger. If I can still do it, that is.'

Dan barely heard this. 'I need one other thing.'

He stood up straight and opened his arms. Billy hugged him, wanting to do it hard – fiercely – and not daring.

'Abra made a good call. I never would have gotten here without you. Now take care of your business.'

'You take care of yours,' Billy said. 'I'm counting on you to drive the Thanksgiving run out to Cloud Gap.'

'I'd like that,' Dan said. 'Best model train set a boy never had.'

Billy watched him walk slowly, holding his hands against his stomach as he went, to the signpost on the far side of the clearing. There were two wooden arrows. One pointed west, toward Pawnee Lookout. The other pointed east, downhill. This one read TO BLUEBELL CAMPGROUND.

Dan started along that path. For a little while Billy could see him through the glowing yellow leaves of the aspens, walking slowly and painfully, his head down to watch his footing. Then he was gone.

'Take care of my boy,' Billy said. He wasn't sure if he was talking to God or Abra, and guessed it didn't matter; both were probably too busy to bother with the likes of him this afternoon.

He went back to his truck, and from the bed pulled out a little girl with staring china blue eyes and stiff blond curls. Not much weight; she was probably hollow inside. 'How you doin, Abra? Hope you didn't get bumped around too much.'

She was wearing a Colorado Rockies tee and blue shorts. Her feet were bare, and why not? This little girl – actually a mannequin purchased at a moribund children's clothing shop in Martenville – had never walked a single step. But she had bendable knees, and Billy was able to place her in the truck's passenger seat with no trouble. He buckled her seatbelt, started to close the door, then tried the neck. It also bent, although only a little. He stepped away to examine the effect. It wasn't bad. She seemed to be looking at something in her lap. Or maybe praying for strength in the coming battle. Not bad at all.

Unless they had binoculars, of course.

He got back in the truck and waited, giving Dan time. Also hoping he wasn't passed out somewhere along the path that led to the Bluebell Campground.

At quarter to five, Billy started the truck and headed back the way he had come.

5

Dan maintained a steady walking pace in spite of the growing heat in his midsection. It felt as though there were a rat on fire in there, one that kept chewing at him even as it burned. If the path had been going up instead of down, he never would have made it.

At ten to five, he came around a bend and stopped. Not far ahead, the aspens gave way to a green and manicured expanse of lawn sloping down to a pair of tennis courts. Beyond the courts he could see the RV parking area and a long log building: Overlook Lodge. Beyond that, the terrain climbed again. Where the Overlook had once stood, a tall platform reared gantrylike against the bright sky. Roof O' the World. Looking at it, the same thought that had occurred to Rose the Hat

(*gallows*)

crossed Dan's mind. Standing at the railing, facing south toward the parking lot for day visitors, was a single silhouetted figure. A woman's figure. The tophat was tilted on her head.

(*Abra are you there*)

(*I'm here Dan*)

Calm, by the sound. Calm was just the way he wanted it.

(*are they hearing you*)

That brought a vague ticklish sensation: her smile. The angry one.

(*if they're not they're deaf*)

That was good enough.

(*you have to come to me now but remember if I tell you to go YOU GO*)

She didn't answer, and before he could tell her again, she was there.

6

The Stones and John Dalton watched helplessly as Abra slid sideways until she was lying with her head on the boards of the stoop and her legs splayed out on the steps below her. Hoppy spilled from one relaxing hand. She didn't look as if she were sleeping, nor even in a faint. That was the ugly sprawl of deep unconsciousness or death. Lucy lunged forward. Dave and John held her back.

She fought them. 'Let me go! I have to help her!'

'You can't,' John said. 'Only Dan can help her now. They have to help each other.'

She stared at him with wild eyes. 'Is she even breathing? Can you tell?'

'She's breathing,' Dave said, but he sounded unsure even to himself.

7

When Abra joined him, the pain eased for the first time since Boston. That didn't comfort Dan much, because now Abra was suffering, too. He could see it in her face, but he could also see the wonder in her eyes as she looked around at the room in which she found herself. There were bunk beds, knotty-pine walls, and a rug embroidered with western sage and cactus. Both the rug and the lower bunk were littered with cheap toys. On a small desk in the corner was a scattering of books and a jigsaw puzzle with large pieces. In the room's far corner, a radiator clanked and hissed.

Abra walked to the desk and picked up one of the books. On the cover, a small child on a trike was being chased by a little dog. The title was *Reading Fun with Dick and Jane*.

Dan joined her, wearing a bemused smile. 'The little girl on the cover is Sally. Dick and Jane are her brother and sister. And the dog's name is Spot. For a little while they were my best friends. My only friends, I guess. Except for Tony, of course.'

She put the book down and turned to him. 'What *is* this place, Dan?'

'A memory. There used to be a hotel here, and this was my room. Now it's a place where we can be together. You know the wheel that turns when you go into someone else?'

'Uh-huh . . .'

'This is the middle. The hub.'

'I wish we could stay here. It feels . . . safe. Except for *those*.' Abra pointed to the French doors with their long panes of glass. 'They don't feel the same as the rest.' She looked at him almost accusingly. 'They weren't here, were they? When you were a kid.'

'No. There weren't any windows in my room, and the only door was the one that went into the rest of the caretaker's apartment. I changed it. I had to. Do you know why?'

She studied him, her eyes grave. 'Because that was then and this is now. Because the past is gone, even though it defines the present.'

He smiled. 'I couldn't have said it better myself.'

'You didn't have to say it. You thought it.'

He drew her toward those French doors that had never existed. Through the glass they could see the lawn, the tennis courts, the Overlook Lodge, and Roof O' the World.

'I see her,' Abra breathed. 'She's up there, and she's not looking this way, is she?'

'She better not be,' Dan said. 'How bad is the pain, honey?'

'Bad,' she said. 'But I don't care. Because—'

She didn't have to finish. He knew, and she smiled. This togetherness was what they had, and in spite of the pain that came with it – pain of all kinds – it was good. It was very good.

'Dan?'

'Yes, honey.'

'There are ghostie people out there. I can't see them, but I feel them. Do you?'

'Yes.' He had for years. Because the past defines the present. He put his arm around her shoulders, and her arm crept around his waist.

'What do we do now?'

'Wait for Billy. Hope he's on time. And then all of this is going to happen very fast.'

'Uncle Dan?'

'What, Abra.'

'What's inside you? That isn't a ghost. It's like—' He felt her shiver. 'It's like a *monster*.'

He said nothing.

She straightened and stepped away from him. 'Look! Over there!'

An old Ford pickup was rolling into the visitor's parking lot.

8

Rose stood with her hands on the lookout platform's waist-high railing, peering at the truck pulling into the parking lot. The steam had sharpened her vision, but she still wished she had brought a pair of binoculars. Surely there were some in the supply room, for guests who wanted to go bird-watching, so why hadn't she?

Because you had so many other things on your mind. The sickness . . . the rats jumping ship . . . losing Crow to the bitchgirl . . .

Yes to all of that – yes, yes, yes – but she still should have remembered. For a moment she wondered what else she might have forgotten, but pushed the idea away. She was still in charge of this, loaded with steam and at the top of her game. Everything was going exactly as planned. Soon the little girl would come up here, because she was full of foolish teenage confidence and pride in her own abilities.

But I have the high ground, dear, in all sorts of ways. If I can't take care of you alone, I'll draw from the rest of the True. They're all together in the main room, because you thought that was such a good idea. But there's something you didn't take into consideration. When we're together we're linked, we're a True Knot, and that makes us a giant battery. Power I can draw on if I need to.

If all else failed, there was Silent Sarey. She would now have the sickle in her hand. She might not be a genius, but she was merciless, murderous, and – once she understood the job – completely obedient. Also, she had her own reasons for wanting the bitchgirl laid out dead on the ground at the foot of the lookout platform.

(Charlie)

Token Charlie hit her back at once, and although he was ordinarily a feeble sender, now – boosted by the others in the main room of the Lodge – he came in loud and clear and nearly mad with excitement.

(I'm getting her steady and strong we all are she must be real close you must feel her)

Rose did, even though she was still working hard to keep her mind closed off so the bitchgirl couldn't get in and mess with her.

(never mind that just tell the others to be ready if I need help)

Many voices came back, jumping all over each other. They were ready. Even those that were sick were ready to help all they could. She loved them for that.

Rose stared at the blond girl in the truck. She was looking down. Reading something? Nerving herself up? Praying to the God of Rubes, perhaps? It didn't matter.

Come to me, bitchgirl. Come to Auntie Rose.

But it wasn't the girl who got out, it was the uncle. Just as the bitch had said he would. Checking. He walked around the hood of the truck, moving slowly, looking everywhere. He leaned in the passenger window, said something to the girl, then moved away from the truck a little. He looked toward the Lodge, then turned to the platform rearing against the sky . . . and waved. The insolent bugger actually waved at her.

Rose didn't wave back. She was frowning. An uncle. Why had her parents sent an uncle instead of bringing their bitch daughter themselves? For that matter, why had they allowed her to come at all?

She convinced them it was the only way. Told them that if she didn't come to me, I'd come to her. That's the reason, and it makes sense.

It did, but she felt a growing unease all the same. She had allowed the bitchgirl to set the ground rules. To that extent, at least, Rose had been manipulated. She had allowed it because this was her home ground and because she had taken precautions, but mostly because she had been angry. So angry.

She stared hard at the man in the parking lot. He was strolling around again, looking here and there, making sure she was alone. Perfectly reasonable, it was what she would have done, but she still had a gnawing intuition that what he was really doing was buying time, although why he would want to was beyond her.

Rose stared harder, now focusing on the man's gait. She decided he wasn't as young as she had first believed. He walked, in fact, like a man who was far from young. As if he had more than a touch of arthritis. And why was the little girl so still?

Rose felt the first pulse of real alarm.

Something was wrong here.

9

'She's looking at Mr Freeman,' Abra said. 'We should go.'

He opened the French doors, but hesitated. Something in her voice. 'What's the trouble, Abra?'

'I don't know. Maybe nothing, but I don't like it. She's looking at him really *hard*. We have to go right now.'

'I need to do something first. Try to be ready, and don't be scared.'

Dan closed his eyes and went to the storage room at the back of his mind. Real lockboxes would have been covered with dust after all these years, but the two he'd put here as a child were as fresh as ever. Why not? They were made of pure imagination. The third – the new one – had a faint aura hanging around it, and he thought: *No wonder I'm sick.*

Never mind. That one had to stay for the time being. He opened the oldest of the other two, ready for anything, and found . . . nothing. Or almost. In the lockbox that had held Mrs Massey for thirty-two years, there was a heap of dark gray ash. But in the other . . .

He realized how foolish telling her not to be scared had been. Abra shrieked.

10

On the back stoop of the house in Anniston, Abra began to jerk. Her legs spasmed; her feet rattled a tattoo on the steps; one hand – flopping like a fish dragged to a riverbank and left to die there – sent the ill-used and bedraggled Hoppy flying.

'*What's wrong with her?*' Lucy screamed.

She rushed for the door. David stood frozen – transfixed by the sight of his seizing daughter – but John got his right arm around Lucy's waist and his left around her upper chest. She bucked against him. 'Let me go! I have to go to her!'

'No!' John shouted. '*No, Lucy, you can't!*'

She would have broken free, but now David had her, too.

She subsided, looking first at John. 'If she dies out there, I'll see you go to jail for it.' Next, her gaze – flat-eyed and hostile – went to her husband. 'You I'll never forgive.'

'She's quieting,' John said.

On the stoop, Abra's tremors moderated, then stopped. But her cheeks were wet, and tears squeezed from beneath her closed lids. In the day's dying light, they clung to her lashes like jewels.

11

In Danny Torrance's childhood bedroom – a room now made only of memory – Abra clung to Dan with her face pressed against his chest. When she spoke, her voice was muffled. 'The monster – is it gone?'

'Yes,' Dan said.

'Swear on your mother's name?'

'Yes.'

She raised her head, first looking at him to assure herself he was telling the truth, then daring to scan the room. 'That *smile*.' She shuddered.

'Yes,' Dan said. 'I think . . . he's glad to be home. Abra, are you going to be all right? Because we have to do this right now. Time's up.'

'I'm all right. But what if . . . it . . . comes back?'

Dan thought of the lockbox. It was open, but could be closed again easily enough. Especially with Abra to help him. 'I don't think he . . . *it* . . . wants anything to do with us, honey. Come on. Just remember: if I tell you to go back to New Hampshire, you *go*.'

Once again she didn't reply, and there was no time to discuss it. Time was up. He stepped through the French doors. They gave on the end of the path. Abra walked beside him, but lost the solidity she'd had in the room of memory and began to flicker again.

Out here she's almost a ghostie person herself, Dan thought. It brought home to him just how much she had put herself at risk. He didn't like to think about how tenuous her hold on her own body might now be.

Moving rapidly – but not running; that would attract Rose's eye, and they had at least seventy yards to cover before the rear of the Overlook Lodge would block them from the lookout platform – Dan and his ghostie-girl companion crossed the lawn and took the flagstone walk that ran between the tennis courts.

They reached the back of the kitchen, and at last the bulk of the Lodge hid them from the platform. Here was the steady rumble of an exhaust fan and the spoiled-meat smell of garbage cans. He tried the rear door and found it unlocked, but paused a moment before opening it.

(*are they all*)

(*yes all but Rose she hurry up Dan you have to because*)

Abra's eyes, flickering like those of a child in an old black-and-white movie, were wide with dismay. 'She knows something's wrong.'

12

Rose turned her attention to the bitchgirl, still sitting in the passenger seat of the truck, head bowed, still as could be. Abra wasn't watching her uncle – if he *was* her uncle – and she was making no move to get out. The alarm meter in Rose's head went from Danger Yellow to Condition Red.

'Hey!' The voice came floating up to her on the thin air. 'Hey, you old bag! Watch this!'

She snapped her gaze back to the man in the parking lot and stared, close to flabbergasted, as he raised his hands over his head and then turned a big, unsteady cartwheel. She thought he was going to go on his ass, but the only thing that fell to the pavement was his hat. What it exposed was the fine white hair of a man in his seventies. Maybe even his eighties.

Rose looked back at the girl in the truck, who remained perfectly still with her head bent. She had absolutely no interest in the uncle's antics. Suddenly it clicked and Rose understood what she would have seen right away, had the trick not been so outrageous: it was a mannequin.

But she's here! Token Charlie feels her, all of them in the Lodge feel her, they're all together and they know—

All together in the Lodge. All together in one place. And had that been Rose's idea? No. That idea had come from the—

Rose broke for the stairs.

13

The remaining members of the True Knot were crowded together at the two windows looking down at the parking lot, watching as Billy Freeman turned a cartwheel for the first time in over forty years (and the last time he'd done this trick, he'd been drunk). Petty the Chink actually laughed. 'What in God's name—'

With their backs turned, they didn't see Dan step into the room from the kitchen, or the girl flickering in and out of view at his side. Dan had time to register two bundles of clothes on the floor, and to understand that Bradley Trevor's measles were still hard at work. Then he went back inside himself, went deep, and found the third lockbox – the leaky one. He flung it open.

(*Dan what are you doing*)

He leaned forward with his hands on his upper thighs, his stomach burning like hot metal, and exhaled the old poet's last gasp, which she had given him freely, in a dying kiss. From his mouth there came a long plume of pink mist that deepened to red as it hit the air. At first he could focus on nothing but the blessed relief in the middle of his body as the poison remains of Concetta Reynolds left him.

'*Momo!*' Abra shrieked.

14

On the platform, Rose's eyes widened. The bitchgirl was in the Lodge.

And someone was with her.

She leaped into this new mind without thinking about it. Searching. Ignoring the markers that meant big steam, only trying to stop him before he could do whatever it was he intended to do. Ignoring the terrible possibility that it was already too late.

15

The members of the True turned toward Abra's cry. Someone – it was Long Paul – said: 'What in the hell is *that*?'

The red mist coalesced into a shape of a woman. For a moment – surely no more than that – Dan looked into Concetta's swirling eyes and saw they were young. Still weak and focused on this phantom, he had no sense of the intruder in his mind.

'*Momo!*' Abra cried again. She was holding out her arms.

The woman in the cloud might have looked at her. Might even have smiled. Then the shape of Concetta Reynolds was gone and the mist rolled at the clustered True Knot, many of them now clinging to one another in fright and bewilderment. To Dan, the red stuff looked like blood spreading in water.

'It's steam,' Dan told them. 'You bastards lived on it; now suck it in and die on it.'

He had known ever since the plan's conception that if it didn't happen fast, he would never live to see how well it succeeded, but he had never imagined it would occur as rapidly as it did. The measles that had already weakened them might have had something to do with it, because some lasted a little longer than others. Even so, it was over in a matter of seconds.

They howled in his head like dying wolves. The sound appalled Dan, but this was not true of his companion.

'*Good!*' Abra shouted. She shook her fists at them. '*How does it taste? How does my momo taste? Is she good? Have as much as you want! HAVE ALL OF IT!*'

They began to cycle. Through the red mist, Dan saw two of them embracing with their foreheads pressed together, and in spite of all they had done – all they were – the sight moved him. He saw the words *I love you* on Short Eddie's lips; saw Big Mo begin to reply; then they were gone, their clothes floating to the floor. It was that quick.

He turned to Abra, meaning to tell her they had to finish it at once, but then Rose the Hat began to shriek, and for a few moments – until Abra could block her – those cries of rage and maddened grief blotted out everything else, even the blessed relief of being pain-free. And, he devoutly hoped, cancer-free. About that he wouldn't know for sure until he could see his face in a mirror.

16

Rose was at the head of the steps leading down from the platform when the killing mist rolled over the True Knot, the remains of Abra's momo doing its quick and lethal work.

A white sheet of agony filled her. Screams shot through her head like shrapnel. The cries of the dying True made those of the Cloud Gap raiding party in New Hampshire and Crow in New York seem puny by comparison. Rose staggered back as if she had been hit with a club. She struck the railing, rebounded, and fell down on the boards. Somewhere in the distance, a woman – an old one, by the wavering sound of her voice – was chanting *no, no, no, no, no.*

That's me. It has to be, because I'm the only one left.

It wasn't the girl who had fallen into the trap of overconfidence, but Rose herself. She thought of something

(hoisted on your own petard)

the bitchgirl had said. It scalded her with rage and dismay. Her old friends and longtime traveling companions were dead. Poisoned. Except for the cowards who had run, Rose the Hat was the last of the True Knot.

But no, that wasn't true. There was Sarey.

Sprawled on the platform and shivering under the late-afternoon sky, Rose reached out to her.

(are you)

The thought that came back was full of confusion and horror.

(yes but Rose are they can they be)

(never mind them just remember Sarey do you remember)

('don't make me punish you')

(good Sarey good)

If the girl didn't run ... if she made the mistake of trying to finish her murderous day's work ...

She would. Rose was sure of it, and she had seen enough in the mind of the bitchgirl's companion to know two things: how they had accomplished this slaughter, and how their very connection could be turned against them.

Rage was powerful.

So were childhood memories.

She struggled to her feet, reset her hat at the proper jaunty angle without even thinking about it, and walked to the railing. The man from the pickup truck was staring up at her, but she paid scant attention to him. His treacherous little job was done. She might deal with him later, but now she had eyes only for the Overlook Lodge. The girl was there, but also far away. Her bodily presence at the True's campground was little more than a phantom. The one who was whole – a real person, a rube – was a man she had never seen before. And a steamhead. His voice in her mind was clear and cold.

(hello Rose)

There was a place nearby where the girl would cease to flicker. Where she would take on her physical body. Where she could be killed. Let Sarey take care of the steamhead man, but not until the steamhead man had taken care of the bitchgirl.

(*hello Danny hello little boy*)

Loaded with steam, she reached into him and swatted him to the hub of the wheel, barely hearing Abra's cry of bewilderment and terror as she turned to follow.

And when Dan was where Rose wanted him, for a moment too surprised to keep his guard up, she poured all her fury into him. She poured it into him like steam.

CHAPTER TWENTY
HUB OF THE WHEEL,
ROOF O' THE WORLD

1

Dan Torrance opened his eyes. Sunlight shot through them and into his aching head, threatening to set his brains on fire. It was the hangover to end all hangovers. Loud snoring from beside him: a nasty, annoying sound that could only be some drunk chick sleeping it off at the wrong end of the rainbow. Dan turned his head that way and saw the woman sprawled on her back beside him. Vaguely familiar. Dark hair spread around her in a halo. Wearing an oversize Atlanta Braves t-shirt.

This isn't real. I'm not here. I'm in Colorado, I'm at Roof O' the World, and I have to end it.

The woman rolled over, opened her eyes, and stared at him. 'God, my head,' she said. 'Get me some of that coke, daddy. It's in the living room.'

He stared at her in amazement and growing fury. The fury seemed to come from nowhere, but hadn't it always been that way? It was its own thing, a riddle wrapped in an enigma. 'Coke? Who bought coke?'

She grinned, revealing a mouth that contained only a single discolored tooth. Then he knew who she was. '*You* did, daddy. Now go get it. Once my head's clear, I'll throw you a nice fuck.'

Somehow he was back in this sleazy Wilmington apartment, naked, next to Rose the Hat.

'What have you done? How did I get here?'

She threw her head back and laughed. 'Don't you like this place? You should; I furnished it from your own head. Now do what I told you, asshole. Get the fucking blow.'

'Where's Abra? What did you do with Abra?'

'Killed her,' Rose said indifferently. 'She was so worried about you she dropped her guard and I tore her open from throat to belly. I wasn't able to suck up as much of her steam as I wanted, but I got quite a lo—'

The world went red. Dan clamped his hands around her throat and began to choke. One thought beat through his mind: *worthless bitch, now you'll take your medicine, worthless bitch, now you'll take your medicine, worthless bitch, now you'll take it all.*

2

The steamhead man was powerful but had nothing like the girl's juice. He stood with his legs apart, his head lowered, his shoulders hunched, and his fisted hands raised – the posture of every man who had ever lost his mind in a killing rage. Anger made men easy.

It was impossible to follow his thoughts, because they had turned red. That was all right, that was fine, the girl was right where Rose wanted her. In Abra's state of shocked dismay, she had followed him to the hub of the wheel. She wouldn't be shocked or dismayed for much longer, though; Bitchgirl had become Choked Girl. Soon she would be Dead Girl, hoisted on her own petard.

(*Uncle Dan no no stop it's not her*)

It is, Rose thought, bearing down even harder. Her tooth crept out of her mouth and skewered her lower lip. Blood poured down her chin and onto her top. She didn't feel it any more than she felt the mountain breeze blowing through her masses of dark hair. *It is me. You were my daddy, my barroom daddy, I made you empty your wallet for a pile of bad coke, and now it's the morning after and I need to take my medicine. It's what you wanted to do when you woke up next to that drunken whore in Wilmington, what you* would *have done if you'd had any balls, and her useless whelp of a son for good measure. Your father knew how to deal with stupid, disobedient women, and his father before him. Sometimes a woman just needs to take her medicine. She needs—*

There was the roar of an approaching motor. It was as unimportant as the pain in her lip and the taste of blood in her mouth. The girl was choking, rattling. Then a thought as loud as a thunderclap exploded in her brain, a wounded roar:

(*MY FATHER KNEW NOTHING!*)

Rose was still trying to clear her mind of that shout when Billy Freeman's pickup truck hit the base of the lookout, knocking her off her feet. Her hat went flying.

3

It wasn't the apartment in Wilmington. It was his long-gone bedroom at the Overlook Hotel – the hub of the wheel. It wasn't Deenie, the woman he'd awakened next to in that apartment, and it wasn't Rose.

It was Abra. He had his hands around her neck and her eyes were bulging.

For a moment she started to change again as Rose tried to worm back inside him, feeding him her rage and augmenting his own. Then something happened, and she was gone. But she would be back.

Abra was coughing and staring at him. He would have expected shock, but for a girl who had almost been choked to death, she seemed oddly composed.

(*well . . . we knew it wouldn't be easy*)

'I'm not my father!' Dan shouted at her. '*I am not my father!*'

'Probably that's good,' Abra said. She actually smiled. 'You've got one hell of a temper, Uncle Dan. I guess we really *are* related.'

'I almost killed you,' Dan said. 'It's enough. Time for you to get out. Go back to New Hampshire right now.'

She shook her head. 'I'll have to – for a while, not long – but right now you need me.'

'Abra, that's an order.'

She folded her arms and stood where she was on the cactus carpet.

'Ah, Christ.' He ran his hands through his hair. 'You're a piece of work.'

She reached out, took his hand. 'We're going to finish this together. Now come on. Let's get out of this room. I don't think I like it here, after all.'

Their fingers interlaced, and the room where he had lived for a time as a child dissolved.

4

Dan had time to register the hood of Billy's pickup folded around one of the thick posts holding up the Roof O' the World lookout tower, its busted radiator steaming. He saw the mannequin version of Abra hanging out the passenger-side window, with one plastic arm cocked jauntily behind her. He saw Billy himself trying to open the crumpled driver's side door. Blood was running down one side of the old man's face.

Something grabbed his head. Powerful hands twisting, attempting to snap his neck. Then Abra's hands were there, tearing Rose's away. She looked up. 'You'll have to do better than that, you cowardly old bitch.'

Rose stood at the railing, looking down and resetting her ugly hat at the correct angle. 'Did you enjoy your uncle's hands around your throat? How do you feel about him now?'

'That was you, not him.'

Rose grinned, her bloody mouth yawning. 'Not at all, dear. I just made use of what he has inside. You should know, you're just like him.'

She's trying to distract us, Dan thought. *But from what? That?*

It was a small green building – maybe an outside bathroom, maybe a storage shed.

(can you)

He didn't have to finish the thought. Abra turned toward the shed and stared at it. The padlock creaked, snapped, and fell into the grass. The door swung open. The shed was empty except for a few tools and an old lawnmower. Dan thought he'd felt something there, but it must only have been overwrought nerves. When they looked up again, Rose was no longer in view. She had retreated from the railing.

Billy finally managed to get the door of his truck open. He got out, staggered, managed to keep his feet. 'Danny? You all right?' And then: 'Is that Abra? Jesus, she's hardly there.'

'Listen, Billy. Can you walk to the Lodge?'

'I think so. What about the people in there?'

'Gone. I think it would be a very good idea if you went *now*.'

Billy didn't argue. He started down the slope, wallowing like a drunk. Dan pointed at the stairs leading to the lookout platform and raised questioning eyebrows. Abra shook her head

(*it's what she wants*)

and began leading Dan around Roof O' the World, to where they could see the very top of Rose's stovepipe hat. This put the little equipment shed at their backs, but Dan thought nothing of this now that he had seen it was empty.

(*Dan I have to go back now just for a minute I have to refresh my*)

A picture in his mind: a field filled with sunflowers, all opening at once. She needed to take care of her physical being, and that was good. That was right.

(*go*)

(*I'll be back as soon as*)

(*go Abra I'll be fine*)

And with any luck, this would be over when she came back.

5

In Anniston, John Dalton and the Stones saw Abra draw a deep breath and open her eyes.

'Abra!' Lucy called. 'Is it over?'

'Soon.'

'What's that on your neck? Are those bruises?'

'Mom, stay there! I have to go back. Dan needs me.'

She reached for Hoppy, but before she could grasp the old stuffed rabbit, her eyes closed and her body grew still.

6

Peering cautiously over the railing, Rose saw Abra disappear. Little bitchgirl could only stay here so long, then she had to go back for some R & R. Her presence at the Bluebell Campground wasn't much different from her presence that day in the supermarket, only this manifestation was much more powerful. And why? Because the man was assisting her. *Boosting* her. If he were dead when the girl returned—

Looking down at him, Rose called: 'I'd leave while you still have the chance, Danny. Don't make me punish you.'

7

Silent Sarey was so focused on what was going on at Roof O' the World – listening with every admittedly limited IQ point of her mind as well as with her ears – that she did not at first realize she was no longer alone in the shed. It was the smell that finally alerted her: something rotten. Not garbage. She didn't dare turn, because the door was open and the man out there might see her. She stood still, the sickle in one hand.

Sarey heard Rose telling the man to leave while he still had the chance, and that was when the shed door began swinging shut again, all on its own.

'Don't make me punish you!' Rose called. That was her cue to burst out and put the sickle in the troublesome, meddling little girl's neck, but since the girl was gone, the man would have to do. But before she could move, a cold hand slid over the wrist holding the sickle. Slid over it and clamped tight.

She turned – no reason not to now, with the door closed – and what she saw by the dim light filtering through the cracks in the old boards caused a scream to come bolting out of her usually silent throat. At some point while she had been concentrating, a corpse had joined her in the toolshed. His smiling, predatory face was the damp whitish-green of a spoiled avocado. His eyes seemed almost to dangle from their sockets. His suit was splotched with ancient mold . . . but the multicolored confetti sprinkled on his shoulders was fresh.

'Great party, isn't it?' he said, and as he grinned, his lips split open.

She screamed again and drove the sickle into his left temple. The curved blade went deep and hung there, but there was no blood.

'Give us a kiss, dear,' Horace Derwent said. From between his lips came the wiggling white remnant of a tongue. 'It's been a long time since I've been with a woman.'

As his tattered lips, shining with decay, settled on Sarey's, his hands closed around her throat.

8

Rose saw the shed door swing closed, heard the scream, and understood that she was now truly alone. Soon, probably in seconds, the girl would be back and it would be two against one. She couldn't allow that.

She looked down at the man and summoned all of her steam-amplified force.

(choke yourself do it NOW)

His hands rose toward his throat, but too slowly. He was fighting her, and with a degree of success that was infuriating. She would have expected a battle from the bitchgirl, but that rube down there was an adult. She should have been able to brush aside any steam remaining to him like mist.

Still, she was winning.

His hands went up to his chest . . . his shoulders . . . finally to his throat. There they wavered – she could hear him panting with effort. She bore down, and the hands gripped, shutting off his windpipe.

(that's right you interfering bastard squeeze squeeze and SQUEE)

Something hit her. Not a fist; it felt more like a gust of tightly compressed air. She looked around and saw nothing but a shimmer, there for a moment and then gone. Less than three seconds, but enough to break her concentration, and when she turned back to the railing, the girl had returned.

It wasn't a gust of air this time; it was hands that felt simultaneously large and small. They were in the small of her back. They were pushing. The bitchgirl and her friend, working together – just what Rose had wanted to avoid. A worm of terror began to unwind in her stomach. She tried to step back from the rail and could not. It was taking all her strength just to stand pat, and with no supporting force from the True to help her, she didn't think she'd be able to do that for long. Not long at all.

If not for that gust of air . . . that wasn't him and she wasn't here . . .

One of the hands left the small of her back and slapped the hat from her head. Rose howled at the indignity of it – nobody touched her hat, *nobody*! – and for a moment summoned enough power to stagger back from the railing and toward the center of the platform. Then those hands returned to the small of her back and began pushing her forward again.

She looked down at them. The man had his eyes closed, concentrating so hard that the cords stood out on his neck and sweat rolled down his cheeks like tears. The girl's eyes, however, were wide and merciless. She was staring up at Rose. And she was smiling.

Rose pushed backward with all her strength, but she might have been pushing against a stone wall. One that was moving her relentlessly forward, until her stomach was pressing against the rail. She heard it creak.

She thought, for just a moment, of trying to bargain. Of telling the girl that they could work together, start a new Knot. That instead of dying in 2070 or 2080, Abra Stone could live a thousand years. *Two* thousand. But what good would it do?

Was there ever a teenage girl who felt anything less than immortal?

So instead of bargaining, or begging, she screamed defiance down at them. '*Fuck you! Fuck you both!*'

The girl's terrible smile widened. 'Oh, no,' she said. '*You're* the one who's fucked.'

No creak this time; there was a crack like a rifleshot, and then Rose the Hatless was falling.

9

She hit the ground headfirst and began to cycle at once. Her head was cocked (*like her hat*, Dan thought) on her shattered neck at an angle that was almost insouciant. Dan held Abra's hand – flesh that came and went in his own as she did her own cycling between her back stoop and Roof O' the World – and they watched together.

'Does it hurt?' Abra asked the dying woman. 'I hope it does. I hope it hurts a lot.'

Rose's lips pulled back in a sneer. Her human teeth were gone; all that remained was that single discolored tusk. Above it, her eyes floated like living blue stones. Then she was gone.

Abra turned to Dan. She was still smiling, but now there was no anger or meanness in it.

(*I was afraid for you I was afraid she might*)

(*she almost did but there was someone*)

He pointed up to where the broken pieces of the railing jutted against the sky. Abra looked there, then looked back at Dan, puzzled. He could only shake his head.

It was her turn to point, not up but down.

(*once there was a magician who had a hat like that his name was Mysterio*)

(*and you hung spoons on the ceiling*)

She nodded but didn't raise her head. She was still studying the hat.

(*you need to get rid of it*)

(*how*)

(*burn it Mr Freeman says he quit smoking but he still does I could smell it in the truck he'll have matches*)

'You *have* to,' she said. 'Will you? Do you promise?'

'Yes.'

(*I love you Uncle Dan*)

(*love you too*)

She hugged him. He put his arms around her and hugged her back. As he did, her body became rain. Then mist. Then gone.

10

On the back stoop of a house in Anniston, New Hampshire, in a dusk that would soon deepen to night, a little girl sat up, got to her feet, and then swayed, on the edge of a faint. There was no chance of her falling down; her parents were there at once. They carried her inside together.

'I'm okay,' Abra said. 'You can put me down.'

They did, carefully. David Stone stood close, ready to catch her at the slightest knee-buckle, but Abra stood steady in the kitchen.

'What about Dan?' John asked.

'He's fine. Mr Freeman smashed up his truck – he had to – and he got a cut' – she put her hand to the side of his face – 'but I think he's okay.'

'And them? The True Knot?'

Abra raised a hand to her mouth and blew across the palm. 'Gone.' And then: 'What is there to eat? I'm really hungry.'

11

Fine might have been a bit of an overstatement in Dan's case. He walked to the truck, where he sat in the open driver's side door, getting his breath back. And his wits.

We were on vacation, he decided. *I wanted to visit my old stomping grounds in Boulder. Then we came up here to take in the view from Roof O' the World, but the campground was deserted. I was feeling frisky and bet Billy I could drive his truck straight up the hill to the lookout. I was going too fast and lost control. Hit one of the support posts. Really sorry. Damn fool stunt.*

He would get hit with one hell of a fine, but there was an upside: he would pass the Breathalyzer with flying colors.

Dan looked in the glove compartment and found a can of lighter fluid. No Zippo – that would be in Billy's pants pocket – but there were indeed two books of half-used matches. He went to the hat and doused it with the lighter fluid until it was soaking. Then he squatted, touched a match, and flicked it into the hat's upturned bowl. The hat didn't last long, but he moved upwind until it was nothing but ashes.

The smell was foul.

When he looked up, he saw Billy trudging toward him, wiping at his bloody face with his sleeve. As they tromped through the ashes, making sure there wasn't a single ember that might spark a wildfire, Dan told him the story they would tell the Colorado State Police when they arrived.

'I'll have to pay to have that thing repaired, and I bet it costs a bundle. Good thing I've got some savings.'

Billy snorted. 'Who's gonna chase you for damages? There's nothing left of those True Knot folks but their clothes. I looked.'

'Unfortunately,' Dan said, 'Roof O' the World belongs to the great State of Colorado.'

'Ouch,' Billy said. 'Hardly seems fair, since you just did Colorado and the rest of the world a favor. Where's Abra?'

'Back home.'

'Good. And it's over? Really over?'

Dan nodded.

Billy was staring at the ashes of Rose's tophat. 'Went up damn fast. Almost like a special effect in a movie.'

'I imagine it was very old.' *And full of magic*, he didn't add. *The black variety.*

Dan went to the pickup and sat behind the wheel so he could examine his face in the rearview mirror.

'See anything that shouldn't be there?' Billy asked. 'That's what my mom always used to say when she caught me moonin over my own reflection.'

'Not a thing,' Dan said. A smile began to break on his face. It was tired but genuine. 'Not a thing in the world.'

'Then let's call the police and tell em about our accident,' Billy said. 'Ordinarily I got no use for the Five-O, but right about now I wouldn't mind some company. Place gives me the willies.' He gave Dan a shrewd look. 'Full of ghosts, ain't it? That's why they picked it.'

That was why, no doubt about it. But you didn't need to be Ebenezer Scrooge to know there were good ghostie people as well as bad ones. As they walked down toward the Overlook Lodge, Dan paused to look back at Roof O' the World. He was not entirely surprised to see a man standing on the platform by the broken rail. He raised one hand, the summit of Pawnee Mountain visible through it, and sketched a flying kiss that Dan remembered from his childhood. He remembered it well. It had been their special end-of-the-day thing.

Bedtime, doc. Sleep tight. Dream up a dragon and tell me about it in the morning.

Dan knew he was going to cry, but not now. This wasn't the time. He lifted his own hand to his mouth and returned the kiss.

He looked for a moment longer at what remained of his father. Then he headed down to the parking lot with Billy. When they got there, he looked back once more.

Roof O' the World was empty.

UNTIL YOU SLEEP

FEAR stands for face everything and recover.

> – Old AA saying

ANNIVERSARY

1

The Saturday noon AA meeting in Frazier was one of the oldest in New Hampshire, dating back to 1946, and had been founded by Fat Bob D., who had known the Program's founder, Bill Wilson, personally. Fat Bob was long in his grave, a victim of lung cancer – in the early days most recovering alkies had smoked like chimneys and newbies were routinely told to keep their mouths shut and the ashtrays empty – but the meeting was still well attended. Today it was SRO, because when it was over there would be pizza and a sheet cake. This was the case at most anniversary meetings, and today one of their number was celebrating fifteen years of sobriety. In the early years he had been known as Dan or Dan T., but word of his work at the local hospice had gotten around (the AA magazine was not known as *The Grapevine* for nothing), and now he was most commonly called Doc. Since his parents had called him that, Dan found the nickname ironic . . . but in a good way. Life was a wheel, its only job was to turn, and it always came back to where it had started.

A real doctor, this one named John, chaired at Dan's request, and the meeting followed its usual course. There was laughter when Randy M. told how he had thrown up all over the cop who arrested him on his last DUI, and more when he went on to say he had discovered a year later that the cop himself was in the Program. Maggie M. cried when she told ('shared', in AA parlance) how she had again been denied joint custody of her two children. The usual clichés were offered – time takes time, it works if you work it, don't quit until the miracle happens – and Maggie eventually quieted to sniffles. There was the usual cry of *Higher Power says turn it off!* when a guy's cell phone rang. A gal with shaky hands spilled a cup of coffee; a meeting without at least one spilled cup of joe was rare indeed.

At ten to one, John D. passed the basket ('We are self-supporting through our own contributions'), and asked for announcements. Trevor K., who opened the meeting, stood and asked – as he always did – for help cleaning up the kitchen and putting away the chairs. Yolanda V. did the Chip Club, giving out two whites (twenty-four hours) and a purple (five months – commonly referred to as the Barney Chip). As always, she ended by saying, 'If you haven't had a drink today, give yourself and your Higher Power a hand.'

They did.

When the applause died, John said, 'We have a fifteen-year anniversary today. Will Casey K. and Dan T. come on up here?'

The crowd applauded as Dan walked forward – slowly, to keep pace with Casey, who now walked with a cane. John handed Casey the medallion with XV printed on its face, and Casey held it up so the crowd could see it. 'I never thought this guy would make it,' he said, 'because he was AA from the start. By which I mean, an asshole with attitude.'

They laughed dutifully at this oldie. Dan smiled, but his heart was beating hard. His one thought right now was to get through what came next without fainting. The last time he'd been this scared, he had been looking up at Rose the Hat on the Roof O' the World platform and trying to keep from strangling himself with his own hands.

Hurry up, Casey. Please. Before I lose either my courage or my breakfast.

Casey might have been the one with the shining . . . or perhaps he saw something in Dan's eyes. In any case, he cut it short. 'But he defied my expectations and got well. For every seven alcoholics who walk through our doors, six walk back out again and get drunk. The seventh is the miracle we all live for. One of those miracles is standing right here, big as life and twice as ugly. Here you go, Doc, you earned this.'

He passed Dan the medallion. For a moment Dan thought it would slip through his cold fingers and fall to the floor. Casey folded his hand around it before it could, and then folded the rest of Dan into a massive hug. In his ear he whispered, 'Another year, you sonofabitch. Congratulations.'

Casey stumped up the aisle to the back of the room, where he sat by right of seniority with the other oldtimers. Dan was left alone at the front, clenching his fifteen-year medallion so hard the tendons stood out on his wrist. The assembled alkies stared at him, waiting for what longtime sobriety was supposed to convey: experience, strength, and hope.

'A couple of years ago . . .' he began, and then had to clear his throat. 'A couple of years ago, when I was having coffee with that gimpy-legged gentleman who's just now sitting down, he asked me if I'd done the fifth step: 'Admitted to God, ourselves, and another human being the exact nature of our wrongs.' I told him I'd done most of it. For folks who don't have our particular problem, that probably would have been enough . . . and that's just one of the reasons we call them Earth People.'

They chuckled. Dan drew a deep breath, telling himself if he could face Rose and her True Knot, he could face this. Only this was different. This wasn't Dan the Hero; it was Dan the Scumbag. He had lived long enough to know there was a little scumbag in everyone, but it didn't help much when you had to take out the trash.

'He told me that he thought there was one wrong I couldn't quite get past, because I was too ashamed to talk about it. He told me to let it go. He reminded me of something you hear at almost every meeting – we're only as sick as our secrets. And he said if I didn't tell mine, somewhere down the line I'd find myself with a drink in my hand. Was that the gist of it, Case?'

From the back of the room Casey nodded, his hands folded over the top of his cane.

Dan felt the stinging at the back of his eyes that meant tears were on the way and thought, *God help me to get through this without bawling. Please.*

'I didn't spill it. I'd been telling myself for years it was the one thing I'd never tell anyone. But I think he was right, and if I start drinking again, I'll die. I don't want to do that. I've got a lot to live for these days. So . . .'

The tears had come, the goddam tears, but he was in too deep to back out now. He wiped them away with the hand not fisted around the medallion.

'You know what it says in the Promises? About how we'll learn not to regret the past, or wish to shut the door on it? Pardon me for saying so, but I think that's one item of bullshit in a program full of true things. I regret plenty, but it's time to open the door, little as I want to.'

They waited. Even the two ladies who had been doling out pizza slices on paper plates were now standing in the kitchen doorway and watching him.

'Not too long before I quit drinking, I woke up next to some woman I picked up in a bar. We were in her apartment. The place was a dump, because she had almost nothing. I could relate to that because *I* had almost nothing, and both of us were probably in Broke City for the same reason. You all know what that reason is.' He shrugged. 'If you're one of us, the bottle takes your shit, that's all. First a little, then a lot, then everything.

'This woman, her name was Deenie. I don't remember much else about her, but I remember that. I put on my clothes and left, but first I took her money. And it turned out she had at least one thing I didn't, after all, because while I was going through her wallet, I looked around and her son was standing there. Little kid still in diapers. This woman and I had bought some coke the night before, and it was still on the table. He saw it and reached for it. He thought it was candy.'

Dan wiped his eyes again.

'I took it away and put it where he couldn't get it. That much I did. It wasn't enough, but that much I did. Then I put her money in my pocket and walked out of there. I'd do anything to take that back. But I can't.'

The women in the doorway had gone back to the kitchen. Some people were looking at their watches. A stomach grumbled. Looking at the assembled nine dozen alkies, Dan realized an astounding thing: what he'd done didn't revolt them. It didn't even surprise them. They had heard worse. Some had *done* worse.

'Okay,' he said. 'That's it. Thanks for listening.'

Before the applause, one of the oldtimers in the back row shouted out the traditional question: 'How'd you do it, Doc?'

Dan smiled and gave the traditional answer. 'One day at a time.'

2

After the Our Father, and the pizza, and the chocolate cake with the big number XV on it, Dan helped Casey back to his Tundra. A sleety rain had begun to fall.

'Spring in New Hampshire,' Casey said sourly. 'Ain't it wonderful.'

'Raineth drop and staineth slop,' Dan said in a declamatory voice, 'and how the wind doth ram! Skiddeth bus and sloppest us, damn you, sing goddam.'

Casey stared at him. 'Did you just make that up?'

'Nah. Ezra Pound. When are you going to quit dicking around and get that hip replaced?'

Casey grinned. 'Next month. I decided that if you can tell your biggest secret, I can get my hip replaced.' He paused. 'Not that your secret was all that fucking big, Danno.'

'So I discovered. I thought they'd run from me, screaming. Instead, they stood around eating pizza and talking about the weather.'

'If you'd told em you killed a blind gramma, they'd have stayed to eat the pizza and cake. Free is free.' He opened the driver's door. 'Boost me, Danno.'

Dan boosted him.

Casey wriggled ponderously, getting comfortable, then keyed the engine and got the wipers to work on the sleet. 'Everything's smaller when it's out,' he said. 'I hope you'll pass that on to your pigeons.'

'Yes, O Wise One.'

Casey looked at him sadly. 'Go fuck yourself, sweetheart.'

'Actually,' Danny said, 'I think I'll go back in and help put away the chairs.'

And that was what he did.

UNTIL YOU SLEEP

1

No balloons or magician at Abra Stone's birthday party this year. She was fifteen.

There *was* neighborhood-rattling rock music slamming through the outdoor speakers Dave Stone – ably assisted by Billy Freeman – had set up. The adults had cake, ice cream, and coffee in the Stone kitchen. The kids took over the downstairs family room and the back lawn, and from the sound of them, they had a blast. They started to leave around five o'clock, but Emma Deane, Abra's closest friend, stayed for supper. Abra, resplendent in a red skirt and off-the-shoulder peasant blouse, bubbled with good cheer. She exclaimed over the charm bracelet Dan gave her, hugged him, kissed him on the cheek. He smelled perfume. *That* was new.

When Abra left to accompany Emma back to her house, the two of them chattering their way happily down the walk, Lucy leaned toward Dan. Her mouth was pursed, there were new lines around her eyes, and her hair was showing the first touches of gray. Abra seemed to have put the True Knot behind her; Dan thought Lucy never would. 'Will you talk to her? About the plates?'

'I'm going outside to watch the sun go down over the river. Maybe you'll send her to visit with me a little when she gets back from the Deanes'.'

Lucy looked relieved, and Dan thought David did, as well. To them she would always be a mystery. Would it help to tell them she would always be one to him? Probably not.

'Good luck, chief,' Billy said.

On the back stoop where Abra had once lain in a state that wasn't unconsciousness, John Dalton joined him. 'I'd offer to give you moral support, but I think you have to do this alone.'

'Have you tried talking to her?'

'Yes. At Lucy's request.'

'No good?'

John shrugged. 'She's pretty closed up on the subject.'

'I was, too,' Dan said. 'At her age.'

'But you never broke every plate in your mother's antique break-front, did you?'

'My mother didn't have a breakfront,' Dan said.

He walked down to the bottom of the Stones' sloping backyard and regarded the Saco, which had, courtesy of the declining sun, become a glowing scarlet snake. Soon the mountains would eat the last of the sunlight and the river would turn gray. Where there had once been a chainlink fence to block the potentially disastrous explorations of young children, there was now a line of decorative bushes. David had taken the fence down the previous October, saying Abra and her friends no longer needed its protection; they could all swim like fish.

But of course there were other dangers.

2

The color on the water had faded to the faintest pink tinge – ashes of roses – when Abra joined him. He didn't have to look around to know she was there, or to know she had put on a sweater to cover her bare shoulders. The air cooled quickly on spring evenings in central New Hampshire even after the last threat of snow was gone.

(*I love my bracelet Dan*)

She had pretty much dropped the uncle part.

(*I'm glad*)

'They want you to talk to me about the plates,' she said. The spoken words had none of the warmth that had come through in her thoughts, and the thoughts were gone. After the very pretty and sincere thank-you, she had closed her inner self off to him. She was good at that now, and getting better every day. 'Don't they?'

'Do *you* want to talk about them?'

'I told her I was sorry. I told her I didn't mean to. I don't think she believed me.'

(*I do*)

'Because you *know*. They don't.'

Dan said nothing, and passed on only a single thought:

(?)

'They don't believe me about *anything*!' she burst out. 'It's so unfair! I didn't know there was going to be booze at Jennifer's stupid party, and I didn't have any! Still, she grounds me for *two fucking weeks!*'

(? ? ?)

Nothing. The river was almost entirely gray now. He risked a look at her and saw she was studying her sneakers – red to match her skirt. Her cheeks now also matched her skirt.

'All right,' she said at last, and although she still didn't look at him, the corners of her lips turned up in a grudging little smile. 'Can't fool you, can I? I had one swallow, just to see what it tasted like. What the big deal is. I guess she smelled it on my breath when I came home. And guess what? There *is* no big deal. It tasted *horrible.*'

Dan did not reply to this. If he told her he had found his own first taste horrible, that he had also believed there was no big deal, no precious secret, she would have dismissed it as windy adult bullshit. You could not moralize children out of growing up. Or teach them how to do it.

'I really didn't mean to break the plates,' she said in a small voice. 'It was an accident, like I told her. I was just so *mad.*'

'You come by it naturally.' What he was remembering was Abra standing over Rose the Hat as Rose cycled. *Does it hurt?* Abra had asked the dying thing that looked like a woman (except, that was, for the one terrible tooth). *I hope it does. I hope it hurts a lot.*

'Are you going to lecture me?' And, with a lilt of contempt: 'I know that's what *she* wants.'

'I'm out of lectures, but I could tell you a story my mother told me. It's about your great-grandfather on the Jack Torrance side. Do you want to hear it?'

Abra shrugged. *Get it over with*, the shrug said.

'Mark Torrance wasn't an orderly like me, but close. He was a male nurse. He walked with a cane toward the end of his life, because he was in a car accident that messed up his leg. And one night, at the dinner table, he used that cane on his wife. No reason; he just started in whaling. He broke her nose and opened her scalp. When she fell out of her chair onto the floor, he got up and *really* went to work on her. According to what my father told my mom, he would have beaten her to death if Brett and Mike – they were *my* uncles – hadn't pulled him away. When the doctor came, your great-grandfather was down on his knees with his own little medical kit, doing what he could. He said she fell downstairs. Great-Gram – the momo you never met, Abra – backed him up. So did the kids.'

'*Why?*' she breathed.

'Because they were scared. Later – long after Mark was dead – your grandfather broke my arm. Then, in the Overlook – which stood where Roof O' the World stands today – your grandfather beat my mother almost to death. He used a roque mallet instead of a cane, but it was basically the same deal.'

'I get the point.'

'Years later, in a bar in St Petersburg—'

'Stop! I said I *get* it!' She was trembling.

'—I beat a man unconscious with a pool cue because he laughed when I scratched. After that, the son of Jack and the grandson of Mark spent thirty days in an orange jumpsuit, picking up trash along Highway 41.'

She turned away, starting to cry. 'Thanks, Uncle Dan. Thanks for spoiling . . .'

An image filled his head, momentarily blotting out the river: a charred and smoking birthday cake. In some circumstances, the image would have been funny. Not in these.

He took her gently by the shoulders and turned her back to him. 'There's nothing to get. There's no point. There's nothing but family history. In the words of the immortal Elvis Presley, it's your baby, you rock it.'

'I don't understand.'

'Someday you may write poetry, like Concetta. Or push someone else off a high place with your mind.'

'I never would . . . but *Rose* deserved it.' Abra turned her wet face up to his.

'No argument there.'

'So why do I dream about it? Why do I wish I could take it back? She would have killed *us*, so why do I wish I could take it back?'

'Is it the killing you wish you could take back, or the joy of the killing?'

Abra hung her head. Dan wanted to take her in his arms, but didn't.

'No lecture and no moral. Just blood calling to blood. The stupid urges of wakeful people. And you've made it to a time of life when you're completely awake. It's hard for you. I know that. It's hard for everyone, but most teenagers don't have your abilities. Your weapons.'

'What do I do? What can I do? Sometimes I get so angry . . . not just at *her*, but at teachers . . . kids at school who think they're such hot shits . . . the ones who laugh if you're not good at sports or wearing the wrong clothes and stuff . . .'

Dan thought of advice Casey Kingsley had once given him. 'Go to the dump.'

'Huh?' She goggled at him.

He sent her a picture: Abra using her extraordinary talents – they had still not peaked, incredible but true – to overturn discarded refrigerators, explode dead TV sets, throw washing machines. Seagulls flew up in startled packs.

Now she didn't goggle; she giggled. 'Will that help?'

'Better the dump than your mother's plates.'

She cocked her head and fixed him with merry eyes. They were friends again, and that was good. 'But those plates were ug-*lee*.'

'Will you try it?'

'Yes.' And by the look of her, she couldn't wait.

'One other thing.'

She grew solemn, waiting.

'You don't have to be anyone's doormat.'

'That's good, isn't it?'

'Yes. Just remember how dangerous your anger can be. Keep it—'

His cell phone rang.

'You should get that.'

He raised his eyebrows. 'Do you know who it is?'

'No, but I think it's important.'

He took the phone out of his pocket and read the display.
RIVINGTON HOUSE.

'Hello?'

'It's Claudette Albertson, Danny. Can you come?'

He ran a mental inventory of the hospice guests currently on his
blackboard. 'Amanda Ricker? Or Jeff Kellogg?'

It turned out to be neither.

'If you can come, you better do it right away,' Claudette said.
'While he's still conscious.' She hesitated. 'He's asking for you.'

'I'll come.' *Although if it's as bad as you say, he'll probably be gone
when I get there.* Dan broke the connection. 'I have to go, honey.'

'Even though he's not your friend. Even though you don't even
like him.' Abra looked thoughtful.

'Even though.'

'What's his name? I didn't get that.'

(*Fred Carling*)

He sent this and then wrapped his arms around her, tight-tight-
tight. Abra did the same.

'I'll try,' she said. 'I'll try real hard.'

'I know you will,' he said. 'I know you will. Listen, Abra, I love
you so much.'

She said, 'I'm glad.'

3

Claudette was at the nurses' station when he came in forty-five
minutes later. He asked the question he had asked dozens of times
before: 'Is he still with us?' As if it were a bus ride.

'Barely.'

'Conscious?'

She waggled a hand. 'In and out.'

'Azzie?'

'Was there for a while, but scooted when Dr Emerson came in.
Emerson's gone now, he's checking on Amanda Ricker. Azzie went
back as soon as he left.'

'No transport to the hospital?'

'Can't. Not yet. There was a four-car pile-up on Route 119 across the border in Castle Rock. Lots of injuries. Four ambos on the way, also LifeFlight. Going to the hospital will make a difference to some of them. As for Fred . . .' She shrugged.

'What happened?'

'You know our Fred – junk food junkie. Mickey D's is his second home. Sometimes he looks when he runs across Cranmore Avenue, sometimes he doesn't. Just expects people to stop for him.' She wrinkled her nose and stuck out her tongue, looking like a little kid who's just gotten a mouthful of something bad. Brussels sprouts, maybe. 'That *attitude*.'

Dan knew Fred's routine, and he knew the attitude.

'He was going for his evening cheeseburger,' Claudette said. 'The cops took the woman who hit him to jail – chick was so drunk she could hardly stand up, that's what I heard. They brought Fred here. His face is scrambled eggs, his chest and pelvis are crushed, one leg's almost severed. If Emerson hadn't been here doing rounds, Fred would have died right away. We triaged him, stopped the bleeding, but even if he'd been in peak condition . . . which dear old Freddy most definitely ain't . . .' She shrugged. 'Emerson says they *will* send an ambo after the Castle Rock mess is cleaned up, but he'll be gone by then. Dr Emerson wouldn't commit on that, but I believe Azreel. You better go on down there, if you're going. I know you never cared for him . . .'

Dan thought of the fingermarks the orderly had left on poor old Charlie Hayes's arm. *Sorry to hear it* – that was what Carling had said when Dan told him the old man was gone. Fred all comfy, rocked back in his favorite chair and eating Junior Mints. *But that is what they're here for, isn't it?*

And now Fred was in the same room where Charlie had died. Life was a wheel, and it always came back around.

4

The door of the Alan Shepard Suite was standing half-open, but Dan knocked anyway, as a courtesy. He could hear the harsh wheeze-and-gurgle of Fred Carling's breathing even from the hall, but it didn't seem to bother Azzie, who was curled up at the foot of the bed. Carling was lying on a rubber sheet, wearing nothing but bloodstained boxer shorts and an acre of bandages, most of them already seeping blood. His face was disfigured, his body twisted in at least three different directions.

'Fred? It's Dan Torrance. Can you hear me?'

The one remaining eye opened. The breathing hitched. There was a brief rasp that might have been *yes*.

Dan went into the bathroom, wetted a cloth with warm water, wrung it out. These were things he had done many times before. When he returned to Carling's bedside, Azzie got to his feet, stretched in that luxurious, bowed-back way cats have, and jumped to the floor. A moment later he was gone, to resume his evening's patrol. He limped a little now. He was a very old cat.

Dan sat on the side of the bed and gently rubbed the cloth over the part of Fred Carling's face that was still relatively whole.

'How bad's the pain?'

That rasp again. Carling's left hand was a twisted snarl of broken fingers, so Dan took the right one. 'You don't need to talk, just tell me.'

(*not so bad now*)

Dan nodded. 'Good. That's good.'

(*but I'm scared*)

'There's nothing to be scared of.'

He saw Fred at the age of six, swimming in the Saco with his brother, Fred always snatching at the back of his suit to keep it from falling off because it was too big, it was a hand-me-down like practically everything else he owned. He saw him at fifteen, kissing a girl at the Bridgton Drive-In and smelling her perfume as he touched her breast and wished this night would never end. He saw him at twenty-five, riding down to Hampton Beach with the Road Saints, sitting astride a Harley FXB, the Sturgis model, so fine, he's full of bennies and red wine and the day is like a hammer, everybody looking as the Saints tear by in a long and glittering caravan of fuck-you noise; life is exploding like fireworks. And he sees the apartment where Carling lives — lived — with his little dog, whose name is Brownie. Brownie ain't much, just a mutt, but he's smart. Sometimes he jumps up in the orderly's lap and they watch TV together. Brownie troubles Fred's mind because he will be waiting for Fred to come home, take him for a little walk, then fill up his bowl with Gravy Train.

'Don't worry about Brownie,' Dan said. 'I know a girl who'd be glad to take care of him. She's my niece, and it's her birthday.'

Carling looked up at him with his one functioning eye. The rattle of his breath was very loud now; he sounded like an engine with dirt in it.

(can you help me please doc can you help me)

Yes. He could help. It was his sacrament, what he was made for. It was quiet now in Rivington House, very quiet indeed. Somewhere close, a door was swinging open. They had come to the border. Fred Carling looked up him, asking *what*. Asking *how*. But it was so simple.

'You only need to sleep.'

(don't leave me)

'No,' Dan said. 'I'm here. I'll stay here until you sleep.'

Now he clasped Carling's hand in both of his. And smiled.

'Until you sleep,' he said.

May 1, 2011 – July 17, 2012

AUTHOR'S NOTE

My first book with Scribner was *Bag of Bones*, in 1998. Anxious to please my new partners, I went out on tour for that novel. At one of the autographing sessions, some guy asked, 'Hey, any idea what happened to the kid from *The Shining*?'

This was a question I'd often asked myself about that old book – along with another: What would have happened to Danny's troubled father if he had found Alcoholics Anonymous instead of trying to get by with what people in AA call 'white-knuckle sobriety'?

As with *Under the Dome* and *11/22/63*, this was an idea that never quite left my mind. Every now and then – while taking a shower, watching a TV show, or making a long turnpike drive – I would find myself calculating Danny Torrance's age, and wondering where he was. Not to mention his mother, one more basically good human being left in Jack Torrance's destructive wake. Wendy and Danny were, in the current parlance, codependents, people bound by ties of love and responsibility to an addicted family member. At some point in 2009, one of my recovering alcoholic friends told me a one-liner that goes like this: 'When a codependent is drowning, somebody else's life flashes before his eyes.' That struck me as too true to be funny, and I think it was at that point that *Doctor Sleep* became inevitable. I had to know.

Did I approach the book with trepidation? You better believe it. *The Shining* is one of those novels people always mention (along with *'Salem's Lot*, *Pet Sematary*, and *It*) when they talk about which of my books really scared the bejeezus out of them. Plus, of course, there was Stanley Kubrick's movie, which many seem to remember – for reasons I have never quite understood – as one of the scariest films they have ever seen. (If you have seen the movie but not read the novel, you should note that *Doctor Sleep* follows the latter, which is, in my opinion, the True History of the Torrance Family.)

I like to think I'm still pretty good at what I do, but nothing can live up to the memory of a good scare, and I mean *nothing*, especially if administered to one who is young and impressionable. There has been at least one brilliant sequel to Alfred Hitchcock's *Psycho* (Mick Garris's *Psycho IV*, with Anthony Perkins reprising his role as Norman Bates), but people who've seen that – or any of the others – will only shake their heads and say *no, no, not as good*. They remember the first time they experienced Janet Leigh, and no remake or sequel can top that moment when the curtain is pulled back and the knife starts to do its work.

And people change. The man who wrote *Doctor Sleep* is very different from the well-meaning alcoholic who wrote *The Shining*, but both remain interested in the same thing: telling a kickass story. I enjoyed finding Danny Torrance again and following his adventures. I hope you did, too. If that's the case, Constant Reader, we're all good.

Before letting you go, let me thank the people who need to be thanked, okay?

Nan Graham edited the book. *Righteously*. Thanks, Nan.

Chuck Verrill, my agent, sold the book. That's important, but he also took all my phone calls and fed me spoonfuls of soothing syrup. Those things are indispensable.

Russ Dorr did the research, but for what's wrong, blame me for misunderstanding. He's a great physician's assistant and a Nordic monster of inspiration and good cheer.

Chris Lotts supplied Italian when Italian was needed. Yo, Chris.

Rocky Wood was my go-to guy for all things *Shining*, providing me with names and dates I had either forgotten or plain got wrong. He also provided reams of info on every recreational vehicle and camper under the sun (the coolest was Rose's EarthCruiser). The Rock knows my work better than I do myself. Look him up on the Web sometime. He's got it going on.

My son Owen read the book and suggested valuable changes. Chief among them was his insistence that we see Dan reach what recovered alcoholics call 'the bottom'.

My wife also read *Doctor Sleep* and helped to make it better. I love you, Tabitha.

Thanks to you guys and girls who read my stuff, too. May you have long days and pleasant nights.

Let me close with a word of caution: when you're on the turnpikes and freeways of America, watch out for those Winnebagos and Bounders.

You never know who might be inside. Or *what*.

Bangor, Maine

Don't miss THE INSTITUTE by Stephen King available from Hodder from September, 2019.

Luke Ellis, a super-smart twelve-year-old with an exceptional gift, is the latest in a long line of kids abducted and taken to a secret government facility, hidden deep in the forest in Maine.

Here, kids who can read minds or make objects move are subjected to a series of experiments. There seems to be no hope of escape. Until Luke teams up with an even younger boy whose powers of telepathy are off the scale, and they create a plan.

Meanwhile, far away in a small town in South Carolina, former cop Tim Jamieson has taken a job working for the local sheriff. Tim's just walking the beat. The quiet life. He doesn't know he's about to take on the biggest case of his career . . .

Turn the page for an extract . . .

First published in Great Britain in 2019 by Hodder & Stoughton
An Hachette UK company

1

A CIP catalogue record for this title is available from the British Library

Hardback ISBN 978 1 529 35539 0
Trade Paperback ISBN 978 1 529 35540 6
eBook ISBN 978 1 529 35542 0

Typeset in Bembo by Palimpsest Book Production Ltd, Falkirk, Stirlingshire

Printed and bound in Great Britain by Clays Ltd, Elcograf S.p.A.

Hodder & Stoughton policy is to use papers that are natural, renewable
and recyclable products and made from wood grown in sustainable forests.
The logging and manufacturing processes are expected to conform to
the environmental regulations of the country of origin.

Hodder & Stoughton Ltd
Carmelite House
50 Victoria Embankment
London EC4Y 0DZ

www.hodder.co.uk

According to the National Center for Missing and Exploited Children, roughly 800,000 children are reported missing each year in the United States. Most are found.

Thousands are not.

1

Half an hour after Tim Jamieson's Delta flight was scheduled to leave Tampa for the bright lights and tall buildings of New York, it was still parked at the gate. When a Delta agent and a blond woman with a security badge hanging around her neck entered the cabin, there were unhappy, premonitory murmurings from the packed residents of economy class.

'May I have your attention, please!' the Delta guy called.

'How long's the delay gonna be?' someone asked. 'Don't sugarcoat it.'

'The delay should be short, and the captain wants to assure you all that your flight will arrive approximately on time. We have a federal officer who needs to board, however, so we'll need someone to give up his or her seat.'

A collective groan went up, and Tim saw several people unlimber their cell phones in case of trouble. There had been trouble in these situations before.

'Delta Air Lines is authorized to offer a free ticket to New York on the next outbound flight, which will be tomorrow morning at 6:45 AM—'

Another groan went up. Someone said, 'Just shoot me.'

The functionary continued, undeterred. 'You'll be given a hotel voucher for tonight, plus four hundred dollars. It's a good deal, folks. Who wants it?'

He had no takers. The security blond said nothing, only surveyed the crowded economy-class cabin with all-seeing but somehow lifeless eyes.

'Eight hundred,' the Delta guy said. 'Plus the hotel voucher and the complimentary ticket.'

'Guy sounds like a quiz show host,' grunted a man in the row ahead of Tim's.

There were still no takers.

'Fourteen hundred?'

And still none. Tim found this interesting but not entirely surprising. It wasn't just because a six forty-five flight meant getting up before God, either. Most of his fellow economy-class passengers were family groups headed home after visiting various Florida attractions, couples sporting beachy-keen sunburns, and beefy, red-faced, pissed-off-looking guys who probably had business in the Big Apple worth considerably more than fourteen hundred bucks.

Someone far in the back called, 'Throw in a Mustang convertible and a trip to Aruba for two, and you can have both our seats!' This sally provoked laughter. It didn't sound terribly friendly.

The gate agent looked at the blond with the badge, but if he hoped for help there, he got none. She just continued her survey, nothing moving but her eyes. He sighed and said, 'Sixteen hundred.'

Tim Jamieson suddenly decided he wanted to get the fuck off this plane and hitchhike north. Although such an idea had never so much as crossed his mind before this moment, he found he could imagine himself doing it, and with absolute clarity. There he was, standing on Highway 301 somewhere in the middle of Hernando County with his thumb out. It was hot, the lovebugs were swarming, there was a billboard advertising some slip-and-fall attorney, 'Take It on the Run' was blaring from a boombox sitting on the concrete-block step of a nearby trailer where a shirtless man was washing his car, and eventually some Farmer John would come along and give him a ride in a pickup truck with stake sides, melons in the back, and a magnetic Jesus on the dashboard. The best part wouldn't even be the cash money in his pocket. The best part would be standing out there by himself, miles from this sardine can with its warring smells of perfume, sweat, and hair spray.

The second-best part, however, would be squeezing the government tit for a few dollars more.

He stood up to his perfectly normal height (five-ten and a fraction), pushed his glasses up on his nose, and raised his hand. 'Make it two thousand, sir, plus a cash refund of my ticket, and the seat is yours.'

2

The voucher turned out to be for a cheesedog hotel located near the end of Tampa International's most heavily used runway. Tim fell asleep to the sound of airplanes, awoke to more of the same, and went down to ingest a hardboiled egg and two rubber pancakes from the complimentary breakfast buffet. Although far from a gourmet treat, Tim ate heartily, then went back to his room to wait for nine o'clock, when the banks opened.

He cashed his windfall with no trouble, because the bank knew he was coming and the check had been approved in advance; he had no intention of waiting around in the cheesedog hotel for it to clear. He took his two thousand in fifties and twenties, folded it into his left front pocket, reclaimed his duffel bag from the bank's security guard, and called an Uber to take him to Ellenton. There he paid the driver, strolled to the nearest 301-N sign, and stuck out his thumb. Fifteen minutes later he was picked up by an old guy in a Case gimme cap. There were no melons in the back of his pickup, and no stake sides, but otherwise it pretty much conformed to his vision of the previous night.

'Where you headed, friend?' the old guy asked.

'Well,' Tim said, 'New York, eventually. I guess.'

The old guy spat a ribbon of tobacco juice out the window. 'Now why would any man in his right mind want to go there?' He pronounced it *raht mahnd*.

'I don't know,' Tim said, although he did; an old service buddy had told him there was plenty of private security work in the Big Apple, including some for companies that would give more weight to his experience than to the Rube Goldberg fuckup that had ended his career in Florida policing. 'I'm just hoping to get to Georgia tonight. Maybe I'll like that better.'

'Now you're talking,' the old guy said. 'Georgia ain't bad, specially if you like peaches. They gi' me the backdoor trots. You don't mind some music, do you?'

'Not at all.'

'Got to warn you, I play it loud. I'm a little on the deef side.'

'I'm just happy to be riding.'

It was Waylon Jennings instead of REO Speedwagon, but that was okay with Tim. Waylon was followed by Shooter Jennings and Marty Stuart. The two men in the mud-streaked Dodge Ram listened and watched the highway roll. Seventy miles up the line, the old guy pulled over, gave Tim a tip of his Case cap, and wished him a real fahn day.

Tim didn't make Georgia that night – he spent it in another cheesedog motel next to a roadside stand selling orange juice – but he got there the following day. In the town of Brunswick (where a certain kind of tasty stew had been invented), he took two weeks' work in a recycling plant, doing it with no more forethought than he had put into deciding to give up his seat on the Delta flight out of Tampa. He didn't need the money, but it seemed to Tim that he needed the time. He was in transition, and that didn't happen over-night. Also, there was a bowling alley with a Denny's right next door. Hard to beat a combo like that.

3

With his pay from the recycling plant added to his airline windfall, Tim was standing on the Brunswick ramp of I-95 North and feeling pretty well-heeled for a rambling man. He stood there for over an hour in the sun, and was thinking of giving up and going back to Denny's for a cold glass of sweet tea when a Volvo station wagon pulled over. The back was filled with cartons. The elderly woman behind the wheel powered down the passenger side window and peered at him through thick glasses. 'Although not large, you look well-muscled,' she said. 'You are not a rapist or a psychotic, are you?'

'No, ma'am,' Tim told her, thinking: But what else *would* I say?

'Of course you would say that, wouldn't you? Are you going as far as South Carolina? Your duffel bag suggests that you are.'

A car swept around her Volvo and sped up the ramp, horn blaring. She took no notice, only kept her serene gaze fixed on Tim.

'Yes, ma'am. All the way to New York.'

'I'll take you to South Carolina – not far into that benighted state, but a little way – if you'll help me out a bit in return. One hand washes the other, if you see what I mean.'

'You scratch my back and I scratch yours,' Tim said, grinning.

'There will be no scratching of any kind, but you may get in.'

Tim did so. Her name was Marjorie Kellerman, and she ran the Brunswick library. She also belonged to something called the Southeastern Library Association. Which, she said, had no money because 'Trump and his cronies took it all back. They understand culture no more than a donkey understands algebra.'

Sixty-five miles north, still in Georgia, she stopped at a pokey little library in the town of Pooler. Tim unloaded the cartons of books and dollied them inside. He dollied another dozen or so cartons out to the Volvo. These, Marjorie Kellerman told him, were bound to the Yemassee Public Library, about forty miles further north, across the South Carolina state line. But not long after passing Hardeeville, their progress came to a stop. Cars and trucks were stacked up in both lanes, and more quickly filled in behind them.

'Oh, I hate it when this happens,' Marjorie said, 'and it always seems to in South Carolina, where they're too cheap to widen the highway. There's been a wreck somewhere up ahead, and with only two lanes, nobody can get by. I'll be here half the day. Mr Jamieson, you may be excused from further duty. If I were you, I would exit my vehicle, walk back to the Hardeeville exit, and try your luck on Highway 17.'

'What about all those cartons of books?'

'Oh, I'll find another strong back to help me unload,' she said, and smiled at him. 'To tell you the truth, I saw you standing there in the hot sun and just decided to live a little dangerously.'

'Well, if you're sure.' The traffic clog was making him feel claustrophobic. The way he'd felt stuck halfway back in economy class of the Delta flight, in fact. 'If you're not, I'll hang in. It's not like I'm racing a deadline or anything.'

'I'm sure,' she said. 'It's been a pleasure meeting you, Mr Jamieson.'

'Likewise, Ms Kellerman.'

'Do you need monetary assistance? I can spare ten dollars, if you do.'

He was touched and surprised – not for the first time – by the ordinary kindness and generosity of ordinary folks, especially those without much to spare. America was still a good place, no matter how much some (including himself, from time to time) might disagree. 'No, I'm fine. Thank you for the offer.'

He shook her hand, got out, and walked back along the I-95 break-down lane to the Hardeeville exit. When a ride was not immediately forthcoming on US 17, he strolled a couple of miles to where it joined State Road 92. Here a sign pointed toward the town of DuPray. By then it was late afternoon, and Tim decided he had better find a motel in which to spend the night. It would undoubtedly be another of the cheesedog variety, but the alternatives – sleeping outside and getting eaten alive by skeeters or in some farmer's barn – were even less appealing. And so he set out for DuPray.

Great events turn on small hinges.

4

An hour later he was sitting on a rock at the edge of the two-lane, waiting for a seemingly endless freight train to cross the road. It was headed in the direction of DuPray at a stately thirty miles an hour: boxcars, autoracks (most loaded with wrecks rather than new vehicles), tankers, flatcars, and gondolas loaded with God knew what evil substances that might, in the event of a derailment, catch the piney woods afire or afflict the DuPray populace with noxious or even fatal fumes. At last came an orange caboose where a man in bib overalls sat in a lawn chair, reading a paperback and smoking a cigarette. He looked up from his book and tipped Tim a wave. Tim tipped one right back.

The town was two miles further on, built around the intersection of SR 92 (now called Main Street) and two other streets. DuPray seemed to have largely escaped the chain stores that had taken over the bigger towns; there was a Western Auto, but it was closed down, the windows soaped over. Tim noted a grocery store, a drug store, a mercantile that appeared to sell a little bit of everything, and a couple of beauty salons. There was also a movie theater with FOR SALE OR RENT on the marquee, an auto supply store that fancied itself the DuPray Speed Shop, and a restaurant called Bev's Eatery. There were three churches, one Methodist, two off-brand, all of the come-to-Jesus variety. There were no more than two dozen cars and farm trucks scattered along the slant-parking spaces that lined the business district. The sidewalks were nearly deserted.

Three blocks up, after yet another church, he spied the DuPray Motel. Beyond it, where Main Street presumably reverted to SR 92, there was another rail crossing, a depot, and a row of metal roofs glittering in the sun. Beyond these structures, the piney woods closed in again. All in all, it looked to Tim like a town out of a country ballad, one of those nostalgia pieces sung by Alan Jackson or George Strait. The motel sign was old and rusty, suggesting the place might be as closed-down as the movie theater, but since the afternoon was now ebbing away and it appeared to be the only game in town when it came to shelter, Tim headed for it.

Halfway there, after the DuPray Town Office, he came to a brick building with ladders of ivy climbing the sides. On the neatly mowed lawn was a sign proclaiming this the Fairlee County Sheriff's Department. Tim thought it must be a poor-ass county indeed, if this town was its seat.

Two cruisers were parked in front, one of them a newish sedan, the other an elderly, mud-splashed 4Runner with a bubble light on the dash. Tim looked toward the entrance – the almost unconscious glance of a drifter with quite a lot of cash money in his pocket – walked on a few steps, then turned back for a closer look at the notice boards flanking the double doors. At one of the notices in particular. Thinking he must have read it wrong but wanting to make sure.

Not in this day and age, he thought. Can't be.

But it was. Next to a poster reading IF YOU THOUGHT MARIJUNA IS LEGAL IN SOUTH CAROLINA, **THINK AGAIN**, was one that read simply NIGHT KNOCKER WANTED. APPLY WITHIN.

Wow, he thought. Talk about a blast from the past.

He turned toward the rusty motel sign and paused again, thinking about that help-wanted sign. Just then one of the police station doors opened and a lanky cop came out, settling his cap on his red hair. The latening sun twinkled on his badge. He took in Tim's workboots, dusty jeans, and blue chambray shirt. His eyes dwelled for a moment on the duffel bag slung over Tim's shoulder before moving to his face. 'Can I help you, sir?'

The same impulse that had made him stand up on the plane swept over
him now. 'Probably not, but who knows?'

Have you read IT? The Number One bestselling novel which inspired two films: IT (2017) and IT CHAPTER TWO (2019)?

Derry, Maine is just an ordinary town: familiar, well-ordered for the most part, a good place to live.

It is a group of children who see – and feel – what makes Derry so horribly diffferent. In the storm drains, in the sewers, IT lurks, taking on the shape of every nightmare, each one's deepest dread. Sometimes IT appears as an evil clown named Pennywise and sometimes IT reaches up, seizing, tearing, killing . . .

Time passes and the children grown up, move away and forget. Until they are called back, once more to confront IT as IT stirs and coils in the sullen depths of their memories, emerging again to make their past nightmares a terrible present reality.

'One of the great storytellers of our time' – *Guardian*

Have you seen these exciting editions
in our classic collection?

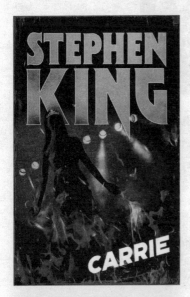

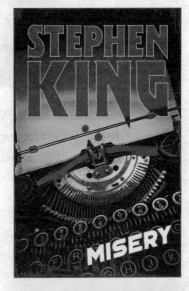

Before DOCTOR SLEEP, there was THE SHINING, a classic of modern American horror from the undisputed master, Stephen King.

Danny is only five years old, but in the words of old Mr Hallorann he is a 'shiner', aglow with psychic voltage. When his father becomes caretaker of the Overlook Hotel, Danny's visions grow out of control.

As winter closes in and blizzards cut them off, the hotel seems to develop a life of its own. It is meant to be empty. So who is the lady in Room 217 and who are the masked guests going up and down in the elevator? And why do the hedges shaped like animals seem so alive?

Somewhere, somehow, there is an evil force in the hotel – and that, too, is beginning to shine . . .

'Obviously a masterpiece, probably the best supernatural novel in a hundred years' – Peter Straub

To find out more about Stephen King please visit www.hodder.co.uk, www.stephenkingbooks.co.uk, www.facebook.com/stephenkingbooks